TEARS OF

A

HUSTLER 2

A
Novel
By

$ILK WHITE

GOOD2GOPUBLISHING

Published by:
GOOD2GOPUBLISHING
7311 W. GLASS LANE
LAVEEN, AZ 85339
www.good2gopublishing.com
QUESTIONS
G2G@GOOD2GOPUBLISHING.COM

THIRDLANE MARKETING: BRIAN JAMES
BRIAN@GOOD2GOPUBLISHING

AUTHOR: SILK WHITE
G2G@GOOD2GOPUBLISHING.COM
FACEBOOK.COM/SILKWHITE212
FACEBOOK.COM/GOOD2GOPUBLISHING
MYSPACE.COM/SILKWHITE
TWITTER@GOOD2GOBOOKS

Copyright © 2008 by $ILK WHITE
Cover designer: Davida Baldwin
Edited by M.S. Hunter
ISBN....978-0-578-04011-0
Typeset by Rukyyah

ACKNOWLEDGEMENTS

First and foremost, I would really like to thank God for blessing me with this gift.

I would like to thank every Silk White fan out there. I truly appreciate your loyalty and patience. I hope you enjoy everything I put out.

Shout out to my home girl Michelle Hunter for all your help and support, I appreciate it. Shout out to my man Tra Verdejo and the rest of the authors that show me luv… Ashley and Jaquavis, my man B. Jones, and shout out to my man Ray and BJ. I want to thank my wife for putting up with me. I know I am a handful, so thank you.

Last but not least, a big shout out to all my brothers and sisters locked up behind the wall…keep ya head up and ya eyes open. It always gets greater later. They can't keep a good person down for long!

PROLOGUE

Once Spanky was in the bathroom, Christie slowly peeled out of her dress and kicked off her heels. She walked freely around the house in nothing but her white thong. Her feet sunk into the plush carpet as she headed to the kitchen to grab a bottle of champagne. On her way back to the bedroom, she nosily placed her ear against the bathroom door. When she didn't hear anything, she began to panic.

"Baby you okay in there?" She asked as she knocked lightly on the door.

Again, no answer came back. Christie quickly reached for the doorknob, only to find out it was locked.

"Baby stop playing around and open up the door," she yelled in a worried tone.

Seconds later, Christie heard a single gun shot go off. Instantly, her heart leaped up into her throat. She quickly took three steps backwards and came forward with a hard lee kick, which busted the door wide open. She slowly melted down to her knees with her mouth hung wide open.

Spanky sat on top of the toilet seat with half of his brains painted on the wall behind him, while the other half rested on his shoulders.

"NOOOOOOO!" Christie screamed at the top of her lungs as she rested her head on Spanky's lap.

"Why did you do this?" She asked herself over and over again, as she cried like a baby. "Why?"

Christie took one last look at Spanky as she slowly made it back to her feet and headed back into the bedroom. She quickly snatched the cordless phone off the charger and dialed 911.

"911, can I help you?" The operator asked nonchalantly.

Yes, "I need an ambulance over here immediately! My husband just shot himself in the head," Christie yelled out in a panic.

"Are you in the house alone?" The operator asked.

"What the fuck does that have to do with anything? Just get me a fucking ambulance over here now," Christie barked into the phone, hanging up in the operator's ear.

"Stupid bitch," Christie said out loud, as she made her way back to the bathroom.

"It's me and you forever boo. I'll always be here for you," Christie whispered as she laid her head back on Spanky's lap.

Thirty minutes later, Christie heard the paramedics banging at the door.

Christie took one last look at Spanky and wiped her eyes as she stood up to answer the door. She quickly rushed to the door even though she knew Spanky was already dead.

The paramedics quickly rushed into the house hoping to save the gunshot victim, but when they reached the victim, they knew they were too late.

Christie couldn't believe what had just happened. A million questions were running through her mind. "Should I have told Spanky about Ali being arrested? Should I have gone in the bathroom with him to comfort him? Is there anything I could have done to prevent this?" She continued to ask herself as the salty tears streamed down her face.

"Just One of Those Days"

Gmoney sat up in bed recovering from his gunshot wound with Coco lying right next to him.

"Baby can I get you anything?" Coco asked, sensing her man was in pain.

"Yeah get me a glass of water so I can take these pain killers."

When Coco returned from the kitchen carrying a glass of water, she and Gmoney both looked on in shock as the reporter interrupted their program.

"Breaking news, the boxer Shawn "Spanky" Martin seems to have committed suicide after losing his title fight last night against James "The Terminator" Johnson. Detectives are still on the scene. We will have more on this story coming up later on the morning news."

"Hell naw," Gmoney said. "I know that wasn't my nigga on the news," he said, not wanting to believe what he just heard.

"You need anything?" Coco asked as she wiggled in her jeans and threw her hair in a ponytail.

"No I'm good, where you going?" "I have to get down to the hospital, so I can be there to support Christie," Coco said, as her eyes started to water.

"Fuck!" Gmoney cursed loudly. "What else can go wrong?" He asked in a defeated tone. "First I got shot, Ali gets locked up, Spanky kills himself, and on top of all that, I ain't making no money because I don't even have a fucking connect!"

"Don't worry baby. Once your wounds heal up, you are going to get it all together," Coco said as she kissed Gmoney on his forehead. "You just take this time and get your rest so when you come back, you can come back strong."

"Thanks boo; you always seem to cheer me up."

"That's my job," Coco replied with a smile. "I'm out baby; call me if you need me."

"Alight, make sure you lock that door," Gmoney yelled out as he grabbed his .45 from under the pillow and sat it within arms reach just in case.

$ilk White

When Coco arrived at the hospital, it was a circus. There were men and reporters all over the place. Some people would do anything to get a story.

When Coco finally made it to the waiting area, she saw Christie sitting in the corner with her face buried in her hands.

She sat down next to Christie and gently began to rub the lower part of her back. "I'm here for you girl," she whispered.

"I shouldn't have told him about Ali," Christie said in between sobs. "It's all my fault."

"It's not your fault. Sometimes shit just happens. This could have happened to any one of us," Coco said sincerely. Seconds later, Freddie stormed up in the hospital crying like a baby. "I knew I should have rode in the limo with y'all! Something in my heart was telling me not to let y'all leave alone!"

"It's not either one of y'alls fault," Coco stated plainly, tired of hearing the two, blame each other for something neither one of them could stop. "Girl you know you can come stay with me and Gmoney until all this blows over if you want," Coco offered.

"That's okay, I think I'm gonna just stay in a hotel for a couple of days and get my mind together," Christie said emotionlessly as she headed for the exit.

Coco made sure Christie and Freddie made it to their vehicles safely before she headed back home. For the entire ride home, Coco prayed out loud for Christie and Freddie. She could only imagine what the two were going through.

"Sometimes it takes something to happen to someone close to you for you to see how blessed you are," Coco thought as she pulled up in her drive way.

When she stepped foot in the bedroom, she saw Gmoney laying in the bed watching a rerun of "Flavor of Love."

"Hey baby, how's Christie holding up?" He asked dryly.

"She's taking it kind of hard, but she's going to be alright," Coco replied as she slid out of her clothes and slid in the bed butt naked and curled up next to Gmoney, where she soon fell asleep.

"Bull Pin Therapy"

"On your feet, dickhead," a red-necked officer barked loudly as he banged his nightstick against the bars on the cell.

Ali stood up and stared coldly at the officer. "You talking to me?"

"Whom else would I be talking to?" The officer capped back. "Put your fucking hands through these bars so I can cuff you dickhead." He made sure he let his last words roll off his tongue.

Ali thought about saying something slick back to the officer. But after the beat down the police gave him when they first brought him down to the station, he decided to bite his tongue and do what he was told.

TEARS OF A HUSTLER 2

Once Ali was cuffed, the officer roughly escorted him to the interrogation room. "Sit down and shut the fuck up," the officer growled as he forcefully sat Ali down in the seat. Two minutes later, Detective Nelson strolled up in the interrogation room puffing on a Winston.

"You have anything you want to tell me?" He asked with an evil smirk on his face. Ali didn't respond.

"Didn't I tell you I was going to end your career?" Detective Nelson chuckled, blowing a cloud of smoke in Ali's face. "After everything we've been through, I'm still going to try to help you," he said as he placed a pen and pad in front of Ali. "We're trying to build a federal case on your friend Gmoney. Help us and we'll help you."

Ali didn't say a word. Instead, he just stared at the detective coldly.

"You're looking at the death penalty. I think you might want to think about this," Detective Nelson paused. "You and your girlfriend killed eight cops. I think you might want to take this deal," Detective Nelson said as he made his exit, giving Ali time to think on it.

All Ali thought about was breaking Detective Nelson's neck with his bare hands. Seconds later, Mr. Goldberg slowly entered the interrogation room. The look on Mr. Goldberg's face told Ali all he needed to know.

"It's that bad huh," Ali chuckled.

"Yeah they talking about giving you and Nancy the death penalty," Mr. Goldberg spoke in a soft voice.

"Write this down," Ali said sliding the pen and note pad to his lawyer. "You tell'em I killed all of those cops and Nancy had nothing to do with any of this."

"You know if you do that, it's not going to be no trial because you basically confessing to all the murders," Mr. Goldberg asked, making sure Ali knew what he was saying.

"Yeah I'll do the time. You just make sure you get Nancy out of this shit hole, and try to get this death penalty dropped, you hear?"

"Will do, anything else?" Mr. Goldberg asked, feeling bad for his favorite client.

"Yeah make sure you let Gmoney know that Detective Nelson and the rest of these racist mufuckas are trying to build a federal case against him. So tell him to move a lil smarter and quieter. Oh and tell him I found out who the snitch is."

"Who is it?" Mr. Goldberg asked with open ears.

"Big Mel," Ali answered with a frown.

"Don't worry. I'll deliver that message personally," Mr. Goldberg said in a matter of fact tone. "Okay so I should have Nancy out of here in 48 hours."

"Oh and can you bring me a few books so I can get my read on?"

"I'll have them up here first thing in the morning. You stay strong you hear," Mr. Goldberg said as he gave Ali a hug before he made his exit.

$ilk White

Once Mr. Goldberg made his exit, Detective Nelson reappeared in the interrogation room. "Change your mind yet?" He asked with an evil smirk on his face.

"I would like to go back to my cell if that's okay," Ali said in bored tone.

"Why don't you use your brain for once in your life? You think we won't be able to build up a federal case on Gmoney by ourselves? I'm trying to help you out. Give us everything on Gmoney and I'll make sure you only have to do 15 years, maybe even 10," Detective Nelson said, looking at Ali for an answer.

"You finished? Can I go back to my cell now?" Ali yawned.

"You a stupid motherfucker," Detective Nelson growled as he stormed out of the interrogation room heated.

"The Good Life."

Rell sat in the living room of his baby mansion, along with Debo and Mad Dog. Rell's crew had really took the streets over, especially since Gmoney didn't have a connect and Ali was locked up. Things couldn't have been better for him and his crew.

"I gotta give you your props," Debo said, giving Rell a pound. "You shut Ali and Gmoney down. Nobody has been able to do that in almost 10 years."

"I can't take all the credit. Them niggaz was weak when we went to war with them. But the main thing is, we're on top now and we have to stay on top. We have to stay hungry and most of all we have to keep the soldiers hungry," Rell said, filling his glass up with vodka. "You two are in charge of security. Make sure y'all keep shit tight. We can't afford no fuck ups."

"Don't worry. We got everybody on their job," Debo announced proudly. "Yo you heard about that nigga who we broke up in the parking lot a couple of months back?"

"Nah, what's up with that chump?" Rell chuckled, thinking about how they assaulted the young man.

"That lil nigga blew his brains out the other night." "Get the fuck outta here," Rell said in disbelief.

"Nah, true story. I saw that shit on the news the other night too," Mad Dog said, speaking for the first time.

"Only weak people kill themselves, so that means he deserved to be dead," Rell said nonchalantly. "But speaking of death, I heard our friend Ali should be heading to the island soon (Rikers Island). Mad Dog I need you to send the word out. Let mufuckas know I got 20 stacks for whoever puts a shank in that cocksucker."

"Consider it done," Mad Dog replied quickly.

"So boss, what you want us to do about Detective Nelson?" Debo asked.

"Nothing yet. We going to keep things going according to plan until that white boy tries his luck and goes against the grain," Rell said in an even tone as he loaded his P89, popped one in the chamber, and rested the firearm in his waistband. "Y'all strap up real quick."

"Why what's up?" Mad Dog asked excitedly, ready to put in some work.

"We gotta go meet up with this spaghetti eating mazurka, Frankie. That slick mufucka tryna raise his prices up since we making so much money. He must be crazy if he thinks I'm paying that shit," Rell said out loud, as the trio made their exit.

* * *

Skip pulled up into Gmoney's driveway in his 2001 Expedition and beeped the horn five times. "This nigga always late," he said to himself.

"You got everything you need?" Coco asked innocently.

"Yeah I got everything," Gmoney replied with a smile.

"You be careful okay?"

"You know I am ma," Gmoney said as he headed for the door.

"Aren't you forgetting something?" Coco said, clearing her throat with a strange look on her face.

"Oh I'm sorry baby," Gmoney said as he came back and placed a soft kiss on Coco's lips.

"Thanks, but I was talking about this," Coco said, holding out a .380 in the palm of her hand.

"Oh shit, good looking out boo!" Gmoney said as he stuck the .380 in his sling that hung around his neck and cradled his arm, as he headed out the door.

"What's good? How's the shoulder holding up?" Skip asked, backing out of the driveway.

"It still hurts a little bit, but fuck all that. What you doing driving while you on the run?"

"Got me a fake I.D.," Skip said calmly as he hopped on the FDR drive.

"How's it looking in the hood?"

"Slow," Skip replied quickly, keeping his eyes on the road. "Knowledge said he's only pulling in about $500 a day."

"Damn, that's it?" Gmoney asked with a frown on his face.

"Yeah that nigga Rell locking shit down because he got the best product out," Skip said matter of fact.

"Who he getting his shit from, Frankie?'

"You know it," Skip said, shooting Gmoney a private look.

"Fuck," Gmoney cursed loudly. "I know there has to be somebody out here with some pure uncut shit. We just not looking in the right places." He sucked his teeth.

"So what we going to do until we find this new connect?"

"We gonna have to go O.T. (out of town) so we can keep the money rolling in.

Smell me? Get back on our old school shit."

"You know I don't give a fuck!" Skip said, as he pulled up to the corner of the projects.

"Call that fool Knowledge and tell him to hurry up."

Skip dialed a number in his phone; spoke briefly, and then hung up. "He said he is on his way now."

Minutes later, Gmoney and Skip saw Knowledge bopping towards the vehicle.

"Hurry the fuck up and stop trying to look cool," Gmoney huffed.

"I'm not trying to look cool. I'm just naturally cool. You dig," Knowledge said playfully as he slid in the back seat.

"You got somebody holding down the block for you?" Gmoney asked.

"Yeah I got some young swoll head nigga holding it down," Knowledge replied.

"Good because I'm going to need you and Skip to round up a few goons and take our operation O.T. until I find us a new connect," Gmoney told the two.

"A'ight, cool. So where we going? Albany, Georgia, Kentucky? Just let me know where we going and it's on and popping," Knowledge said from the back seat.

"Florida," Gmoney said in an even tone. "That chick I bagged from the club the night I got shot, Ashley, she said she has an apartment out in Florida. So I want y'all to set up shop in her apartment and get this money."

"A'ight, bet that shit sound like easy money," Skip said, shrugging his shoulders.

"Yeah but I don't want y'all going out there on some cowboy shit. Y'all niggaz go out there on some low key, laid back shit and get this money. Ashley is going to have all the drugs and guns in her car. All y'all have to do is follow her in separate cars, dig?"

"How long are we staying out there?" Knowledge asked.

"For a month," Gmoney replied quickly. "I should be done found a connect by then."

"So where we headed now?" Knowledge asked.

"Skip is dropping me off at Mr. Goldberg's office. He left me a message talking about he needed to holla at me. After he drops me off, I want y'all to go pack y'all shit and get ready for this trip."

* * **

Rell entered the small diner with Debo and Mad Dog in tow. As soon as Rell entered the small restaurant, he saw Frankie sitting in a booth in the back of the diner.

"Glad you could make it on such short notice," Frankie said, forcing a smile on his face.

"Yeah, yeah, yeah, fuck all this bullshit! Let's get stra'ight down to business.

What's up with you raising your prices?" Rell asked, not hiding the fact that he didn't like the Italian man.

"I'm not raising the prices that high," Frankie protested.

"Listen if it ain't broke, then don't fix it," Rell shot back.

"Listen Rell, my peoples are having a little trouble getting the stuff in," Frankie said, sipping on his coffee.

"That don't have shit to do with me. You go take that shit up with Detective Nelson, that's between y'all two. I'm not paying no increase because you scared to talk to Detective Nelson!"

"You don't have no choice. You're going to have to pay the increase, that's just how the game goes," Frankie said nonchalantly, shrugging his shoulders.

With the quickness of a cat, Rell reached over the table and slapped the shit out of Frankie. "You must got shit twisted around here," Rell growled as he as shot to his feet, snatching his P89 from his waistband. "You don't tell me what fucking choices I have," he said as he slapped Frankie twice across his face, but this time he did it with the toast (gun) in his hand. Once other diners saw the gun, they quickly exited the small diner.

"Open ya fucking mouth," Rell growled, taking off the safety as he placed half of the barrel in Frankie's mouth. "I'm not paying these high ass prices. You make those other clowns pay extra, you understand?" Frankie nodded his head.

"And if any of your spaghetti eating friends have a problem, y'all know where to find me," Rell said as he gave Frankie one last slap across his face. "Bitch ass nigga," Rell said over his shoulder as he peeled four, hundred dollars bills off of his huge knot of cash and handed it to the waitress. "Sorry about the trouble I caused," he said as the trio made their exit.

"I can't stand that fake mafia motherfucker," Rell huffed as he placed a blunt between his lips.

"He really tried to make us pay extra for some shit he don't want to take up with Detective Nelson," Rell said to no one in particular.

Don't even worry about that slick hair cocksucker. If he even think about retaliating, I'm going to take care of him personally," Debo said, never taking his eyes off the road.

"Retaliate," Rell echoed. "I wish he would."

* * **

"What's up? You wanted to see me?" Gmoney asked, stepping inside Mr. Goldberg's office.

"Yeah I was just on my way to go visit Ali. Why don't you come take a ride

$ilk White

with me?" Mr. Goldberg said, looking at Gmoney for a response.

"Cool let's roll," Gmoney said as he followed Mr. Goldberg to his car.

"Where they got Ali, in the tombs?"

"Nah they just transferred him to Rikers Island," Mr. Goldberg answered. Gmoney and Mr. Goldberg sat in the visiting room patiently waiting for Ali to come from up stairs. Ten minutes, later Ali came through the visiting room door wearing the gray D.O.C. (Department of Corrections) jump suit. "My nigga what's good?" Ali smiled as he gently gave Gmoney a hug, not wanting to hurt his injured arm. "I'm still standing," Gmoney replied with a smile. "I'm sorry about what happen to your brother."

"He gonna be a'ight, he's a tough kid."

"What are you talking about?" Gmoney raised an eyebrow.

"I heard he got knocked out," Ali said clueless.

Gmoney lowered his head as he began quietly. "Ali after the fight was over, Spanky went back home and killed himself," Gmoney said, refusing to make eye contact with Ali.

"Yo don't play around like that," Ali said with fire in his voice.

"True story," Gmoney said in a frail voice. Ali looked over at Mr. Goldberg.

"I am too busy to watch the news." Mr. Goldberg shrugged his shoulders in shock. "Fuck!" Ali cursed loudly as he jumped to his feet and flipped the small table over that was in front of him.

Immediately, four C.O.'s came over and roughly escorted Ali out of the visiting room.

Gmoney and Mr. Goldberg just sat and watched the four C.O.'s escort Ali to the back. "I don't think you should have told him that shit stra'ight up like that," Mr. Goldberg suggested.

"I thought he knew about it already," Gmoney said, regretting having to be the one to break the news to Ali. For the entire ride back home, the two rode in tense silence.

"It was something I had to tell you," Mr. Goldberg said, finally breaking the silence. "Oh yeah, the last time I went to see Ali he told me to tell you he found out who the snitch was."

"Who?" Gmoney asked, giving the lawyer his full attention.

"Big Mel," Mr. Goldberg said, glancing over to see Gmoney's facial expression. Gmoney sucked his teeth. "I knew that nigga was snitching the whole time."

"I kind of suspected he was snitching myself," Mr. Goldberg said in agreement.

"It's all good. Gimme 72 hours and his body will pop up floating in one of these rivers. Mark my words," Gmoney assured his lawyer and long time friend.

"What ever you do, just make sure you do it discreetly," Mr. Goldberg said as he pulled up in front of Gmoney's house. "You know I'm going to cover my ass," G-money winked at Mr. Goldberg as he disappeared through the front door of his house.

CHAPTER 1 ROAD TRIP

"Y'all ready?" Ashley asked, loudly popping her gum.

"Yeah we ready," Knowledge answered as he watched Ashley's fat ass jiggle from side to side as she swayed towards the car. "Damn Gmoney stay with the good quality smuts."

"Stop worrying about some ass and start focusing on getting this money," Skip checked him.

"Damn what's wrong with you? I'm just having a lil fun," Knowledge huffed as he slid in the passenger seat of the Benz.

"Just stay focused, we already got enough problems," Skip reminded him.

Ashley pulled up along side Skip and beeped the horn. "Y'all ready?"

"We about to follow you right now, and make sure you keep your music to a minimum," Skip said, making the engine come alive.

Ashley sucked her teeth as she slowly pulled out into traffic. She drove a green Mazda 626. Skip and Knowledge followed her in a Benz, and a van full of soldiers followed the Benz.

"Yo son we going to shut this town down when we get there," Knowledge boasted as he placed a Newport between his lips.

"Remember Gmoney said to go out here on some laid back shit."

"Damn why don't you loosen up?" Knowledge hissed as he reclined his seat back.

"Listen I can't afford no slip ups. And if you slip up, that means I slipped right along with you," Skip told him.

"A'ight, a'ight I feel you. I ain't gon slip," Knowledge said, pulling hard on his cigarette. "We just gonna go out here and get this money, maybe even some pussy if we get lucky," he said, laughing hysterically, nudging Skip the whole time.

Skip did his best to block out all the ignorant shit Knowledge was talking about. The only thing on his mind was his wife April. "I wonder what she's doing right now," he thought as he cruised along the dark highway. His thoughts were rudely interrupted when he felt Knowledge nudging him again.

"Yo these country bitches be having the stupid fat asses, know what I'm saying?"

"Yeah," Skip replied emptily as he pulled out his cell phone and dialed April's number.

* * **

$ilk White

"Come and eat," April yelled as she piled spaghetti on two plates and set them down on the table.

"What you cook mommy?" Little Michael asked, licking his lips for extra emphasis.

"Your favorite; spaghetti and meat balls," April answered as she poured her and him a glass of apple juice. "Bow your head for prayer."

After a short prayer, April and Michael began attacking their food like animals. "Damn I think I out did myself tonight," she boasted, looking at Little Michael for a compliment. "Is something wrong?" She asked, sensing something was wrong.

"Is daddy coming home for dinner?" Little Michael asked innocently.

"Not tonight sweetheart," April answered quickly. She knew this conversation would present it self sooner than later.

"What about tomorrow?"

April cleared her throat before she spoke. "Michael your father won't be coming home for a while. He has to stra'ighten out a few things in his life. He'll be back. And if I know your father like I think, he'll be back sooner than we both expect."

"Are you and daddy getting a divorce?" Little Michael asked, twirling his fork around in his spaghetti.

"Damn these kids are too fucking smart nowadays," April said to herself, looking around the kitchen formulating a response. "No baby we're not getting a divorce. Me and your father are just working out a few things. Once everything is worked out, your father will be back, I promise."

"Okay, can I go to my room now?" Little Michael asked dryly.

"You don't want to finish eating your food?"

"Okay go empty your plate," April said as she watched Little Michael empty his plate and stomp off to his room. Times like this, April wished Skip were home so he could be the one to answer their child's questions, instead of her always having to be the bad guy. Before April could get up from the table, she heard her cell phone ringing. She looked at the caller I.D. and saw Skip's name flashing across the screen. April was about to answer it, but then decided to just send Skip stra'ight to the voicemail. April loved Skip, but she knew he still wasn't ready to give up his lifestyle. Until then, she had nothing to say to him.

* * * *

"Damn," Skip cursed loudly when he got April's voicemail. Please record your message after the beep beeeep…

"Yo when you gon' stop playing these fucking games? I know you see my number on the fucking caller I.D. You know what? Fuck you!" Skip said, ending the call.

"Problems at home?" Knowledge questioned.

"What else is fucking new?" Skip huffed. "Bitches ain't shit but problems," he said out of frustration.

"Don't sweat it. It happens to the best of us."

"But I don't get it; I buy her everything she wants. She lives in a nice ass house and drives two nice cars. She don't have to do shit but go to school," Skip hissed. "I would love to stay home all day and get taken care of. Shit if a bitch is paying for all my shit, you wouldn't hear a peep out of me. As long as she ain't out selling her ass, I don't care. Smell me?"

"I feel you. But you know chicks don't think like that. They be wanting all that romantic bullshit," Knowledge chuckled. "Every chick that has a drug dealer for a boy friend will always say she liked it better when you didn't have money. But that's only because now they already got everything they wanted, and now they bored living in that big ass house. Chicks are crazy. No matter how hard we study them we'll never understand them," Knowledge said, lighting up another cigarette.

"That's the most non-ignorant shit you said all night," Skip said, giving Knowledge a pound.

"Yeah bitches are crazy, but we wouldn't be shit without them," Knowledge said, staring blankly out the window.

"I know that's right," Skip agreed as he kept a small distance between the Benz and the Mazda he was tailing.

CHAPTER 2 WELCOME HOME

Coco quickly dressed and dressed Little Ali in his cutest outfit. "You ready to go see your mommy?" She asked in a baby voice.

"What time is Nancy supposed to be released?" Gmoney asked as he loaded his .45.

"Mr. Goldberg said anytime between three and five," Coco answered as she headed to her car, carrying Little Ali in his car seat.

When Coco finally reached the prison, she was happy to see Mr. Goldberg waiting there for her.

"You got here right on time," Mr. Goldberg said, looking at his watch. "She should be released in about 15 minutes."

Thirty minutes later, Nancy was finally released from the facility. "Thank you so much," Nancy said gratefully as she gave Mr. Goldberg a big hug.

"No problem," he replied nicely.

"And thank you sooo much," Nancy said as she gave Coco a big bear hug.

"I brought somebody to see you," Coco smiled as she placed Little Ali in his mother's arms.

"Awww look at my baby," Nancy sang, placing kisses all over the baby's little face.

"Come on let's get you to the crib so you can shower and change those filthy clothes," Coco said as she slid back in the driver seat of her vehicle.

"Y'all drive safely okay? And if y'all have any problems or questions just give me a call," Mr. Goldberg said politely as he made his way over towards his vehicle.

"I'm glad you home girl," Coco said as she pulled out into traffic.

"Yeah I just wish Ali could have come home with me," Nancy said as a tear escaped her eye.

"Ali is a soldier. He took all that time so you could be free, and I'm pretty sure he wouldn't want to see you crying right now," Coco said as she slowed down for the yellow light.

"I know, but it's hard. I love that man to death. We was just about to get married," she said as the tears started pouring. "It seems like every time things start going good for me, somebody or something always snatches it away from me."

"That's life! Shit like that happens every day," Coco said in an even tone. "For example, when Gmoney got shot, he could have easily died. Shit just happens and we all gotta just roll with the punches."

"I know I'm trying to be strong, but it's hard."

"You need to count your blessings. You and Ali could have easily been killed in that sting, but both of y'all are still alive," Coco said, trying to cheer her best friend up.

"Trust and believe I'll be at every visit; me and Little Ali."

"That's what I'm talking about. You just gotta make the best out of your situation," Coco said, pulling up in her driveway.

"Yeah you right. I just love Ali so much and I miss him already," Nancy said, wiping her eyes. "And thanks for letting me stay here until I get everything together."

"Don't mention it. We got more than enough space," Coco said as the two entered the house.

"Hey what's up jail bird," Gmoney joked as he kissed Nancy on the cheek.

"Hey what's up G," Nancy replied dryly.

"Keep ya head up girl. We all know Ali not going to have no problems behind the wall," Gmoney said as he poured himself a drink.

"Oh yeah, I forgot to ask you, did Spanky win his fight that night?" Nancy asked.

"Oh shit, I forgot you ain't been around no T.V. while you was in the joint," Coco said as she poured herself a shot of Henny before she continued. "Umm… Spanky got knocked out in the fight."

"Damn, I know the only reason he lost was because his arms weren't a hundred percent," Nancy said, shaking her head. "It's all good. I know he going to come back strong."

"Nah, he won't be making a comeback," Coco said, downing the liquid fire in one gulp.

"I know Spanky didn't retire after one loss," Nancy said, looking at Coco for a response.

"No, he didn't retire. After the fight, he killed himself."

"Get the fuck outta here!" Nancy said in disbelief.

"True story," Coco said, looking down at the floor.

"Damn that's crazy. How is Christie holding up?"

"Not sure. We can go and check up on her tomorrow and see how she doing," Coco suggested.

"Definitely, I'm about to go hop in the shower and get out of these clothes," Nancy said as she handed Little Ali to Coco and headed for the bathroom.

CHAPTER 3 THE PROBLEM

Detective Nelson pulled up in front of Frankie's mansion with an attitude. "I wonder what this guy is going to complain about now," he said out loud, as he rang the doorbell. Seconds later, one of Frankie's big bodyguards answered the door. "Outta my way," he huffed as he brushed past the security guard, and headed towards the huge living room where he saw Frankie sitting on the leather sofa, along with another Italian man sitting next to him with a long slick looking ponytail.

"Okay what seems to be the problem?" Detective Nelson chimed as he helped himself to a glass of stra'ight vodka.

"That fucking moolie, Rell, is out of control. Either you handle him or I will," Frankie said, still upset and embarrassed about what Rell did to him in the small diner.

"What happened?" Detective Nelson asked, flopping down on the couch. "I go down to meet this prick in a small diner so I can discuss the new prices with this idiot, and the fucking moolie sucker punches me out of the blue for no reason," Frankie continued his rant. "Then this fucking cocksucker sticks a fucking gun in my mouth. Can you believe this shit?" Detective Nelson couldn't help but laugh.

"I'm glad you think this is so fucking funny," Frankie said angrily, pouring himself another drink. "I hope you start laughing when you turn on the morning news and see that fucking moolie on your screen," he threatened.

"Don't get your panties in a bunch; I'm going to go talk to him."

"Fuck a talk," Franked snapped. "Let me kill that black son of a bitch and you just find you somebody to take his place."

"I wish it was that simple. You see Rell and his crew bring in too much money to just cut him off," Detective Nelson said nonchalantly.

"So what are you telling me that this cocksucker can just go around doing whatever the fuck he wants?" Frankie asked, raising an eyebrow.

"I told you I was going to talk to him. And don't worry; I'll make him pay the extra since he attacked you. Will that make you feel better?"

"I would feel better if Rell was dead," Frankie said irritated. "Do you trust me?" Detective Nelson asked with an evil smirk on his face.

"I guess," Frankie remarked snidely.

"Alright then, I said I'm going to handle it. So just sit back, collect this money, and be cool alright?"

"Okay," Frankie said, giving the detective a half smile. Once Detective Nelson made his exit, Frankie quickly turned his gaze at Jimmy. "This moolie has got to go."

"Just give me the word and it's done," Jimmy said nonchalantly, as if taking someone's life was an everyday thing.

Jimmy was an Italian hitman who loved his job a little too much. Frankie heard Jimmy was the best of the best, so he hired him after Rell had assaulted and embarrassed him. "I want this whacked. But at the same time, I can't afford to fuck up the money," Frankie said in deep thought. "Fucking moolie brings in tons of money."

"Okay then why don't you let me send him a message?" Jimmy said as his ponytail flapped every time he turned his head.

"You know what? That might be a good idea," Frankie said, rubbing his hands together.

"I think maybe I should take out one of his family members or somebody who's close to him," Jimmy suggested.

"Yeah, but I'm not sure if he has any family."

"Don't worry. I'll tail him for about a week and find out who he's close to," Jimmy said as he stood to leave.

"Okay keep in touch with me," Frankie said, noticing some form of chest protector poking through Jimmy's dress shirt, as he stuck his arms through his blazer and headed towards the exit.

Frankie knew what Jimmy was capable of, and he also knew Rell would definitely get the message loud and clear.

* * **

Before Detective Nelson went home, he made a quick pit stop in the Bronx, near Hunts Point. Detective Nelson cruised slowly down the block until he saw exactly what he was looking for. The young black prostitute stood on the corner wearing a tight spandex top advertising her large breast. The mini skirt she wore exposed the bottom of both of her ass cheeks, and her clear stiletto's made her calf and legs look even more voluptuous.

Detective Nelson pulled up in front of the young lady and beeped the horn. The prostitute swayed towards the vehicle, throwing a little extra switch in her walk. The passenger window rolled down and the prostitute gladly stuck her head through the window.

"What's up? You looking for a good time?" She asked, seductively licking her lips.

"I'm looking for a good blow job. Could you steer me in the right direction?"

"Look no further. You found the cream of the crop and I got some bomb pussy too," she added.

"Oh really," Detective Nelson replied, sizing the young lady up.

"You not a cop are you?" The prostitute asked suspiciously.

"Yes I am," Detective Nelson replied. "But I'm not looking to arrest anybody, just looking for a good blow job."

"Okay well you don't mind paying up front then do you?"

"Not a problem," Detective Nelson said, handing the young lady a crumbled up fifty-dollar bill.

The prostitute stuffed the money in her little purse and slid in the passenger seat with the Detective.

When Detective Nelson pulled up in front of his brown stone apartment, he noticed a familiar face standing in front of his building. "What the fuck are you doing here?" He grunted as he approached his building with the young prostitute on his heels.

"You don't look too happy to see me," Big Mel said smugly.

"Can't you see I'm a little busy?" Detective Nelson said, nodding his head towards the young prostitute.

"Fuck that! That shit can wait. You owe me something and I'm here to collect," Big Mel told him in a cold tone.

"What are you talking about?" Detective Nelson asked, faking ignorance.

"You told me if I helped you get rid of Ali, in return you would give me a hundred thousand dollars in cash and a few spots for me to put product in," Big Mel refreshed the Detective's memory.

"Oh yeah I did tell you that didn't I?"

"Listen I ain't got time for these games. I want my money and I want it now," Big Mel declared.

"Well I don't have the money right now," Detective Nelson shot back. "I'll have your money sometime this month."

"I need my money now detective!"

"I don't have it. What do you want me to do? Pull it out my ass," Detective Nelson hissed as he tried to brush past the big man.

With the quickness of a snake, Big Mel pulled a metal pipe from his back pocket. He swung the pipe so hard that one could hear it cutting through the wind until it made contact with Detective Nelson's head.

Detective Nelson's body quickly collapsed, loudly smacking the hard concrete. Before the prostitute could scream, Big Mel covered her mouth with his gloved hand. "I'm not going to hurt you, okay?"

The prostitute nodded her head yes.

"I'm going to take my hand off your mouth and you better not scream," Big Mel said, slowly releasing his grip from the young prostitute's mouth.

"Hopefully this will keep you quiet," he said, handing the young lady a hundred dollar bill.

"Thank you so much for not hurting me," the prostitute said gratefully as she quickly disappeared around the corner.

Big Mel quickly scanned the block. Once he was sure that the coast was clear, he unarmed the detective, then scooped him up and tossed him over his shoulder. He carried the detective up a flight of stairs until he reached his apartment.

Big Mel let the detective's body slam viciously on the floor as he searched through his pockets until he found his keys. He quickly unlocked the door and dragged Detective Nelson inside the apartment by his ankles. "Punk ass white boy," Big Mel chuckled as he handcuffed Detective Nelson with his own cuffs.

Once Detective Nelson was cuffed, Big Mel searched the apartment high and low looking for the stash. He flipped over Detective Nelson's mattress and his eyes lit up. "Jackpot," He mumbled as he saw the entire box spring covered with money. Big Mel didn't have time to count the money, but from the looks of it, it had to be between twenty to forty thousand dollars.

Big Mel grinned wickedly as he stuffed as much money as he could in a pillowcase. When it was all said and done, Big Mel had four pillowcases filled with money.

Big Mel was about to make his exit, but stopped directly in front of the door when he heard Detective Nelson mumble something. "I'm going to enjoy watching you die," he grumbled with fire dancing in his blue eyes.

"What you fail to realize detective is that I'm already dead. How long you think I got until Gmoney or somebody from the crew finds me? I should have never dealt with you in the first place. Ali was a good brother and he always looked out for his own. Now because of me, he's sitting in a fucking cage," Big Mel said, disgusted with himself.

"You going to wish you was in a fucking cage when I get finished with you bitch," Detective Nelson huffed as he did his best to try and get to his feet, but it was no use.

"Did you just call me a bitch?" Big Mel asked, doing a 180. "You heard me loud and clear bitch," Detective Nelson barked, not backing down.

Before the last word left Detective Nelson's mouth, Big Mel was already in motion. He roughly pulled Detective Nelson's pants down to his ankles and removed the metal pipe from his back pocket.

"What the fuck are you doing?" Detective Nelson yelled in panic. "I'm about to show you who the real bitch is," Big Mel shot back as he viciously shoved the metal pipe up Detective Nelson's ass.

Detective Nelson's face turned bloodshot red as he howled in pain.

"That was for my man Ali," Big Mel said as he grabbed the four pillowcases and made his exit, leaving Detective Nelson laying on the middle of the floor, handcuffed with a pipe hanging out his ass.

CHAPTER 4 A THOUSAND MILES AWAY

Ali sat on the bus shackled down like an animal. His hands were shackled in front of him, while his right ankle was shackled to another inmates left ankle. Ali hated living in a cage like an animal, but at the same time, it was all part of the game. Ali always knew it was a possibility he would have to do some time, and he took his life sentence like a man. Mr. Goldberg had gotten him out of the death penalty, but he couldn't get him out of the life sentence.

Ali had prepared himself as best as he could mentally to do this time, but it's kind of hard to prepare yourself to NEVER COME HOME AGAIN.

While the other inmates went to sleep, Ali stayed up for the entire ride. When the bus finally pulled up to the facility, Ali swallowed hard as the barb wired fence opened allowing the bus to enter.

"Here we are boys. Gladiator school," the red face officer chuckled. All of the inmates remained on the bus until the C.O. directed them to exit the bus. Once inside the facility, the C.O. made all the inmates go inside the intake cell until further notice. After about 30 minutes of listening to the warden of the facility talk about nothing, the inmates had to strip butt naked and be searched before being sent to their cell.

"Let's go," a husky C.O. announced as he escorted Ali to his cell.

Ali was expecting to have a big, strong, greasy looking cellmate, but instead his cellmate turned out to be a midget. The C.O. forcefully pushed Ali in the cell and slammed it shut.

When the midget saw Ali enter the cell, he immediately hopped off his bunk. "Listen; let me let you know how shit works around here. You don't fuck with me and I won't fuck with you a'ight? And I hope you don't be snoring and farting and shit or we gon have some problems," the midget said, looking Ali up and down.

"My man, check this out. I aint trying to hear all that bull shit you talking about, smell me? Just stay out my way and don't fuck with none of my shit and we stra'ight," Ali said as he tossed his shit up on the top bunk.

"This my house," the midget said, patting his chest. "You don't tell me what's going on, I tell you."

Without thinking twice, Ali kicked the midget in his face. Once the midget was on his back, Ali forcefully planted his knee in his chest pinning him down. "If I hear another word out of you, I'mma break your fucking face," he threatened.

"Nah you can't just come up in here regulating shit. I been here for eight years," the midget huffed.

"Do whatever you want to do. Just don't bother me," Ali said as he took his knee off of the midget's chest.

The midget quickly hopped back on his feet. He thought about trying his luck, but decided against it. "Well we both gotta live here, so I guess we better make the best of it," the midget said as he hopped back on his bunk.

Ali unpacked a few of his things, then climbed up to his top bunk, and laid flat on his back. "So what's your name," he asked, breaking the silence.

"Everybody calls me Lil Bit," the midget spoke proudly.

"So what's your story?"

"What you mean?" Lil Bit asked defensively.

"What you in for?" Ali rephrased the question. "I got caught with three bricks in my trunk."

As Ali listened to the midget speak, he noticed he had a strong down south accent. "Yo, where you from?"

"Florida," Lil Bit responded.

"So how you get locked up in New York?"

"I was working for this girl named Pauleena. I'm sure you've heard of her," Lil Bit raised an eyebrow. "She got shit locked down in Florida, but now she's expanding her operation to New York. She getting money out here from mainly wholesale, but she really looking for a spot so she can get some of that break down money."

"Yo, I heard rumors about Pauleena, but I thought that was just street gossip," Ali said staring blankly at the ceiling.

"Nah she's real, sexy as fuck too," Lil Bit added.

"How long you been working for her?"

"Mmmm… about five years before I got locked up. But fuck all that. What's ya name and what you in for?" Lil Bit reversed the conversation.

"Everybody calls me Ali."

"I heard of you. You that brother that was giving all the niggaz in the hood jobs and shit. I also heard you killed 15 cops who tried to bust up in your crib."

"Nah it was only eight cops," Ali corrected him.

"You know your name was even ringing out in Florida?"

"Word?" Ali asked, shocked.

"Yeah, it was talk about some up north cat getting crazy money and giving back to the community. The word was your crew was kind of like the black mafia," Lil Bit chuckled.

"The black mafia huh," Ali echoed. "Is that a compliment?"

"What? Fosho!"

"Thanks I guess," Ali said with a smile.

"Pauleena would always talk about how she wanted to hook up with you and your crew. I think she kind of admired you," Lil Bit said in an even tone.

"Word?"

"Yup, she got the most high quality shit in America," Lil Bit boasted.

"In America, huh?"

"The shit used to be so pure, we had to stomp on the shit just so the fiends wouldn't O.D., I swear to God."

"Well I wish we could of hooked up before I got locked up, plus I been out the game for a while."

"Out the game?" Lil Bit hopped out of his bed in shock. "You can never get out. You know that!"

"Yeah and I also know you can't over stay your welcome in the game either," Ali capped.

"Yeah I hear you," Lil Bit replied, as he laid back down on his bunk.

"What I was trying to do was build something; you know what I'm saying? Instead of buying jewelry, cars, and spinning rims, I invested my money into the businesses. That way it would bring me more money, and give more black people jobs because I only hired black people, who couldn't get jobs because they had felonies, or they didn't graduate from school, smell me?"

"Yeah that's some deep shit."

"If more drug dealers and people period, would do shit to help their community, the world be a better place; then maybe it wouldn't be so many mufuckas sitting in jail."

"Yeah, you a deep brother. Hopefully everybody will wake up sooner or later," Lil Bit said, as he opened up his King Magazine.

"Yeah hopefully," Ali said as he drifted off to sleep.

CHAPTER 5 NEW GUN IN TOWN

"Here take this," Knowledge huffed as he handed the crackhead the amount of crack he paid for and shoved him out the back door. "Damn these mufuckas is filthy," Knowledge complained. "Shit, I thought the fiends in New York was bad; God damn!"

"Nigga you been complaining since we got here," Skip huffed, shaking his head.

"I'm just saying yo, I gotta wash my hands every 10 minutes," Knowledge continued to rant.

Skip had set everything up lovely. He turned Ashley's apartment into a trap house. The fiends came in through the back door, got served, and exited the same way they came in. Two shooters occupied one of the upstairs bedrooms and looked out for any signs of trouble. Skip also had Suge standing in the doorway.

Suge was 6'7 and weighed 360 pounds; his job was to make sure no fiends got out of hand. Everybody called him Suge because he favored Suge Knight.

"I told you this shit was going to be a piece of cake," Knowledge said out loud, as he waited for the next customer to show up.

Skip was about to respond, but lost his train of thought when he saw Ashley walk into the kitchen wearing nothing but some boy shorts and a bra. "Yo why don't you put some fucking clothes on?" Skip said, crumbling up his face.

"This is my motherfucking house. I can wear whatever I want to wear. Plus it's hot as fuck in here," she shot back in a sassy tone.

"Why don't you have some respect for yourself?" Skip sucked his teeth in disgust.

"If you don't like it, then don't look," Ashley said, snaking her neck. "Plus I don't think Gmoney would appreciate it if he knew you had your eyes glued to his stuff," she said as she swayed back towards the steps.

"Fuck that. You can walk around however you want. I don't mind," Knowledge said as he hungrily eyed the beautiful woman who stood before his eyes.

"You shut your pervert ass up. This pussy right here," she slapped her ass, "belongs to Gmoney!"

"Bitches is too bold nowadays," Skip hissed as he pulled out his cell phone and dialed April's number, only to get sent stra'ight to the voicemail again.

"Yo my dude, I'm about to run to the store down the block real quick. You want anything?" Knowledge asked, placing his 9mm in the small of his back.

"Nah, I'm good. Good looking though," Skip replied, his mind stuck on his wife and son.

$ilk White

* * * *

"Damn, shorty ass is stupid fat," Knowledge said out loud as he turned around to look at the woman's ass who was leaving the store as he entered. "I love these country bitches," he said loudly as he grabbed the items he desired.

All the women in the store gave him salty looks for the last comment he made, but Knowledge paid them no mind.

"Fuck this shit," Knowledge huffed as he nonchalantly skipped the line and tossed his items on the counter. "Yo fam, let me get some Skittles and some Newport's B."

"Ummmm… there is a line back here," a dark skin lady said loudly, as she sucked her teeth.

"Oh yeah, and let me get a lighter too," Knowledge said, ignoring the woman who stood behind him.

"Excuse me sir?"

"Fuck outta here," Knowledge said, directing his attention to the woman. "Damn, I'm just tryna get some cigarettes."

"Well you need to wait in line like everybody else," the lady said, raising her voice.

"Listen bitch, I don't do lines! Now excuse my back," Knowledge said, turning his back to the lady so he could pay for his shit and go.

"Bitch?" she echoed. "Who the fuck you calling a bitch? You don't want me to go get my baby daddy, because if I go get him all hell will break loose up in this store. You better act like you got some sense fuck nigga!"

Knowledge sighed loudly, as he slowly turned around and backslapped the lady. "Now go get ya baby daddy!"

"You done fucked up now," the lady said as she exited the store still holding the side of her face.

* ** *

"Stupid ass bitch," Knowledge mumbled as he stepped back in the house.

"What's wrong?" Skip asked, sensing something was wrong.

"I just had to smack the shit outta some bitch at the store," Knowledge said with a bit of venom in his voice.

"You stupid," Skip exhaled. "You just don't get it," he lightly scolded him.

"Nah, shorty was up in the store wilding for no reason," Knowledge said, trying to sound convincing.

"You better hope she don't come back with nobody," Ashley said, sitting on the couch cross-legged. "Cause niggaz play with them choppers out here," she told him.

"Nobody asked you all that," Knowledge said as he shot her a cold stare.

"Yo, just stay in the fucking house from now on," Skip huffed.

"Damn, why you acting like a lil bitch?"

Skip was about to respond, but decided he didn't want to waste his breath.

** * *

Roy and three other men sat at a round table outside in the middle of the hood playing spades.

"Damn it's hot as fuck out here," Roy said, wiping the sweat from his forehead. The four men sat in the shade, but somehow the sun still took its toll on them.

Roy sat at the table with no shirt on, studying his hand. To the average person, Roy looked like a regular person. But everybody who knew him, knew he was one of the biggest drug dealers in Florida and one of, if not the most, vicious and violent men in America. Each man had their pistols on the table within arm's reach. Roy wrote down the score on a small piece of paper when he noticed an elderly woman approach the card game.

"Excuse me. I'm looking for someone who goes by the name Roy," the old lady said innocently. "How you doing ma'am? How can I help you?" Roy asked, giving her his undivided attention.

"Umm…you don't know me, but I was told if I had any problems to come see you," she said in a frail voice.

"So what's up?" Roy asked.

"My husband has a bad drug problem. He stole my rent money and now my rent is two months behind. If I don't pay my rent tomorrow, they going to put me out in the street."

"How much you need?"

"About $1,800," the old lady told him.

Roy looked over at his right hand man, Bumpy. "Pay the lady."

Bumpy quickly pulled out a big wad of cash and peeled off 20, one hundred dollar bills, and handed it to the elderly woman.

"God bless you Roy. Thank you so much," the old lady said as she kissed Roy on his cheek, as she walked away thanking the Lord.

"Damn that's the fifth rent you done paid this month," Bumpy huffed.

"You talking like that money is coming out of your pocket," Roy exhaled.

"I'm just saying, it seems like people are just trying to use you," Bumpy protested.

"Chill out bro," Roy said as he shuffled the cards.

Roy couldn't do nothing but chuckle. His right hand man Bumpy was one of the cheapest mufuckas in the world. He got the name Bumpy because his face was covered with nasty looking bumps. He had a face only a mother could love, but Roy and Bumpy been friends ever since the second grade. And when it came to gunplay, Bumpy was one of the best.

"How many books you got?" Bumpy asked as he noticed the familiar Dodge Charger come to a screeching stop.

Evet slid out of the driver seat with a hurt look on her face.

"What's up baby?" Roy asked focusing on the hand that he was dealt.

"Some hoe ass nigga just slapped me while I was at the store," Evet growled.

"Slapped you," Roy's brow furrowed at that last comment.

"Yeah, for no reason too," she added, still rubbing her face. "And he had a New York accent."

"A'ight, go in the house. I'mma take care of it," Roy said with a gesture of dismissal. Once Evet was in the house, Bumpy spoke. "How you want to handle this?"

"Round up a couple of soldiers and teach them fuck niggaz a lesson," Roy said in a calm voice. "I'mma go and make sure Evet is a'ight."

Bumpy quickly rounded up three soldiers, popped the trunk on the old school Cadillac, and removed three A.K.'s.

"Let's go take care of this business," Bumpy grumbled as he slid in the passenger seat. Once the car was filled, the Cadillac cruised to its destination.

* * * *

Skip sat on the couch along with Ashley, watching an episode of Martin. "Yo this nigga funnier than muthafucka," Skip laughed loudly.

"Damn, it aint that funny," Ashley sucked her teeth.

"Just shut up," Skip said mockingly.

Ashley sighed. "I need a drink."

"Get me one too," Skip chimed.

"Fuck outta here," Ashley yelled over her shoulder.

She returned from the kitchen carrying two glasses in one hand and a bottle of Remy in the other. Before she could make it back to the couch, bullets came flying through the windows and doors.

Skip quickly tackled Ashley and covered her from danger. The gunshots sounded like a marching band drum line stood outside of the apartment.

The two shooters who stood upstairs immediately opened fire on the old school Cadillac. Once the gunshots slowed up, Knowledge quickly shot to his feet, stormed outside, and emptied the clip of his 9mm at the Cadillac's taillights. "Pussies!" he yelled as he watched the Cadillac bend the corner.

"Yo get this money and drugs up outta here," Skip ordered as he held his Desert Eagle down by his side.

Suge quickly headed upstairs to do as he was told.

"Get ya ass up and put on some clothes," Skip said, helping Ashley up off the floor. "Two soldiers got hit," Suge said, with three duffle bags in his hands.

"A'ight listen. When the cops get here, just tell them you live here alone and somebody just did a drive by," Skip said as he and the rest of the crew slid out the back door and made their getaway.

CHAPTER 6 BACK FROM THE DEAD

Big Mel sat in his small, one bedroom apartment counting the money he just stole from Detective Nelson. Big Mel felt good about what he did to the crooked cop. His heart told him he should have killed the detective, but something inside of him decided that torturing the man would be better. The thing that bothered Big Mel the most was Ali. He was like a big brother to Big Mel and setting him up only made Big Mel feel worse and worse every time he thought about it.

Sitting on the couch next to Big Mel was a M16 Rifle and a Teflon vest. He knew half of the world was probably looking to kill him so on site, he would be prepared to throw down if need be. Big Mel had a lot of things on his mind, but his main objective was to make Detective Nelson's life as miserable as possible.

A huge smile appeared on Nancy's face when she saw Ali walk through the visiting room doors.

"Hey baby! I missed you so much," Nancy screamed as she jumped up in Ali's arms. "Hey boo," Ali said as he hugged Nancy tightly.

"So how's everything?" Nancy asked as the two sat down.

"I can't complain," he replied dryly.

"You ain't been having no problems up in here right?" Nancy asked nervously.

"Nah, I've been cool."

"Do you have a cellmate?"

"Yeah, my cellmate is a midget."

"A midget?" Nancy chuckled.

"Yeah, he's cool. I'm just making the best out of a bad situation," Ali shrugged.

"Did you hear about Spanky?"

"Yeah, I heard. I refused to go to the funeral," Ali said, looking down at the floor. "I can't look at my baby brother in a box."

"I understand," Nancy said, as she rubbed his back for comfort.

"Hey shit happens," he sighed. "First Big Mel snitches on me, then my brother kill himself right before I was supposed to get married." Nancy didn't know what to say, so instead, she just rubbed his back.

"What's up with little Ali?"

"Oh I was going to bring him, but he got a cold and I didn't want to bring him out in this kind of weather."

"Okay that's cool," Ali said, as he noticed some big diesel guy ice grilling him.

"You know him?" Nancy asked, noticing how the big man was staring at Ali.

"Nah, not that I know of," Ali shrugged his shoulders. "I probably killed somebody in his family or something," Ali said, taking a guess.

"Oh my God baby! Please try to stay out of trouble," Nancy pleaded.

"It's impossible to stay out of trouble in a place like this," Ali said, returning the big man's stare.

"That guy looks like he been working out since he was a baby," Nancy said, scared that the big man was going to hurt her fiancé'.

"It's all good," Ali said, redirecting his attention back to the queen that sat before him.

"You just be careful in this place, okay?"

"You know I got you boo," Ali told her as the C.O. announced that visiting hours were over.

Ali gave Nancy a big hug and kiss before he headed in the back, where each inmate had to strip butt naked and get searched.

* * * *

"How was your visit?" Lil Bit asked Ali, as soon as he entered the cell.

"It was cool, I guess."

"You take any flicks?"

"Nah, not this time," Ali said, hopping up on his bunk.

"A few of my chicks used to come see me the first year, but after that, it was a wrap. They all stopped coming one by one, slowly but surely," Lil Bit said, with a little bit of hurt in his voice.

"Don't let that bother you. You'll be outta here soon."

Lil Bit chuckled. "Yeah, in about eight more years."

"It could be worse. You could have got life," Ali remarked. "Fuck all that. I'm about to go to chow. You rolling?"

"What they having?"

"Pizza," Lil Bit said, throwing his shirt on.

"Yeah, I'll roll with you," Ali said, as he hopped off his bunk.

Five minutes later, every one's cell popped open and each inmate stepped out their cell and stood in line. After walking down a few flights of stairs, Ali and Lil Bit reached the mess hall (cafeteria).

As usual, the shit was noisy and packed. Ali stood on line and noticed the big diesel guy from the visiting room a few heads ahead of him and Lil Bit.

"Yo who is that big, ugly, diesel muthafucka?" Ali asked Lil Bit.

"Oh that's just Knock Out," Lil bit answered nonchalantly.

"Knock out?"

"Yeah, they call him that because where ever he punches you at, you gonna be knocked out. Why, y'all got beef?"

"I don't know. He was just staring at me while I was on my visit."

"That's not good," Lil Bit said, shaking his head.

"Fuck that! I'm about to go see what's popping!"

"Chill! Wait until we get back to the staircase," Lil Bit said, grabbing Ali by the wrist.

"Fuck that. I ain't waiting for him to make his move first," Ali said, jerking his arm loose. Ali quickly skipped the line and crept up on Knock Out from behind, with Lil Bit on his heels. With all his might, Ali swung and landed a vicious hook to the back of Knock Out's head.

With the reflexes of a wild animal, Knock Out turned around already in a swinging motion. Ali ducked the punch right on time. Knock Out's punch knocked out the guy who stood behind Ali.

Ali quickly followed up with a hook to the body and an upper cut to the big man's chin. The punches had no effect on the big man.

Knock Out grabbed Ali and with almost an effortless toss, Ali was airborne.

Once Lil Bit saw his cellmate crash on top of a table, he quickly threw two upper cuts below Knock Out's belt. Knock Out picked Lil Bit up with one hand and punched him across the mess hall.

By this time, Ali had made it back to his feet. Before Knock Out could make his way over to Ali, a well-known inmate named Loco, sliced Knock Out's face from behind with a street razor.

Before Knock Out knew it, Ali and Loco had him on the floor stomping him out. Seconds later, the turtles (Police in riot gear) came rushing in the mess hall. Every inmate immediately dropped down to the floor; no one wanting to get shot with a rubber bullet.

The officers quickly handcuffed Lil Bit, Ali, Loco, Knock Out, and two other inmates who was about to jump into the fight. The officers escorted them to the box and locked down the entire prison.

CHAPTER 7 HERE COMES THE BULLSHIT

Coco laid on the king-sized bed butt naked on her stomach, propped up on her elbows, watching a reality show with a blunt in between her fingers. She laughed at how silly people on T.V. acted, when she heard the front door slam. Seconds later, Gmoney entered the room. "Hey baby," he said, as he kissed Coco on the lips and removed the blunt from her fingers.

"What up G? I made dinner, but I'm sure you probably ate already."

"Yeah, I had Chinese food while I was out," Gmoney said distractedly, as he slowly and gently massaged and played with Coco's exposed pussy.

"She missed you too," Coco replied, as she felt her pussy getting wet instantly. Two minutes later Gmoney felt Coco's warm mouth all over his dick. Coco did her best to deep throat Gmoney's dick as she started off kissing and licking the head. By this time Gmoney had entered two fingers inside Coco's sopping wet pussy.

"Damn," Coco moaned with her mouth still full. Gmoney's fingers felt so good that she could feel herself releasing in his hand. Gmoney then placed his straining erection against her mouth and began guiding her head back and forth at a fast pace, until he couldn't take it anymore and exploded in her mouth.

Coco greedily swallowed every last drop then watched as Gmoney headed for the shower. Coco laid on the bed exhausted from her sexual escapade, as JayZ flowed through the speakers at a low volume, when the ringing house phone caught her attention. "Hello," Coco answered in lazy tone.

"Can I speak to Gmoney please?" a woman asked with a slight attitude.

"Who the fuck is this?" Coco asked nastily.

"This is Ashley," she answered in a slick tone. "Remember me? I met you at the hospital," she said, rubbing it in.

"Oh the high priced hooker? I remember you," Coco said, taking a shot.

"Listen, I don't have time to play games with you. Where's Gmoney? I been calling his cell phone and he ain't answering."

"Bitch it's obvious he's avoiding your calls for a reason," Coco said hotly. "I figured you must have been around him tagging along like always. Just tell him to call me. It's an emergency and don't forget the name is Ashley," she said, hanging up in Coco's ear.

"Fucking bitch," Coco cursed loudly, as she headed towards the bathroom. Before she could enter, Gmoney was coming out. "Damn, you could at least have enough respect for me and not give bitches the house phone number," Coco huffed, rolling her eyes.

"What the fuck are you talking about?" Gmoney asked, confused.

"Why the fuck does that bitch Ashley have our home number? What the fuck is this shit about?" she said, folding her arms in front of her.

"It's nothing boo. Ashley is out of town with Skip and Knowledge getting that money. I told her only to call the house if it was an emergency from a landline," Gmoney explained.

"Do I look stupid to you," Coco asked, trying to suppress the tears of anger that were starting to form in the corner of her eyes.

"Look don't start, because I ain't even trying to hear that bullshit tonight," G-money said, waving her off. "You know what? I don't need this shit," Coco hissed, as she began packing her things.

"What the fuck you doing?" Gmoney asked, looking on in shock.

"Something I should have done a long time ago," Coco said, as she continued to pack her shit.

"You know what? I'm sick and tired of you complaining about every fucking thing," Gmoney barked, as he stepped in Coco's closet and grabbed as much of her clothes as he could carry, and threw her belongings out in front of the house. The whole time Gmoney never noticed the van that stood across the street. Several FBI agents sat in the van snapping pictures of Gmoney from every angle.

"Don't touch my shit! I can carry it by myself," Coco yelled out as she quickly wiggled her fat ass in a pair of skintight jeans.

"What's going on out here?" Nancy asked, stepping out of her room.

"Girl, I can't stay here anymore. If I stay, he's only going to continue to step all over me," Coco said as her titties swung around freely. "Well, if you leaving then I'm leaving too," Nancy said as she handed Coco her bra from off the floor.

"Nah, I don't want you traveling all around in this weather with the baby," Coco said, as she grabbed a few more of her things and headed for the door.

"Gmoney, what happened?" Nancy asked, trying to defuse the situation.

"I give this girl the world and all she do is complain. Let her take her ass out there for a while, and then maybe she'll realize how good she had it!"

"You can't just put her out in this kind of weather," Nancy said on her friend's behalf.

"Fuck that she gotta go," Gmoney said, swatting in Coco's direction.

"I ain't going nowhere, until you give me some money," Coco declared.

"Here, you greedy bitch," Gmoney yelled as he tossed 15 thousand dollars down from the second floor of the huge house. "Is that enough, you fucking spoiled gold-digger?"

Coco didn't respond. She just picked up the neatly rubber band stacked money and made her exit.

Once outside, Coco tossed the money and the rest of her belongings in the trunk of her Lexus. She then slid in the driver's seat and made the engine come to life. But before she left, she wasn't going to leave quietly. Coco slid out the Lexus and picked up a brick that sat at the end of the driveway and tossed it through the windshield of G-money's Range Rover. "Muthafucka," she chuckled, as she quickly slid back in the driver seat of the Lexus and backed out of the driveway.

The entire time, the FEDS took pictures of every thing that went on.

* * **

"Come on!" Mad Dog yelled, leaning against the shinny black limousine. Seconds later, Rell stepped out of his house with an opened bottle of Moet in his hand, with Debo in tow.

"Happy born day my nigga," Mad Dog said, giving Rell a pound followed by a hug.

"It's my birthday, every day," Rell replied, as the trio slid in the back of the limo. "I'm just happy I made it another year on this earth to celebrate," Rell said, as he guzzled from the bottle.

"You heard about Detective Nelson?" Mad Dog asked.

"Nah, what's up with that chump? He was supposed to pick up his money last week, but he never showed up," Rell said.

"You ain't going to believe this shit," Mad Dog said, looking at his two partners. "I heard a soldier from Ali's crew broke into Detective Nelson's crib, beat him up, robbed him, and then shoved a pool stick up his ass."

The trio immediately erupted into laughter.

"Get the fuck outta here," Rell said, waving Mad Dog off.

"Nah, I'm dead ass. That's the word on the street," Mad Dog said, sipping slowly from his glass.

"Damn, that's fucked up," Rell chuckled, looking at his watch. "I know his ass hole is burning!" The trio erupted into laughter again.

When Rell and his crew entered the club, it wasn't jammed packed. But slowly but surely, the club began to fill up. Rell and his crew made their way to the V.I.P. section, where they ordered drinks.

The whole time Rell never noticed Jimmy sitting in the V.I.P. section next to him, along with a couple of Spanish women. Rell sat nursing a drink, bobbing his head to the music the DJ was playing, when he noticed a fine ass white girl. "Damn," Rell whispered as he admired the woman's long blonde hair and ocean blue eyes. Everyone who was close to Rell knew he had a weakness for white women. It was just something about them, not to mention they didn't complain and have an attitude every five minutes.

Debo and Mad Dog hated the fact that Rell always dated white women instead of black women, but Rell was the boss so it wasn't much they could do about it. "To each his own," is what the two would always say.

Debo shook his head, as he watched Rell snake through the crowd in pursuit of the white girl. "Excuse me. I don't mean to bother you," Rell said as he grabbed the white girl by her wrist. "It's my birthday and I would love for you to join me in my V.I.P. section for some drinks," he said in a well-spoken manner.

"Sure no problem," Blue eyes said, after she sized up the man that stood before her.

"I spotted you from across the room and I just had to say something to you," Rell told her, as he handed her a glass of champagne. "Thank you," she said, accepting the drink. "You're not too bad looking yourself."

"So what's a beautiful woman like yourself doing in a place like this?" Rell asked, guzzling from his bottle.

"My friend dragged me out the house. I'm not really a party person," Blue eyes chuckled lightly, as she sipped from her glass.

"I can tell," Rell replied, undressing the young lady with his eyes.

"So, what's your name?"

"Everyone calls me Rell."

"Nice to meet you Rell; everyone calls me Heather." She batted her eyes innocently, as she shook Rell's hand.

"That name definitely fits that pretty face," Rell flirted, as he kissed the top of Heather's hand.

"Thanks," Heather said, blushing, as she sat crossed legged.

Meanwhile, Jimmy sat watching Rell's every move. He had to give it to Rell; the man knew how to have a good time. Jimmy watched as Rell had a conversation with the young lady. He then looked over to where Debo and Mad Dog stood. Two sexy divas had their full attention. He decided now was the perfect time to make his move. "Excuse me ladies. I'll be right back," Jimmy said, as he snaked his way through the crowd slipping his black gloves on his hands. Once outside, Jimmy removed the .380 that rested in his ankle holster, along with the silencer that rested in the small of his back. He quickly screwed on the silencer as he approached Rell's limousine. "Hey you can't park right here."

"Why not?" The limo driver asked defensively.

Jimmy quickly shoved the .380 in the driver's face and pulled the trigger twice.

TEARS OF A HUSTLER 2

As if nothing happened, Jimmy walked off to his vehicle and disappeared into the night, leaving the limo driver slumped over the steering wheel.

* * * *

Heather sat in the V.I.P. section still talking to Rell when she noticed her friend signaling that she was ready to leave.

"Well it was nice talking to you, but my friend is ready to go and I'm driving so…."

"Can I get your number before you go?" Rell asked, as he smoothly removed his cell phone from its case.

"Sure," Heather said, as she punched her number inside his cell phone. "You better use it too." She winked as she and her friend disappeared in the crowd.

Rell watched Heather's ass switch from side to side before she disappeared through the crowd. "Damn, I gotta hit that," he said to himself, as he pictured the two going at it in his mind.

"Let's get up outta here. Its dead in here," Debo said noticing every body making their exit one by one.

When the trio made it outside, the cool breeze quickly assaulted them.

"Damn its brick (cold) out here," Rell mumbled, as he tapped on the hood of the limo so the driver could unlock the doors. "Yo open the fucking door," Rell yelled, as he walked over to the driver's window.

"Oh shit," Rell growled, as he quickly removed his p89 from his waistband. "Somebody shot my fucking driver."

"Why the fuck would somebody shoot our driver?" Debo asked, holding his Desert Eagle with two hands as his eyes swept the parking lot.

"Fuck that. Get inside the limo until the cab gets here just in case the shooter is still out here," Mad Dog suggested as he held open the back door.

Rell quickly hopped in the back of the limo and out of the line of fire.

When the cab finally arrived, Rell and Debo quickly slid in the back seat. Mad Dog stayed at the scene and waited until the cops arrived, since the limo was rented in his name.

"Who the fuck would go out and shoot our driver?" Debo asked as he and Rell entered the baby mansion.

"I don't even know who has the balls to do some shit like that," Rell said, as he headed over to the mini bar. "We already took care of Ali and Gmoney so it couldn't have been them," Rell said in deep thought.

"Probably some new jack trying to make a name for himself," Debo said, trying to figure out the mystery.

"Nah, that wasn't the work of an amateur," Rell said, downing the liquid fire in one gulp.

"We just gotta be cautious until we get to the bottom of this," Debo said.

"Don't worry, I'mma figure this shit out," Rell said in a serious tone.

CHAPTER 8 PAIN IN THE ASS

Detective Nelson laid on his bed flat, on his stomach, looking at the blank T.V. screen. Only evil and murderous thoughts ran through his mind. Detective Nelson had a mugshot picture of Big Mel lying right next to him. Every time he looked at it, the more he wanted to kill Big Mel. The detective hadn't slept in a week. Instead, he stayed up all night spinning the barrel on his .357 Magnum thinking about how was going to kill the big man when he caught him.

Detective Nelson didn't mind the fact that Big Mel had robbed him. He didn't like how Big Mel had tampered with his manhood; for that, Big Mel had to die a slow and painful death.

"Why are we hiding from these niggaz like some bitches?" Knowledge huffed, as he paced back and forth in the hotel room.

"Why don't you shut the fuck up and stop complaining? We still getting money so what's the big deal?" Skip grunted, as he served a crack head, and then sent him back on his way.

"It's not about the money. It's about standing our ground," Knowledge continued his rant.

"Listen, Gmoney will be here in about an hour. Take it up with him when he get here," Skip said, ending the conversation. Forty-five minutes later, Skip heard a loud knock at the door. When he answered it, Gmoney stood on the other side.

"What's good?" Gmoney asked; as he stepped in the hotel room, giving each man dap.

"So what's the plan?" Knowledge asked, thirsty to let his gun do the talking for him.

"Who's this guy who tried to smoke y'all?" Gmoney asked.

"Some cat named Roy," Skip answered. "I did a little research on dude and from what I hear he's the real deal."

"That's what I like to hear," Gmoney smiled. "Everybody strap up."

"What's the plan?" Suge asked, as he handed Gmoney a .45.

"Simple. I'mma go talk to the cat," Gmoney said, checking the magazine on his gun. "Either he's going to lead us in the right direction to get some bomb work, or we gon post up across the street from his block."

"They don't do the block thing too much out here. These niggaz be having the trap houses poppin," Knowledge informed Gmoney.

"I don't give a fuck how they make their money. Bottom line is I want in,"

Gmoney said as he and his crew made their exit, only leaving behind two soldiers, so they could serve any customers that showed up at the hotel.

* * * *

"Yeah we shot that whole shit up," Bumpy boasted, as he studied his hand.

"You think them city niggaz got the message?" Roy asked, as he poured himself a shot of Bacardi 151.

"I guess, because they ain't pumping out of that apartment no more," Bumpy said, throwing out a card.

As Roy went to count his team's books, he noticed two cars and a minivan pull up back to back.

"Looks like we got company," Roy announced, as he stood and grabbed his p89 from off the table. Bumpy, and the two other men who stood at the table, quickly cocked their weapons and stood in front of Roy.

Gmoney and Skip slid out of the Benz while Knowledge, Suge, and the rest of the goons stayed put.

"I'm looking for Roy," Gmoney said politely.

"Why? What's the play?" Bumpy asked, with a pistol in each hand.

"Are you Roy?" Gmoney asked.

"It doesn't..."

"Well then shut the fuck up," Gmoney said, cutting the ugly man off.

Bumpy took a step closer, then decided to stay his distance when he saw Skip's hand inch toward his waistband.

"How can I help you gentlemen?" Roy asked, stepping forward.

"I'm Gmoney and this is my home boy Skip. If it's not a problem, I would like to have a word with you alone, if that's okay."

"No problem. Just let my man pat you down real quick," Roy replied in a smooth tone. Immediately, Bumpy removed Gmoney's .45 from his waist.

"What's on ya mind?" Roy asked placing his p89 in the small of his back as the two stepped out of ear range.

"Well it's like this," Gmoney began. "I know you running a smooth operation and I'm not trying to interfere with any of that. I'm just trying to get in where I fit in, you dig?"

"I hear you bro. But I'm telling you now, this town ain't big enough for both of our crews," Roy said with little emotion.

"I agree. That's why I'm here to ask you for a favor."

"What kind of favor?" Roy raised an eyebrow.

"Well as you can tell, me and my crew is from New York," Gmoney paused momentarily. "Basically, I would like for you to introduce me to your connect, if that's not a problem. You introduce me, I take the work back to New York, and you never see me again. But if I can't find a connect, then you just gonna have to do what you gotta do cause we ain't leaving this bitch empty handed," Gmoney said in a determined tone.

Roy chuckled. "I admire your courage. Most people wouldn't have the balls to do some wild, cowboy shit like this. So I'm gonna tell you what I'm going to do for you," he paused. "Since my connect lives in upstate New York, I'm going to call her and ask if she ever heard of a Gmoney and if she would consider doing business with you. If she says cool, then you good, but if she say it's a no go, then I'm going to blow your head off," Roy said calmly as he pulled his p89 from the small of his back. "And my goon squad will take care of the rest of your crew."

Gmoney was about to come back with a slick remark, but when 30 men came running out of the apartment that he and Roy stood in front of, all carrying choppers, he held on to his thoughts. Immediately, two of the gunmen aimed their A.K. 47's at G-money face, while the rest of the shooters quickly unarmed Skip and surrounded the vehicles.

Roy shot Gmoney a good luck glance as he pulled out his cell phone and stepped off to the side.

Gmoney thought about reaching for the gunman's rifle, but the murderous look in the teenager's eyes quickly changed his mind. All Gmoney could do was wait it out and hope for the best.

After being on the phone for about 20 minutes, Roy walked over to Gmoney with a smile on his face. "Well looks like you're a certified gangsta," he said, sticking his p89 back in the small of his back. "It's cool," Roy announced, motioning for his goon squad to lower their weapons. "We all friends here."

"No hard feelings, but business is business," Roy said, extending his hand.

"I can dig it," Gmoney said, shaking the gangsta's hand that stood in front of him.

"My connect said she been wanting to do business with you and your partner Ali for quite some time. They just didn't know how to approach you or your wild crew."

"Is that right?"

"Yeah tell your crew to make themselves at home. I own this whole apartment complex, so they're welcome to relax in any apartment they want; as long as it's on this side," Roy said, making a gesture with his hand.

"You own this whole shit?" Gmoney asked in shock.

"Yeah, I bought it from some crackers who was over charging tenants. So I bought it and rented out the apartments for much more affordable prices. Plus I control all the money that comes in and out of here feel me?"

"I can dig it. You getting the best of both worlds yeah," Gmoney nudged him.

"You getting tenants rent, then if they want to get high, you right there to clean house."

"Exactly," Roy replied with a wink. "Let me take you on a little tour around here."

"So you second in charge?" Bumpy asked Skip.

"Yeah," Skip replied, giving the ugly man dap.

"You and your homey got a lot of heart coming down here in the chopper zone like that." "Desperate people do desperate things," Skip replied, shrugging his shoulders. "The reason I'm giving you a tour around here is because my connect wants you to join the family," Roy said. "Nah, I don't know about all that. I got my own family, no disrespect; you know what I'm saying?" "My partner would take it as a token of appreciation if you would consider." "Who the fuck is this secret connect?" Gmoney huffed as he placed a blunt between his lips. "I'm pretty sure you heard of Pauleena, the queen of the south right?" "The name sounds familiar, but I'm not really a south person, you dig?"

"I hear you bro," Roy said, as he led Gmoney to an apartment where two men stood in front, guarding the door. Roy nodded his head and immediately the two men stepped to the side so their boss and his friend could enter.

"Welcome to the trap house," Roy announced with open arms. "This is where the fiends come in at," he said, pointing to the back door, which led to a dirt path. "Up here is where the money goes until my pick up man picks it up. He's scheduled to make pickups every 30 minutes, just in case the jack boys are feeling lucky," Roy said, pointing to one of the rooms upstairs. "The next room is the lookout room. I keep shooters in each room, but in this room, I have at least four shooters; that makes five in all. So if a muthafucka robs this spot and get away, he definitely earned it; feel me," Roy laughed.

"I can dig it," Gmoney replied.

"I got 15 trap houses all throughout this city, and that's not including all the other ones I'm responsible for out in Atlanta and Texas. To make a long story short, I got the south on lock, but Florida is my home town."

"Damn, y'all down south niggaz is smarter than I give y'all credit for," Gmoney admitted.

"Basically what I'm trying to say is, if you join the family you'll be getting some of this trap money."

"And what do y'all want in return?" Gmoney asked, sensing something fishy was going on.

"When we go see Pauleena tomorrow, she'll explain everything."

CHAPTER 9 PRAISE THE LORD

April laid on the bed, staring up at the ceiling. Ever since Skip left, she found it hard for her to sleep at night. Every time she closed her eyes she, would think and wonder if Skip was all right. April wanted to answer Skip's phone calls so bad, but she knew if she did, he would more than likely sweet talk his way back into her life, and continues to live the same lifestyle. April refused to live like that another day. All that street thug shit was now a thing in the past.

April's thoughts were interrupted when she heard a light knock on her bedroom door. "Come in," she yelled, already knowing who it was.

Little Michael entered the room rubbing his eyes. "Mommy can I have some cereal?"

"You sure can," April replied, as she slid out of her comfortable bed, and headed for the kitchen. "After you eat your cereal, go wash up and put on your dress clothes. We going to church today."

"Aww mommy I hate church," Little Michael sucked his teeth.

"Why? What's wrong with church?" April asked, placing her hand on her hip.

"It be so boring."

"Okay I'll make a deal with you. If you come, I'll let you bring your PSP," April said, extending her hand.

"You got yourself a deal," Little Michael said, shaking his mother's hand.

Once April had convinced Little Michael into coming to church, she went in her closet and pulled out an expensive dress that she only wore once when she and Skip went to some fancy restaurant.

"Yeah, I think I'm going to roll with this one," she told herself, liking how the dress tightly hugged her hips, and showed off her curvy figure.

When April pulled up in the church's parking lot, it was jammed packed. "Damn, I'll have a better time finding a parking spot at a club then at church! Ain't that a bitch?"

Before April and Little Michael entered the church, April handed Michael a five dollar bill. "Make sure you put that in the collection plate."

"Why every time we come to church we always gotta put money in the stupid basket?" Little Michael asked with a frown.

"Because that's how you get your blessings," April answered quickly, as she grabbed him by the wrist and entered the house of the Lord.

* * **

$ilk White

Ali sat in a naked cell all by himself staring blankly at the wall. To take his mind off of being in the box or SHU (special housing unit) as the police called it, Ali reminisced on all the good times he had before he ended up in the shit hole he was in. He thought about all the good foods he ate, and he definitely thought about all the pussy he'd gotten over the years.

So far, Ali had been in isolation for 68 eight days and counting. Jail was already a horrible and boring place to be, but being in the box only made the time drag even more. Ali was in deep thought thinking about some pussy, when he heard somebody lightly tapping on his cell.

"I figured you were lonely in here, so I brought you something to read," a female C.O. said, sliding two books through the little slot.

"Thank you, but I'm not really a big reader," Ali said, making his way over to the cell door so he could read the C.O.'s nametag. "But I do appreciate it Ms. Ruby."

"Oh please call me Crystal," she insisted.

"Crystal Ruby? What kind of name is that?"

"That's what my mom's named me." She smiled, looking into Ali's eyes.

Ali could tell that this chick was a hood chick by the way she talked and handled herself. Ali quickly looked away. He knew how much he loved hood girls, and Crystal was definitely a hood chick, but she was also a dime. What stood out about her was she stood six feet tall which was kind of tall for a female, but she was definitely sexy with it.

"If you give those books a chance I'm pretty sure you will love them," Crystal said, trying to make small talk.

Ali picked up the two books: Married to Da Streets by Silk White and Hood Rat by K'wan. "Both of these titles sound interesting. I think I'm going to check em out," Ali said gratefully.

"Well I guess I better be going now, talk to you later." Crystal waved goodbye as she strolled down the tier.

"Talk to you later Ms. Ruby," Ali said, as he leaned his face against the bars, so he could get a good look at Crystal's healthy ass as it jiggled up and down through her uniform pants with every step she took. "Damn," Ali said, shaking his head. From the looks of things, he could tell that the C.O. wore a thong under her uniform pants.

Ali quickly erased the nasty thoughts from his mind as he sat on his bunk and picked up one of the books that Crystal had just brought him.

* * **

Once service was over, April patiently waited for most of the people to make their exit so she could have a word with the pastor. "Michael sit right here until I come back."

Michael nodded his head, as he continued playing his PSP.

"Hey Pastor," April said, as she gave him a hug.

"Hey April, how have you been? I haven't seen you in service for a while. Is everything okay?" Pastor Jackson asked, with a look of concern.

"Well not really," she answered, looking at the floor.

"Tell you what, how about I come over to your house tomorrow and you tell me all about it, because I have to run over to the hospital real quick to pray for one of my members who has cancer," Pastor Jackson said, handing April a piece of paper and a pen so she could write down her address.

"I'll be home all day tomorrow so you can drop by anytime," April said, handing Pastor Jackson the paper with her address on it.

"Okay, I'll see you tomorrow. You go in peace," he said as he and a deacon made their exit.

JayZ bumped through the Benz speakers, as Skip pulled into the airport parking lot. "Yo, you heard what Hov just said?" Skip asked, with his face crumbled up.

"Yeah that nigga killed that shit," Gmoney said, bobbing his head to the beat.

"A'ight, this what we doing," Gmoney said, grabbing everybody's attention. "Me, Skip, Knowledge, and Suge is flying. We'll meet the rest of y'all at the spot when y'all touch down."

With that being said, a soldier quickly exited the van and slid in the front seat of the Benz.

Roy and Bumpy looked on from the sideline.

Once on the plane, the six gangstas made small talk with one another.

"Everything a'ight?" Gmoney asked, looking at Skip.

"Nah, B. I think I'm out," he replied.

"What you mean?" Gmoney asked, leaning forward.

"I can't do this no more," Skip sighed. "I gotta go straighten shit out with April and my little man."

"Yo, what kind of shit is that?" Knowledge hissed.

Gmoney quickly hushed him. "It's about time you started using your head," Gmoney said as he gave Skip a hug. "You should have been out the game. You got more to lose than any of us," he reminded Skip.

"Yeah I think I'm going to move to Canada and start over fresh," Skip said. "Plus out there I'll have a clean record."

"Anything I can do to help just let me know," Gmoney said as he gave Skip a pound.

"Knowledge, time for you to step up to the plate," Gmoney announced.

"That's what I been waiting for," Knowledge said in a cocky tone as he gave Suge dap.

$ilk White

"Be careful what you ask for. People always think they missing something when they on the outside looking in. But when they get in, they realize they ain't been missing shit," Skip said, shooting Knowledge a private glance.

When the plane finally landed, Gmoney, Knowledge, and Suge all gave Skip a hug and said their goodbyes as they watched Skip hop in a cab.

"That's a real motherfucking soldier right there," Gmoney said, as his eyes got a misty as he watched the cab's taillights bend the corner.

Once the cab was out of eyesight, Gmoney quickly slid in the back of the limousine with the rest of the crew.

"Take us to Pauleena's mansion," Roy ordered as he opened up a bottle of Henny and poured himself a glass. "Y'all make y'all self at home."

* * **

"Pull over right here real quick," Skip told the cab driver as he quickly ran up on a brother who was selling roses on the corner. "Let me get two dozen of these shits," Skip said, handing the man a hundred dollar bill. "Keep the change brother," he said as he slid back in the back seat of the cab. For the entire ride, Skip thought about the look on April's face when he handed her the roses and tell her he was out the game. I hope she's cool with moving to Canada, Skip thought out loud, as the cab pulled up to the dingy apartment building. "Here you go papi keep the change," Skip said, handing the cab driver a hundred dollar bill.

Skip hopped up the flight of steps with a smile on his face. He couldn't wait to tell April the good news. As soon as Skip entered the apartment with his key, his smile quickly melted into a frown as he heard a man's voice coming from the living room.

What the fuck is going on in here?" Skip growled as he entered the living room. "Babes what are you doing here?" April asked, jumping up in shock. "Fuck all that, what is this nigga doing here?" Skip asked, taking a step closer to the man sitting on the couch. "This is the pastor from the church," April blurted out as she stepped in front of Skip, doing her best to keep him away from the pastor.

"What the fuck is he doing in my house?" Skip huffed as he pushed April out of his way.

"Listen brother, I just came over here to pray for your wife," Pastor Jackson said as he stood up.

"Well you should have been praying for yourself!"

"The only person I fear is God," Pastor Jackson shot back, raising his voice.

"So you think God can stop me from punching you in your face right now?" Skip asked, balling up his fist.

Before the pastor got a chance to reply, Skip had already caught him with a two-piece to the chin, dropping him off of impact.

Skip went in to stomp the pastor out, but April had grabbed him by the waist trying to hold him back.

"Get the fuck off me," Skip growled as he turned and slapped April down to the floor.

"Daddy what are you doing?" Little Michael asked, peeking down the hallway to see what all the commotion was.

"It's okay Mike. Go to your room. Everything is fine," Skip said, pasting a fake smile on his face. In that split second, Pastor Jackson quickly made it to his feet and threw Skip in a chokehold from behind.

"I'm about to send you straight to hell you son of a bitch," Pastor Jackson snarled, as spit flew from his mouth with every word he spoke. Pastor Jackson quickly dropped to the floor and wrapped his legs around Skip's waist applying more pressure. Once Little Michael saw the pastor put his father in a chokehold, he quickly ran to the phone and dialed 911.

"Let him go!" April yelled, as she tried to pry Pastor Jackson's arms from around Skip's neck.

April looked over and saw Skip gasping for air as his face turned red as an apple. She knew she had to do something and do it fast. With not many options left, April quickly ran to the kitchen and grabbed a knife. Without thinking twice, she jabbed the knife in Pastor Jackson's side three times until he released the hold he had on Skip's neck.

"You fucking bitch! I'm going to kill you!" Pastor Jackson grumbled, as he slowly made his way towards April with the devil in his eyes.

"Just leave," April yelled as tears ran down her face.

"I am after I lay hands on you," Pastor Jackson said in a deadly tone. His mouth had gone dry and sour, his hands curled into fists. As he came forward, she retreated a step. Everything seemed to be going slow inside April's head, but it must have all happened in less than a minute.

"Just leave! If you come any closer, I'm going to stab the shit outta you," April yelled as she backed into the wall, clutching the knife with two hands.

Skip slowly made it back to his feet and grabbed the glass vase from off the coffee table. The vase whistled through the air as it violently shattered over the pastor's head, dropping him instantly.

"Gimme that knife," Skip demanded. "I'm about to skin this nigga alive," he said with venom dripping from his voice.

Seconds later, two cops busted through the front door with their weapons already drawn. "FREEZE!"

Skip stood over Pastor Jackson's sprawled out body with the knife glittering in his hand.

"Don't make me do it," one of the officers yelled, halfway squeezing on the trigger.

"Baby please put down the knife," April begged.

With a defeated look on his face, Skip dropped the knife. Immediately, the two officers roughly tackled Skip and cuffed him.

"All I came over here to do was make up with you," Skip said in a low pitch voice. "I brought you roses and all that. Then I come home and you got a man sitting in the living room," he said in an unsteady voice.

"Baby I told him to come over here so he could pray for our marriage," April said in a weak and shaking voice as she saw the brief look of hurt flashed across her husband's face.

"Fuck that praying shit. You know I'm not just going to leave my family hanging," Skip fumed. "Now I gotta spend time in a fucking cage because you wanted this faggot to pray for us," he said, shaking his head involuntarily.

Seconds later, Pastor Jackson finally made it back to his feet still a little dizzy. "I want to press charges," he said pin wheeling his arms to keep his balance.

"Officer, what's the charges?" April asked. Her face wore a cautious, startled expression.

"Not certain yet ma'am. Your husband could be charged with assault or maybe attempted murder; it depends," the officer answered politely.

"Fuck," April cursed loudly knowing that everything that had just happened was partly her fault, not to mention Skip was already on the run.

"Mommy why they got daddy in hand cuffs?" Little Michael whined as he hugged her leg.

"It's just a misunderstanding baby," April cried openly as she and Little Michael watched as the police took Skip away.

CHAPTER 10 PAULEENA

Gmoney slid out limo with a smile on his face. "I can definitely see myself in a crib like this real soon," he said to himself as he admired the huge mansion. In front of the mansion, two Muslim brothers stood holding down the entrance. Each man wore a black suit, along with a red bow tie.

"What's up J," Roy said, extending his hand to one of the Muslims. The Muslim looked at Roy's hand as if he had just rubbed it in some shit. "How can I help you brother?"

"We here to see Pauleena," Roy said, looking the two Muslims up and down.

"Name please?" the shorter Muslim asked, speaking for the first time.

"What you talking about? I was just here last week. Why y'all acting like I'm some kind of new nigga?"

"Name please?" the short Muslim asked, again as he cracked his knuckles.

Roy frowned, but answered regardless. "Roy." Immediately, the taller Muslim spoke into his earpiece. "Yeah we got a Roy outside. He says you're expecting him." Seconds later, the taller Muslim turned to face Roy. "Sorry about that brother, just doing my job," he said, as he lightly frisked, each man one by one, before he allowed him to enter. The taller Muslim then escorted the men to a room at the end of the hallway. "Knock before you enter," he said in a deep voice as he returned back to the front to rejoin his partner.

"Knock, Knock, Knock!"

"Come in," a deep voice boomed from the other side of the door. Roy and Bumpy entered the office confidently as Gmoney, Suge, and Knowledge brought up the rear.

Gmoney saw a very attractive Spanish looking woman sitting behind a mammoth oak desk with a seven-foot Muslim standing by her side. The seven-foot monster stood with his hands clasped in front of him. With the jacket from his suit removed, his twin .45's sat comfortably under his arms in the shoulder holster.

"I delivered just like you asked me to," Roy said, kissing the back of Pauleena's hand.

"That's why I love you," Pauleena replied with a smile. "Now which one of these handsome gentlemen is Gmoney?" she asked as she stood up and slowly walked from behind the desk. Once Pauleena was in Gmoney's full view, he studied her from head to toe. His eyes immediately locked when they came in contact with her horse ass. The tight black spandex she wore didn't help the situation at all.

"I'm Gmoney," he said raising his hand.

$ilk White

"It's a pleasure to finally meet you," Pauleena said shaking his hand. "So who are these two gentlemen?" she asked, looking at Knowledge and Suge.

"This right here is my number two man, Knowledge."

"Nice to meet you Knowledge," Pauleena greeted him.

"And this is my main muscle right here, Suge."

"Nice to meet you Suge."

"The pleasure is all mine," Suge replied with a warm smile.

"Roy, I need a favor."

"What up?"

"Could you and Bumpy please take these two gentlemen out to the bar so I can have a word with Gmoney alone?"

"No problem," Roy said as he, and Bumpy escorted Suge and Knowledge to the bar area of the mansion.

"I'm glad you could make it on such short notice," Pauleena said, pouring her and Gmoney a glass of Remy.

"It's all good. My ears are always open when it comes to money," Gmoney said, gladly excepting the drink.

"Okay let's get straight down to business then," Pauleena said as she sat on the couch cross-legged next to Gmoney. "From what I hear, you and your partner Ali had the streets on lock until Detective Nelson made Frankie stop supplying y'all with work. That's when Rell got his hands on the product y'all used to have and ran with it."

"How the fuck do you know all that?" Gmoney asked a little puzzled.

"I'm like the F.E.D.S. I know everything," she chuckled. "But basically, I brought you here because I know we can help each other."

"How you figure?" Gmoney asked, sipping the liquid fire.

"Simple, I want you and your crew to join my family," Pauleena paused to take a sip. "You will never have to worry about finding a connect ever again. I get my shit straight from the Cuban's pure uncut shit."

"Damn, you the answer to all my problems then," Gmoney chuckled. "Only problem is I'm hot right now, the
F.E.D.S. is all over me and I wouldn't want to bring any of my heat down on you; Smell me?"

"The F.E.D.S. are the least of my worries sweetie. I got a few judges and district attorney's on my payroll. We all family, one hand wash the other."

"What about all the trap houses, you got pumping in the south?"

"You join our family and you'll get a piece of all the action. Plus when I hit you with that bomb work, we going to shut down the entire Harlem area; not to mention upstate New York, like Buffalo and Syracuse," Pauleena said, pointing to the floor. "My boy Roy got more than enough soldiers on stand by for anything. For instance, like that little problem you got with Rell. I can get that handled for you, along with that cocksucker Detective Nelson just like that," she said, snapping her fingers for extra emphasis.

"Nah, I gotta handle Rell myself," Gmoney told her.

"I know you got your pride and everything, but you gonna have to be smarter about your decisions especially with the F.E.D.S. on your back."

"Yeah you right about that," Gmoney agreed. "Well it looks like we have ourselves a deal. I would love to join the family."

"You made a good decision," Pauleena said, leaning over to give Gmoney a hug.

Gmoney embraced Pauleena tightly until he felt his cell phone vibrating on his hip. Before Gmoney could reach for his cell phone, the seven-foot monster was already in motion. The big man quickly grabbed Gmoney's wrist with one hand, clutched the back of his neck with the other. "Don't move!" His voice boomed like thunder.

"Malcolm," Pauleena said, giving him a look that said its okay. The seven-foot monster quickly released his grip.

"Fam, don't put ya hands on me again," Gmoney said in a cold tone as he answered his phone. "Yeah who dis?"

"It's me Skip."

"What's good, you changed your mind already?" Gmoney said playfully.

"Nah, I'm in jail," Skip said in an uneven tone.

"Get the fuck outta here," Gmoney said in disbelief.

"True story."

"How? I was just with you?" Gmoney asked.

"I went to the crib trying to surprise April with the good news, and I found her in the living room with a preacher."

"A preacher?" Gmoney echoed. "Them niggaz be the biggest freaks."

"I be knowing."

"So what you did to that clown?" Gmoney asked, already knowing how bad his long time friend's temper was.

"I tried to kill that fucking faggot," Skip told him. "How did everything go with the Pauleena chick?"

"Everything is good on this side," Gmoney said, not wanting to talk about that, especially on a jail line. "I'm gonna send Mr. Goldberg down there first thing in the morning."

"A'ight good looking. I'm about to get comfortable for my little vacation, just hold me down on the commissary end."

"You know I got you," Gmoney told him.

"A'ight, I'mma keep in touch my nigga, one."

"One."

"Everything a'ight?" Pauleena asked, sipping from her glass.

"Nah, a good friend of mine just got knocked." (Locked up)

"What's his name? I might can have my peoples pull some strings."

"Nah, he gon have to sit for this one," Gmoney said, shaking his head. "He was already on the run."

"Damn, he gon definitely have to hold that down," Pauleena agreed. "I want you to start thinking before you react"

"What you mean?" Gmoney asked confused.

"I mean let the soldiers do their job, that's what we pay them for, you going to have to stop letting your pride and temper get the best of you."

"Yeah, you right."

"Two weeks with me and you'll be looking at the game in
a totally different way," Pauleena told him. "We'll just have to see about that."

"What's the word on the streets?" Rell asked, flipping through the daily newspaper. "We still haven't heard shit on who could have killed our driver," Debo shrugged his shoulders.

"Nobody ain't heard nothing?"

"I put the word out and nothing came back yet," Debo said. "I still think you should stay in the house until me and Mad Dog get to the bottom of this."

"Fuck outta here. Rell don't hide from nobody," he grunted, speaking of himself in third person.

"Nah, I'm not saying for you to be hiding out, I'm just thinking it would be safer to get to the bottom of this shit first," Debo said humbly.

"I don't pay you to think, I pay you to bust heads," Rell shot back.

Before Debo could respond, somebody rang the doorbell. Debo quickly grabbed his shotgun that rested on the coffee table as he headed towards the door. He looked through the peephole and let out a sigh of relief when he recognized the person standing on the other side.

"Detective Nelson, what a pleasant surprise."

"Out of my way shit face," Detective Nelson barked as he brushed past the big man.

"How can I help you detective?" Rell asked, folding his hands in front of him.

"I need you to help me find this scum bag named Big Mel, he used to run with Ali and Gmoney before we shut them down." "A'ight, I'll see what I can do."

"No, make it happen," Detective Nelson fumed.

"Be easy, I said I got you," Rell said. "I heard about what happened to you."

"That bastard is going to pay with his life," Detective Nelson spat.

"I'll have something for you by the end of the week," Rell told him.

"Cool, you got that for me?" Detective Nelson said, shooting Rell a private glare.

"Yeah, Debo go get Detective Nelson his money," Rell ordered. "So what are you going to do when you find this fucker?"

"You don't even want to know," Detective Nelson said with venom dripping from his voice. "I'm about to go check out this address I got for him. I doubt if he'll be there, but I'm going to go check it out anyway when I leave here."

"I'll have an address for that cocksucker in a week, but I'm going to need a favor too," Rell said, turning to face the Detective. "Somebody killed my driver last week and I need you to find out if it's something serious or not. I didn't get a word from the streets, so I'm not taking this too serious; you dig?"

"I'll look into that for you," Detective Nelson said, taking the duffle bag from Debo. "I'll see y'all in about a week," he said as he filed for the door.

CHAPTER 11 ISOLATION

"Ninety-nine… a hundred," Ali huffed out of breath as he got up from doing some pushups. Ali stretched his arms, and then splashed some water on his face when he heard a light tapping on his cell door. When he turned around he saw Ms. Ruby standing admiring him.

"Hey what's up Crystal?" Ali greeted the young C.O.

"I'm surprised you remembered my name," Crystal blushed. "Did you finish those books yet?"

"Yeah both of them shits were fire."

"I told you, you would like em," Crystal said, checking out how good Ali looked in his wife beater. "Can I tell you something?" She asked in a little schoolgirl voice.

"Yeah, what up?"

"I'm so embarrassed."

"Embarrassed about what?" Ali asked, moving towards the cell door.

"I feel so silly telling you this, but I had the biggest crush on you."

"You knew me before I came here?" Ali asked.

"Nah, I didn't know you. I'm from Buffalo." She chuckled. "But when I go clubbing, me and my girls always go to the city. One night I was at the club with my home girl and you and your crew strolled up in there as if y'all owned the place. The first time I saw you, I knew I wanted you."

"So why you ain't holla at me?"

"I was scared. Most high status guys like to disrespect women and I thought you were just like the rest, but when I spoke to you last month when I brought you those books, I found out you were different."

"Nah, I would never disrespect a black queen, unless she's asking to be disrespected you dig?"

"Yeah, I feel you. I'm just upset I had to finally meet you like this," Crystal said, looking in Ali's eyes.

"Yeah me too," Ali quickly looked away.

"When do you get out the box?"

"Next week finally," Ali replied gladly.

"That's good news, I gotta get outta here, but I guess I'll be seeing you around," Crystal said in a seductive tone.

"I guess so," Ali said, returning her stare.

"Catch you later," Crystal said as she spun on her heels and walked off.

Once Ms. Ruby was gone, Ali threw some more cold water on his face to try to calm his hormones down. Ali felt bad for flirting with another woman. He knew it wasn't right, but the dog in him tried to convince him that flirting wasn't cheating. After 20 minutes of racking his brain, Ali laid on his bunk until he drifted off to sleep.

* * **

Detective Nelson pulled up in front of the address he had for Big Mel with three officer dressed in street clothes along with him. Each man had a murderous look on their face, as they approached the apartment building. "Whoever get the shot on this cocksucker first, take it," Detective Nelson ordered, as he removed his .357 from its holster as the foursome entered the building. Detective Nelson eased along the wall holding his .357 with two hands as he gave the other officers a silent signal with his hands.

Detective Bradley shot the lock off the door, then placed his back against the wall as the two plain clothes soldiers ran in the apartment, followed by Detective Nelson. After a quick search, the officers found that the apartment was empty.

"It's all clear," Detective Bradley yelled, holding his shotgun.

"What do we do now boss?" One of the officers asked.

"Send a message," Detective Nelson said with a sharp edge in his voice.

The three officers looked on as Detective Nelson pulled a lighter from his pocket. With a light flick, the first thing Detective Nelson set on fire was the curtains followed by the kitchen tablecloth, and the old looking sofa. Before the flames could maximize, Detective Nelson and his officers smoothly made their exit.

"This is just the beginning," Detective Nelson said heatedly as he pulled out unto traffic. "I'm going to make this cocksucker suffer," he continued his rant.

"I told you, you should have never started doing business with those animals. These fucking guys would sell crack to their own family members, no way you can trust guys like that," Detective Bradley spoke openly.

"This is not about trust, it's about money," Detective Nelson said, giving Detective Bradley a private glare. "Money talks and bullshit walks a marathon."

"You right about that," Det. Bradley agreed.

Detective Nelson got ready to say something else, but his ringing cell phone momentarily paused the conversation. "Yeah who's this?" He answered.

"This is the captain speaking, where's your location?" He asked.

"Not far, I'm cruising through Harlem right now. Why what's up?" Detective Nelson chimed as he slowed down for the yellow light.

"Get to the station A.S.A.P. I need to have a word with you. It's urgent," the Captain said in a stern voice.

"I'm on my way," Detective Nelson said, ending the conversation.

$ilk White

Twenty minutes later, he strolled confidently inside the precinct snacking on a glazed donut.

"The captain wants to see you in his office," the desk officer said the minute he laid eyes on Detective Nelson.

"I'm heading that way now," Detective Nelson replied with a smile. As soon as he stepped in the office, he saw the captain sitting back in his chair with a nasty look on his face.

"Hey what's up captain? What's so important that it couldn't wait until later?" He asked as he helped himself to a seat.

"We have a problem," the Captain said in a low tone.

"What else is new?"

"No, we have a serious problem," the Captain said, turning to face Detective Nelson. "Your friend Gerald has got to go."

"Who, Gmoney?" Detective Nelson asked intensely.

"Yes Gmoney," the captain answered swiftly, letting the name roll off his tongue.

"Why? Ali is already behind bars. I got a medal for that collar. What is that not good enough?"

"Listen, a lot of people want this guy fried, a lot of heavy hitters if you know what I mean," the captain said, raising an eyebrow.

"I thought the F.E.D.S. were already building a case on that cocksucker?" "They are, but they're taking too long. My people are upset because they haven't been able to get shit on him."

"Bullshit, he goes to court in two months. He's bound to get three and a half years tops," Detective Nelson said, his voice sounding very firm and sure of it.

"Fuck three and a half years! The people over my head want this guy either in a cell with no key or in a fucking bag," the captain said with a lot of emotion. "They're really upset because Ali wouldn't give up no information on nobody in his organization, not to mention somebody else from their organization just got arrested and didn't say a word."

"What's the guy's name who just got arrested?" Detective Nelson asked.

"If I'm not mistaking I think it was Skippy or Skipper."

"Skip, yeah I know him," Detective Nelson chuckled. "So what do you need me to do?"

"I need you to take Gmoney down like you did Ali, but I would appreciate it if you put a bullet in his head."

"But he's no longer a factor. Their dynasty is done." Detective Nelson said, sitting up in his chair.

"It doesn't matter. The people over my head want him dead, and I'm over your head, and I want you to kill this cocksucker by any means necessary; no questions asked," the captain said, laying seven big stacks of money on his desk. "So what's it going to be?"

Detective Nelson chuckled as he stuffed the stacks of money in his jacket pocket and made his exit.

The F.E.D.S. stood on the roof taking pictures of Gmoney and the warehouse he held his meetings at.

Gmoney slid out of his Range Rover and looked over both shoulders as his construction Timberlands sunk into the fresh white snow. As Gmoney headed towards the entrance, the wind whined louder and began to flutter the collar of his jacket. "Damn it's fucking brick out here," he said blowing on his hands in an attempt to keep them warm.

"What's good my niggaz?" Gmoney said as he entered the warehouse. "Let's get straight down to business," he said, rubbing his hands together greedily. "We got the new product ready. Now I need all of y'all to get out and spread the word that we're back and we ain't going nowhere; you dig?" He paced the floor. "Give out some samples to the main customers so the word can spread faster."

"Don't even worry about it. You know I'mma get the hood back poppin again," Knowledge boasted.

"Oh yeah and make sure y'all watch ya steps, cause the word on the streets is the F.E.D.S. are trying to build a case on us, or should I say me," Gmoney chuckled. "Just hold it down out there in them streets," he said as he watched as his crew all exited from the back of the house going to handle their business.

"What y'all doing here?" Gmoney asked, looking at Roy and Bumpy.

"Pauleena asked us to follow you around, just to make sure you don't have any unnecessary problems, if you know what I mean," Roy grinned devilishly.

"Why you think I keep this guy around for?" Gmoney said, nodding his head towards Knowledge.

"Not my business, I work for Pauleena and she told me and Bumpy to make sure we keep you out of harms way," Roy replied.

"Fuck it more muscle won't hurt," Gmoney shrugged his shoulders. "When shit pop off, I just hope y'all be on point," Knowledge said, talking indirectly.

"We shoot first and ask questions never," Roy replied flashing a mouth full of gold.

"Fuck all this thinking shit. Let's go to the club and celebrate," Gmoney told his crew as each man headed out the door.

"So how do you feel knowing that any day the F.E.D.S. can pick you up?" Roy asked.

$ilk White

"Fuck the F.E.D.S!" Gmoney barked. "All cops are stupid. They're only as good as their snitch; if muthafuckas didn't run they mouths every time they get locked up, shit would be sweet right now."

"True story," Knowledge added as he turned onto the highway.

"Oh shit," Gmoney said out loud, as he pulled out his cell phone and quickly dialed a number.

On the third ring, a woman with a soft voice answered. "Hello?"

"Nancy what's up? This Gmoney, you busy?"

"Nah, I'm up fooling around with this baby," she said in a stressed tone. "Why? What's up?"

"I was just calling to see if you were still going to see Ali tomorrow?"

"Of course I am. You know he just got out of the box today so I gotta bring him his snacks and shit," Nancy said as she cradled the phone between her ear and shoulder.

"A'ight, when I get home tonight, remind me to give you five gees to put on his books."

"I'll remind you if I'm still awake when you get in, cause you know how late you be coming in sometimes," Nancy reminded him.

"Yeah, I be knowing. Tell you what, when I get in I'mma put the money on the kitchen table a'ight?"

"Okay, that's cool."

"Oh yeah, did Coco call the house?" Gmoney asked, trying not to sound thirsty.

"No. I don't know why you trying to be so tough. Just call the girl, damn! You know you want to," Nancy said, putting Gmoney on the spot.

"Come on, you know I can't do that," Gmoney pressed. "I know that's your friend but she be bugging."

"Sometimes love make people act a lil crazy, but you know that girl loves you and I know you love her."

"I do but she gotta understand in this kind of business, I need a girl who is understanding and will always hold me down no matter what happens. In the back of my mind, I need to know that she'll be there no matter what."

"Well it's kinda hard to ask for all that when you got bitches blowing up your house phone. Then on top of that, the bitch got the nerve to be poppin shit," Nancy said sternly.

"But that comes along with the business; smell me? She know none of them bitches, don't mean shit to me," Gmoney said defensively. "But yo, we going to speak more about this later a'ight?"

"A'ight later," Nancy said as she ended the conversation.

Knowledge pulled up in the club's parking lot and tapped the horn twice trying to get the attention of a pack of sexy looking ladies. "What's good Mami?" He yelled, with his head hung half way out the window. The ladies smiled but kept it moving.

"Catch 'em when you get inside," Gmoney said out loud.

"You know I am," Knowledge replied as he placed the gear in park and let the engine die.

As soon as the foursome stepped foot in the club, they were quickly attacked by the heat mixed with the smell of strong weed. Gmoney quickly made his way to the V.I.P. section, where he sent the nice looking waitress to the bar to get him two bottles of champagne. Gmoney came out to celebrate and that's just what he planned on doing. His crew was out setting shop back up; he had the best connect in town so he planned on getting fucked up, especially since he had extra muscle with him.

"Good looking ma," Gmoney yelled over the blaring music as the waitress handed him two bottles of champagne buried in a bucket of ice. He poured himself a glass of champagne and lit up a blunt as he bobbed his head to the tunes the D.J. was playing.

"Get the fuck outta here," Gmoney chuckled as he noticed two white guys wearing suites and dark shades slowly walking past the

V.I.P. section. "Yo these fucking crackers must think we ain't got no kind of sense," he said, nudging Bumpy.

"They must want you bad," Bumpy replied.

"People always want what they can't have, especially cops," Gmoney said, pointing his middle finger up to the two agents.

"You might have to fuck around and leave town for a little while," Bumpy said, not liking the looks of the agents.

"If they had anything on me, they wouldn't be following me around all fucking day," Gmoney said, sipping on his champagne. "Fuck the F.E.D.S! They can suck a dick with aids on the tip!" He erupted into laughter.

Gmoney's laugh quickly turned into a frown as he saw Coco moving through the crowd with a group of men. "That fucking bitch!" Gmoney growled as all his thoughts turned into anger, as rage flashed in his eyes.

Five minutes later, Knowledge entered the V.I.P. section. "Yo, I just saw Coco with that boxing cat who knocked Spanky out over there," he said pointing.

"Who, the Terminator?" Gmoney asked, shooting to his feet.

"Yup," Knowledge said, adding fuel to the fire. Without thinking twice, G-money left his V.I.P. section and headed to where the Terminator, Coco, and his entourage sat enjoying themselves.

"What the fuck is you doing?" Gmoney growled as he approached the group's table. Two of the Terminator's bouncers made to get up, but the Terminator held them steady.

"I'm having some drinks with a few friends," Coco huffed. "What's the big

$ilk White

deal?"

"Listen," Gmoney paused. "Get ya ass up. We going home!"

"Nah, I'm chilling, I just got here," Coco said slyly.

"Get ya ass up and let's go!" Gmoney snarled.

"My dude, the lady said she don't want to go with you," the Terminator said, getting up from his seat.

"What!" Gmoney's face crumbled up instantly. "This my bitch," he said as he grabbed Coco up out her seat by her hair.

The Terminator charged Gmoney, but Knowledge quickly stepped in between the two as he attempted to bust a Corona bottle over the Terminator's head. The Terminator partially blocked the bottle and countered with a quick sharp uppercut that dropped the street thug instantly.

Roy quickly pulled out his p89 and roughly pushed Gmoney and Coco towards the exit. When Bumpy saw the scuffle break out, he didn't hesitate to pull his .45 from his waistband. He immediately aimed his firearm at the man's head, who knocked Knowledge out. Bumpy partially squeezed the trigger, but held up when he remembered the F.E.D.S were in the building. He knew if he murdered the man in the club, it would definitely fall back on Gmoney. Bumpy had to make a decision and make it quick. Not sure what to do, Bumpy quickly took his aim off of the stranger's head and raised the gun to the ceiling and let off four thunderous shots in rapid succession. Immediately, everybody in the club ducked down when they heard the shots ring out. A stampede quickly broke out as innocent club goers climbed over one another trying to squeeze out the exit.

Once all hell broke loose, Bumpy grabbed Knowledge and did his best to get him to safety. Knowledge lost and regained his vision at least two times as Bumpy helped him to the exit. Right before the two could reach the exit, the two agents quickly blocked their path. "Freeze!" One of the agents yelled.

Bumpy quickly pushed Knowledge to the floor as he raised his pistol. Before he could get it passed his waist, the two agents had already opened fired on the ugly man. The shots quickly lifted Bumpy off his feet. But before he hit the wet club floor, he managed to get one shot off. The shot shattered one of the agent's collarbone, sending him crashing to the floor howling in pain.

Bumpy hit the floor, shook once, and then died. Knowledge laid on the floor next to Bumpy. All he could do was watching Bumpy's life drain from his body.

"Don't fucking move!" The agent yelled as he aimed his pistol in Knowledge's face, holding it with two hands. "Turn over on your stomach," the agent ordered as he hand cuffed Knowledge, then gave him a quick pat down. "You got a license for this?" He asked, removing the Glock from Knowledge's waistband. Knowledge didn't respond. He was a loud nigga, but he knew when to keep his mouth shut.

TEARS OF A HUSTLER 2

* * * *

"Get off me!" Coco struggled to break away from Gmoney's grip.

"You better shut ya fucking mouth right now!" Gmoney warned. Roy quickly placed his p89 on top of the front tire of an unknown vehicle. "Gimme ya heat," he said as he took Gmoney's pistol and did the same with it.

"What the fuck was you doing with those clowns?" Gmoney hissed.

"What does it matter?" Coco asked in a bored tone.

"I knew you wasn't nothing but a smutt," he said as he mushed her and headed towards his Range Rover.

"You the smutt! I've always been faithful to you!" Coco yelled in the middle of the parking lot as she watched Gmoney and the man with the southern accent hop in the Range Rover and storm out the parking lot like a bat out of hell.

CHAPTER 12 BACK IN POPULATION

When Ali walked through the visiting room doors, Nancy could see the look of stress covering his face. His whole body language was different. It was as if he wasn't the same man. Ali used to always be happy and full of joy; that Ali was long gone.

"Hey baby. How they treating you in here?" Nancy asked as she cupped Ali's unshaven face and gently placed seven to ten kisses on his lips.

"I'm still standing, so I guess I'm okay." He smiled weakly.

"Well no matter what, you know I will always be here for you," Nancy said, placing her hands on top of his.

"Thanks boo, I appreciate it."

"You don't have to thank me. I'm just doing my job," she said sincerely. "So why were you fighting?"

"Some clown I was beefing with out on the streets put a hit out on me," Ali said nonchalantly.

"Are you serious?" Nancy asked nervously.

"I don't want to talk about that right now," Ali said, looking over at Lil Ali sleeping peacefully in his stroller.

"Just promise me you'll be careful."

"I got you baby."

"I brought you some snacks and Gmoney gave me five gees to put on your account," Nancy said, changing the subject.

"What Gmoney been up to?"

"I don't know, but I heard him yelling at somebody on the phone this morning," Nancy chuckled. "He's always yelling at somebody."

"You gotta be tough in a tough business."

"Oh yeah, I heard Skip got locked."

"Word?" Ali asked in shock.

"Yeah, I heard April was fucking some preacher while Lil Michael was in the house, and Skip walked in on them," she said, shaking her head.

"Damn! He going to have to sit for a while," Ali sighed. "You sure April was fucking the preacher?"

"That's the word that's going around," Nancy shrugged her shoulders.

"What's up with Christie?"

"I don't know. Nobody heard from her since the incident," Nancy said looking away. "I called her a few times but I never get an answer."

"A'ight I need you to go pay her a visit and make sure she's alright."

"I'm on it."

"Then I need you to start looking for a new place."

"Why?" Nancy asked.

"Because I said so; plus I don't want you nowhere around anybody who's on a lot of people's death list. It's bad enough I almost got you killed."

"Baby you know I'll take a bullet for you," Nancy chuckled as she heard the fat faced C.O. yell "Visiting hours are over!"

"Okay, I'll see you the same time next week. Hopefully next time big head will be awake," she motioned towards Lil Ali getting his sleep on.

"It's all good baby, get home safe," Ali said, cuffing both of Nancy's ass cheeks as the two engaged in a long kiss.

"I love you baby," she purred as she tried to squeeze the life out of Ali when she hugged him.

"I love you too babe," Ali said, before he headed towards the exit. Nancy walked out of the facility and prepared her mind for the long, lonely ride home.

* ** *

"How was your V.I.? Lil Bit asked, doing mini pushups.

"It was cool," Ali replied. "I just hate the sad look on her face every time it's time for her to leave."

"Yeah, I used to hate that shit too," Lil Bit said, as he noticed somebody standing in the doorway of their cell. "What's good, can I help you?" Lil Bit said, throwing his hands up.

"I need to holla at Ali for a second," the man declared.

Ali looked over at the man and noticed it was the same dude who had helped him out during his fight. "Yeah, what's poppin?" Ali asked, stepping out of the cell.

"I know you don't know me or nothing like that, but I'm Loco," he said, extending his hand.

"Ali," he said, accepting Loco's hand. "I appreciate what you did for me a couple months back."

"Ah don't mention it. I owed you that," Loco smiled. "My little cousin was heading down the wrong path, and my sister told me some cat named Ali gave him a job, and ever since he been on the right path. I also heard if anybody had any problems you were the man to see."

"I personally don't know your cousin, but I do my best to hold down the hood," Ali said truthfully.

"Ever since I heard about you and what you been doing with the community, I wanted to be down with your organization," Loco said, giving Ali his props.

Ali chuckled. "My organization is out on the streets. So when you get out, go holla at my man Gmoney if you wanna join the family."

"Of course you don't have an organization up in here… yet!" Loco raised an eyebrow. "You just got here, but you already have the power. All you need are the soldiers; that's where me and all my blood homies come in at." He grinned devilishly.

"What you have in mind?" Ali asked, leaning against the rail.

"It's like this; I got a few of my homies in here pumping some dog food for me (dope). With you on my side, we can go far. Plus, I heard its a little bounty on your head. Fuck with me, and me and my crew will hold you down."

"A'ight, let me think about this," Ali said.

"You won't have to do nothing, just sit back, and get paid," Loco said, looking at Ali for a response.

"It's sound good. I think we can do business," Ali said, shaking Loco's hand.

"Everything is set up lovely. No way can shit get fucked up."

"Yeah the plan sounds bullet proof," Ali said, looking over the rail down at two cats playing chest. "Yo, you think you can get me a banger (shank)?"

"Not a problem, I'll have one of my mans swing by later on with that," Loco told him. The two men spoke for about two hours before the two-headed back to their cells so the C.O. could do his count. "On the count!" The C.O. yelled, in a southern redneck accent as he watched all the inmates head to their cells. Once he finished his count, he made his announcement. "Count clear!"

Seconds later, all the inmates went back to their regular routines.

"Yo, I'm about to make some tuna fish sandwiches. You want in?" Lil Bit asked, heading out the cell.

"Nah, I'm good," Ali answered, lying down on his bunk. He laid in his bed wishing he were home with Nancy, laid up in some pussy. Ali didn't realize all the small things that he took for granted on the streets would come back to haunt him while he sat in a cell.

CHAPTER 13 HOW YOU DOING

"I'm so glad you could finally make some time for me," Heather said, smiling at Rell.

"Sorry it took so long for us to hook up, but an unexpected problem came into play," he replied with a smile.

"Yo, where we headed?" Mad Dog asked, looking at the couple through the rear view mirror.

"What are you in the mood for?" Rell asked as he faced Heather.

"Ummm… I can go for some Italian food."

"Cool, Mad Dog take us to that nice Italian restaurant that we rode past the other day."

"You talking about that shit downtown?" Mad Dog asked as he switched lanes.

"Yeah, you know that one I'm talking about," Rell spat as he slid his hand on Heather's thigh. Heather wore an expensive looking silver dress. The front was cut was so low that her nice sized breast threatened to spill out. To go along with the dress, she wore a nice pair of diamond earrings with a thin necklace. To complete her outfit, she wore a pair of silver three-inch pumps.

"I see you don't waste no time," Heather said, addressing Rell's hand on her thigh, but at the same time, she didn't ask him to move it.

"Time is my worst enemy," Rell countered smoothly, as he stared off into her blue eyes. That was a nice come back," Heather said with a smile, as she felt it getting a little moist between her legs.

"So do you always date black guys?"

"Wow what kind of questions is that?" She chuckled.

"Nah, I'm just asking because I'm not sure what you may be used to, because I'm gonna be myself. I don't hold nothing back, what you see is what you get."

"And I don't want you to hold nothing back," Heather said, placing her hand on top of Rell's. "So have you dated a lot of white women?"

"Ummm… actually I do," Rell said. "Not saying I don't like black women, it's just I have easier time trusting white women instead of black women."

"That must be something from your past, because I know you didn't get like that overnight."

"Yeah, but I don't want to get into all that right now. My main focus tonight is you," Rell sensually whispered in her ear. "That's what I like to hear," Heather said, matching Rell's stare.

Mad Dog just shook his head as he pulled up directly in front of the restaurant.

$ilk White

"Be easy with this muthafucka," he said, tossing his keys to the valet parking guy.

* * * *

"So you shot his fucking driver?" Frankie asked, shoving a meatball in his mouth.

"Yeah you told me to send a message, so that's what I did," Jimmy said in an even tone.

"Yeah, but I think I might need you to send another message that grabs his attention," Frankie said, biting into a piece of garlic bread.

"Consider it done," Jimmy replied with little emotion. Taking a life wasn't a big deal to Jimmy. He could care less. His goal was to be the best in his line of work.

"I know that fucking moolie damn near shit his draws when he saw a bullet in his drivers head," Frankie laughed with a mouth full of food.

"I doubt it," Jimmy said, wiping his mouth with a napkin. "Me and him are no different. We are both killers, so the site of blood doesn't bother us. The only difference between us is I'm a professional killer," he said, giving Frankie a wink.

"Fuck that moolie. He's got some big fucking balls," Frankie chuckled. "Putting his hands on me, he must have wanted to die."

Jimmy shook his head and enjoyed a glass of wine as Frankie continued to go on and on about the situation. Seconds later, Rell strolled up in the restaurant arm and arm with Heather, along with Mad Dog closely on their heels.

"I don't believe this shit!" Frankie said, tapping Jimmy to get his attention. Jimmy looked at Rell and chuckled, "speaking of the devil."

"What the fuck is that chick doing with that moolie?" Frankie said in a disgusted tone.

"Looks like they're on a date," Jimmy pointed out as he helped himself to another glass of wine.

"That's disgusting," Frankie growled, as he no longer had an appetite. "Fucking niggers should stick to their own kind."

"This ain't the 40's anymore," Jimmy reminded his friend.

"Fuck that, now I really want you to teach this chump a lesson."

"Will do," Jimmy said nonchalantly as he threw on his shades and stood from his seat. "Have my money for me in the morning," he said with a smile, as he headed for the exit.

"Don't worry you'll get your money," Frankie yelled out as he watched the natural born killer make his exit.

Rell sat looking over the menu when he noticed an Italian man wearing dark shades walk past his table icing Heather.

"Damn he was all in your mouth," Rell said out loud.

"Well can you blame him?" Heather asked, batting her eyes.

"Good point," Rell chuckled as the waitress approached their table.

Once the trio ordered their food, the waitress quickly disappeared back into the kitchen.

"So what do you do for a living?" Heather asked curiously.

"Oh shit," Rell chuckled. "Umm…I'm an entrepreneur."

"Entrepreneur?" Heather echoed.

"Yeah, is something wrong with that?" Rell asked defensively.

"No that's cool," Heather said, as the waitress returned to the table carrying three plates.

"So what do you like to do for fun?"

"Anything that's fun or exciting basically," Heather replied, giving Rell the "I'm down for whatever" eye.

Rell quickly picked up on the hidden message. "That makes two of us," he flirted. While Rell was talking, Heather slipped her foot out of her shoe and began rubbing her foot up and down his leg. Rell couldn't help but get into beast mode. "Yo, I'm ready to get up outta here, what about you?" He said, looking at Heather for a response.

"I thought you would never ask," Heather said, downing the last corner of wine left in her glass.

Rell dropped a few bills on the table as the trio quickly made their exit. The whole time, Rell or Mad Dog never noticed Frankie sitting in the cut in the back of the restaurant.

* * **

"Damn, this where you live?" Rell asked looking at the fancy house, as Mad Dog pulled up.

"It sure is."

"Damn boss man, her crib is just as big as yours," Mad Dog said as he placed the vehicle in park.

"I can wait to give you a tour," Heather whispered as she slid out of the back seat.

"Yo, I'mma call you in the morning so you can come pick me up a'ight?"

"You sure you don't want me to stay out here until the morning?" Mad Dog asked sternly.

"Nah, I'm good."

"You, sure you trust that bitch enough to stay here all night?" Mad Dog raised an eyebrow.

"On second thought, I want you to stay put. I'mma go in there, bust her ass like a lobster tail real quick, then I'mma be out," Rell said as he gave Mad Dog a pound.

"A'ight handle your business," Mad Dog said, sliding Rell a condom.

As soon as Rell stepped into the house, Heather was all over him. "I've been waiting for this since the moment I laid eyes on you," Heather whispered as she darted her tongue in and out of Rell's mouth. Immediately, Rell scooped Heather up off of her feet.

"Damn daddy," she screamed as she wrapped her legs around Rell's waist. Rell slowly sucked on Heather's neck as he made his way down to her firm breast. He roughly snatched down the top of her dress and popped one of her titties in his mouth. He sucked on her titties as if he was dying of thirst and her breast were the only source of water.

"Oh shit!" Heather moaned and cursed loudly as she felt her pussy throbbing from anticipation. "I wanna taste you," she whispered in Rell's ear as she worked his dick into stiffness with her free hand.

Rell roughly turned her around, spread her legs, and thrust his dick into her hot, sopping wet pussy. Heather bit her bottom lip and hissed as Rell slid in and out of her. He pushed hard and fast, burying himself as far into her body as he could go. "You like that?" Rell grunted as he pulled Heather's hair back.

"Yes, I love it…." Heather sighed.

Rell gripped her small waist and began to hammer into her harder and harder until he exploded.

"Damn, you ain't tell me you had it like that," Heather said catching her breath.

"I thought you knew," Rell countered smoothly. "But yo let me get up outta here."

"Where you going?"

"I have to go take care of some business," Rell said, sliding his p89 back in his waistband.

"Okay babes, be careful out there, and call me when you get home," Heather said as she walked Rell to the door.

"A'ight, I got you ma," Rell winked before he bopped towards the awaiting vehicle.

"Damn, it took you long enough," Mad Dog hissed. "What the fuck was you doing in there; making love?" he teased.

"You know I don't play no games when it comes to pussy," Rell reminded his homey.

The entire time, Jimmy laid on his stomach on a roof a block away from Heather's house. He whistled tunelessly as he set up his 30caliber assault rifle. Jimmy zoomed in on Mad Dog's head as he let the crosshair follow the vehicle as it cruised along the empty streets.

"So how was it?" Mad Dog asked, nudging Rell with his elbow as he kept his eyes on the road.

"The pussy was a'ight," Rell chuckled as he lit up a roach that laid in the ashtray.

"I knew it," Mad Dog said with authority. "See if she got any friends next time."

"You know I got you," Rell countered, blowing out a cloud of smoke.

Before Rell could say another word, he heard the driver window shatter as he felt a warm liquid splash across his face. He looked over to his left and saw Mad Dog slumped over the steering wheel. Before Rell could figure out what was going on, the vehicle swerved into a parked car and flipped over 12 times.

"Bullseye!" Jimmy said out loud, as he unscrewed the silencer from his riffle. He quickly broke down his riffle, placed it back in its chest, and fled the scene. Two minutes later, Rell regained full consciousness. "Fuck!" he cursed loudly as he unlocked his seatbelt and violently crashed onto the ceiling of the S.U.V. He had a deep gash above his right eye, along with a huge knot on the corner of his head. Rell crawled out of the front windshield as fast as he could, in fear the vehicle might explode. "Muthafuckas!" He cursed as he snatched his p89 from his waistband and let off six rounds into the air. Rell looked down at Mad Dog and quickly turned away. "It's on," he said to himself as he headed back in the direction of Heather's house.

Heather answered the door and jumped out of fright. She saw Rell standing on the other side of the door with blood running down his face. Immediately, she thought he had been shot, especially since she heard gunshots just moments ago. "Baby are you okay?"

"Yeah I'm fine. I just need to use your phone real quick," Rell said as he brushed past her and grabbed the cordless phone. On the fourth ring, Debo finally picked up. "Hello?"

"I told you I wasn't bugging. Somebody is trying to kill me!" Rell said hotly.

"What?"

"Yo, wake the fuck up!" Rell barked into the receiver. "Muthafuckas just killed Mad Dog!"

"Who?"

"I don't fucking know, but I'm betting it's the same person who killed my driver. Whoever he is, this muthafucka is a professional."

"Where you at? I'm coming to pick you up," Debo said as he pulled out a pen and jotted down the address. "A'ight I'll be there in 20 minutes. Don't move until I get there."

"Say no more," Rell said as he hung up the phone.

"Are you okay?" Heather asked again, as she poured some alcohol on a paper towel and applied it to the cut above Rell's eye.

"Ahww shit!" Rell growled as he pushed Heather's hand away. "I'mma be a'ight," he told her.

"Who in the world could have done something like this?" Heather wondered out loud.

"I don't know, but whoever it was, is going to pay with their life," Rell huffed, his voice sounding very firm and sure of itself.

CHAPTER 13 THE MAKEOVER

"You gonna really have to start laying low," Roy said as he slowed down for the yellow light.

"I don't know how to slow down," Gmoney said, lighting up a clip from the ashtray. "How do you slow down when you're living the fast life?"

"I don't know, but you gon have to do something," Roy said as he turned up the windshield wipers. "This kind of heat is not good for business; I think that's why Pauleena wants to meet with you."

"Listen, with all due respect, Pauleena is not the one out in the streets making sure things run smoothly. No, I don't stand on the corner and sell the drugs myself. I'm the man behind the scene and everybody knows the muthafuckas behind the scene always have the most work to do," Gmoney said sternly.

"I hear you bro," Roy said as he noticed flashing lights in the rear view mirror. "The fucking cops behind us." "Fuck!" Gmoney cursed as he removed his .45 from his waistband and placed it in the hidden compartment in the dashboard.

"Here," Roy said as he handed Gmoney his p89. Gmoney quickly tossed the guns inside the stash box as Roy pulled over to the side of the road. "Ain't shit in the trunk right?" Gmoney asked nervously.

"Nah, we good," Roy assured him.

Detective Nelson slowly eased his way to the passenger door, while Detective Bradley made his way towards the driver's door.

"What seems to be the problem detective?" Gmoney asked, only cracking his window.

"Get out of the fucking car!" Detective Nelson demanded.

"For what? It's pouring down out there," Gmoney huffed.

"Don't make me have to tell you again," Detective Nelson warned.

Roy quickly slid out of the driver seat and held an umbrella over Gmoney's head as he eased out of the passenger seat. "Let's cut straight to the chase. What the fuck do you want from me?" Gmoney asked in a bored tone.

"I'm here to make a deal with you," Detective Nelson said in an even tone.

"I'm not a snitch, you know this already."

"I'm not asking you to snitch," Detective Nelson said, sliding a Winston between his lips.

"Then what the fuck do you want from me?" Gmoney asked curiously.

"I need you to do us both a favor and leave town immediately."

"Fuck outta here," Gmoney chuckled. "I ain't going nowhere, you leave town."

$ilk White

"Listen, why don't you stop being so stubborn and quit while you ahead? You done made enough money. Leave town and never come back. Go see the world and enjoy that money."

"And if I don't?" Gmoney challenged.

"Either I'm going to blow your brains out, or I'm going to put you in jail for the rest of your life just like I did your friend Ali."

Gmoney chuckled before he responded. "Detective Nelson your job is to try to lock me up, and my job is to not get locked up. It's obvious I'm better at my job then you are at yours." He raised an eyebrow. "If you don't want to see me no more, then get some evidence and build a case."

"Some people just don't know how to quit," Detective Nelson said, shaking his head. "Don't say I never tried to help you," he said as he flicked his cigarette and headed back to his unmarked car, with Detective Bradley on his heels.

"Fuck outta here with that shit," Gmoney growled as he slid back in the passenger seat.

"I don't know what that muthafucka is up to, but he's definitely up to something," Roy said as the engine rattled and the car rolled out into traffic.

* * **

Roy pulled up in front of Pauleena's mansion and let the engine die as he and Gmoney made their way to the front door. Once again, the two Muslim brothers who guarded the door gave them problems. "How I can I help you brother?" The shorter one asked.

"You already know who we here to see," Roy hissed.

"Hold your arms out please," the taller one spoke for the first time.

Roy and Gmoney did what they were told so they could get the bullshit over with as soon as possible. The two Muslim guards frisked the two thugs before letting them enter.

"I'm going to put a bullet in the back of that short muthafucka's head one of these days," Gmoney said as the two reached Pauleena's office. Before Roy got a chance to knock on the door, Pauleena had already opened it.

"Gentlemen, so glad y'all could make it. Come in," she said as she stepped to the side. "Malcolm, get these gentlemen something to sip on please."

The seven-foot monster gave Gmoney a nasty look before he headed over to the mini bar and fetched a bottle of champagne.

"So what's so important that I had to rush over here at nine o'clock in the morning in this nasty weather?" Gmoney asked as he sipped from his glass.

"What the fuck happened to Bumpy?"

"The cops…"

"I'm talking to Gmoney," Pauleena said as she quickly hushed Roy.

"Well basically we was in a night spot and shit got a little out of hand," Gmoney shrugged his shoulders nonchalantly.

"That's it? Shit just got out of hand?" Pauleena asked with a bit of venom in her voice.

"Shit happens."

"Well next time make sure shit just don't happen. Bumpy was a good brother and I don't like losing my men," Pauleena said in a matter of fact tone.

"I hear you."

"Well, basically what I called you over here for is to give you a makeover."

"A makeover?" Gmoney echoed. "What kind of makeover?"

"Not the kind of makeover you thinking about," Pauleena said, downing her drink. "You hotter than a fire cracker and we have to do something to get this heat off of you and keep it off of you."

"So what did you have in mind?"

"I'm going to take you and Roy shopping," Pauleena said with a smirk on her face.

"Shopping?" Roy said as he turned and faced Gmoney.

"Yeah shopping, come on let's make it happen. The limo is out front waiting for us," Pauleena said as she headed for the door with Roy and Gmoney in tow.

Malcolm searched underneath and all around the limo for anything suspicious before he allowed Pauleena to enter.

"Where's your home boy Knowledge?" Pauleena asked, popping open another bottle champagne.

"He's in the hood getting that new product out on the streets."

"How's it going so far?"

"Everything is good. He said the streets is buzzing about this new product," Gmoney said as he split open a Dutch Master and dumped the guts inside the wastebasket.

"That's what I like to hear."

"Me and my niggaz been had the streets. All we lacked was the banging product," Gmoney said.

"Getting the streets back is not the problem. Keeping them boys (cops) off your ass is the problem."

"So how do you plan on keeping Rosco (cops) off my ass?" Gmoney chimed.

"Simple; first I'm going to take you and Roy to go pick up some suits. Then, you two are going to stick with me so y'all can stay outta trouble."

"Hang with you? Nah, I ain't tryna be doing a whole bunch off girl shit you dig?" Gmoney said, taking a long drag from his blunt.

"Girl shit, what the fuck you talking about? We partying tonight. This nigga got me fucked up," Pauleena said as she gave Malcolm a pound. Malcolm didn't respond, instead he just grinned.

"Knowledge strolled through the housing projects like he owned them, with Suge following closely behind him.

"Finally shit is back to normal," Knowledge said out loud as he saw a fiend stretched out on the bench with caked up slime on both corners of his mouth.

"Yeah that new product Pauleena hit niggaz off with is poppin," Suge said as him and Knowledge entered the building.

"I know. This the third time today we picking up money from the stash crib," Knowledge said as the two stepped off the elevator. "Yo what the fuck is you doing?" He barked as he saw a young hustler serving a crackhead in the hallway.

"I'm getting this money," the young hustler replied in a cocky tone.

Knowledge sighed loudly as he turned and snuffed (punched) the young hustler. "Don't let me catch you serving muthafuckas in the hallway. What if I was the cops? Ya stupid ass would be in jail right now."

"You right, my fault," the young hustler said just above a whisper, with his head down.

"Make all sales in the staircase or inside an apartment from now on, a'ight?"

"I got you," the young hustler said as he disappeared in the "B" staircase.

"Stupid ass young nigga," Knowledge huffed as him and Suge headed to the door they were looking for. "Now we gon have to switch up the stash crib."

"For what?" Suge asked as he did a special knock on the door.

"Cause it will make me feel better," Knowledge replied as a big man holding an Uzi, sporting an afro beard opened the door.

"Come on; let me get this bread so I can be out. I ain't got all day," Knowledge complained. The big man didn't respond, instead, he just went to the back room and fetched a nice sized duffle bag. "The way this shit is moving, I'mma probably be giving you another call in a couple of hours."

"A'ight bet, oh and I'mma need you to switch this stash crib too; immediately."

"Say no more," the big man replied, as he walked Knowledge and Suge to the door.

"Yo, keep shit running smoothly and we won't have no problems you dig?" Knowledge yelled over his shoulder as he made his exit.

CHAPTER 14 FAMILY

Nancy walked out of her new condo and slid in the driver seat of Ali's Lexus. She popped JayZ in the C.D. player as she pulled out of the driveway. She fished around her purse for her ringing cell phone as she stopped for the red light. "Hello?" She answered.

"What's up boo?"

"It's about time you called me. I been waiting for your call all day," Nancy replied with a slight attitude.

"I had to wait for these crackers to do the count," Ali told her.

"I was just joking baby. How was your day so far?"

"Okay I guess," Ali chuckled. "Will I be getting a letter from you today?"

"Of course."

"Okay, then my day will be much better," Ali said with a smile.

"Don't play with me. You know I write you a letter every night before I go to sleep," Nancy reminded him.

"Thanks, I appreciate it." "You don't have to thank me for that; I'm just doing my job."

"I know. I just want you to know I appreciate it. But anyway, what you getting into today?" Ali asked.

"I'm on my way to Christie's house so I can check up on her. I haven't heard from her since that thing happened."

"Christie is family and we always take care of family," Ali said in a firm tone.

"I'm on it boo. I was thinking we could go get our nails and hair done."

"That sound's cool. But yo, this phone is about to cut off so I'mma hit you up later on tonight a'ight?"

"Okay babes, I love you. Be careful in there," Nancy said as she blew Ali a kiss through the phone.

"I love you too; one," Ali said as he hung up the phone and headed back towards the day room. On his way to the day room, Ali bumped into Lil Bit and Loco.

"What's good my niggaz?" Ali said, giving both men pounds.

"Chilling," Loco replied quickly.

"Why y'all posted up right here?" Ali asked.

"Six new inmates supposed to be coming up in here soon," Loco said, hog spitting on the floor. "I like to see the new inmates when they first come in to make sure it's nobody I had beef with when I was out on the streets."

"Makes sense," Ali said as he posted up next to the two thugs. Ten minutes later, an officer escorted eight new inmates through the gated door.

"Oh shit," Ali said out loud, as he saw Skip in the middle of the line of new inmates. After the officer had escorted Skip to his cell, Ali made his way over.

"Yo, if you wanna live here, you gonna have to pay rent lil nigga," Ali growled disguising his voice.

Skip quickly spun around ready for action. A smile appeared across his face when he saw who was standing behind him. "Oh shit! I was about to knock you the fuck out," he chuckled as he gave Ali a pound followed by a hug.

What you doing up in here? I heard you killed a preacher," Ali laughed.

"I should have killed his ass," Skip said, thinking back on the night, which he lost his freedom. "Fuck it. What's done is done; I got six years to figure out what I'm going to do when I get up outta here."

"Well look on the bright side; at least you know you getting out," Ali exclaimed.

"Yeah can't cry over spilled milk," Skip agreed.

"Me and my man got a lil something going on in here, so you gon be a'ight," Ali assured him.

"I see you don't waste no time setting shit up."

"Time doesn't wait for no one. Plus word is, Rell got some paper on my head," Ali chuckled. "So you know I'm on point."

"That nigga Rell is pussy. You know I'mma hold you down up in here. I wish somebody would try some shit," Skip said with a lot of emotion.

"I ain't worried about that clown. But yo, my cell is right over here. When you finish unpacking, come over and holla at me."

"I got you," Skip said as he gave Ali a hug.

* * * *

Nancy pulled up in front of Christie's crib and couldn't believe her eyes. She saw two big men kick open Christie's front door and barge in. Not knowing what was going on, Nancy quickly jumped out of the Lexus and ran to the front door as fast as she could in her heels. Once Nancy reached the front door, she saw one of the big men pistol-whipping Christie.

"Hey what's going on in here?" Nancy screamed as she ran to Christie's aid. "This bitch owe us $15,000 dollars and we're here to collect," one of the big men said, aiming his gun at Nancy. "Hold on! There must be something we can do," Nancy pleaded.

"Unless you got $15 gees cash on you, then we ain't got shit to talk about. If she go then you gotta go too. Can't leave no witnesses you know."

Nancy didn't know what she was going to do, but she knew she had to do something, and do it quick. "Here take the Lexus," she said as she handed the big man her car keys.

"You a good friend. I would never give up my vehicle for a dirty ass crack head bitch," the big man said as he gave Christie one last kick. With that being said, the two men made their exit.

"I'm so sorry Nancy. Please forgive me," Christie sobbed with her head hung low.

"Sorry my ass! You better tell me what the fuck is going on, and you better start talking now," Nancy growled.

"I needed something to take my mind off of my problems."

"So you go out and smoke crack?"

"Don't come up in here judging me," Christie said, rolling her eyes.

"Don't judge you?" Nancy echoed. "Until you pay me back for that Lexus, I can do all the judging I want!" She snarled.

"You just like everybody else," Christie sobbed as she got up and headed for the bathroom. The first thing Nancy noticed when Christie walked off was the fat ass she once had no longer existed. She couldn't believe how Christie let herself go like that. Not only were Christie's good looks fading away, but so was her way of living. The house was filthy. Not to mention, everything in the house that was valuable had been sold or either pawned.

Nancy peeked through the cracked bathroom door and saw Christie's reflection through the mirror. Seeing her friend crying and at her worst point made Nancy's heart melt. "Stop that crying. You know whatever you need I got you. I'm here to help, we family," Nancy said, draping her arm around Christie's neck.

"I need you to help me get this monkey off my back," Christie said shamefully.

"You don't have to explain," Nancy sighed. "Get your things. You coming with me to my house until you get this situation under control."

"Thank you so much Nancy. I really appreciate this," Christie slurred.

"Stop thanking me, we family. Now go get ya shit ready while I call a cab," Nancy said as she pulled out her Blackberry and called a cab.

CHAPTER 15 DANCING WITH THE STARS

"I feel like a fucking idiot with this suit on," Gmoney hissed.

"You look fine. You just not used to it yet," Pauleena smirked.

"Ain't nothing I see myself getting used to smell me?" Gmoney said as the limo pulled up in front of the fancy club.

"I'll bet the ladies will love it," Pauleena winked as she slid out the back of the limo.

Gmoney stepped in the club and immediately grabbed two glasses of champagne off a passing waiter's tray.

"You a straight up alcoholic," Roy said as he watched Gmoney guzzle down the champagne.

"Fuck that. I need to get right up in this bitch," Gmoney slurred as he noticed a fine sister sitting over in the corner by herself.

"Yo Roy, you see shorty over there?" Gmoney said, nodding in the woman's direction.

"Yeah, what about her?"

"I gotta go holla at her," Gmoney said as he wiped the corners of his mouth.

"She looks expensive." Roy raised an eyebrow.

"It ain't tricking if you got it," Gmoney said over his shoulder as he headed in the diva's direction. As Gmoney approached the PYT (pretty young thing), he could tell she was one of those classy type chicks that's used to being spoiled.

"Excuse me is this seat taken?" Gmoney asked politely.

"No you're welcome to sit down," the diva said in an uninterested tone.

"I'm Gmoney," he introduced himself, extending his hand.

"Gmoney?" The diva chuckled. "I know your mother didn't name you G-money."

"Nah, basically I got the name because I'm a "G" and I love money; so the name was perfect for me."

"I guess," the diva said as she shook his hand weakly.

"I didn't catch your name."

"Because you didn't ask for it," the diva shot back.

"Damn ma, why you being so cold?" Gmoney asked as he sipped on his champagne. The diva chuckled before she responded. "Because I meet guys like you all the time and I already know what you all about."

"Sorry sweetheart, but you don't know nothing about me. I'm a one of a kind brother. There's only one Gmoney."

"I know you the type of brother who's used to getting what he wants, when he wants it. I also know guys like you are not used to hearing the word "NO." So yes, I think I know what you're all about," the diva said in a matter of fact tone.

"You want me to tell you what I know?" Gmoney asked, not waiting for a response. "I know you love and are used to the finer things in life. And I also know that you could use a real man in your life. I can also tell you ain't been fucked well in a while, and I mean fucked gooood!" Gmoney said, dragging out the word. "All I'm saying, is how can you win if you don't play the game? I can promise you, you ain't never met a guy like me before…smell me?"

"I be nervous when it comes to guys because they all talk a good one."

"Baby I can walk it like I talk it and play it how I say it," Gmoney said, undressing the diva with his eyes.

"My name is Destiny," the diva said, extending her hand.

"Nice to meet you Destiny," Gmoney smiled as he grabbed two more glasses of champagne off the waiter's tray, and handed one to Destiny.

"So what's your real name? I know your mother didn't name you Gmoney."

"Nah, my real name is Gmoney A.K.A. the bad guy," he told her as he sipped from his glass. The whole time Destiny was talking, Gmoney was checking out her merchandise. His eyes first locked on her silky straight hair that hung down to the middle of her back, her bang stopped right above her eyebrows. Next, Gmoney's eyes made it to Destiny's full lips that were covered with strawberry lip-gloss.

"I'll be right back. I'm going to the little girls' room," Destiny said flirtatiously as she stood up and headed in the direction of the restroom. Knowing that Gmoney was watching, she made sure she threw a little extra switch in her walk.

Gmoney sat back and watched Destiny's fat ass jiggle up and down with each step she took. "Damn, I definitely gotta shagg that," he said out loud as he finished his drink.

Roy sat on the sideline sipping on some champagne as he kept a close eye on Pauleena. Pauleena had raised Roy since he was 12 years old. When Roy's mother died from a stroke, Pauleena took the young boy under her wing and schooled him. Now 13 years later, Roy was one of the highest paid and most feared men in America. As Roy played the sideline, he noticed an Italian man approach Pauleena. He was about to head over there, but decided against it when he saw Malcolm step in between the two.

"How may I help you?" Malcolm asked as he patted the Italian man down if front of everyone.

"No need to pat me down. I would just like to have a word with Ms. Pauleena."

"And who might you be?" Pauleena chimed as she slowly sipped from her glass.

$ilk White

"The name's Frankie," he said, extending his hand.

Pauleena looked at the man's hand as if he had just pulled it out of the toilet. "So how can I help you?" she said, leaving Frankie hanging.

"Word on the streets is you pushing a lot of coke," Frankie said, undressing the nice figured woman with his eyes.

"Yeah and?"

"Yeah and me and my people have a problem with that," Frankie shot back as he continued to eye the sexy woman hungrily.

"I'm not sure if you heard or not but I don't deal with problems; I start 'em," Pauleena said in an even tone.

"Listen bitch…I don't know who you think you are, but it's obvious you don't know who your fucking with," Frankie said as he popped his collar. "In this city, I'm the supplier of suppliers. And anything in this city must come through me first, understand?"

"What the fuck is going on over here?" Gmoney asked as he walked up. "Frankie I know you not over here giving my girl problems?"

"Oh I didn't know she was with you G," Frankie said, copping a plea. "Why didn't you say you was with Gmoney?" he asked, looking over at Pauleena for an answer.

"Yo, did he disrespect you?" Gmoney asked.

"He sure did," Pauleena said with a smirk on her face.

Before the words could leave Pauleena's mouth, Gmoney had already crashed a half-empty champagne bottle over Frankie's head. Pauleena quickly turned her head so no shattered glass would get in her eyes.

"Get ya punk ass up. Don't ever disrespect her again, you hear me?" Gmoney growled as he took everything valuable that Frankie had in his pockets before Malcolm tossed the Italian man outside the club, and onto the curb.

"You know that cocksucker?" Pauleena asked in a salty tone as she helped herself to another drink.

"Yeah, he used to be me and Ali's old connect," Gmoney replied as he noticed Destiny return from the restroom. "I think I might need to borrow that limo tonight," he said, feeling a little buzzed from the champagne. Pauleena looked over in Destiny's direction and knew what Gmoney's plans were for the night. "Go ahead and enjoy yourself," Pauleena said with a wink as she turned to face Malcolm. "I'm going to need you to call up our second driver."

Malcolm didn't speak. Instead, he replied with a quick head nod.

"Is everything alright?" Destiny asked as she noticed blood dripping from G-money's hand.

"Yeah everything is cool. I had to rough some cat up real quick," Gmoney said nonchalantly as he wrapped his hand up with a few napkins. "Listen baby, I'm about to get up outta here. Would you like to join me?"

"I don't think that would be a good idea."

"Come on ma, don't be like that. We could grab a bite to eat, some chicken, steak, whatever you want."

"I am a little hungry," Destiny said, looking at her wristwatch. "Do you have chicken in your house?"

"Yeah I got some of everything in my crib," Gmoney replied.

"Oh okay because I don't eat a lot of peoples cooking and I don't eat out either. So if you got chicken at your crib, then I'll hook us up a meal," Destiny suggested.

"That sounds like a plan. Let me grab our coats and we out," Gmoney said as he headed over to the coat check. When Gmoney returned, the two quickly fled for the exit. When they stepped outside, they noticed it was now snowing badly.

"Oh I love the snow," Destiny said out loud, taking in the view.

"I can dig it," Gmoney said as the driver opened up the back door to the limo so Gmoney and his lady friend could enter.

"This is nice," Destiny said, looking around.

"My motto is live everyday like it's your last. You never know when it's your time to go, so I'm just enjoying my life," Gmoney shrugged his shoulders.

"I ain't mad at that," Destiny said, making herself more comfortable.

"So what was a fine young thing like you doing up in that bushy ass club?"

"I'm a classy kind of girl. All those other spots be too rowdy. But don't get it twisted, I'm still hood all day," Destiny said with authority. The limo driver pulled up in front of Gmoney's condo and placed the limo in park. Gmoney never took chicks he first met to his main crib, always to the condo.

"Damn, you got a nice spot," Destiny said as she slid out of the back seat of the limo.

"You only live once so I might as well live it up," Gmoney said as he led Destiny to the front door.

"What's good? You want me to give you a tour around this joint?"

"Nah, you can just show me where the kitchen is so I can get started on dinner," Destiny replied, trying to hide her interest in Gmoney.

"A'ight, just walk straight through the living room and you can't miss it. I'mma go slip into something a little more comfortable," Gmoney said as he headed upstairs to the second level of the condo.

Destiny walked through the living room and was surprised how good the man was living. "Damn, this brother got a fireplace and everything," she said to herself as she finally entered the kitchen. Ten minutes later, Gmoney returned back downstairs wearing a wife beater, a pair of Red Monkeys, and some slippers.

"Yo, you got everything you need?"

"Yeah I found everything," Destiny said, checking out all Gmoney's tattoos on the low.

"A'ight I'mma be in the living room getting my drink on," Gmoney said as a blunt hung from the corner of his mouth. "You want me to get you a drink?"

"Yeah, you got Alize'?"

"Yeah I got you," Gmoney said as he made his way over to the stereo. Destiny's body jumped slightly when she heard DJ Khaled "Brown Paper Bag" blast through the speakers. Once Destiny realized what song was playing, she immediately began to bob her head as she continued to season the chicken.

Gmoney headed over to his mini bar area and fixed him and Destiny drinks. As he fixed their drinks, Pauleena's word struck a chord within him. "Slow down. What's the point in making all this money if you never get to enjoy it?"

Gmoney took one step in the kitchen and looked at Destiny's nice sized ass, and made up his mind that he would now start to enjoy his money instead of raise hell.

"Here's your drink ma," he said, handing her a glass of Alize'.

"Thanks."

"No, thank you. It's been a while since I had a gorgeous woman cooking for me in my kitchen."

A smirk danced on Destiny's lips. "Are you just telling me what I want to hear or are you serious?"

"Do I look like the type of nigga who play games?" Gmoney asked, downing the Henny in one gulp.

"Hold on, let me take a good look at you," Destiny said as she turned to face Gmoney. Before she could come back with a slick response, Gmoney grabbed the back of her neck and kissed her passionately. Twenty seconds later, Destiny's hands were all down Gmoney's monkeys (jeans) fondling his lovestick. She quickly worked him to stiffness.

"Let me see what you working with," Gmoney slurred.

Destiny quickly complied, as she turned off the stove and lead Gmoney to the living room and shoved him on the couch. She quickly slid out of her dress, and slowly and sensually began to gyrate her hips to 50 Cent's song "Amusement Park." She palmed her full breast and pulled at her tender brown nipples as she continued to entertain G-money.

"You just gonna sit there and watch me all night?" Destiny hummed in a challenging tone. With that being said, Gmoney immediately backed out (pulled out his pipe) "Don't talk me to death," he told her.

Gmoney sat back and watched Destiny take his erected member into her warm mouth and wrap her juicy lips around his shaft. As Gmoney began to fuck Destiny's mouth, she felt her pussy began to warm and moisten.

Destiny's mouth felt so good that Gmoney grabbed the back of her head, and begged her not to stop as he slowly glided in and out of her mouth.

"You like that daddy?" Destiny asked as she rubbed her clit, and then stuck her fingers in Gmoney's mouth. After a few more minutes of sucking, Gmoney couldn't take it anymore. He aggressively turned Destiny around, rolled on a condom, and entered her pulsating pussy.

"Oh shit…" she sighed and panted in pleasure as she took the dick the best she could.

"Don't cry now," Gmoney grumbled as he slid deeper and deeper inside her tight hole.

"That's right. I want you fuck me just like that," Destiny said through clenched teeth as she threw the ass back. Gmoney grabbed Destiny's waist as he watched her ass slap back and forth against his torso. After about 20 minutes of getting her back dug out, Destiny crawled away from Gmoney's back shots.

"What's wrong?" Gmoney asked.

"I'm about to suck the shit out of your dick," Destiny slurred as she quickly removed Gmoney's condom and threw his dick right back in her mouth. Once Gmoney felt Destiny's mouth on his dick, he moaned and cursed loudly. Destiny gingerly licked, sucked, and kissed his dick as she made her way to his shaft, then his balls. Gmoney just sat back and watched Destiny's performance.

Destiny jerked and pulled on Gmoney dick as she sucked on it, making loud slurping noises until he finally exploded in her mouth. 15 minutes later, the two were both passed out on the couch.

CHAPTER 16 PUTTING IT IN

"Yo slow this muthafucka down!" Knowledge barked. "You tryna get us pulled over before we hit the spot?"

"My fault. It's so much snow on the ground I can't even see the lines in the streets," Suge said.

"Well maybe if you take off those fucking sunglasses and slow this muthafucka down, you'll be able to see something," Knowledge told him.

The young killer who sat behind Suge chuckled.

"What the fuck you back there laughing at?" Suge huffed, feeling embarrassed. "I bet you won't be laughing in 15 minutes."

"I always show up when it's time to perform," Shorty said from the back seat.

"Don't get mad at youngin cause you got them stupid ass shades on," Knowledge laughed as he placed a pair of white latex gloves on his hands.

"Fuck all that. Is Gmoney alright with this hit?" Suge asked, focusing hard on the road.

"It doesn't matter. He put me in charge, so the choice is mine and we doing this shit point blank," Knowledge said as he loaded his 12gauge pump shotgun. "It's time to give that faggot a wakeup call anyway. He probably thinking we forgot about his bitch ass," he said in between puffs of his Newport. "Nigga really think he gon' put some Jamaicans up in one of our old spots, get the fuck outta here," he said heatedly.

"Well you know I'm down for whatever," Suge said as he pulled over a block away from the pizza shop on the corner.

"So what's the plan?" Shorty asked from the back seat.

"Listen Shorty, just shut the fuck up, and follow our lead a'ight?" Suge growled as he rolled down his ski mask, placing his shades over the mask.

"What the fuck? Take them shits off," Knowledge huffed.

"Chill! These my good luck sunglasses," Suge hissed. "How the fuck is my shades bothering you?"

"This nigga got on a ski mask with sunglasses," Knowledge said out loud to no one in particular, as he exited the vehicle shaking his head. Knowledge made it a few steps away from the pizza shop before he rolled down his ski mask. "Let's do this," Knowledge entered the pizza shop, and quickly headed straight to the back door.

"Hey no one go back there," the cashier grumbled in a heavy accent. A split second later, Suge entered the pizza shop and knocked out the cashier's front teeth with his .45. In a quick motion, Suge hopped over the counter and emptied out the register.

Knowledge entered the back room that read "Employees Only." He entered the room and as soon as he turned to his left, a tall man with long dreadlocks stood in front of his shotgun. "Where the shit at?"

"What you talk bout?" the Jamaican asked, faking ignorance. With no trace of emotion, Knowledge pulled the trigger sending the Jamaican's brains splashing all over the wall. Suge heard the loud gunshot and prayed that Knowledge was okay. His job was to guard the front door. The only thing that kept him from running to the back was discipline.

The head Jamaican sat in his office in the back counting money until he heard a thunderous gunshot ring out. From how loud the gunshot was, he could tell the gunman was close. The Jamaican quickly grabbed the AR15 that rested under his desk. "Pussy boys wanna cum fuck wit me? Don't know who dem fucking wit!" He grumbled as he cocked the machine gun and aimed it at the door.

Knowledge slowly eased towards the door with caution. He slowly placed his ear to the door to see if he could hear whether someone was inside. Before he could remove his ear from the door, about eight shots flew through the door missing Knowledge by a fingernail.

"Me a blood clot gorilla! You no wanna fuck wit me pussy boy!" The Jamaican yelled as he slowly eased towards the door coming from an angle. Suge almost shitted on himself when he heard a loud series of gunshots go off. He knew right off the back that it couldn't have been Knowledge because those shots came from some type of machine gun.

Once the shots flew through the door, Knowledge quickly laid his shotgun on the floor and removed his .40 cal from the small of his back. On the count of three, he pointed his arm at the door and let off five shots in rapid succession.

Once the Jamaican heard the gunman return fire, he quickly pulled the trigger as the gun rattled in his hand.

Knowledge was about to return fire, until he saw two big suitcases sitting over in the corner. Something about two suitcases in the corner of a pizza shop didn't seem right to Knowledge. Without thinking twice, Knowledge grabbed the two suitcases and headed back towards the front of the pizza shop. When Knowledge came from out the back, Suge almost shot him. "Damn nigga I almost shot you," Suge exhaled.

"Take them stupid ass sunglasses off then maybe you'll be able to see," Knowledge joked as he handed Suge one of the suitcases. The two men stopped dead in their tracks when they heard six shots go off. "Where the fuck did those shots come from?" Knowledge asked.

"Them shits came from outside" Suge replied as he dashed outside to find Shorty standing by the car with his 9mm smoking. Suge looked over on the ground and saw two men with dreadlocks laid out on the concrete.

"Come on we out!" Suge yelled as him and Knowledge both ran to the getaway

$ilk White

car and slid in, each man holding a suitcase.

"Yo Shorty punch this shit," Knowledge yelled from the back seat. Before Knowledge could get his words out, Shorty got behind the wheel and gunned the engine.

CHAPTER 17 LONG TIME NO SEE

"Hold on I'm coming," Nancy yelled as she got up from off the couch and went to see who was banging on her door. She looked through the peephole and quickly opened the door. "Hey girl, what's up? Where the fuck you been?"

"Girl I been all over the place," Coco replied as she kissed Nancy on the cheek. "I came through to check on you and the baby."

"The baby is taking a nap right now, but come sit down and tell me what you been up to," Nancy said as the two sat on the couch.

"You got a minute, because this is going to take a while," Coco said as she pulled a blunt out from her purse.

"You always up in the middle of some shit," Nancy said, thirsty to hear the gossip.

"First of all, I know you heard about what happened between me and Gmoney cause it was all over the streets," Coco said, taking a long drag from the blunt.

"How am I going to hear anything? You know I don't be in the streets," Nancy said, reminding her.

"Well after me and Gmoney broke up, I started messing with this boxing cat name "The Terminator.""

"The same Terminator who knocked Spanky out?" Nancy cut in.

"Yeah that's him, but I didn't find out he was the guy who knocked out Spanky until after we had been seeing each other for a while," Coco said, trying to clean it up.

"You knew if Gmoney found out, he was going to flip. Spanky was family," Nancy pointed out.

"I know, but he's out fucking whoever he wants. Why can't I do the same?" Coco protested.

"Because you're fucking the guy who knocked Spanky out, causing him to kill himself...that's not a good look!"

"But anyway, let me tell you what happened," Coco said, quickly changing the subject. "I'm in the club chilling with my boo, minding my business, when this fool G-money walks over to our table with all his boys with him, talking about what the fuck am I doing in here with this guy. I told that nigga you don't got no muthafucking papers on me. I can see who the fuck I want." Coco over exaggerated, spicing up the story.

"Then what happened?"

"Gmoney grabs me by my hair and starts to drag me out the club. So once my man saw what was going on, he knocked like three of Gmoney's boys out," she lied. "Then two seconds later, bouncers were everywhere breaking up the fight."

$ilk White

"Girl you is crazy," Nancy said, shaking her head in disbelief.

"But yeah, the Terminator is mad cool, and he loves to be around me," Coco boasted.

"Stop saying that name so loud. Christie is in the back room sleeping," Nancy warned.

"Oh word? What she doing here? I'm about to go wake her ass up. I ain't seen her in months," Coco said with a smile on her face.

"Trust me you don't want to go back there."

"Why, what's wrong?" Coco asked, sensing something was wrong.

"I went to go check up on Christie the other day to see how she was doing. But when I got there, two big men were beating the shit out of her and threatening to kill her; talking about she owed them all kinds of money."

"You lying!"

"Lying? I had to give up Ali's Lexus just so they wouldn't kill the both of us," Nancy said in a low voice.

"That's crazy," Coco said, covering her mouth in shock. "She fucking around with that dope?"

"Crack, I think," Nancy replied with a look of hurt on her face.

"So you letting her stay here until she get her shit together right?"

"Of course, she's family," Nancy replied as she picked up the ringing cordless phone. "Hello?" She answered.

"Hey baby what's up?"

"Nothing baby, I was just thinking about you. How was your day?"

"Why do you always ask me that when you know where I'm at?" Ali asked.

"Sorry baby…I just wanted to see how your day was," Nancy said, sucking her teeth.

"How is Christie doing?"

"She's doing okay. She's in the room resting right now," Nancy answered.

"Whatever needs to be done, I need you to do handle that for me," Ali paused briefly. "We have to make sure Christie gets her shit together."

"I got you. Christie is family," Nancy replied.

"And we always take care of family, remember that. But anyway, this phone is about to cut off. When you coming to see me?"

"I'll be up there tomorrow, baby. Why? You miss me?"

"What you think?"

"I don't know. Why don't you tell me," Nancy flirted in her sexy voice.

"How about I show you how much I miss you tomorrow when I see your fine ass?"

"That sounds like a plan to me baby. Always know that I love you and can't wait to see you tomorrow. You want me to wear a skirt?"

"Yeah wear a skirt and make sure you wear a thong too. Okay baby, I love you too. I gotta go," Ali said as he ended the conversation.

"Everything good back in the town?" Skip asked.

"Yeah you know...regular shit," Ali replied as he noticed the husky C.O. heading in his direction.

"Hey Ali you got a visit," the C.O. announced.

"I wonder who the fuck could be coming to see me?" Ali said out loud, turning to face Skip. "I just spoke to Nancy and she's in the crib chilling with Coco.

"Maybe it's one of your side joints," Skip replied.

"I been up in this muthafucka for a year and a half and the only person who comes to visit me is Nancy," Ali said as he gave Skip a pound and headed over to the C.O. so he could escort him down to the visiting room. When Ali reached the visiting room, the C.O. escorted him to the plexi glass area.

"Yo what's good? I'm not in the box, why do I have to sit behind a glass?" Ali asked curiously.

"Your visitor requested this kind of visit," the C.O. barked. "Now go have a seat at table number four."

Ali took his seat behind the thick plexi glass and waited patiently for his visitor to make their presence known. When Ali's visitor showed his identity, Ali's face quickly turned into a mask of anger. Big Mel sat on the other side of the plexi glass and picked up the phone. Ali paused briefly before he picked up the phone.

"You got some big ass balls coming up here...no homo," Ali said in a humble tone.

"Listen...I know you probably want me dead, but just let me explain..."

"Explain what?" Ali growled cutting Big Mel off. "Nigga I took care of you and your whole fucking family, and this is what you do to me?"

"I know I fucked up," Big Mel whispered with his head down in shame. "I was just jealous of you."

"Jealous of what? Whatever was mines was yours, so don't hit me with that bullshit," Ali said, waving him off.

"You had the one thing that we couldn't share. You had power," Big Mel said as a tear rolled down his cheek. "I wanted to be you so bad that I didn't know what else to do."

"So you put me in here?" Ali said with a chuckle. "If this glass wasn't between us, I would fuck body (kill) you."

"I know you would," Big Mel said, breaking eye contact. "Well I just came to ask for your forgiveness and I left five gees on your books."

"Five gees?" Ali echoed. "So you thought you was going to leave FIVE gees on my books and I was going to forgive you? That's what you thought?"

Before Big Mel could respond, Ali got up and started banging the phone against the glass. "You a fucking dead man walking," Ali yelled as two correctional officers roughly escorted him out of the visiting room.

CHAPTER 18 FLAMBOYANT

Knowledge parked his Benz in the club's parking lot, reached over, and opened up the glove compartment. Inside sat neat stacks of money placed in rubber bands. Knowledge quickly grabbed four stacks, placing two in each pocket. Parked two spots away was Suge, along with three young wild soldiers.

"I never knew this club even existed," Knowledge said as he gave Suge and the rest of the goon's pounds.

"I heard Pauleena owns this shit," Suge pointed out.

"Oh word? I wonder what Gmoney wants to holla at me about," Knowledge said, thinking out loud.

"Probably about all the trouble you been causing," Suge replied as the crew started towards the entrance. Before Knowledge and his crew reached the entrance, he noticed an all-black limousine pull up to the curb. Seconds later, Roy slid out the back seat, followed by Gmoney and about seven soldiers.

"Knowledge what's good my man?" Gmoney asked, giving him and Suge both pounds.

"You know…living the fast life," Knowledge replied with a smile.

"That's what I like to hear. Let's go up in here and do what we do," Gmoney said, draping his arm around Knowledge's neck.

Once inside the club, Gmoney and his crew were treated with V.I.P. treatment as usual. After about 15 minutes of chilling, the V.I.P. section was flooded with gold diggers and groupies.

"Hello do I know you?" A woman who was half-naked asked Knowledge.

"I don't know. Do you?" Knowledge responded, sipping on some Henny.

"Well I can't really get a good look at your face," the woman said, hinting towards the blue Mets hat that came down over Knowledge's eyebrows.

"Fuck all this small talk," Knowledge said as he grabbed the woman's wrist and pulled her down on his lap. As the night went on Gmoney sat back and took mental notes on little things that were going on.

"Shout out to my nigga Gmoney and Knowledge over in the V.I.P. area living it up," the DJ shouted over the mic, giving them a shout out. Gmoney sat back enjoying his blunt of haze as he half listened to what the chick in his ear was talking about. Seconds later, Roy came over and whispered in Gmoney's ear.

"Yo it's some clown over there demanding that he speak with you right now."

Gmoney looked over Knowledge's shoulder and took a close look at the man. "Nah, I never seen that fool before in my life," he confirmed.

"So you want me to send him on his way?" Roy asked impatiently.

"Nah, let him through so I can see what this chump talking about," Gmoney instructed as he filled up his flute with champagne. As the man approached the table, Gmoney noticed the man's big muscles.

"What's good fam?" the big man said as he gave Gmoney a pound and helped himself to a seat. "I know you don't know me and all that, but my name is Q."

"How can I help you Q?" Gmoney asked in an uninterested tone.

"Listen…I'mma keep it funky with you. I just came home from doing eight years up in Elmira and I'm fucked up."

"So what you want? A job?" Gmoney asked in between puffs.

"A job?" Q echoed with a little chuckle. "Nah, I don't need a job, but I could use a new car and a couple of dollars if you know what I mean," he said with a raised eyebrow.

"Okay let me get this straight. You want me to buy you a car and give you money, is that correct?"

"Absolutely!" Q replied, helping himself to a drink.

"And why the fuck would I do that? I don't even know you," Gmoney fumed.

"Because if you don't, I'mma have to bet on my bullshit. And trust me, you don't want that," Q said in a calm tone. "I got over a hundred shooters on my team ready to do whatever, so let me know how you wanna play it. And word on the streets is you the police number one target so you don't need this heat I'mma about to bring down. Get what I'm trying to say?"

"I hear you," Gmoney said, blowing out a cloud of smoke. "Just let me know how much money you need and what kind of car you want and it's yours"

"That's what I'm talking about," Q said with a smirk. "I'll just take 50 thousand for now and a new Lexus."

"No problem. You'll have it before the night is out," Gmoney told him as he refilled his flute with more champagne.

"A'ight cool. I'mma go fuck with a few of these bitches in here, but I'll be back in about an hour," Q said as he patted Gmoney on the back and headed for the dance floor. Once Q left, Gmoney signaled for Knowledge to come over.

"What's good?" Knowledge asked as he sat down.

"You seen that clown I was just talking to?"

"Yeah, what about him?"

"I'm going to need you to get rid of him tonight!" Gmoney told him.

"Not a problem," Knowledge replied as a smirk played on his lips.

"You need me to go with him?" Roy asked, noticing something was wrong. "You a'ight?"

"Nah, I'm not alright. Everything is all fucked up," Gmoney exhaled in an even tone. "This shit is fucking whack!"

"What you talking about?" Roy asked confused.

"How we living is whack," Gmoney growled. "Everyday the shit Ali used to tell me is starting to make more and more sense." He paused to fix himself another drink.

"What you mean? You have everything a person could ask for." Roy pointed out.

"What do I really have? Tell me Roy what do I have?"

"Everything!" Roy replied.

Gmoney looked around the club formulating a response. "Is this what you call everything?" He asked, no longer sipping from his flute, but instead, swigging from the bottle. "All this stress and drama, and all I got is a big ass house that I live in alone. I got five cars and don't bring half of them shits out; A whole bunch of jewelry that I can't even wear at the same time; All this champagne and liquor I drink just to throw it up and piss it out. I got a condo and two apartments that I only slept in twice. So what's this shit really all about? Then on top of that, now I got muthafuckas trying to extort me just because."

"Shit could always be worst," Roy said as he noticed Pauleena stroll up in the club with about four Muslim brothers behind her.

"Shout out to Pauleena, who just stepped in the building. You already know what it is!" The DJ said, shouting her out over the mic.

"Fuck you doing here?" Gmoney asked as he gave Pauleena a hug.

"Damn, I gotta have permission to come in my own club?" Pauleena joked as she dismissed the gold digger who was sitting next to Gmoney and took her seat.

"Nah, I'm just fucking with you, with ya sexy ass," Gmoney flirted openly.

"You so fresh," Pauleena giggled as she slid him something on the low.

"What the fuck is this?"

"Oh shit! You gon finally give me some of that sweet pussy?" Gmoney grinned.

"In your dreams sweetie," Pauleena said flatly. "It's a surprise. It's just a little gift from me to you."

"That's what's up," Gmoney said as he noticed the dirty looks Malcolm was giving him. "Yo…why the fuck this big, ugly nigga always looking all in my face?" Gmoney barked, rising to his feet.

"Brother I will kill you with my bare hands," Malcolm growled, taking a step forward.

"Listen you two, chill the fuck out. We all on the same team," Pauleena said, defusing the situation.

"What's good? Everything alright over here?" Knowledge asked with a blunt hanging from the side of his mouth.

"Yeah everything is cool, but I think it's time to take care of that thing we talked about earlier."

"I'mma get on that right now. I'mma scream at you when it's all said and done," Knowledge said as he gave Gmoney a pound and kissed Pauleena on the cheek.

Q sat at the bar, sweet-talking some chick when he felt some one tap him on the shoulder. "Come on let's take care of this business," Knowledge said, not waiting for a response. Once outside the club, one of Knowledge's soldiers pulled up in a royal blue Buick.

"Here, stay close behind us," Knowledge whispered as he handed Suge the keys to his Benz. "Yo come on. I ain't got all day," Knowledge sucked his teeth as he slid in the back seat of the Buick.

"Watch how you talk to me before I come back there and smack ya fucking head off!" Q snarled as he hopped in the passenger seat. It took everything inside of Knowledge to control his temper.

"Lil niggaz mouths' is reckless nowadays," Q continued.

* * **

"Your spot always be having the baddest bitches," Gmoney said out loud. "I wouldn't have it any other way," Pauleena replied with a smile.

Gmoney grabbed a bottle of champagne and began to guzzle it as he felt his phone vibrating. Immediately, he recognized that the call was being made from Nancy's house.

"Yeah what's good?" he yelled into the receiver.

"Yo, where you at?" Nancy yelled so Gmoney could hear her over the loud music.

"I'm at the club right now."

"Oh, well go to the bathroom so you can hear because I got Ali on the other line."

"A'ight I'm going right now," Gmoney said.

"Hurry up so I can click over."

"Yo I'll be right back," Gmoney said as he snaked through the crowd, heading towards the bathroom. As Gmoney squeezed through the crowd, Pauleena noticed two dirty looking men creeping up on Gmoney from behind. From the filthy, thick beards they sported, Pauleena figured it wasn't a coincidence. Without thinking twice, she pulled her 9mm from her handbag and moved through the crowd as fast as her three-inch heels could take her, with Malcolm in tow. As soon as Gmoney entered the bathroom, he looked under each stall, making sure he was alone.

"Put my man on the phone," he said excitedly.

"Hold on," Nancy said as she quickly clicked over.

"Hello?" Ali's voice boomed through the phone.

"My nigga, what's good? You been getting the money I been sending you?"

"Yeah I got it."

"It's nothing, but how you holding up in there?" Gmoney asked.

"I'm standing strong. Ya man Skip up in here with me."

"I heard, I heard. But yo, I'mma be up there next weekend to see y'all."

"That's what's up. How you holding up out there?" Ali asked.

"Everything is cool. The team is still moving and getting stronger than ever."

Before Gmoney could say another word, he heard the bathroom door bust open. When he turned around, all he saw was two big cannons in his face.

"You already know what this is!" One of the gunmen growled as he snatched Gmoney's IPhone from out of his hand.

"Ya man getting robbed right now," the gunman said into the receiver as he tossed the phone over in the corner.

"Take whatever y'all want," Gmoney said as he continued to guzzle from his bottle.

"This nigga must think we playing," the other gunman said as he slapped G-money in the face with the ratchet.

"Look at me! I know you remember me," the man said as he unarmed Gmoney. "Let me refresh your memory. My cousin Victor, you put him in a wheelchair about a year ago," he growled as his partner stripped Gmoney of all his valuable belongings.

Seconds later, the two gunmen heard the bathroom door bust open. Before they knew what was going on, Pauleena was already in motion. Two hollow point messengers of death found a home in the first gunman's chest and neck, dropping him instantly. Not knowing what to do, the second gunman aimed his pistol at Pauleena. But as he pulled the trigger, Gmoney managed to grab his arm and redirected the bullet.

Pauleena and Malcolm sat in the doorway watching as Gmoney and the gunman battled to get control of the gun. Pauleena was getting ready to shoot but decided to hold fire, not wanting to hit GMoney by mistake.

GMoney and the gunman scuffled for about 30 seconds before a single shot went off ending the scuffle. A smile appeared on Pauleena's face when she saw the gunman drop down to his knees and cough up blood.

"You thought you was going to rob me muthafucka?" Gmoney said calmly as he emptied the whole clip in the gunman's face. Seconds later, six big bouncers came running into the bathroom.

"Pauleena is everything okay?" One of the bouncers asked.

"Yeah everything is cool. I'm just going to need y'all to get rid of these bodies for me," Pauleena said nonchalantly. "Make sure you take em out back and clean up this mess too," she ordered as she, Gmoney, and Malcolm exited the bathroom.

$ilk White

"Yo I'm about to get up out of here," Gmoney said, shaking his head.

"Do that. You look like you could use some rest."

"A'ight I'mma call you tomorrow," Gmoney said as he kissed Pauleena on the cheek.

"Okay. Oh and don't forget to go check out the gift I got you," Pauleena said with a wink.

Gmoney dug down in his pocket and pulled out the hotel key that she gave him earlier. "A'ight I got you. This better not be no whack shit either or else I'mma be tight," he said as he exited the club and slid in the back of his limo.

* * * *

"So where you from?" The driver asked.

"Queens," Q replied quickly.

"Oh word? My cousin lives out there. What part you from?"

"Why the fuck does it matter what part I'm from?" Q barked.

"Nah, I was just asking."

"Well stop asking me all these fucking questions," Q snarled. Knowledge sat in the back listening to Q disrespect his young soldier. Once Knowledge thought they were far enough away from the club, he pulled out his .380 and shot Q in the back of his head.

"OH SHIT!" Damn you could have at least gave me a warning." The driver yelled, still a little startled.

"Sorry, but I couldn't stand hearing his mouth for one more second," Knowledge chuckled from the back seat.

"Damn nigga you farted?"

"Nah, I ain't fart"

"So what the fuck is that smell?"

"It's a dead nigga in the front seat. His muscles are relaxed so he probably shitted on himself, now pull over," Knowledge said, schooling the young soldier. Once the driver pulled over, him and Knowledge quickly exited the Buick. "Where the fuck is this guy? I told him to stay right behind us," Knowledge said out loud. Seconds later, Suge pulled up. "Damn y'all standing over in the cut I almost didn't see y'all."

"If you take those stupid ass shades off, then maybe you might be able to see," Knowledge hissed as he and his young soldier slid in the vehicle.

"Nigga you know I always wear my shades when I go on a job," Suge huffed as he gunned the engine, fleeing the crime scene.

* * * *

Gmoney stepped off the elevator on the fourth floor of the hotel and strolled down the hallway until he found the room he was looking for. Before he pulled out the key, he felt his cell phone vibrating on his waist. He looked at the caller I.D. and saw that it was Knowledge calling him. "Yeah what's up?" He answered.

"It's done!"

"A'ight bet, I'll holla at you later," Gmoney said, quickly ending the conversation. Not wanting to be bothered, he turned his phone off and pulled the room key out of his pocket. He slid the card through the door and the green light flashed, signaling for him to enter. Gmoney drew his .45 as he slowly entered the room with caution. Once inside the room, Gmoney noticed two beautiful ladies laid across the bed wearing nothing but thongs.

"Are you Gmoney?" the darker one out of the two asked seductively.

"The one and only," he answered as he hungrily eyed the two women.

"Damn Pauleena didn't tell us you was this fine," the light-skinned one said openly. "I'm Nicole and this is Zora," she said, pointing to her friend. "I want you to just sit back and just enjoy yourself," Nicole said as she pushed Gmoney onto the love seat as she climbed back on the bed with Zora.

Gmoney sat back in the love seat and watched as Zora and Nicole began to tongue kiss in front of him. His manhood quickly stiffened as he continued to watch the two women kiss and explore each other's body. After a long kiss, Nicole slid Zora's thong off and slowly began to rub and massage her clit. Zora moaned and cursed loudly as she felt her pussy began to warm and moisten. "Come eat my pussy," she demanded. Nicole complied as she thrust her tongue inside Zora's warm pussy, and then alternated between tongue- fucking her and sucking on her clit. Zora gasped, sucking in air through clenched teeth.

Gmoney sat back, shaking around the ice in his glass as he continued to watch the show.

"Oh shit…" Zora sighed as she grabbed Nicole's head and begged her not to stop. Seconds later, Zora's body tensed as she began to climax. Once the two finished eating each other out, they turned their attention and focus on Gmoney. By this time, his dick was already rock hard.

"Take those clothes off now!" Zora demanded as she and Nicole stood over him watching his every move. Without hesitation, Gmoney peeled his clothes off. He sat back and watched as Zora and Nicole fought to see which one was going to suck his dick first.

Zora won the battle and slowly began to lick around the rim of his dick with the tip off her tongue, while Nicole dipped her head beneath his balls and started licking in a circular motion. Zora and Nicole both licked and sucked all over Gmoney's shaft and head. And once he came, the two fought to taste his fluids. No matter how many times Gmoney came, Zora and Nicole got his dick back hard and took turns riding it over and over again until the sun rose the next day.

CHAPTER 19 SLAVERY

"Yo let me get two of them shits," an inmate said as he handed Skip a 50-dollar bill. Skip took the money and handed the inmate two small bags of dope.

"This some good shit you got. If you keep this shit, I'll have my girl start bringing me more money," the inmate said as he opened up his package.

"You already know we only keep the best!" Skip yelled over his shoulder as he exited the man's cell and headed down the tier.

"Hey boy!" Sang an unfamiliar voice.

Skip stopped and noticed a white, baldheaded man with too many tattoos approaching him.

"What's up?" Skip asked, taking a defensive stance.

"Boy have you lost your fucking mind?" the white man growled. "This is my fucking territory. I know you not dumb enough to be selling on my property without paying rent, and even more importantly, without my permission."

"Listen…I don't know what y'all skinheads got going on…."

"Who the fuck you calling a skinhead?" the white man growled, getting all up in Skip's face. "My name is Rose," he yelled in Skip's face.

Skip was about to steal on the skinhead until a C.O. strolled up. "Is everything alright over here?" he asked, looking at Rose and Skip.

"Yeah everything is cool," Rose said with a warm smile. "Listen you black bastard, I better not catch you slinging on my property again, or that's your ass," he snarled as he walked off.

"I'm so scared!" Skip yelled as Rose walked off. "Punk ass white boy," he said out loud, as he headed straight for Ali's cell.

Ali sat in his cell shooting the breeze with Lil Bit when Skip walk up in his cell.

"Yo some skinhead just pressed me, talking about I can't sell nothing without his permission and if he catch me slangin again, its gonna be a problem."

"Which skinhead?" Ali asked in an even tone.

"That bitch ass cracker standing in the middle," Skip said, pointing at the pack of skinheads standing together. "Oh that's Rose. He's the leader of the Aryan Nation," Lil Bit announced. "A'ight, I'm about to go over there and holla at that clown," Ali said as he threw on his white pants.

"Where the fuck you get those pants from?" Skip asked.

"These crackers got ya boy working in the mess hall (kitchen)," Ali said sourly. "Yo y'all wait right here, while I go holla at these skinheads mufuckas," He said as he headed towards where the Aryan Nation stood.

"Yo which one of y'all fools is Rose?" Ali asked, approaching the group.

"Who the fuck wants to know?" One of the skinheads shot back.

"Who's asking?" Ali fumed.

"I'm Rose, how can I help you?"

"I need to speak to you in private?"

"Right this way," Rose said as he led Ali inside his cell. "I'm listening."

"You had some words with my man earlier. What was that all about?" Ali asked, getting straight to the point.

"Your man was out of line earlier. I caught him on my property."

"How you figure?"

"What you mean how I figure? I caught the cocksucker slinging on my property. He's lucky I didn't kill his ass," Rose said, placing a cigarette in his mouth.

"I don't fuck with none of your peoples, so don't fuck with mine," Ali declared.

"You got some big ass balls nigger!" Rose said, blowing smoke in Ali face. "You a new jack in here boy! You ain't been here for two full years. I heard you were big time while you were on the streets, but in here you ain't shit but a number big time sumbitch," he growled inches away from Ali's face.

"It's on you, however you wanna play it; just let me know," Ali said with a smirk on his face.

"Boy you dumber than you look," Rose chuckled as he watched Ali walk off.

"Yo Ice Pick come here," Rose called out.

"What's up?" Ice Pick asked, cracking his knuckles.

"It's time to teach the new jack how to play with the big dogs," Rose raised an eyebrow.

CHAPTER 20 WORLD WAR III

"So you sure it was one of Gmoney's boys who robbed the pizza shop?" Rell asked, his brown eyes glittering dangerously.

"Me never forget a face," the Jamaican said in a mellow tone; yet it was firm.

"A'ight, so it was them who been trying to get at me," Rell said in deep thought.

"Let me know me what to do cuz you know me got a hundred yardies ready to lick shots," the Jamaican said, making a gun with his finger for extra emphasis.

"I want Gmoney dead," Rell stated harshly.

"Just give me the word," the Jamaican said with a bugged out look on his face. "Blood clot pussy boys killed my brotha."

"A'ight round up your soldiers and go take care of this situation. I want you to take out as many of them as you can. I don't care if they with their wives, girlfriends, kids or whatever," Rell said as he studied the Jamaican in front of him.

"You no worry, Dirty gonna show you how me turn it up," Dirty said as he filed for the door.

* * * *

"Here's $20,000. I want Gmoney dead. And once you're done with him, I want you to kill that Pauleena bitch," Frankie said, handing Jimmy the money.

"This ain't enough," Jimmy said flatly.

"Once you get rid of Gmoney, you'll get the rest of the money."

"I thought you and Gmoney were cool?" Jimmy asked.

"We were until he cracked a bottle over my fucking head," Frankie exclaimed loudly.

"I'll kill anybody as long as you paying for it," Jimmy said with a smile.

"That's why I pay you the big bucks," Frankie countered as the two busted out laughing.

CHAPTER 21 THE SPOTLIGHT

Knowledge's Benz pulled up directly in front of the club bumping Camron's Killa Season CD. He stepped out of the Benz wearing a black, short cut mink with the hood, along with plenty of jewelry. As soon as he stepped foot on the curb, Suge and about seven soldiers awaited his arrival.

"What's good my niggaz?" Knowledge said as he and his crew headed straight for the entrance. "I heard they got some bad bitches up in this spot."

"Hell yeah, these bitches be looking like porn stars," Shorty replied, looking like a pervert.

"Did you bring me what I asked for?" Knowledge questioned.

"Yeah it's right here," Suge said as he handed Knowledge a book bag. "That's $10,000 in one's just like you asked."

"A'ight good looking baby," Knowledge said as he handed each soldier a stack of singles. "Y'all niggaz enjoy yourselves and have a good time, I know I am."

Once all the strippers saw Knowledge and his crew enter the club, they immediately swarmed him and his crew like sharks who smelled blood. "Hey what's up big time?" A dark skin stripper with a stupid fat ass spoke. "I ain't seen you in here for a while."

"You know I had to get my one, two on. But with an ass that fat, you know I was coming back," Knowledge said as he pulled the stripper down onto his lap.

"What will you be drinking?" A topless waitress asked seductively as she approached the two.

"Let me get a vodka and orange juice and get the lady whatever she's drinking," Knowledge said as he stuck a 50-dollar bill down in the waitress's shorts.

"Thank you baby and what will you be drinking?" The waitress asked looking at Felisha for a response.

"I'll have the same thing he's having," she replied as she straddled her legs around Knowledge's waist and began to slowly gyrate her hips to the music the D.J. was playing.

"That's what I'm talking about," Knowledge slurred, still feeling a buzz from the small bottle of Henny he consumed earlier in the night.

"Just tell momma how you want it and it's all yours," Felicia whispered in Knowledge's ear as she took it in her mouth.

"You know I want some of that bomb ass head and of course you know I can't let you go without busting that ass," Knowledge grinned as he cupped both of her ass cheeks with a firm grip.

$ilk White

"You know I got you," Felicia said, thinking back on the first time her and Knowledge had sex. Felicia and about five of her coworkers had met Knowledge and a few of his boys at a hotel when they got off work. All she could remember was ass and titties everywhere, unlimited bottles of champagne and Knowledge fucking the shit out of her and her best friend who laid next to her.

"You know I'm down for round two," Felisha said, matching Knowledge's stare. The conversation was momentarily paused when the waitress reappeared carrying two drinks.

"Good looking ma. Keep the change," Knowledge said with a wink. The waitress just smiled as she turned and headed back towards the bar; throwing a little extra switch in her walk so Knowledge could see what she was really working with. Knowledge made a mental note to get the Spanish waitress's number before he left.

"So how you wanna do this at a hotel or did you have something else in mind?" Felisha asked as she felt Knowledge's manhood began to rise underneath her.

"We can do it like the last time," Knowledge replied with a smirk.

"So when do you want to be out?"

"Let my homies have a little more fun, then we can roll," Knowledge said as he looked over Felisha's shoulder and saw Suge, Shorty, and the rest of the crew toss dollars like it was nothing.

"That's what I'm talking about," Suge slurred as he slid a hand full of dollars into the stripper's thong, who stood in front of him bent over.

* * * *

Meanwhile, across the street from strip club sat a white van. "As soon as dem blood clot pussy boys come out, I want y'all to rinse ya gun in their face," Dirty said, giving his five soldiers simple instruction.

"What's good? You ready to get up out of here?" Knowledge asked, turning to face Felicia. "I was born ready," Felicia replied. "Let me go change and grab a few of my girls then we can be out." "A'ight bet. Don't have me waiting all day," Knowledge said as he slapped Felicia's ass as she walked off. Once Felicia disappeared inside the dressing room, Knowledge quickly made his way over to the bar. As he approached, he noticed some john talking to the Spanish waitress.

"Here's a hundred dollars now get lost," Knowledge said, tossing the hundred-dollar bill at the john's chest.

"Damn you throw paper away just like that?" The waitress asked with a raised brow.

"You can't take it to Heaven or Hell with you, so you might as well spend it,"

Knowledge replied with a smile.

"Uhmm… Excuse me, but I believe I was talking to the lady first," the john said, tapping Knowledge on his shoulder.

Knowledge ignored the man and continued on with his conversation. "So you got a number that I can reach you at?"

"Hey asshole, I was talking to the lady first," the john growled as he grabbed Knowledge by his shoulder and spun him around. "I said…"

"You said what muthafucka!" Knowledge snarled.

"Oh I'm sorry Knowledge. I didn't know that was you," the john said, copping a plea.

"Yo get the fuck out my face," Knowledge quickly dismissed the john. "Yo, you good?" Shorty asked with his hand on his 9mm.

"Yeah everything good, just some chump who made an honest mistake," Knowledge hissed as he turned his attention back towards the topless waitress. "Like I was saying before I was rudely interrupted," Knowledge continued smoothly. "Let me get your name and number before I get up outta here."

"The name's Jamie," she replied as she scribbled down her number on a napkin and slid it over the counter.

"You'll be hearing from me soon," Knowledge said, stuffing the napkin down in his pocket as he, his entourage, Felicia, and a few of her coworkers headed for the exit. Once outside, the cool air slapped Knowledge and his crew in the face.

"Damn it's kinda nippy out here B," Shorty said out loud, as he zipped up his jacket.

"This that good football weather right here," Suge said as he noticed a white van cruising through the parking lot.

Suge quickly reached for his hip until he noticed one of the strippers had dropped her cigarettes. As the stripper bent over to pick up her cigarettes, her ass grabbed the attention of Knowledge and his entire crew. By the time Suge looked back up, he saw the side door of the van open with three men with long dreadlocks hanging out the side. Each man held a firm grip on a machine gun.

"Oh shit it's a hit!" Suge yelled as he quickly pulled his pistol from his waist.

Once Dirty saw Knowledge and his crew were not on point, him and his shooters immediately opened fire on whoever was standing outside at that time. Knowledge's eyes lit up when he saw a van full of Jamaicans. He quickly snatched his .40 from the small of his back, but it was a little too late. Bullets were already flying through the air.

One of Knowledge's soldiers quickly tackled him in an attempt to protect him. In the process, the soldier took four bullets in his back and rib cage area.

"Fuck!" Knowledge cursed loudly as he rolled the dead body off of him and returned fire.

$ilk White

Dirty and his crew tore up the whole front of the strip club before the van stormed out of the parking lot, burning rubber as it bent the corner. Once the bullets finished ringing out, Shorty shot to his feet and tried to chase the van down the street, sending shots in its direction with his 9mm. When Knowledge finally made it back to his feet, he saw all of his soldiers sprawled out on the ground, along with Felicia and her crew. "Where the fuck is Suge?" Knowledge thought out loud, as he searched all the bodies that laid before him. "Ahw hell naw!" Knowledge said in a weak voice as he saw Suge laid out on the concrete with two bullets holes in his chest. "You a'ight?" Knowledge asked as he knelt down by Suge's side.

"It was all my fault. I seen it coming," Suge slurred as he broke into a coughing fit.

"Do me a favor; try not to talk," Knowledge said as he pulled out his cell phone and called for an ambulance.

"You know why this happened right?" Suge asked in a frail voice. "Because I didn't have my shades on," he said with a bloody smile.

Knowledge couldn't help but chuckle. "You and them damn glasses," he said, shaking his head. "Just hang in there. You gonna make it."

Seconds later, Suge's body began to shake uncontrollably. His eyes stared off into space as the life drained from his body. "Fuck," Knowledge whispered as he watched his friend die in his arms.

"AWWW SHIT!" Shorty huffed as he returned to the scene and saw Suge laid out on the concrete leaking. "Come on B. We can't stay here," he said as he heard the sirens getting louder and louder. "I ain't leaving him like this," Knowledge declared as he held his friend's hand.

"We ain't leaving him because he's already gone!" Shorty said, placing a hand on Knowledge's shoulder. "If we don't leave now, then all three of us gonna be gone you dig?"

Knowledge slowly let go of Suge's hand as he dug down in Suge's left front pocket.

"Come on man. What the fuck you doing?" Shorty yelled as he watched Knowledge take his sweet time. "Fuck this shit," he yelled as he jogged towards his truck. Knowledge searched Suge's pockets until he found what he was looking for. He pulled out Suge's sunglasses and placed them on his face. "My nigga I'mma see you when I see you. But know that whoever did this is going to pay with their fucking life."

"Yo come the fuck on!" Shorty yelled, beeping the horn as he pulled up directly in front of Knowledge. Knowledge took one last look at Suge before he got up and slid in the passenger side of the vehicle. Once he was inside, Shorty put the pedal to the metal.

CHAPTER 22 HEAT

"What's so fucking important that I had to get out my bed at five o'clock in the morning?" Gmoney asked with a slight attitude.

"I have something I want to show you," Pauleena replied with a wicked grin on her face.

"What's that?" Gmoney asked as he noticed that Pauleena had on a wife beater, army pants, and a pair of combat boots.

"Right this way," she said as she led Gmoney, Roy, and Malcolm into the next room. As soon as Gmoney entered the room, he noticed a man with long dreadlocks tied to a chair in the middle of the room. From the bruises on his face he could tell that he probably been getting fucked up for the past 24 hours. "So what's his story?" Gmoney asked, with little emotion.

"I see somebody ain't been on the job," Pauleena chuckled. "Did you know that Suge was murdered last night?"

"Get the fuck outta here," Gmoney said fanning her off.

"You don't believe me? Why don't you call up your friend Knowledge?"

Without hesitation, Gmoney dialed Knowledge's number. On the fifth ring, Knowledge answered.

"Yoooo where the fuck you been? I been trying to call you all night. Some fuck boy niggaz rolled up and dumped on us, muthafuckas took Suge out."

"Fuck!" Gmoney cursed loudly. "A'ight I don't wanna talk about this over the phone. I'mma get up with you later on tonight," Gmoney said, hanging up in Knowledge's ear.

"Fuck all this low profile shit," Gmoney huffed. "This riding around in limo's and shit ain't me."

"Okay just be prepared for all the heat that's going to come down on you," Pauleena warned. "This game is all about longevity."

"I can dig it," Gmoney replied dryly. "So who's this cocksucker?" he said, looking towards the Jamaican tied to the chair.

"One of my people's hit me up, talking about they heard this fool bragging about how him and his crew had just hit up Knowledge and his crew."

"So did you get any info out of this chump?"

"Nothing serious, all he told me was there's a big contract on your head," Pauleena replied.

"My head?" Gmoney asked with a smile.

"Yes sir."

"What else is new?" Gmoney said nonchalantly as he shrugged his shoulders. "So what you wanna do with this mop head muthafucka?" "It's your call," Pauleena said, looking at Gmoney for his response.

"A'ight I got mad shit I gotta take care of today, so I'm going to try to get up with you later," Gmoney said calmly as he kissed Pauleena on the cheek. Then he pulled out his .45 and walked over towards the Jamaican. Without a trace of emotion, Gmoney emptied the entire clip in the Jamaican's body as he turned and filed for the exit. "Yo y'all be easy. I'm out."

Once she was sure Gmoney was gone, Pauleena spoke. "I like that guy, muthafucka got a lot of heart."

"I don't like him. That wild muthafucka is going to get us all locked up," Malcolm huffed as he grabbed a bottle of vodka and helped himself to a shot.

"Oh shut up Malcolm. You don't like nobody," Pauleena said, waving him off. "But Roy, we got a little problem that I'm going to need you to take care of for me."

"What's up?" Roy asked from the sideline.

"A little trouble back home," Pauleena began. "Some guy named Big Time called himself opening up three trap houses on our territory. I'mma need you to go out there and make an example out of this guy."

"Consider it done," Roy replied with a grin. "I was starting to get homesick anyway."

CHAPTER 23 RESPECT

"Thanks for meeting me here on such short notice," Gmoney said as he glanced at the menu in front of him.

"My pleasure, I ain't seen you in mad long," April replied with a smile.

"How's Skip holding up in there?"

"He's cool, making the best out of a fucked up situation."

Before Gmoney could reply, he noticed two FBI agents sit at a table directly across from him and April. "Look at these dick heads."

"Damn, them crackers ain't going to stop until they catch ya ass," April chuckled.

"Well, let them keep trying and I'll keep getting money until they succeed," Gmoney began quietly. "I got one of my goons dropping off a little paper in your trunk right now."

"Right now?" April said, looking over her shoulder.

"Yeah it's kind of hard for me to move around with all this heat," he said, nodding his head towards the two FBI agents.

"I can dig it."

"How's the lil man?"

"Oh he's cool, getting big," April said.

"That's cool, but I got a couple of things I need to take care of so I'mma have to cut this a little short. I just wanted to make sure you were straight financially," Gmoney said with a wink as he stood up.

"Ok, well keep in touch. My number is still the same. I'mma stay here and enjoy my dinner, especially since it's already paid for," April said with a warm smile.

"I know that's right," Gmoney said as he kissed April on the cheek. "Ok come on muthafuckas. Let's roll," he said as he knocked on the table that the FBI agents sat at. Being caught off guard and not knowing what to do, the two agents quickly shot to their feet and stormed out of the restaurant; not wanting to lose sight of their main suspect.

"This nigga gonna always be crazy," April said out loud as she shook her head.

* * * *

"Damn that's the fifth time the D's (detectives) done circled this bitch," Knowledge said out loud as he and his crew stood 20 deep in the lobby.

"Yeah that's because Shorty shot some kid from around here the other day," one of the youngins informed him.

$ilk White

"Speaking of the devil," Knowledge said as he saw Shorty on the other side of the door, waiting for somebody to buzz him in.

"Yo it's crazy out there B," Shorty said as he handed a box of dutches to a nobody who just wanted to be down. "Yo roll up," he said as he turned to face Knowledge. "I just saw the D's go in the next building. So more than likely, they going up on the roof so they can take some pictures of us."

"Yeah them muthafuckas been on they job lately," Knowledge hissed. "I had to lose a tail they had on me earlier."

"We just gotta stay on point," Shorty said as he pulled his 9mm from his waistband and handed it to one of the shooters who stood close by.

"Let me get your ratchet too," the shooter said, looking at Knowledge with his hand out.

"Oh shit. Here this nigga come," Knowledge huffed as he smoothly passed off the ratchet.

"Hey Knowledge can I have a quick word with you?" Carl asked innocently. Carl was a big time drug dealer back in the eighties. After giving the system 15 years of his life, he wisely changed his life for the better and left the game alone.

"What's good my nigga?" Knowledge said as he gave Carl a pound.

"I just need a minute of your time."

Knowledge sucked his teeth. "Come on B. I don't wanna hear all that preaching shit right now. I'm about to make moves."

"This shit is only going to take a second," Carl insisted.

"Okay, okay what do you want to talk about?" Knowledge asked in an uninterested tone.

"Why is there 25 brothers standing in my lobby?"

"It's raining outside and we just chilling. What the fuck is the problem?"

"Just chilling right?" Carl said with a raised brow as he saw one of Knowledge's workers serve a fiend right in front of the elevator.

"Why you acting like Mr. Goody Goody?" Knowledge hissed. "When I was a little kid, it was you I wanted to be like. I saw all the fine women, the jewelry, cars. And most importantly what I admired the most, was how people respected you," he reminded Carl.

"But look at me now," Carl said sternly. "It took me 15 years behind bars to realize none of that shit matters when you sitting in a cell. I lost all my money, all my hoes, and most importantly, my family. The people I thought had my back really didn't, you dig? I'm just trying to keep you from learning the hard way like I did."

"Listen Carl, no disrespect, but you lived your life. Now I'm just tryna live mine," Knowledge said as he took a long drag from his blunt.

"A'ight I'm done preaching to you," Carl said irritated. "I'm just gonna leave you with something to think about," Carl leaned closer to Knowledge's ear. "When you dancing with devil, you better pray you don't have two left feet."

"I don't dance; I just two step," Knowledge shot back as he and his crew busted out laughing.

"I hear you brother," Carl yelled over his shoulder as he headed across the street to get him a pack of cigarettes.

"That nigga always trying to kick some knowledge," Shorty said in between puffs.

"Carl is a good dude," Knowledge said as he let Carl's words sink in.

"Oh shit 50!" A look out yelled.

"Yo y'all niggaz put that shit out," Knowledge ordered as he saw Detective Nelson heading towards the building with two plain clothed cops behind him.

"My man Knowledge," Detective Nelson hummed. "Long time no see. I know you haven't forgot the procedures that quick," he said as he roughly threw Knowledge against the wall.

"What the fuck is this about?" Knowledge questioned as he felt the detective forcefully spread his legs apart.

"You telling me you forgot about the murder, you just committed the other day?" Detective Nelson said, fishing for information.

"Murder?" Knowledge echoed with his face crumbled up. "You mistaking me for somebody else."

"I don't think so," Detective Nelson said as he threw the cuffs on Knowledge's wrist as tight as possible.

"This some bullshit," Shorty said as him and the rest of the entourage looked the plain clothed cops up and down.

"You feeling froggy boy?" Detective Bradley growled as he placed his hand on the Beretta that rested in his holster.

"What the fuck you gon do with that?" Shorty asked with a smirk on his face.

"I wish that white boy would!" A soldier yelled out from the background.

"Come on lets go. We'll be back for the rest of these mooks later," Detective Nelson said as him and Detective Bradley escorted Knowledge out of the building.

"Who the fuck you calling a mook, you dirty ass white boy?" Shorty shot back as he and the rest of the crew followed the plain clothed cops to their unmarked vehicles. As Detective Nelson escorted Knowledge to his vehicle, Knowledge saw Carl on his way back to the building with a cigarette hanging out of his mouth. Carl didn't speak. Instead, he just shook his head as he walked past the young soldier.

* * **

$ilk White

Gmoney slid out the passenger side of the Yukon and saw Shorty and a few other soldiers standing in front of the building they usually hung out at. "Yo keep this muthafucka running," he told his driver as he and two of his shooters headed towards the front of the building where Shorty stood. "Shorty what's good? Where the fuck that nigga Knowledge at?" Gmoney asked as he gave the young man a pound.

"The D's just picked him up like an hour ago."

"Say word?"

"Word…that same cop that was on ya ass," Shorty said in between puffs. "His bitch ass came over here harassing niggaz for no reason."

"You know that's how they do," Gmoney said in a calm tone as he noticed a blue van parked across the street. "Mufuckas is watching us right now," he said, nodding towards the blue van.

"Damn I didn't even notice that van," Shorty admitted. "It's all good. Just stay on point," Gmoney said as he covered his mouth with his hand as he continued to speak. "You know them white niggaz be reading lips and shit. But I'm going to swing back around here in a couple of days. I want you to run shit until Knowledge is released. Think you can handle that?"

"I won't let you down," Shorty replied with his hand covering his mouth.

"A'ight I'm out. Try to stay out of sight until some of this heat dies down," Gmoney said as he turned and headed back towards the Yukon.

"Take me to Mr. Goldberg's office," Gmoney ordered as he leaned his seat back and turned the volume back up, as his driver headed to the next destination.

* * * *

"So what do you have to tell me?" Detective Nelson asked as he sat across the table from Knowledge. "The same thing I always tell you," Knowledge said with a smile. "Go fuck yourself."

"Wow that was funny. You should be a comedian," Detective Nelson said as he placed a tape recorder on the table. "Do you know a man named Suge?"

"Negative," Knowledge answered quickly.

"You sure about that?" Detective Nelson asked with a smirk on his face.

"Yup."

"So who is this standing next to Suge in this picture?" Detective Nelson asked as he slid Knowledge a picture of him and Suge together.

"I've never seen either one of these men before in my life," Knowledge replied with a straight face.

"So you're telling me that's not you in that picture, standing next to your friend Suge?"

"I told you already I don't know no Suge! And I've never seen either one of those men in the picture you just showed me."

"Oh really?" Detective Nelson began. "So I guess this isn't you either, huh?" he said as he pressed play on the tape recorder.

"Yoooo where the fuck you been? I been trying to call you all night. Some fuck boy niggaz rolled up and dumped on us, mufuckas took Suge out."

"Fuck! A'ight I don't wanna talk about this over the phone. I'mma get up with you later on tonight."

Detective Nelson stopped the tape with a smile on his face. "That's you and that scum bag Gmoney. Now stop fucking around and tell me what the fuck happened to Suge," Detective Nelson growled, getting all up in Knowledge's face.

"Where's my lawyer?" Knowledge said in a bored tone. Seconds later, a fist smashed into his face like a blunt object, causing Knowledge to fall out of his chair. Out of reflex, Knowledge quickly shot back to his feet and caught Detective Nelson with a series of combinations to the head, sending him crashing back into the wall. Knowledge was getting ready to go in for the kill, until Detective Bradley and two uniform officers stormed in the room; turning it into a four on one. They beat Knowledge until he passed out from the pain.

"You don't look so tough now," Detective Bradley fumed as he felt a puffy bruise forming under his eye.

CHAPTER 24 TEMPTATION

Nancy walked through the double doors of the visiting room in a good mood. It had been a whole week and she couldn't wait to see her man. Before Ali entered the visiting room, Nancy went over to the vending machine and got Ali some microwavable hot wings, some snacks, and a blue Gatorade. Seconds later, Ali came bopping through the visiting room door with a warm smile on his face.

"Hey daddy," Nancy said like a little schoolgirl as she jumped up in his arms.

"Hey baby I missed you," Ali whispered as he hugged his wife tight, as she wrapped her legs around his waist.

"Damn this week felt like a month," Nancy whined like a baby.

"I know," Ali replied. "But we gon be a'ight."

"So how you been?"

"I can't complain, but I did make some connections up in here."

"Baby I know you not up in here doing what I think you doing," Nancy said, shaking her neck.

"Nah, just listen before you start tripping," Ali said as he looked over both shoulders. "Now listen, I got this C.O. that's going to let me get a cell phone up in here."

"Who is she?" Nancy asked with fire in her eyes.

"Why do you automatically assume it's a lady C.O.?"

"Because I know you Ali."

"What is that supposed to mean?"

"That means a girl is gonna be a girl no matter where she's at. You should know that by now."

"Shut your mouth for a second and just think. Wouldn't you like to talk to me like at around two a.m.?"

"Yeah…"

"Yeah so stop acting like that then. You know these crackers shut down the phone at 11:00 a.m.," he reminded her.

"I know daddy. Sorry for acting like that. It's just that you be in here all day with that bitch, and I only get to see you once a week," she said, pouting like a baby.

"You talking like the bitch be in my cell with me all day," Ali said, giving her a strange look. "She's just a C.O. that works here, who tryna look out for a brother."

"I understand babe."

"A'ight, so when you come up here next week, bring me one of those prepaid Boost Mobile joints," Ali instructed, as one of the C.O.'s signaled that his visit was over.

"You know I got you daddy," Nancy said as she hugged Ali tight as she threw her tongue in his mouth.

"I'mma call you later on tonight," Ali said as he slapped Nancy ass as he watched her make her exit. When Ali made it back to his unit, he saw Skip and Loco standing in front of his cell chopping it up.

"My niggaz, what's good?" Ali said, giving both men a pound.

"Just chilling, how was the visit?" Loco asked.

"It was cool. The cell phone is on its way," Ali replied nonchalantly.

"How do you do it?" Loco asked, shaking his head.

"Do what?" Ali asked.

"Still be cool knowing you never gonna get out this bitch alive."

"It's all a part of the game," Ali said. "I knew the rules before I started playing. Plus, they can't break me because they ain't make me."

"Yo let's hit up the yard real quick," Skip quickly changed the subject.

"Why, what's up? You need to see somebody?" Loco asked.

"Yeah that big six, six nigga said he needed to holla at Ali about something."

"What big six, six nigga?" Ali asked.

"You know that big quiet nigga that always be working out all the time," Skip said, trying to refresh Ali and Loco's memory.

"Oh a'ight, I know who you talking about now," Ali said as the trio headed down to the yard.

"Why the fuck are the cops fucking with me and my crew so hard?" Gmoney huffed as he and Mr. Goldberg sat parked in Gmoney's new Lexus coupe.

"Because they want to see you fall," Mr. Goldberg replied quickly. "What, you forgot about all the cases you and your crew beat?"

"Damn them crackers don't forget shit, huh?"

"Not a thing," Mr. Goldberg replied quickly.

"What's up with Knowledge?"

"Oh they don't have nothing on him. He'll be out before the night is out," Mr. Goldberg said, leaning back in his seat. "But you and your crew going to have to leave them cell phones alone. If you need to talk to someone, have a face to face meeting because the F.E.D.S are on y'all hard!"

"A'ight, I got you. When you go to the courthouse to get Knowledge out, you tell him to come straight to my office ASA fucking P," Gmoney ordered as he tossed his cell phone out the window.

For the entire ride home, Nancy sang along with her new Mary J. Blige CD. No matter how far away Ali was, every time Nancy went up to the prison, something about seeing her man made her feel good. Before heading home, Nancy made a quick stop at

$ilk White

the Chinese restaurant to pick up some food for her and Christie. She had been gone for almost the whole day and she damn sure didn't feel like cooking shit, so Chinese it was.

Nancy pulled up in her driveway and smiled. "Damn it feels good to be home," she said out loud, as she glanced at her watch. "Let me hurry the fuck up," she told herself, knowing that Ali would be calling the house in 30 minutes. She quickly stuck her key in the lock and entered her crib. "I got us some Chinese food. You better come get it while it's...." her words got caught in her throat when she saw that her living room was completely naked. "I know this bitch didn't," Nancy growled as she searched the entire house looking for Christie. "Fuck!" Nancy cursed loudly. "This bitch even took the phone out of the wall," she said out loud, shaking her head. Not only did Christie clean out her crib, but now she couldn't even talk to Ali because the house phone cord was snatched out of the wall. She quickly pulled out her cell phone and dialed a number. On the fourth ring, Coco picked up her in a friendly mood. "Good evening, Coco speaking," she sang.

"Bitch, I just got robbed!"

"Robbed?" Coco echoed, sitting up in her bed. "Get the fuck outta here."

"I'm dead ass, I just got back from seeing my boo. And when I got home, my whole place was cleaned out." "So you don't know who did the shit?"

"Nah, but I know when I catch Christie, I'm going to whip her ass," Nancy said with venom dripping from her tone. "I let this bitch in my crib and this what she turn around and do to me? Nah fuck that! Crackhead or no crackhead, she getting her ass whipped."

"You know what you need?" Coco said, not waiting for Nancy to reply. "You need to go out and clear your mind. Swing through so we can talk about it, then later we can go out and have a few drinks."

"I'm coming over, but I don't know about the drinking part," Nancy told her best friend as she ended the conversation.

CHAPTER 25 BRING IT BACK

"Damn what the fuck happened to you?" Gmoney asked, noticing all the scrapes and bruises on Knowledge's face.

"I punched that bitch ass Detective Nelson in his mouth, and then he and his home boys jumped me," Knowledge said, shrugging his shoulders.

"Why were you arrested?"

"Muthafuckas been following me around all day," Knowledge said. "And they got our phones tapped. That faggot Detective Nelson played back a recording of me and you talking on the phone."

"That phone shit is dead," Gmoney said, tossing Knowledge a beeper. "We taking it back old school." "I feel you," Knowledge said as he examined the beeper closely.

"007 means to meet me here and 008 means to come straight to Pauleena's crib, a'ight? The only people who have this number are me and Pauleena."

"A'ight, cool. Oh yeah I almost forgot to tell you while I was in the can, I ran into this clown who say he used to work for Rell."

"And?"

"And he told me that Rell got a safe in his girlfriend's house, holding a couple hundred thousand."

"Who's this girl?" Gmoney asked in a calm voice.

"Some white girl. I got the address if you want it."

"Nah, hold on to it. I want you and Shorty to go over there get that money and bring it back."

"What about the white girl?" Knowledge asked.

"Kill her," Gmoney answered with no trace of emotion. "I tried to let bygones be bygones, but this muthafucka don't know when to stop," Gmoney paused. "He dropped Suge, so one of his gotta fall."

Knowledge wanted to tell Gmoney it was his fault that Suge got murdered, but decided to remain silent and let Rell take the blame. "A'ight, I'mma go get on that right now." "A'ight when you done, swing by Pauleena's club." "Say no more," Knowledge said, quickly making his exit.

"Why the fuck would somebody rob their own friend?"

"You have to remember Christie is not the one thinking. That crack is doing all the thinking for her," Coco said, taking a long drag from her blunt.

"Yeah I know. But fuck all that, she gotta get her ass whipped for this shit,"

$ilk White

Nancy said as she watched Coco get dressed. "Damn where's the rest of your outfit?"

"My man like's to see his boo in as less as possible," Coco said with a wink.

"Well I hope y'all have fun because I don't think I'm going."

"What? You have to go. I already told James you were coming," Coco declared.

"Don't you mean the Terminator?" Nancy said, rolling her eyes for extra emphasis.

"Damn, you still tripping over that shit that happened to Spanky?" Coco asked dryly. "James isn't the one who killed Spanky, Spanky killed Spanky," she said reminding Nancy.

"Yeah, but that's easy for you to say because you not the one engaged to Spanky's brother," Nancy pointed out.

"Damn, it ain't like I'm trying to hook you up with one of his friends. I'm just asking you to go out with ya girl for a couple of drinks."

"I don't have nothing to wear."

"I got you covered," Coco said as she headed into her closet. When she returned, she was carrying a silver tube dress.

"Here I haven't even worn this shit yet. Try not to stain it all up. I know how you do," she joked. "Now that you mention it, I think I do need to get out the house," Nancy said, holding up the dress. "Trust me you going to love this spot," Coco said with a smirk.

* * * *

"You think there's gonna be mad bitches at the club tonight?" Shorty asked, putting on some rubber latex gloves.

"Pauleena stay with mad bitches in her club," Knowledge replied as he threw on his hoody and drew the strings. "You ready to do this?"

"Yeah I'm tryna hurry up and get to the club," Shorty said as he quickly loaded his revolver and slid out of the passenger seat of the stolen Buick. As Knowledge walked up on the house, he noticed the "ADT" security sign outside the door.

"We got 10 seconds to find this bitch," Knowledge said, nodding towards the sign.

"I'll take the downstairs," Shorty replied as he aimed his revolver at the front lock and shot it off. Once inside the house, Shorty quickly ran through the living room with his pistol in hand in search of the woman, while Knowledge quickly raced up the stairs taking two steps at a time.

When Knowledge reached the top of the steps, he kicked in the first door he saw. Lucky for him, he saw Heather sitting up, looking startled with a book in her hand. "Get your ass up," Knowledge snarled as he grabbed a hand full of Heather's blonde hair.

"What do you want from me?" Heather asked in a weak and shaking voice.

TEARS OF A HUSTLER 2

"First I want you to answer this phone and say everything is okay," Knowledge whispered as he placed his 9mm to the white woman's head and passed her the ringing cordless phone.

"Hello?" She answered.

"Hello ma'am, my name is Scott and I'm calling from "ADT" home security. I see your alarm just went off. Is everything okay?"

"Yes I'm fine. I just got home and I must have triggered the alarm by mistake."

"Okay ma'am. Would you like me to send a patrol car through there just to make sure everything is alright?"

"No, that won't be necessary," Heather said, trying to remain calm.

"Okay ma'am. Enjoy the rest of your night."

"Okay you too," Heather said as she hung up. "Okay now what's this all about? You want money?"

"Nah bitch, we want Rell's money!" Shorty growled as he entered the bedroom.

"I don't know what you talking about," Heather lied with a straight face.

"Word?" Knowledge said as he quickly slammed Heather down on the bed and placed a pillow over her face.

POOOOW! Knowledge's 9mm barked as he let off a shot two inches away from Heather's head. "I'm gonna ask you one more time, where's it at?"

"Alright, alright. It's down in the basement, in the dryer," Heather sobbed.

"You better not be lying," Knowledge said as Shorty headed downstairs towards the basement.

"I'm not lying. Just please don't kill me," she pleaded.

Five minutes later, Shorty came back upstairs holding a garbage bag.

"We good?" Knowledge asked.

"Yes sir," Shorty replied with a smile.

With that being said, Knowledge quickly turned and placed the pillow back over her face and pulled the trigger again, but this time he didn't miss.

"Let's get out of here and hit up the club," Shorty said as he and Knowledge fled the murder scene.

Gmoney pulled up in front of the club two trucks deep. He slid out the back seat of the Expedition looking brand new; he wore all black so his jewelry could stand out more.

"Gmoney my main man, how you feeling tonight?" the bouncer at the front door asked, trying to make small talk.

"So far, so good," Gmoney replied as he and his entourage brushed past the bouncer and headed inside the club. Once inside the club, Gmoney and his crew headed towards their regular V.I.P. section. To Gmoney's surprise, Pauleena was already sitting on one of the couches with Malcolm standing behind her looking over the crowd.

$ilk White

"Glad you could finally make it," Pauleena said with a warm smile.

"Wasn't even sure if I was going to come out tonight. I been on my depressed shit lately," Gmoney said, taking a seat next to Pauleena.

"What's on your mind?"

"I'm just trying to adapt to walking around without my strap, smell me?" G-money said as he took a long drag from his blunt. "I'm not used to depending on someone else to protect me, you dig?"

"It's all a part of the game," Pauleena said as she kept her eyes on a husky man who stood over by the bar. "When the heat is on, we gotta get low. Remember, we playing chess, not checkers," she raised an eyebrow.

"Don't get it twisted. I ain't tripping; I just think I need a vacation."

"Don't we all," Malcolm cut in.

Gmoney didn't reply. Instead, he just gave Malcolm a dirty look before he continued. "Like I was saying," he huffed. "This heat is making it extra harder for me to move around how I want to."

"Yeah them muthafuckas got it out for you hard!" Pauleena agreed. "You know that husky nigga over there standing by the bar?" she asked, pointing towards the bar.

"Nah, why what's up? You want me to go over there and check him out?"

"Nah, you don't need no more attention drawn to you. Remember?" Pauleena said, shooting Gmoney a private look.

"Yo, money standing by the bar…get him the fuck outta here. He's giving me the creeps," Pauleena ordered as she watched two of her Muslim soldiers head towards the bar to handle their business.

"You paranoid or something? That man was just over there minding his business, trying to get his drink on," Gmoney said, popping open a bottle of champagne.

"I don't give a fuck what he was over there doing. He was giving me a bad vibe so he gotta go," she said, holding out her glass so Gmoney could refill it. "Plus, I been having nightmares for the past couple of days."

"Nightmares?" Gmoney chuckled.

"Yeah for the past couple of nights, I've been having some real bad dreams."

"Word? With all the security you got, you scared of a little bad dream?" Gmoney said laughing. "Don't worry baby, I ain't gonna let nothing happen to you," he teased.

"In my dreams, you are the one always getting killed…not me," Pauleena said in a serious tone.

Gmoney's smile quickly faded away. "Damn that's crazy."

"I know."

"I knew you liked me, but I didn't know you was having dreams about the kid," Gmoney joked.

"That's your problem; you always joking," Pauleena said as she watched her soldiers escort the husky man out of the club. "It's always better to be safe than sorry."

"I can dig it," Gmoney replied as the two touched glasses and continued to exchange words.

* * * *

"Come on girl, James is outside waiting on us," Coco yelled out.

"Damn, can I make sure my lip gloss is poppin before I go out?" Nancy said with a slight attitude. When the two stepped foot outside, Nancy saw a stretched limo park in front and immediately wanted to hit a u turn. "Stop acting like that. Let's go and have a good time," Coco said as the driver got out and opened the door for the two beautiful sistahs.

"Hey boo," Coco sang as she slid in the limo and kissed the Terminator on the cheek.

"What's good? Who's your friend?" The Terminator asked, looking over at Nancy.

"Damn, gimme a second. This is my best friend Nancy, Nancy this is James."

"The Terminator," he corrected her as he kissed the back of Nancy's hand.

"Nice to meet you," Nancy said, giving him a half smile as she jerked her hand back.

"And this is my bodyguard, Rodney," the Terminator said, nodding towards the six-nine monster.

"Damn Coco! Why you ain't tell me your friend was so fine?" Rodney said, openly undressing Nancy with his eyes.

"Because she already got a man."

"A real man," Nancy cut in.

"You tryna say I ain't real?" Rodney asked. Nancy didn't answer. Instead, she just stared blankly out the window. "Bitch you don't hear me talking to you?" Rodney snarled.

"Bitch? Nigga you must be high right now talking to me like that," Nancy said, rolling her eyes. "You better get this big, ugly ass nigga out my face. I'll make one phone call and get ya big ass smoked.

"You threatening me?" Rodney's voice boomed as he inched over towards Nancy.

"Rodney you better not touch her! That's my word," Coco said as she grabbed Rodney's arm so he wouldn't hit her friend.

"Get ya hands off me bitch!" Rodney growled as he backslapped Coco. Coco's head snapped back so hard that both of her earrings flew out of her ear.

Nancy reached in her purse to grab her pepper spray, but before she knew what was going on, Rodney's massive hands was around her neck.

"That's enough!" The Terminator yelled out. "Yo pull over."

Once the limo driver pulled over, the Terminator spoke calmly. "Y'all bitches get the fuck out. I can't stand no ghetto bitches," he said in a disgusted tone as he opened the door.

"That's how you gon do me James?" Coco whined with tears in her eyes.

"Get the fuck out," he said coldly.

"Fuck him! We don't need this bullshit," Nancy said as she grabbed Coco's wrist and exited the limo.

"Stupid ass bitches!" Rodney yelled out the window as the limo pulled off.

"I can't believe them niggaz just tried to O.D. on us," Nancy said, shaking her head.

"It's all your fault," Coco said, giving Nancy an ugly look. "I know you mad because your man is in jail, but that don't give you the right to fuck up my shit."

"Excuse me?" Nancy said, placing her hands on her hips.

"You heard me; you didn't want me with James cause of what happened to Spanky."

"Oh, so that's why he called you a bitch right?" Nancy said sarcastically.

"This kind of shit always happens to me," Coco said as she broke down in tears. "I'm never going to be able to find a good man who just love's me for me."

"Just be patient," Nancy said as she pulled Coco close to her and hugged her.

"I'm sorry for coming at you like that," she sobbed.

"Don't worry about it. Let's get us a cab before we freeze to death out here," Nancy said as she noticed a black Benz heading straight for the curb. "Watch out!" She yelled as she and Coco quickly hopped back on the curb.

"What the fuck y'all doing out here?" Knowledge said from the driver side of the Benz.

"Hey Knowledge, we need a ride home," Nancy said, walking towards the Benz; not waiting for an answer.

"Damn, where y'all coming from dressed like that?" Shorty asked, noticing Nancy's thick sexy legs and fresh pedicure toes.

"We were on our way to that new club a few blocks away."

"Oh word...that's where we was going too. Y'all sure y'all want to go home? We just right around the corner from the club." Knowledge said, looking at Nancy through the rear view mirror. "Nah me and my girl had a rough day. I think we should go home."

"Nah, fuck that. We already here so we might as well do the damn thing," Coco said, drying her eyes.

"Damn, what's wrong with you? Your man whipped that ass?" Knowledge chuckled.

"At least he didn't knock me the fuck out," Coco shot back.

"Fuck you! That bitch ass nigga snuck me," Knowledge protested.

"Again, right?"

"Nancy you got too much class to be hanging around with trash like this," he said, talking as if Coco wasn't sitting right there.

"Well don't talk to me since I'm so trashy," Coco sucked her teeth.

Knowledge pulled up in front of the club and as usual, it was flooded with people. When the bouncer saw Knowledge, he quickly gave him a pound and let him, and whom he was with enter the club and walk around the metal detector.

"Oh shit, Gmoney and Pauleena already up in here," Shorty said, pointing towards the V.I.P. section.

"I'm not going over there," Coco said, looking at Nancy.

"Why not?"

"Because I don't want to see Gmoney," Coco said shamefully. "I understand," Nancy said as she reached out and tapped Knowledge's arm. "We gon just chill right here."

"What?" Knowledge said, looking confused. "We bout to go straight to V.I.P., you know how we do!"

"We'll be over there in a little while," she lied. "Me and my girl about to hit up the dance floor," Nancy said as she rocked back and fourth to the beat.

"A'ight, you want me to send a bottle your way?"

"Nah, that won't be necessary. We straight," she told him.

"A'ight, I'mma be right over here if you need me," Knowledge said as him and Shorty snaked their way through the crowd.

"Prime time, what's goodie?" Knowledge joked as he gave Gmoney, then Pauleena a pound.

"Gmacking and gstacking," Gmoney replied smoothly. "How did that other thing play out?"

"Like taking candy from a baby," Knowledge smiled. "Got that bitch ass nigga for 20 stacks," he said, not mentioning the 30 thousand that he and Shorty took off the top.

"When is that old school ass nigga going to realize he can't see me?"

"When you kill his ass!" Pauleena cut in. "That's the type of nigga that every time you see him, it's going to be a confrontation. And that's not good for business."

"That nigga don't want no problems with us," Knowledge said, helping himself to a drink.

"Oh yeah? What do you think Suge would say about that?" Pauleena said as she got up and walked off, not waiting for a response.

"Yo where you going?" Gmoney called after her.

"I gotta pee," she yelled over her shoulder as Malcolm and two other Muslim brothers escorted her to the ladies room.

"Man! That bitch don't know nothing about the streets," Knowledge said once Pauleena was out of earshot. "She knows more than you think," Gmoney said as he grabbed a bottle of champagne, popped open the cork, and took a deep swig. "She's a straight go getta."

"Speaking of go getta's," Knowledge paused briefly to take a look at the ass of some Spanish chick. "I picked up Nancy and Coco on my way over here."

"Say word?" Gmoney said in disbelief.

"Dead ass, they over there," Knowledge said, pointing towards the two sexy divas.

"Why you ain't bring them over to the V.I.P. section?"

"I tried but Nancy said they was good on the dance floor," Knowledge explained.

"I'll be right back," Gmoney said as he got up and headed towards where Nancy and Coco stood.

One of Pauleena's Muslim security guards cleared a path through the crowd as Gmoney followed closely behind him like a running back.

"Ahw shit," Coco sighed. "Here this nigga come."

Nancy looked up and saw Gmoney approaching. "Long time no see," she yelled over the bumping music.

"What's goodie?" Gmoney smiled, opening his arms for a hug.

"You," Nancy replied as she slid in Gmoney arms and gave him a hug.

"Yo let me holla at your girl real quick. We got everything in the V.I.P. section," Gmoney said as he watched Nancy squeeze through the crowd heading for the V.I.P. section.

"So what's good?"

"Nothing!" Coco replied in a nasty tone.

"The Terminator is over there. Why you ain't over there with him?" Gmoney said, pointing towards the V.I.P. section on the other side of the club.

"Because I'm not," Coco growled, still feeling the effects of getting played. "Well you're welcome to join me and the fam if you want," Gmoney offered.

"Thanks, but no thanks. I'm cool right here," Coco answered, looking down at the floor.

"Why the fuck you acting like this for?" Gmoney asked, clearly disappointed.

"You know why," Coco yelled, as her eyes got watery.

"We both out here dealing with people we don't want to deal with, because you couldn't keep your dick in your pants!"

TEARS OF A HUSTLER 2

"That's what this is about?" Gmoney asked looking in Coco's eyes.

"That's what it's always been about Gerald," Coco said, trying to make a point. "I ain't never been with one guy my whole life until I met you. You changed my whole way of thinking. For once in my life, I felt loved," she sobbed.

Gmoney looked at Coco's make up running down her face from the tears and felt bad for her. "You want to give this another try?"

"I want to, but I know you ain't never going to change."

"We going to make this work," Gmoney smiled warmly. "What ever happened in the past is the past," he told her.

"Okay, I missed you so much daddy," she sobbed burying her face in Gmoney's chest.

"I missed you too," Gmoney said, cupping Coco's ass while he hugged her, drawing lustful looks from some of the club goers nearby. "Let's go get us a drink," Gmoney exhaled as the two headed for the V.I.P. section. Knowledge and Shorty eased their way through the crowd searching for something to slide, when Knowledge saw a familiar face. "Yo is that the Terminator right there?" He asked, pointing towards the V.I.P. section.

"Hell yeah that's that bitch ass nigga!" Shorty replied, heating up the already hot situation. "What's good, you want me to clap that fool?"

"Nah, you wilding. That shit will get Pauleena's club shut down," he reminded Shorty. "But I am going to go over there and say hello," Knowledge said, unable to drop the fact that another man had knocked him out cold.

Rodney sat next to the Terminator entertaining a couple of young tenders, when he noticed two men heading for the entrance of their V.I.P. section. "Whooooa, whooooa can I help you brothers?" Rodney asked, stepping in front of the two men.

"Yeah you can start by moving the fuck out of my way," Knowledge huffed as he attempted to brush past the six-nine monster.

"Nigga is you crazy?" Rodney barked as he grabbed Knowledge by the throat and shoved him back a few feet. Before Rodney could release his grip on Knowledge's throat, Shorty had already had his revolver trained on the big man. "Put ya motherfucking hands up," he warned.

Rodney looked in the young man's eyes and could tell he wasn't bluffing. Knowledge quickly regained his balance and snatched his 9mm from his waistband. "What's up now big man?" He said in a calm voice as he proceeded to bash the big man's face in with the burner, while Shorty kicked and stomped on the big man's ribs until four big bouncers came running over to break up the fight.

Pauleena sat in the V.I.P. section having a word with Gmoney, when she noticed people on the dance floor shift to one side of the floor. "Somebody over there getting it poppin," she said, shooting to her feet.

$ilk White

"I hope it's not one of our peoples," Gmoney said, looking for Coco and Nancy just in case they had to make a quick dash for the exit.

"More than likely it is," Pauleena said, standing on her tiptoes trying to see over the crowd. Seconds later, Pauleena and Gmoney saw a bouncer escorting Knowledge and Shorty out of the side door of the club.

"I'mma go check on them. I'll be right back," Gmoney whispered in Coco's ear as he headed for the exit. Once again, the Muslim guard cleared a path while Gmoney followed close behind. Once Gmoney was gone, Pauleena sat right next to Nancy. "So you're Ali's fiancé huh?" She asked, looking Nancy up and down.

"Yeah is that a problem?" Nancy asked defensively.

"Not at all sweetheart," Pauleena said as she crossed her legs getting more comfortable. "I just wanted to introduce myself. I'm Pauleena," she said, extending her hand.

"Nice to meet you," Nancy said as she shook her hand with little to no effort.

"And I take it you're Gmoney's girl," Pauleena said, facing Coco. "Or at least one of them," she smirked.

"No, I'm his main bitch sweetheart," Coco shot back, rolling her eyes.

"I bet you are," Pauleena chuckled as she helped herself to another drink.

Coco sucked her teeth. "Listen bitch, I don't know who you are but you better watch your little mouth or else," she warned.

"Or else what?" Pauleena asked as she slid her .380 from her handbag and stood over Coco. "Yeah you ain't talking that tough shit now," she chuckled. "Don't let the dress and heels fool you. I will abuse both of y'all bitches up in here."

Nancy and Coco shot Pauleena nasty looks, but neither one said a word.

* * * *

"Yo what happened in there?" Gmoney asked.

"I saw that bitch ass nigga, the Terminator and I made a move," Knowledge said louder than he had to. Before Gmoney could respond, the Terminator came storming out of the club with security escorting him and Rodney to their limo.

"Bitch ass nigga," Knowledge said under his breath as he watched the Terminator being escorted out of the club like a coward.

"Listen you going to have to slow down with all that wild-wild west shit. Its motherfuckers probably watching us right now," Gmoney said, looking over both shoulders. "If you gonna do something, do it wisely; not with two hundred witnesses around."

"Yeah you right. My fault, I wasn't thinking," Knowledge said, giving Gmoney a pound.

"A'ight, y'all be safe. I'mma get back inside before I freeze to death," Gmoney joked as he headed back inside.

The whole time, Jimmy sat parked six cars down chain smoking, while keeping a close eye on his target. Little did Gmoney know that Jimmy wasn't his only problem. A white van sat parked at the other end of the parking lot, watching Gmoney's every move. Seven Jamaicans sat in the white van; each man holding an automatic weapon.

Gmoney bopped back towards the V.I.P. section to get his jacket and grab Coco and Nancy. When he reached the V.I.P. section, he noticed both Coco and Nancy had frowns on their face. "What's wrong?" He asked.

"Your friend over here pulled a gun out on us and we don't appreciate it," Nancy said with an attitude.

"Who Pauleena?" Gmoney asked in shock.

"Yeah that bitch right there," Coco snarled, pointing at Pauleena.

"Yo what's good? My fam said you backed out on them. What's that all about?" Gmoney asked, approaching Pauleena.

"Awh, I was just fucking with them bitches. It ain't about nothing," Pauleena said nonchalantly. "Well don't fuck around like that," Gmoney said firmly.

"I got you G. I was just having a little fun, it won't happen again," she said as she gave him a hug and a kiss on the cheek.

"A'ight I'm about to breeze. Call me tomorrow," Gmoney said, using his thumb and pinky to make a phone with his hand as he walked off. Once outside, Coco was still heated. "If that bitch ain't have that gun, I would have gave her a work out."

"Let that shit go," Gmoney said as his driver pulled the Yukon up to the curb. "I'm going to follow you," the Muslim security guard said as he walked in the direction of his vehicle.

"A'ight I'mma wait for you," Gmoney said, looking over both shoulders before he slid in the passenger seat of the Yukon. Once the Yukon pulled off, the Muslim security guard followed closely behind in a Honda.

Jimmy sat patiently as he watched the white van quickly pull off in pursuit of its target.

Jimmy smoothly flicked his cigarette out the window as he threw the car in gear, and continued to follow his target around until the time was right.

CHAPTER 26 BACK HOME

"Make that ass clap for me," Big Time instructed as he laid back on the motel bed watching the dark skin stripper shake her ass for him. The stripper sucked her teeth as she did what she was told to do. She hated her job, but she had to do what she had to do for that paper. She didn't look at herself as a prostitute; more like an entrepreneur.

"Yeah that's what I'm talking about," Big Time mumbled as he stroked his penis openly. "Come over here and get this vanilla outta me."

The dark skin stripper loved to suck dick, but not when the dick belonged to a two hundred and sixty pound pig. "You sure you can handle that daddy?" She asked, looking at Big Time for a comment.

"Bitch get over here and suck this dick," Big Time growled. "You talk too damn much; I don't pay you to talk."

Big Time was a big, black, ugly muthafucka. He sported a beard like the rapper, Rick Ross. He may have been big and ugly, but his long paper kept him with a bad bitch.

The stripper took Big Time's whole dick in her mouth as she slowly guided her head up and down, the whole time making a loud slurping sound. She then spit on his rod and sucked it off. After about 20 minutes of sucking, Big Time couldn't take it anymore. He had to get a shot of that pussy. "Bring that ass over here," he demanded as he rolled a condom on his dick.

The stripper seductively licked her lips as she climbed on top of him, straddling her legs on each side of him as she slipped him inside of her. "Damn daddy…" she sighed as she began riding his dick slowly.

Meanwhile, outside in the hotel parking lot, Roy sat in an old station wagon, along with two of the finest women Pauleena could find for the job.

"So what you need us to do?" Jessica asked, looking at herself in the compact mirror she held in her hand.

"All I need y'all to do is grab the attention of those two stiff's right there," Roy said, nodding towards the two bodyguards who stood by, guarding the door.

"That's it?" Jessica asked, looking at Roy as if he just said something in a different language.

"Take care of that and I'll do the rest," Roy said, sliding his hands in a pair of black leather gloves.

"Watch us work," Jessica said as her and Keisha slid out of the station wagon.

Roy watched closely as Jessica and Keisha made their way up the stairs and over towards the bodyguards.

"Damn why you ain't tell me these niggaz was gon be so fine?" Jessica said out loud as her and Keisha approached the two bodyguards.

"Whoa, whoa where y'all think y'all going?" The no neck bodyguard asked sternly.

"This room 42 right?" Jessica asked sarcastically. "Big Jah sent us over for the party."

"Nah, it's not no party over here sweetheart," No Neck said, hungrily eye balling the two half-naked women who stood in front of him.

Once Jessica and Keisha had the two bodyguards' attention, Roy made his move. He tossed his hood over his head, screwed a silencer on his 9mm, and slid out the station wagon, taking the steps to the other side of the building. He had moved with the swiftness and silence of a cat hopping up the steps.

"What you mean it's no party over here?" Jessica rocked back on her heels. "Me and my girl came here to put on a show, and we don't get paid unless we perform," she placed her hands on her perfectly curved hips. "So somebody better tell us something."

"Listen I don't know who told you it was a party over here, but they lied to you," No Neck said, hypnotized by Jessica's large breast that threatened to spill out of her top. "But I tell you what," he moved in closer. "I get off like around two. So if you give me your number, I'll be more than gladly to pay you and your friend to perform," he said with a smirk.

Meanwhile, Roy eased up behind the two guards. His arms were fully extended and locked in place at the elbow; with both hands, he gripped the 9mm tightly. "HEY!" he said in a calm tone. Before the two bodyguards could turn around, a bullet pierced through both men skulls, killing them instantly. Roy was about to tell Jessica and Keisha to go back to the car, but they were already three steps ahead of him. He watched both of their fat asses jiggle as they hurried down the stairs.

* * **

Big Time felt himself getting ready to cum as the dark skin stripper's big titties bounced and slapped him in the face. Just as Big Time was coming, he heard the room door bust open. "What the fuck?" He growled as he bucked his midsection, tossing the stripper off the bed. He desperately reached for the .357 that laid on top of the nightstand. Big Time quickly jerked his hand back as a bullet grazed his knuckles. "Fuck is this all about?" Big Time asked, looking up at the hooded man.

"You know what this is about," Roy spoke calmly. "Pauleena gave you simple instructions; stay on your side of town and we won't have no problems. But no, you wanna be a greedy muthafucka," Roy said as he emptied his clip in the big man's chest.

"Damn! It's about time you got here. I was just about to throw up," the dark skin stripper said as she scooped her clothes up from off the floor and hurried out the room.

$ilk White

Back in the station wagon, Roy made the engine come to life and then pulled out of the hotel's parking lot.

"Damn, all that action just turned me on," Jessica said out loud, wiping some make believe sweat from her forehead.

"I couldn't tell by the way you took off back there," Roy joked.

"Fuck that! I ain't getting killed for nobody," Jessica said as she spat her gum out the window.

"Shut your mouth or either put something in it," Keisha teased from the back seat, tired of hearing Jessica talk nonsense.

"That's not a bad idea," Jessica said seductively as she unzipped Roy's zipper. "What you doing?" Roy asked, trying to keep his eyes on the road. "I'm about to make you cum in less than four minutes," Jessica replied as she stroked his dick with her hand. "I got a hundred you can't make him cum in less than four minutes," Keisha challenged. "I got a hundred on that too," Dark skin said, jumping in on the bet.

"What? Y'all bitches must have forgot who I be," Jessica said, looking at the two ladies in the back seat. "Let me know when to start."

Keisha waited for about 20 seconds. "Okay now!"

"With that being said, Jessica dove in head first; bobbing her head up and down, going about two hundred miles an hour as she sucked the shit out of Roy's dick. The station wagon swerved slightly as Roy lost control of the wheel for a second, as he filled Jessica's mouth with his fluids. "Oh shit," Roy whispered.

"Where my money at?" Jessica said proudly as she held out her hand.

CHAPTER 27 IGNORANCE IS BLISS

Big Mel stepped out of his raggedy, one bedroom apartment and looked down both hallways before locking the door. After being locked in the house for six months, it was time for Big Mel to go out and stretch his legs. Before he stepped off the stoop, Big Mel tossed his hood on top of his head, zipped up his jacket and headed for the train station.

Big Mel placed his back against a wall as he waited patiently on the platform for the number two train to arrive. The whole time, he kept his hand in his jacket pocket, where his finger rested on the trigger of his .45

Big Mel couldn't remember the last time he rode the train. But with his situation and all, the train was the safest form of transportation for him. He boarded the train and stood defensively against the door, making sure he was in perfect position to see everything and everyone; not taking anything for granted. Big Mel stood up for the entire ride.

"You like this bracelet?" Knowledge asked as he slowed down for the yellow light.

"Yeah that shit is hard," Shorty said from the passenger seat, admiring the thick diamond filled bracelet. "How much that run you?"

"Nine stacks," Knowledge boasted as he saw two thick honeys crossing the street. "Damn ma, do fries come with that shake?" Knowledge yelled as he rolled down his window.

The two dimes both turned back and smiled, but neither stopped.

"Yo, y'all need a ride?" Knowledge asked, pulling up to the curb.

"Nah, we good," the two said in unison.

"Two beautiful ladies like y'all shouldn't be out here walking at this time of night," Knowledge said as he and Shorty slid out of the Benz.

"We'll be a'ight. The train station is right there," the lighter one out of the two spoke openly.

"I know, but I'll feel better knowing that I got you two ladies home safe and sound, smell me?"

"Why don't you give me your number and I'll call you when I get home," light skin said in a sexually charged voice.

"A'ight cool," Knowledge licked his lips as he tried to memorize his phone number, which he only used for pleasure.

Meanwhile, Shorty was leaning against the Benz, storing the dark skin girl's number in his phone.

$ilk White

When the train finally reached Big Mel's stop, he quickly exited and heading up the stairs. Once he reached the top of the steps, Big Mel noticed two guys who seemed to be talking to their girls. He paid them no mind and continued on about his business. As Big Mel made it to the other side of the street, he heard gunshots and shattering glass, as he snatched out his .45 and dove behind a parked car. "What the fuck?" He yelled as the car that he used as a shield, alarm blared in his ear.

"Don't take my number if you not going to use it," Knowledge flirted as he noticed a suspicious big man with a hoody walk past. He paid him no mind and continued to get his mack on. Shorty on the other hand studied the big man closely. He knew he saw the big man before; he just couldn't put a name to the face. After two minutes of searching his memory, the name popped into his head. "Big Mel," he whispered to himself. "Y'all ladies get up out of here," Shorty ordered as he pulled his revolver from his waistband. The two dimes quickly hurried down the subway steps, each not wanting to get hit with a stray bullet.

Once Knowledge saw his partner pull his strap, he quickly pulled out his 9mm and asked. "Who?"

"Big man right there," Shorty said as he let off two shots in the big man's direction. Big Mel quickly sprung from behind the parked car and threw four reckless shots over his shoulder as he ran down the block.

Once Knowledge saw the big man running freely down the street, he stood wide-legged in the middle of the street, aimed his 9mm, and took his best shot. Bak, Bak, Bak, Bak!

When the smoke cleared, Knowledge saw the big man bend the corner.

"Damn, how the fuck did you miss him?" Shorty asked with a confused look on his face.

"I had to hit him at least twice. That's a big nigga! He ain't gon just fall down from two shots," Knowledge said, trying to sound convincing.

"Whatever," Shorty said, waving him off. "Whenever I shoot a nigga, they always fall."

"Don't disrespect my aim," Knowledge said calmly as he and Shorty tossed their guns down the sewer drain, slid back in the Benz, and pulled off.

Big Mel turned the corner and found himself on a lit up street. He touched his arm and felt warm blood. One of Knowledge's bullets seemed to graze his arm. "Fuck!" Big Mel growled as he hog spit on the ground. Going outside didn't seem like such a good idea after all. Big Mel walked down the block until he came across a strip club. Other than a few sleazy prostitutes, Big Mel couldn't remember the last time he saw a good quality woman. Thinking with his little head instead of the big one, he entered the strip club.

"Can I see some I.D.?" The bouncer asked, looking Big Mel up and down suspiciously. The bouncer studied the I.D. closely before handing it back to the big man. Once Big Mel was inside the club, the bouncer pulled out his cell phone and dialed up a familiar number.

"So how are you and the captain getting along?" Detective Bradley asked, running through a red light. "Is that a joke?" Detective Nelson chuckled. "He wants G-money in a jail cell upstate somewhere."

"So what's your plan?"

"We going to have to take it back to old times and get grimey with these street thug motherfuckers," Detective Nelson said emotionally. "Just like we took Ali off the streets, we have to do his partner the same way. Only problem is, now that the F.E.D.S. are on Gmoney's back, it's going to be a little tougher to really play ball with this prick."

"When we do shit, we just have to make sure we cover our asses and we'll be fine," Detective Bradley said, glaring over at his partner.

"Hold on," Detective Nelson said, sitting up straight. "Isn't that Knowledge's Benz right there?"

"I'm not sure," Detective Bradley retorted, squinting his eyes to get a better look.

"Run his plates," Detective Nelson ordered as he checked the rounds in his .357. "If it's registered to a woman named Deseray Tommis, then that's our man."

Less than four minutes later, Detective Bradley had the results. "Yup Deseray Tommis," he said with a smirk as he threw on the bright red light, signaling for the Benz to pull over.

"Awww shit," Knowledge huffed as he saw the flashing lights in his rear view mirror. "The boys behind us. Don't look," he said in a paranoid tone. "You clean?"

"Yeah all I got is this 50 sack of piff (haze) on me," Shorty said as he opened up the small plastic bag, and tossed the pretty looking buds in his mouth, chewed it up, and swallowed it.

"You a nasty motherfucker," Knowledge said seriously, as he pulled over.

"You think they pulling us over for the shooting?"

"Not sure, but we clean anyway. By the way, who was that nigga we was shooting at?" Knowledge asked, never taking his eyes off the rear view mirror.

"That was the big nigga who snitched on Ali. When I was a look out, I remember Ali coming through the hood with that clown." Shorty said, reflecting back to when he was a look out.

Before Knowledge could respond, Detective Bradley was already tapping on his window with his flashlight.

"Roll the goddamn window down asshole!" Detective Bradley rumbled.

"What seems to be the problem officer?" Knowledge asked with a grin.

"Step out of the vehicle please," Detective Bradley spoke in an even tone. "Slowly," he barked, placing his hand on his weapon. Knowledge and Shorty slowly exited the vehicle.

"What's a midget like you doing working for Gmoney?" Detective Nelson said with a smirk as he roughly patted the shorter man down.

"Ya moms said my size is just right," Shorty shot back.

"Oh yeah?" Detective Nelson smiled. "I know a lot of guys in the pin going to think you the perfect size too," he said as he slapped the cuffs on Shorty and made him sit down on the curb, next to Knowledge.

"What the fuck? We ain't even do shit! This is harassment!" Knowledge yelled from the curb.

"Shut the fuck up!" Detective Bradley barked. "We know you two shit heads had something to do with a shooting that went on a few blocks back."

Shorty sucked his teeth. "We don't know shit about no shooting."

"You don't?" Detective Nelson cut in. "I bet y'all know something about a boxer and his bodyguard getting assaulted in a night club last week."

"Nope!" Knowledge said blandly. "Don't know nothing about that either."

"You want to know a little secret?" Detective Nelson leaned in closer to Knowledge's ear and whispered. "The bodyguard y'all assaulted wants to press charges." Knowledge was about to protest, but decided against it. "Again, right?" He said mockingly.

"Y'all son of a bitches swear y'all so tough," Detective Bradley huffed as he cracked Knowledge and Shorty both in the head with his flashlight.

Detective Nelson was about to join in on the beating, until he heard his cell phone ringing. "Yeah," he answered in an aggravated tone.

"I got the info on that cat who shoved a pipe up your ass," the caller said in a light chuckle.

"Who the fuck is this?"

"You got the bread?" The caller asked.

"Yeah I got the bread," Detective Nelson quickly answered.

"A'ight, cool. Meet me in front of the Foxy Lady Gentlemen's Club," the caller said, ending the conversation.

"Why the fuck do your friends call you Knowledge?" Detective Bradley asked. "Because you the dumbest motherfucker I've ever met."

"Radio in for another squad car to pick these two assholes up," Detective Nelson said, pulling Detective Bradley to the side. "I just got a call. Somebody know the whereabouts of that scum bag Big Mel."

"Let's go send that worthless nigger to hell," Detective Bradley said as he noticed the squad car pull up to the scene.

"I'm going to need you to take these scum bags down to the station for me," Detective Nelson said, flashing his badge to the uniform cops. "Just put them in a holding cell until I get there. Me and my partner have to go take care of something."

"No problem detective," the uniform cop said, talking to Detective Nelson's departing back.

"Where we going?" Detective Bradley asked once he was behind the wheel.

"Four blocks over," Detective Nelson said with ice in his tone. "That gentlemen's club called The Foxy Lady."

Five minutes later, Detective Bradley pulled up across the street from the gentlemen's club.

"Wait right here," Detective Nelson said as he slid out the vehicle and jogged across the street towards the entrance of the club. The big bouncer saw the red-faced, white man jogging towards the entrance and figured that had to be his man. "Detective Nelson?" He asked curiously.

"Yeah," Detective Nelson flashed his badge. "You the guy who called?"

"Yeah, the man you looking for is inside. Now when do I get paid?" The bouncer asked greedily.

"Give me your phone number and I'll have that delivered to you later on tonight. By the way, how did you get my number?"

"Rell gave it to me a while back, when he was up in here," the bouncer replied as he gave the detective his phone number. "Good work," Detective Nelson yelled over his shoulder as he headed back to his awaited vehicle.

Big Mel took a wet paper towel and wiped the little specks of blood off his arm. "Fuck!" He growled, looking at his reflection in the mirror. Not only was his arm hurting, but he also didn't have a clue who the two thugs who shot at him were. Before Big Mel left the bathroom, he removed the clip from his .45 and shoved in a fresh full clip. He popped one in the chamber and placed the .45 back in his pocket as he smoothly exited the restroom.

Big Mel sat off in a private corner in the back of the club, making sure he could see everything and everyone.

"So how you want to handle this?" Detective Bradley asked, plucking the ashes from his cigarette out the window.

"We wait!" Detective Nelson whispered as he held a tight grip on his .44 magnum, and never took his eyes off the entrance of the club.

Forty-five minutes later, Detective Nelson saw Big Mel cautiously stroll out of the club. Looking over both shoulders before he walked, Big Mel headed back towards the train station, moving at a quick pace.

"Pull up on this cocksucker from behind, nice and slow," Detective Nelson said with a murderous look in his eyes.

"You got it," Detective Bradley replied as he shifted the car in gear.

A smile appeared on Big Mel's face when the train station lights came into his sight. Big Mel had one thing on his mind, and one thing only; and that was getting to the train station and making it home safe. Within a second, Big Mel's worst fear became a reality. A thunderous sound sent chills up his spine. His brain was telling him to turn around and bust back, but his body just wouldn't comply. Two shots to Big Mel's back sent him violently crashing down to the concrete. The cold cement told Big Mel that he wasn't dreaming.

"Well, well, well, looks like this hide and seek game has finally come to an end."

Instantly, Big Mel recognized the voice. "It's about time," he chuckled, before spitting out blood. "I thought you stopped looking for a second." Shattering glass seemed to wipe the smile off his face. "What the fuck you doing?" Big Mel whispered as he struggled to turn his neck, only to find Detective Nelson standing over him with the end of a broken ridget beer bottle in his hand.

"Oh hell naw," Big Mel screamed out in fear. "Just kill me muthafucka!"

"I am," Detective Nelson countered as he roughly pulled down Big Mel's pants. As if on cue, Detective Nelson forcefully jammed the ridget beer bottle up Big Mel's ass.

"Ahwwww," Big Mel howled in pain.

"In the Bible, it says what goes around comes around," Detective Nelson whispered as he aimed his .44 magnum at Big Mel's head and pulled the trigger twice.

CHAPTER 28 IT'S ON

Knock, Knock, Knock. Debo waited patiently on the other side of the door for an answer.

No answer came back.

Debo quickly pulled out his Desert Eagle. "You alright in there?" He yelled as he knocked on the door again.

"Come in," a voice from behind the door called.

Debo entered Rell's office and found him sitting behind his desk, talking on the phone.

"What can I do for you?" Rell asked as he hung up the phone and turned to face his best friend, slash bodyguard.

"I got some bad news," Debo said, taking his eyes off Rell and looking down at the floor.

"I'm listening," Rell said. His eyebrows rose slightly.

"It's Heather," Debo began quietly. "They found her dead in her house."

A small grin appeared across Rell's face. "Nah impossible, I just spoke to her last night," he said in disbelief. Debo didn't reply. He just slid the daily newspaper from his back pocket and tossed it on Rell's desk. On the front page, was a picture of Heather with the words: "Innocent woman robbed and murdered," in bold letters.

Rell quickly shoved the newspaper off his desk and onto the floor out of frustration. "Find out who did this," he demanded as he banged his fist on top of his desk.

"Gmoney and his peoples," Debo answered. "I already passed the word on to all the soldiers to tool up."

"Nah," Rell said shaking his head. "This muthafucka has gone too far. I gotta handle this myself," he said as he pulled his p89 from out of the top drawer. "Fuck sending the goons after Gmoney, I'm going to kill him myself. This ain't business no more, it's personal!"

"I can't let you take on Gmoney and his crew alone," Debo protested.

"I must do this alone," Rell said louder than he had to, as he got up and fetched his Teflon vest. "I'm from the old school," he said as he strapped on the bulletproof vest.

"I'm not just going to sit around and watched you take on an army by yourself," Debo said, not taking no for an answer.

"You know what?" Rell asked, staring at Debo. "I could use a driver."

"I got you covered," Debo said with a smile on his face.

"Make sure you call Maurice and let him know he's the man until this shit blows over."

"I got you," Debo said as he quickly pulled out his cell phone, doing what he was told.

Rell threw a hooded sweatshirt over his vest, followed by an all-black army jacket. "Make sure you let Maurice know if he needs some muscle, to call up those wild ass yardies," Rell said as he shoved six extra clips into his pocket. "I got you covered boss."

** **

"Pull over right there on the corner," Knowledge said, pointing to three thugs, standing on the corner.

Without thinking twice, Shorty did as he was told.

"What's good my niggaz? How it's looking out here?" Knowledge asked as he smoothly slid out of the Lexus rubbing his hands together.

"It's looking marvelous," a deep voice man answered as he gave Knowledge a pound.

"You got that for me?" Knowledge asked as he coolly glanced at his watch.

"Yeah of course," the deep voiced man answered as he and Knowledge headed inside the building they stood in front of. Once inside the building, deep voice pulled out a key and headed for the mailboxes. He stuck his key in the lock and pulled out a big wad of cash that had a money clip around it, and handed it to Knowledge.

"This $4,700?" Knowledge asked with a raised brow. "I don't have to count it do I?"

"Don't even come at me like that," Deep voice said as he nudged Knowledge. "I'll have the other half for you tomorrow."

"A'ight, cool. You be safe out here," Knowledge said as he gave deep voice a pound, and slid back in the Lexus and peeled off into the night.

** **

"That bitch Gmoney has to fall!" Rell said as he stared blankly out the passenger window.

"Don't worry. We gon drop all them fools one by one," Debo said as he stopped for the red light.

"In about two more blocks, we should be approaching one of Gmoney's corners," Rell said calmly as he cocked back his p89.

** **

"Nah I can't do nothing with 17," Deep voice huffed, not even looking at the fiend who stood in front of him.

"Come on I been copping from y'all niggaz since forever," the fiend protested. "Hook a brother up."

"Hook you up?" Deep voice echoed, getting frustrated. "You got 10 seconds to get up out my face... eight, nine," he started to count as he watched the fiend walk off mumbling something under his breath. "Don't come back until ya paper grow a few inches," he yelled out as he hog spit on the ground. "It's too fucking cold out here to be playing games," he said to no one in particular. Deep voice pulled out his cell phone and was about to call his shorty until he saw a heavily tinted whip cruising down the block at a slow speed. "Yo hold that down I think that's five-o," he yelled out to his two partners.

** **

"That's them right there?" Debo asked with fire dancing in his eyes.

"Yeah, that's them. Slow this motherfucker down," Rell ordered as he rolled down his window, and stuck his p89 out and let it bark.

Ten gunshots later, Debo gunned the engine, fleeing the scene. On the corner, the three workers laid lifeless in front of the building they worked out of.

CHAPTER 29 SEX IN THE AIR

Ali laid on his bunk, reading an article in the new Don Diva magazine until he heard a loud commotion coming from outside his cell. "What the fuck?" He said out loud, as he slid off his bunk, and headed out his cell to see what all the fuss was about. Outside the cell, Skip had some white kid hemmed up, fishing through his pockets. "Where my money at?" Skip asked with a sharp edge in his voice.

"I don't have it," the white dope fiend slurred.

"Yo what's the problem?" Ali asked, approaching the two men.

"This bitch owe us two hundred dollars and he don't wanna pay."

"Because I don't have the money," the white boy pleaded.

"You had the money. But instead of paying what you owe, you went and copped some shit from Rose," Skip said, blowing up the spot.

"Let him go," Ali said in an even tone.

"What?" Skip asked, giving Ali a strange look.

"I said let him go," Ali repeated himself.

"What the fuck was that about?" Skip asked once the white boy was out of earshot. "That's like the seventh fiend we lost this week."

"Better product always wins," Ali said, looking over at Rose and the Aryan Nation family playing cards. "And right now, Rose has the better product."

"Well we need to tell Loco to get some better shit," Skip suggested.

"Fuck Loco. He don't know shit about good quality dope. He just tryna make a couple dollars," Ali said as he headed in his cell and reached in his pillowcase to pull out the Nextel that Nancy brought him a few weeks ago. Ali dialed a number and sat on his bunk waiting for the person on the other end to answer.

"Hello," Nancy answered in a happy tone.

"Hey bae, what's up?"

"Nothing, I'm just lying on the couch watching T.V., I was just thinking about you," she said, switching her position on the couch.

"I was thinking about you too. But check it out, I need a favor."

"Whatever you need, you know I got you," Nancy replied.

"I need you to tell Gmoney that I need some dog food (dope)."

"Dog food?" Nancy echoed. "What's that?"

"He'll know what it is when you tell him," Ali said quickly.

"Okay I got you boo." "So what you got on right now bae?" Ali asked in a seductive tone.

"I'm just laying here wearing your favorite; a red thong and matching bra."

"Mmmmm…Damn bae, you got your man dick harder than learning how to play the piano," Ali flirted.

"I wish you were here right now so I could suck and fuck the shit out of your dick," Nancy said in her sexiest voice.

"Nah, don't even worry about that. I worked something out with one of the C.O.'s up here. Next time you come up here, make sure you bring four hundred dollars, and the C.O. gonna let us slide off in one those trailers that they got for the married people."

A broad smile appeared across Nancy's face. "For real?"

"True story, and make sure you wear those red pumps I like,"

"I got you daddy," Nancy sang like a little schoolgirl.

"But I gotta get ready to go to work baby. I'm going to call you as soon as I get off."

"Oh yeah…I forgot they got you working in the kitchen," Nancy said, suddenly remembering.

"Yeah you know how these crackers play. But let me go, I'mma scream at you later. Love you."

"I love you too baby," Nancy said, blowing him a kiss through the phone.

"A'ight one," Ali said, ending the conversation.

"So what's up?" Skip asked with a puzzled look on his face.

"We wait," Ali said plainly. "I just put in the order. Give it a week and we'll have a new supply. But for now, we keep pumping the shit we got until the new package arrives."

"A'ight cool," Skip said. The two men quickly turned around when they heard a C.O. banging on the cell door with their nightstick.

"What's up Ali?" Crystal sang in a seductive tone.

"Ain't nothing Ms. Ruby. I'm just chilling. How you feeling?" Ali said, returning her stare.

"I been good; just a little tired," she said, playfully stretching her arms.

"Yo I'mma head back to my cell. I'll holla at you later," Skip said as he exited the cell. Before he left, he made sure he turned and took a peek at Crystal's healthy ass. "Damn," he said under his breath as he visualized the two of them having wild sex in his mind.

"So what's going on Ms. Ruby, how can I help you?" Ali asked.

Crystal placed her hands on her hips. "I thought I told you to call me Crystal?"

"Oh yeah my bad," Ali apologized with a warm smile.

"Anyway the warden wants to see you, so he sent me to come get you."

"Fuck the warden wanna see me for?"

"I have no idea," Crystal replied with a puzzled look on her face.

$ilk White

"A'ight, come on. Let's be out," Ali said as he grabbed his green button up shirt, threw it on, and followed Crystal as she led the way.

Meanwhile, Rose sat over in the day room playing cards, watching Ali's every move. Once the C.O. escorted Ali out of the housing unit, Rose made his move. He looked over at Ice Pick and gave him the go-ahead nod.

"I got you," Ice Pick said with a nod of understanding, as he stood up from the table and headed over to where Lil Bit stood with his back turned, talking to a customer. As Ice Pick got closer to the midget, he slid an ice pick with tape wrapped around the handle from his back pocket. In a smooth motion, Ice Pick jabbed the ice pick in Lil Bit's back twice as he continued to walk by like nothing never even happened. Instantly, Lil Bit's eyes lit up as he felt the sharp object pierce through his back. He immediately dropped to his knees, clawing at his back.

"So have you read any new books lately?" Crystal asked, making small talk as she and Ali strolled down the empty hallway.

"Nah, not lately. I got a few new joints, but I haven't read them yet," Ali replied as Crystal led him through the empty kitchen, and into a small storage closet.

"What the fuck…." Before Ali could get the words out, Crystal had planted his back against the wall and began slobbering him down, as she massaged his dick through his green Dickie pants with her free hand.

Ali was about stop her, but decided to just go with the flow. Having a lady C.O. on his team comes with plenty of benefits.

Crystal slowly eased her way from Ali's lips, down to his nice-sized dick. "Damn you backed up I see," she said as she held his balls in her hand and slowly began to lick them in a circular motion. When she finally made it to his dick, she slowly put the head in her mouth and began licking around the rim of his dick with the tip of her tongue. Ali threw his head back as he stroked the back of Crystal's neck while she handled her business. After about six minutes of sucking, Crystal rose to her feet. "Fuck me Ali. We don't have that much time," she said as she handed him a condom.

Ali quickly rolled on the condom, pulled Crystal's uniform pants and thong down to her ankles, and began fucking the shit out of her.

Crystal bit her bottom lip with her hands wrapped around her ankles as Ali slid in and out of her at a steady pace. Ali stood with the screw face as he watched his dick disappear in and out of the correctional officer's wet, juicy pussy.

When Ali felt himself getting ready to cum, he instantly gripped her small waist and began to hammer into her harder until he filled his condom with his fluids.

"Damn, I ain't know it was like that," Crystal said as she slid her thong back up in the crack of her ass.

"Yo you wilding. If we get caught, you gon lose your job and I'm gonna get my ass whipped," Ali said, knowing how them crackers upstate got down.

"Be easy," Crystal said in a relaxed tone. "No one will ask us no questions when they see you with me," she said, motioning towards the shield right above her left breast.

Ali shrugged his shoulders. "Fuck it; I ain't stressing it if you ain't."

"I ain't stressing shit. I know you just better keep your mouth shut," Crystal warned, giving Ali a look that could kill.

"That's the last thing you gotta worry about," Ali assured her as the two headed back down the empty hallway. When the two returned back to the housing unit, Crystal noticed that the place was on lock down. "What the fuck done happened now?" She thought out loud, as one of her coworker buzzed her and Ali in through the metal door.

"What happened?" Crystal asked curiously.

"An inmate got stabbed in his back...again," the white officer said sarcastically with a smirk on his face. "Who are you and what's your name?" The officer asked in a bored tone as he turned and faced Ali.

"Ali, I'm up in cell 38," he told the officer.

"Cell 38 huh?" The officer said, trying to find Ali's name on the clipboard he held. "Looks like your bunkie is the inmate that got stabbed," the officer said as a smirk danced across his lips.

"You got 20 seconds to get to your cell," the officer said as he pressed a button behind his desk that opened up Ali's cell. Ali didn't respond to the ignorant officer. Instead, he just headed straight to his cell. As he headed up the corridor, he gave Crystal a private glance. She returned his glance and gave him a short head nod in return before she was taken out of her zone by the other officer's gruff voice.

"Fucking animals," he said in a disgusted tone.

"Motherfuckers can't go a day without killing one another."

"I know what you mean," Crystal said over her shoulder, rolling her eyes. She couldn't stand how most of the staff working at the facility treated the inmates. Just because the men were incarcerated, doesn't mean they should get treated and talked to like animals.

"You have a good night Ms. Ruby," the white officer said as he closely watched the nice shaped woman's ass cheeks bounce up and down with each step she took.

"Good night," Crystal replied as she stepped on the other side of the metal door.

Ali reached his cell and noticed all of Lil bit's belongings were gone. "Fuck!" He yelled out loud. Ali didn't know what went down, but he knew he would soon find out, and someone was gonna have hell to pay.

CHAPTER 30 DON'T PLAY WITH ME

Carl stepped out of the cab with his eight-year-old son, fast on his heels.

"I can't wait to get upstairs so I can play this new Madden," Little Bobby sang happily.

"You better get all the practice you can get, because once I get a hold of the controller, you know you going down," Carl chuckled as he nudged Little Bobby.

"You can't beat me no more daddy."

"We'll see," Carl said with a broad smile on his face. As the two made it closer to the building, Carl's smile quickly faded into an ugly frown.

"Daddy why are those men always standing in the lobby of our building every night?" Little Bobby asked innocently.

"I wish I knew," Carl said, trying to hide the anger in his tone.

"Yo pass that shit nigga!" Knowledge hissed as he snatched the blunt from a nondescript, who stood in the lobby. "Big lip muthafucka," he said as everybody in the lobby busted out laughing.

"Yo where that Henny at?" Shorty asked louder than he had to.

"Ain't no more," a soldier wearing a durag replied.

"It's 20 muthafuckas in this lobby. Somebody about to run to the liquor store," Shorty said, looking around for a victim. Over in the corner, he saw a scrawny kid leaning against the wall trying to look cool.

"Yo fam," he called out. "It's time for you to make that liquor run," Shorty said, pulling out a thick stack of money. "Bring me what you can with this," Shorty said as he handed the kid two hundred dollar bills. "And don't be all day either," he said, showing off for the 10 chicks who stood in the lobby with the rest off the hoodlums.

As the scrawny kid made his exit, Carl and Little Bobby stepped through the entrance.

"Carl what's good my dude?" Knowledge said, extending his hand to give Carl a pound. Carl looked at Knowledge's hand as if it had some kind of virus on it. "Ain't nothing good," he said as if he was about to bring it to Knowledge.

"Daddy, can we go upstairs now?" Little Bobby asked, as he broke down into a coughing fit from the cloud of weed smoke that hung in the air.

"Come on," Carl growled as he grabbed Little Bobby's hand and led him towards the elevator.

"What's his problem?" Shorty asked openly.

"I don't know, but he bout to get his ass whipped in a minute," Knowledge said loud enough so Carl could hear him.

TEARS OF A HUSTLER 2

Seconds later, a well-known fiend came storming in the building talking as if he was in a loud club. "Let ya boy get five of them thangs. And don't try to give me no shake like you niggaz did last time," Odog said, putting on a scene like usual. Immediately, a young runner served the fiend right there in the lobby in front of everybody.

"Come on son, let's take the stairs," Carl said with a cold edge in his voice as him and Little Bobby disappeared in the staircase. "Come on man," Odog complained. "You ain't got nothing bigger than this? Bad enough I ain't get six for 50," he grumbled, looking at the small bags as if they had a disease on them.

"Throw that nigga an extra one so he can get the fuck up outta here," Knowledge said as he made his way over to where the fine ladies where standing.

"Damn I'm lucky. I'm not a one woman man," Knowledge said, rubbing his hands together as he circled the women looking at each one from head to toe.
"What's that supposed to mean?" A light skin girl with a healthy ponytail asked, batting her eyes. Before Knowledge could reply with a slick come back line, he heard the girls scream, then a loud gunshot go off. Knowledge quickly spun around with the quickness of a cat with his hammer already drawn. Carl came busting out of the staircase door wearing a hoody and a .357 in his hand. A young lady screaming grabbed Shorty's attention, causing him to reach for his waist.

Carl quickly sent a shot to the ceiling, freezing the young man in place. Not wanting to get hit with a .357 bullet, Shorty quickly threw his hands up in surrender as Carl slid behind him, and pressed the barrel of the traypound to the back of his head.

"What the fuck you doing?" Knowledge yelled as he inched forward with two hands on his 9mm that was aimed at Carl's head.

"Take another step and you gonna have to mop this chump up off the floor," Carl threatened with ice in his voice as he watched the chicks, and bitch ass niggaz almost kill themselves breaking for the exit. By now, every soldier in the lobby had their guns trained on the once cool cat named Carl.

"What the fuck is this shit about?" Knowledge asked, pondering on taking the headshot.

"I asked you ignorant fools nicely to stop slanging in front of this building," Carl snarled. "People's kids, mothers, grandmothers, even baby mother's walk in and out of this building every day. Why should they have to see y'all smoking, drinking, and standing around with y'all pants hanging off y'all asses all day?"

"Nigga fuck all that. What do you want?" Knowledge asked as if Carl was becoming an annoyance.

"Talking to you fools is useless. Now I want to talk to the man," Carl said with authority.

$ilk White

"Nah, now you wilding," Knowledge hissed. "Put that fucking gun down before I pop ya head off!" He growled as he took another step closer.

"Pop this nigga already. What you waiting for?" Shorty yelled from the chokehold. Knowledge sighed loudly. "Yo let me use you phone," he said to one of the goons.

"Why? Let's just kill this chump," the goon shot back.

"I can't just kill him. I've known this mazurka since I was a lil shorty," Knowledge huffed as he snatched the cell phone from the goon's hand. Knowledge punched in some numbers on the phone and handed it back to the soldier. "A'ight, I just paged him. Now we just gotta wait for him to show up."

"I missed you so much," Coco sang like a little schoolgirl as she and Gmoney sat in the Jacuzzi together, getting their relax on.

"I missed you too," Gmoney replied as he sipped from his glass of Henny, as the multiple jets massaged his body. Having Coco back in his life made Gmoney feel good inside. He really loved Coco and hated wondering if she was okay, or not when the two were separated.

"Pour me a cup of that. A bitch is parched over here," Coco said playfully as she nudged Gmoney with her foot.

"Keep your crusty feet to yourself," Gmoney said, playfully swatting her foot away as he reached for the bottle of Henny.

Coco sucked her teeth. "Crusty?" She echoed. "Nigga please, ain't a damn thing crusty on my body," she said in a matter of fact tone.

"I know crusty when I see it," Gmoney nodded and sipped some more.

"That's your word?" Coco said with a wisp of a smile. Her naked body was dripping wet as she slowly walked over to the corner where Gmoney sat. "Is this crusty too?" She asked, placing her left leg on the outside rim of the Jacuzzi, leaving her freshly waxed pussy in Gmoney's face. Gmoney cleared his throat as he sat face to face with Coco's juicy pussy. "Can I help you?" He asked as he sat his glass down next to his .45 that rested within arm's reach.

"I don't know, can you?" Coco said as one of her eyebrows rose. Not being the type to back down from a challenge, Gmoney immediately burried his head between Coco's legs; licking and sucking all of her juices away, forcing her to cum quicker than she wanted to.

"Damn!" Coco moaned and cursed as she grabbed his head, and begged him not to stop. Two minutes later, Coco's body tensed as she began to climax for him yet again.

"Stand your ass up," Coco demanded as she held Gmoney's rock hard dick with two hands and gingerly licked, sucked, and tongue kissed his dick. She made sure she slurped all the water off of his dick before she opened her mouth as wide as she could.

TEARS OF A HUSTLER 2

She was only able to take in half of his dick, before letting it slide back out the side of her mouth; making a loud slopping sound. For the next 10 minutes, Coco sucked the shit out of Gmoney's dick; the whole time, making loud slurping noises until he finally exploded in her mouth.

"I see I still got the title," Coco boasted as she wiped her mouth with the back of her hand.

"You know you the champ bae," Gmoney said out of breath, as he reached for his beeper that was vibrating uncontrollably. "What the fuck?" He said out loud, as he looked at his beeper with a weird look on his face.

"What's wrong babe?" Coco asked with a look of concern.

"Somebody just beeped me with my old building number."

"The building in the projects?" Coco asked.

"Yeah...it must be Knowledge, because I know Pauleena wouldn't be up in the projects," Gmoney said out loud, as he got up and stepped out of the Jacuzzi butt naked.

"So I guess we ain't going out to eat then, huh?" Coco asked innocently.

"Yeah we still going. I'mma just swing by the projects real quick to see what's good," he told her as he started getting dress.

When Gmoney and Coco made it downstairs, they saw the four men, who was supposed to protecting them, gathered around the flat screen T.V. playing Madden.

"Fuck is y'all niggaz doing?" Gmoney barked, causing the four men to jump; one of them even pulled out his ratchet.

"My bad. I was just busting this clown ass in Madden," Eraser Head spoke up. He got the name because he had a square head and a skinny face, which made him look like an eraser.

"Strap up! We gotta go swing by the projects real quick," Gmoney said, looking down at his beeper, which was now vibrating again.

Gmoney and Coco slid in the back of the Yukon, while Eraser Head occupied the passenger seat, and another goon made the Yukon come to life with a turn of the key. The other two goons hopped in an all-black Honda and tailed the Yukon, as the two pulled out into the street.

Jimmy sat a block away in a station wagon, puffing on a cigarette, looking like his nerves were shot. "That ass is mines as soon as you come back," he whispered as he flicked the cigarette butt out the window. Jimmy sat back and watched the white van full of Jamaicans pull out right after the Yukon and Honda pulled off. "Fucking amateurs," he hissed as he sat and continued to wait patiently for his victim to return.

"Why the fuck are we going to the projects anyway?" Eraser Head asked.

"Something is up," Gmoney answered calmly.

"Knowledge paged me "911" three times already."

$ilk White

"I hope everything is alright," Coco added. "Especially, with the heat that's on y'all."

"Man fuck the police," Gmoney said with conviction. "I don't touch no drugs and I don't carry a gun on me no more. So if them mufuckas wanna follow me around all fucking day, then by all means, let 'em."

"I think you starting to cool off though, because I haven't seen an unmarked car on us in a few days," Eraser Head said.

"Yeah them boys been quiet lately, but you know that's how they do. They want us to think shit is all-good, hoping we slip up. And as soon as we do, they gonna be right there waiting for us," Gmoney said as the Yukon pulled up to the curb in front of the projects. Just by looking out the window, Gmoney could see about 15 to 20 people standing in the lobby. "Yo, you got an extra strap on you?"

"You know I do," Eraser Head answered quickly.

"Let me get that thang," Gmoney said, reaching his arm over Eraser Head's shoulder.

Without thinking twice, Eraser Head slid Gmoney a pearl handled .380.

"A'ight bae, wait right here. I'll be right back," Gmoney said as he kissed Coco on the cheek. "You too," he said, turning to face the driver. "Keep this motherfucker running," he ordered as him and Eraser Head made their way to the building. As Gmoney got closer to the building, he made out a man with a hoody, holding a gun to somebody's head. "I don't know what's going on, but I'm only talking for 10 minutes. If shit ain't settled by then, take the shot," Gmoney said in a calm tone as the two entered the building.

"Fuck going on up in here?" Gmoney asked, realizing the man who held the .357 was his longtime friend, Carl.

"I been asking your partner over here for a few weeks now to move from in front of this building, slanging poison."

"This nigga lying!" Knowledge cut in.

Gmoney quickly hushed him. "Talk to me Carl. Why did you call me down here? Time is money, and I don't have neither to waste."

"I want you to get these dudes away from my building," Carl demanded.

Gmoney eyed him suspiciously. "So that's what you called me down here for?" He asked, not giving Carl a chance to answer. "Listen I'm a busy man. Do I come down to your job telling you how to handle your business?" He asked sounding irritated.

Carl managed to muster a grin. "When you was coming up, I raised you like you was my little brother; now this how you talk to me?"

"You ain't been the same ever since you got out of jail. It's like that shit made you get soft."

"You think I'm soft now?" Carl asked, digging the nose of the .357 even further into the back of Shorty's head.

"You remember the law of the streets right?" Gmoney raised an eyebrow. "You only pull that strap if you gon use it."

Carl took his time responding. "Trust me, I know what time it is," he beamed. "You have a gift and you using it for evil. All of these young men out here look up to you. They'll do anything you say. But instead of using that power to help uplift brothers, you got them out here selling drugs for you and killing each other."

"And you had the same gift back in the day, and what did you do with it? Not a motherfucking thing," Gmoney said, answering his own question.

"G, I'm here so you can learn from my mistakes. Plus, it's not like you pressed for cash," Carl said, nodding towards the diamond bracelet on Gmoney's wrist. "What I'm trying to say is, if you want to throw your life away cool; but don't take all these brothers down with you."

"Listen Carl, please put the gun down. It's not necessary. We can talk like two men," Gmoney tried to reason in a mellow tone.

"Promise you'll move your men out of this building and all this shit will be over." "This shit ain't never going to be over," Knowledge growled from the sideline. Carl gave Knowledge a cold stare, and then turned his focus back on Gmoney. "Promise me that and we have no more problems. I don't want my son coming home from school to see y'all in here smoking weed, and selling drugs. We all need to come together and…."

Before Carl could finish what he was saying, Eraser Head had pulled out his .38 and popped Carl in the shoulder. The impact from the shot caused Carl to drop his gun as he hit the lobby floor.

Carl desperately tried to reach for the .357, but within a blink of an eye, Shorty, Knowledge, and the rest of the crew was stomping the shit out of him.

"Move out the way so I can body this stupid nigga!" Shorty yelled as he picked up the .357 from off the floor.

"Nah hold that down," Gmoney said walking over to where Carl laid, clutching his wounded shoulder. "If any of my soldiers catch you in this project again, you die; simple as that. Do we have an understanding?"

Carl gave Gmoney a bloody smile before responding. "Motherfucker you better kill me now while you got the chance. Cause if I ever see you again, you fucking history," he spat.

Gmoney just chuckled as he stood up to leave. "If anybody ever see this fool in the hood again, I want y'all to terminate his fucking contract."

"Bitch ass nigga! No matter how hard you try, you'll never be Ali," Carl yelled at Gmoney's back.

Gmoney ignored that last comment as him, Eraser Head, and Knowledge left the building, while the rest of the goons went back to kicking and stomping on Carl's ribs and head.

"Don't ever call me down here for some shit like this again," Gmoney growled.

"Nah, I was gonna pop money head off, but I know you been knowing son forever, so I didn't want to violate...smell me?" Knowledge told him.

"If that nigga ain't with us then he's against us," Gmoney said blankly. "I'm out, hold it down out here. And you and the soldiers get up outta here before five-o come through this joint," he said as he gave Knowledge a pound.

"Yeah, I'm about to get up outta here in a minute. I'm about to head to club "Spy" and grab me a nice lil Spanish thing," Knowledge said, rubbing his hands together.

"Any word on who popped those three kids who worked for us?" Gmoney asked curiously.

"Nah not yet, but I got a few goons looking into that as we speak," Knowledge assured him.

"A'ight bet. I'm out. Scream at me if anything," Gmoney said as he disappeared into the back seat of the Yukon.

"Is everything okay?" Coco asked with a concerned look on her face.

"It's all good," Gmoney replied as he handed Eraser Head back the .380.

"Baby, Nancy just called me a minute ago," Coco said, turning to face Gmoney.

"Word? What she talking about?"

"Nothing. She told me Ali called her and said he needs you to get him some dog food," Coco told him.

"Damn, he know I don't fuck with no dope," Gmoney said out loud. "Yo, change of plans. Take me to Pauleena's crib."

The driver didn't reply. He just nodded at Gmoney through the rear view mirror.

CHAPTER 31 A TIME TO KILL

Rell looked up blankly at the ceiling. He hadn't been able to sleep in almost three days. All he could think about was when and how he was going to kill Gmoney. Lil Wayne's song "I Feel Like Dying" hummed through the small speakers on the dresser. Music seemed to somehow always make Rell feel better inside, but this time it wasn't working. Nothing or no one was going to change Rell's mind or how he felt.

Rell reached over and grabbed the p89 Ruger from off the pillow next to him. He closely examined the pistol as he played out the scene on how he was going to kill Gmoney in his mind. A wicked smile appeared on his face when he envisioned himself popping Gmoney's head clean off his shoulders. The ringing of his cell phone quickly put an end to the brutal vision going on in his mind. "Yeah," he answered, already knowing who it was from glancing at the caller I.D.

"What are you doing?" Detective Nelson's voice boomed on the other end of the phone.

"Nothing right now. Why, what's good?"

"What's good is that I got some good news for you."

"Lay it on me," Rell said as he sat straight up in the bed.

"One of my informants just tipped me off to one of Gmoney's stash cribs over out in Brooklyn. He told me its Gmoney and Pauleena's stash crib. I haven't been able to find this Pauleena chick in the system, but if she's a player, I'm definitely going to get a heads up on her. Long story short, let me know if you want to take the stash crib. Cause if not, I'll take the motherfucker down myself," Detective Nelson said, waiting for a response.

"Nah, this one is all mines," Rell replied with ice in his voice.

"Alright, if I get anymore leads, I'll be sure to contact you," Detective Nelson said, ending the conversation on that note.

"It's on now!" Rell said out loud with a weird grin on his face, as he hopped up off the bed and threw his war clothes back on.

"Y'all wait right here. I won't be gone long," Gmoney said, looking at Coco and his driver as he, and Eraser Head headed for the entrance of Pauleena's mansion.

"Gmoney is here to see you," Malcolm's voice boomed, waiting for Pauleena's approval to let him in.

Pauleena didn't respond. She just nodded her head yes. "Gmoney what's good?" She greeted the smooth hustler with a warm smile.

"Ain't shit...just needed to holla at you about something," Gmoney said,

$ilk White

noticing Pauleena fumbling through some sort of folder or portfolio.

"Can you believe this old ass man is one of the biggest heroin dealers," she said out loud, looking at a personal picture of the old dealer. "This motherfucker is filthy rich," she chuckled, handing Gmoney the small photo.

"Romelo?" Gmoney said, reading the name under the picture out loud. "I heard about this cat."

"What did you hear?" Pauleena asked curiously.

"I heard the motherfucker don't take no shit. And I also heard he a real flashy O.G." Pauleena laughed before speaking again. "Well I can't wait to meet him."

"Meet him for what?"

"I was figuring since we got the coke and crack sewed up, we might as well start expanding. Plus, you know what they say," she paused. "Ain't no money like dope money."

Gmoney chuckled. "If it's going to increase my bank account, then count me in."

"Yeah, I definitely will." Pauleena said, still studying the older man's photo. "I'm throwing Roy a surprise birthday party at this club out in Miami. Everybody who's anybody will be there, so I'm hoping I can catch this old mazurka up in there and rap with him a taste."

"That old nigga live in Miami?" Gmoney asked.

"Nah, he's originally from New York. But when he started getting paid, he copped this big ass house in upstate New York; Syracuse I think."

"That's cool, but I'm getting ready to bounce. I had something to tell you. Oh yeah," Gmoncy suddenly remembered. "I got a message from Ali. He said he needs a good heroin supplier."

"You see, great minds think alike," Pauleena said with a wink.

"When you hook up with that old mazurka, be sure to hit me up so I can get a chick to smuggle that up there for my man."

"You know I got you, but yo, you heard about ya man's man?" Pauleena asked, putting fire to the end of her blunt.

"Who you talking about?"

"Some cat that goes by the name Big Mel."

"Yeah that's the faggot who snitched on Ali. What about that bitch ass nigga? I hope you got an address for me," Gmoney's eye's tightened with interest.

"No need for all that," Pauleena spoke in a calm tone. "Niggaz found his ass laid out in a ditch over there around Fordham road, with his asshole all cut up, and shit."

"Damn, who did him in like that?"

"Word on the streets say it was your friend, Detective Nelson," Pauleena told him.

TEARS OF A HUSTLER 2

"Every dog has his day I guess," Gmoney chuckled as he and Eraser Head filed for the exit.

"True indeed," Pauleena said over the rim of her glass as she watched Gmoney and his goon make their exit.

"Sorry about that bae," Gmoney apologized as he slid back in the back seat.

"It's all good," Coco replied, not wanting to argue over something so petty.

"Yo take us to my man Ali's restaurant," Gmoney ordered from the back seat.

"I got you boss," the driver said, pulling out of the mansion's drive way.

Trey sat at a small table in the kitchen, counting a table full of money. "Damn B. This a lot of shit to be counting by myself," he huffed out loud.

"I'll help you," Big Steve said with a devilish smile on his face.

"Nigga you must be crazy," Trey said seriously. "You Brooklyn niggaz got sticky fingers. I ain't getting smoked for you. I'd rather get smoked for something I do myself."

"Scary ass Harlem nigga," Big Steve capped back. "Who told you to talk? Just stand there and hold that gun like you get paid to do," Trey said half-jokingly.

"I'm holding this gun to protect ya punk ass. If I wasn't holding this gun, all the jack boys in New York would be up here robbing ya punk ass."

Trey was about to come back with a slick reply, until he heard something tapping against the living room window. "What the fuck?" Trey said out loud, as he pushed away from the table, pulling his .380 from the small of his waist, as he and Big Steve went to go investigate. The reason the two men were so startled was because they were on the fourth floor.

"This nigga must be crazy," Trey hissed as he looked out the window and saw a crack head throwing little pebbles up at the window. "Throw another fucking rock and see what happen," Trey yelled as Big Steve opened up the window.

"Suck my dick!" The crack head shouted before he took off sprinting up the block, never looking back.

As the two men watched the crack head takeoff up the street, the front door getting blown off the hinges caught their attention. Big Steve quickly went for his baby Uzi, but he was a little too slow. As soon as Rell saw the big man attempt to reach, he pulled the trigger on his shotgun, sending Big Steve hurling backwards through the window. Trey immediately froze up once he saw his longtime friend get executed in that fashion.

"Drop that piece before I turn your head into velvet," Rell threatened, aiming the barrel of the shotgun at the young hustler's forehead.

"Why? You just gon shoot me anyway," Trey protested.

"You must got me confused with a man that repeats himself," Rell replied with a sharp edge in voice. Seeing death in the man's eyes, Trey quickly did as he was told.

Once Rell saw that the young man was unarmed, he jabbed him in the face with the ass of his gun, sending Trey crashing to the floor.

"What a motherfucker like you doing up in here with all this money and product?" Rell asked with a smirk on his face.

Trey didn't answer; he just shot the stick-up man an evil look.

"Well since you don't know, I'mma just have to take it off your hands," Rell's chuckled as he pulled out a garbage bag from his back pocket, and swept all the money from off the table inside of it. "You make sure when you see that faggot Gmoney, you tell him Rell is responsible for this. Oh yeah, and tell him I said from now on, I'm coming myself. I ain't sending no soldiers or nothing; just me," he paused briefly to light up a Newport. "More than likely, I'll be seeing you again. Cause if I know your boss like I think I do, then he's never going to man up and come see me."

"Gmoney gonna fuck ya ass up when he catch you," Trey spat out of hurt pride.

"Again, right?" Rell said, giving the young hustler a comical look. "Tell that bitch nigga I'll be waiting," he said as he exited the same way he entered.

Once Trey was sure the gunman was gone, he quickly exited the apartment before the cops could arrive. His first stop was to the nearest pay phone.

"This shit better be good because I'm hungrier than a motherfucker," Eraser Head grumbled as he slid out of the Yukon.

"Ali's restaurant got the best food in town," Gmoney said proudly as he, Coco, and Eraser Head headed towards the restaurant's entrance.

"Damn that's fucked up," Eraser Head said, shaking his head. "You could have at least let that man come inside and get something to eat."

Gmoney looked at Eraser Head as if he had a bad taste in his mouth before he spoke. "I pay that mazurka to drive. What if we gotta run up outta here? I ain't got time for a nigga to be fumbling around with the keys and shit. It's too risky, not to mention you know who is with us," he said, nodding towards Coco.

"You know who my ass!" Coco snapped. "Don't play with me. If shit jump off, I know how to handle myself."

"Oh yeah, I forgot you was a coldblooded killer," Gmoney joked as the trio entered the restaurant. Once the staff saw Gmoney enter the restaurant, they treated him and his guest with the royalty treatment.

"Right this way," the hostess said, as he led the trio to a nice table over by the side window. "Your waitress will be with you in one second," he said politely as he headed back to his post.

"I want to be just like Ali when I grow up," Eraser Head said like a school kid. "Nigga getting paid even while he in the can."

"He's a perfect example that hard work definitely pays off," Gmoney said as he watched the young, dark skin waitress approach their table with two bottles of champagne in a bucket of ice, along with three champagne flutes.

"How you doing today gorgeous?" Eraser Head said, seductively giving the waitress the, what's-good eye.

"I'm good," she replied, trying to keep it professional. "Are y'all ready to order yet?"

Coco was getting ready to order, but Eraser Head beat her to the punch. "Yes I'll have steak medium rare, some yellow rice, and your number on the side," he said with a warm smile.

The now blushing waitress returned the man's smile as she nicely replied. "Steak medium rare and yellow rice coming right up."

"What about my last order?" Eraser Head pressed.

"I'll see what I can do," the waitress smiled as she focused her attention on Coco and Gmoney. "Are y'all ready to order?"

"Yeah I'll have the same thing my man ordered," Gmoney said.

"And I'll take the steak too. But instead of yellow rice, I'll have macaroni and cheese," Coco said politely as she handed the waitress back the menu.

"Coming right up. Oh and girl I love the shoes," the waitress said as she spun on her heels and headed back towards the kitchen. Eraser Head made sure he watched every step the waitress took until she disappeared through the double doors. "Damn she got a fatty, right G?"

Gmoney was about to answer until he saw the murderous look that Coco was giving him.

"You know I only got eyes for my boo," he quickly tried to clean up his last statement.

"Don't play with me Eraser Head, cause you know I will fuck your friend up in here," Coco said in a joking matter, but was dead serious.

Over on the other end of the restaurant, Ashley exited the restroom and spotted Gmoney sitting over at a table next to the window with some chicken head sitting way too close to her soon to be man. Without thinking twice, Ashley pulled down her purple mini skirt as far as it could go, trying not to look slutty as she made her way towards the trio's table.

I got a shorty gimme her number when she come back." Eraser Head said, looking to lure Gmoney into an easy bet.

"No bet," Gmoney said, waving off his personal bodyguard.

Gmoney looked up over the rim of his champagne flute and almost choked when he saw the familiar face heading in his direction.

When Ashley's expensive purple, open toe heels stopped in front of the trio's table, even Ray Charles could see that some shit was about to go down. "What's up G baby? I been trying to get in touch with you all day to let you know I just got back in town today," she said with a smile. Her eyes briefly took in his company, and then came back to him. "But I guess you was busy," she said distastefully as she let her eyes roll over Coco.

"Yeah I been a lil tied up today. How come you didn't leave me a message?" Gmoney replied, trying not to let the panic slip through his tone.

"And who is this?" Ashley asked, gesturing her fingers towards Coco.

Gmoney tried to hurry up and respond, but he was too late.

"Who am I? Bitch who the fuck are you? You coming over here interrupting our shit," Coco fumed.

"I'm Ashley," she said as she gave Coco the once over and wasn't impressed at all. "I believe we spoke on the phone before," she said, refreshing Coco's memory.

Out of the two women, Ashley was the prettier one, but Coco didn't fall far behind in looks or ass.

"Listen I'm not going back and forth with a nondescript. Now if you don't mind, why don't you go back and do whatever it was you was doing," Coco said, dismissing Ashley as she fanned her away with the back of her hand.

"First of all, watch how you talk to me you little ragamuffin before you get punched in the face," Ashley said so loud that she started getting stares from a few other diners.

He being a fiend for action, Eraser Head sat back watching the exchange with a broad smile on his face.

"Excuse me; what did you just call me?" Coco said in an even tone as she pushed away from the table and stood up.

"You heard me bitch!" Ashley said as she smoothly slipped out of her purple heels. She now stood 5'5 flat footed.

"Yo chill the fuck out!" Gmoney said as he stood in front of Ashley.

"You better teach your lil girlfriend some manners, before she get her ass tow-up," Ashley snarled in her down south accent.

"Lil girlfriend?" Coco echoed as she tried to lunge at the country girl, but G-money was there to block her path. Once Coco got close enough, Ashley threw a wild punch over Gmoney's shoulder missing Coco by inches, but the impact from the swing caused her to knock off Gmoney's hat by accident. Ashley went to take another swing at Coco, but as she swung, somebody caught her arm in mid-swing. She turned around to find a tall white man holding her arm, flashing his FBI badge with his free hand. His partner stood off in the rear with a cold look on his face.

"Miss, grab your shoes and please come with us," the agent said politely as they escorted Ashley out of the restaurant.

"Damn them motherfuckers was sitting right next to us," Eraser Head said with a shocked look on his face. "You think they heard anything?"

"Nah, we wasn't talking no important shit…thankfully," Gmoney said as he placed his hand over his mouth to hide his words. "I guess everything happens for a reason," he said humbly as he looked at Coco then headed for the exit.

"I know that's right," Eraser Head chuckled as he snatched one of the bottles of champagne off the table, as he and Coco followed Gmoney's lead. When Gmoney made it outside, he saw Ashley cursing out the two agents from across the street.

"Bitch is crazy," he said out loud, as he slid in the back seat and prepared himself to hear Coco curse him out for the entire ride home.

Gmoney stared blankly out the window, while Coco did what she did best…complain.

"Damn if you gon have bitches on the side, you could at least have them under control!" Coco exhaled. "Do I have guys running up on you questioning you?"

"No" Gmoney replied dryly.

"You know why?"

"No, please tell me," Gmoney huffed.

"Cause I got too much class to let some shit like that happen," she continued to rant without even taking a breath. "Then on top of that, you ain't even fucking with no dimes. You out here fucking with these low-class, bottom of the barrel bitches."

"Nah you bugging. Shorty was on point," Eraser Head said, jumping in the conversation from the front seat.

"Shut up!" Coco snapped as she slapped Eraser Head in the back of his neck.

"Yo, G it looks like we got some company," the driver said, reminding everyone he was still in the vehicle.

"Word? What it's looking like?" Gmoney asked, looking straight ahead.

"Looks like a white van. That bitch been tailing us since we left the restaurant," the driver said, looking at Gmoney through the rear view mirror.

"You want me to drop you off at one of our stash houses, so you'll be alright until this shit pop off?" Gmoney asked in a smooth tone as he looked over at Coco waiting for a response.

Coco looked at him as if he was talking in a different language. "Nah I'm good. You know I ride or die with my man."

A broad smile appeared on Gmoney's face as he placed his hand on top of hers. "Yo swing by the projects real quick. If the van follows us up there, then we know what time it is," Gmoney ordered.

"So what you doing later ma?" Shorty asked the Hispanic woman that stood in front of him.

"Nothing, I'm about to go upstairs and cook dinner for my son. Then after that,

$ilk White

I'm free. Why, you coming through?"

"That sounds like a plan," Shorty said, licking his lips. "Ya baby daddy ain't gon be home right? Cause I don't want to have to twist money shit back," he said, making a gun with his fingers.

"Nah, you know I ain't with all the drama and bullshit," the Hispanic chick said in a heavy accent as she placed a hand on Shorty's chest. "You promise you gon come through tonight, cause last time you had me waiting up all night," her voice changing to a whining, nagging note.

"Yeah ma. You know I'mma come through and toss ya lil ass up," Shorty said nonchalantly.

"A'ight make sure you bring some dutches, because I got a 50 of that sticky."

"I got you ma. Say no more," Shorty said as he noticed Gmoney's Yukon pull up to the curb and beep the horn. "Gimme one second," he told her as he made his way over to the Yukon. When Shorty reached the Yukon, the back window immediately rolled down.

"Youngin what's good?" Gmoney smiled as he gave Shorty a pound.

"You already know, on the grind. But what brings you down here? Did one of my peoples mess up the count?"

"Your count is always straight," Gmoney said, rubbing his beard. "Yo how many goons you got out here with you?"

"About four or five," Shorty replied quickly.

"A'ight strap up, and meet me at my crib in 10 minutes."

"Why, what's up?" Shorty asked curiously.

"You see that white van a block away?"

"Yeah, what about it?" Shorty asked as he smoothly took a glance at the white van.

"That motherfucker, been following us around for the last hour. I'm heading to my crib now. I want you to leave here in 10 minutes," Gmoney ordered.

"You sure it's not the boys?" (Cops)

"Nah, I'm positive it's not the fuzz," Gmoney said in a calm tone. "I'm heading to the crib now. If y'all roll up, and them niggaz in the van ain't made they move yet, you know what to do."

"I got you," Shorty said as he slid his hands into his black leather gloves.

"Where that nigga Knowledge at?" Gmoney asked curiously when he didn't see him nowhere around.

"Him and a few other goons headed over to the Bronx to go check up on Trey," Shorty told him.

"Trey?" Gmoney echoed, searching his memory trying to put a face with the name. "Oh yeah Trey," he suddenly remembered. "What happened to him?"

"Somebody rolled through there and shot up the stash crib, killed all the muscle, and took everything else."

"Make sure Knowledge holla at me when he get to the bottom of that shit. I'll see you in 10 minutes," Gmoney said as he gave Shorty a pound. As the Yukon pulled away from the curb, seconds later so did the white van.

* * **

Rell sat across the street in a tinted out Honda, watching Knowledge and a few other guys talking to Trey a half block away from the crime scene. Yellow tape, detectives, and reporters were everywhere; not to mention, everybody within a three-block radius stood behind the yellow tape being nosey. Throughout all the chaos, Rell kept his focus on Knowledge and his crew.

"Yo what the fuck happened to Big Steve?" Knowledge asked with four goons standing behind him.

"Some nigga that call himself Rell shot the door off the hinges, shot Big Steve out the fucking window, then took all the money, and the little bit of work we had up in there," Trey said making several different hand gestures.

"Rell?" Knowledge echoed with his face crumbled up. "I know you ain't let that bitch ass nigga rob you?"

"I was about to go for my strap, but that nigga had the drop on me. What the fuck was I suppose to do?" Trey fumed.

"Don't worry about it. We gon catch that faggot," Knowledge said, looking over Trey's shoulder at a few uniform officers coming in their direction.

"I'm banging out next time B. word," Trey said in a matter of fact tone.

Knowledge arched his brow. "Next time?" He chuckled. "Nigga you get paid to collect money, and hold down the stash crib. We gon setup another stash crib for you tomorrow. But this time, you gon have a lil more muscle with you, you dig? Let the shooters do their job, you just make sure you do yours."

Trey was about to reply, but he paused briefly to let the uniform officers pass. "I'm just saying, my pride not gon just let that nigga get away with that shit like that"

Knowledge let out an aggravated breath. "Nigga shut the fuck up and let us do our job," he growled, poking his finger in Trey's chest. "Nigga you should have popped the fuck off when you had the chance," he said as he and his four shooters hopped in his all black Expedition. Knowledge made the Expedition come to life with a turn of the key. Immediately, Styles P. song "Super Gansta" came blaring through the speakers. Seconds later, the truck tires squealed as the truck bent the corner.

Once Rell saw the Expedition pull off, he quickly caught the light so he could keep up with the shooters. Instead of sitting back and waiting for the shooters to come after him, Rell decided to go after the shooters. It was a gutsy move, but what did he have to lose?

"You young motherfuckers don't know who y'all fucking with," Rell said out loud, as he continued to follow the all black Expedition.

Once Jimmy saw Gmoney's Yukon pull back into the driveway, he screwed the silencer on his fully automatic Israeli Uzi, as he continued to wait for the perfect opportunity to strike.

"As soon as you get in the house, I want you to go straight upstairs," Gmoney ordered as he and Coco slid out the back seat. "Hide under the bed until I tell you otherwise," he said as he pulled Coco along. Once inside the house, Gmoney watched as Coco jogged up the stairs, doing as she was told. He and Eraser Head then immediately headed over to his gun closet. Gmoney snatched open the closet doors and a big smile appeared on Eraser Head's face. "Damn nigga, you got enough guns to supply a small army."

"Better safe than sorry," Gmoney exhaled as he strapped on a Teflon vest over his white thermal shirt. "Yo, hand me that Beretta and that A.K. with the banana clip," he said with his hand out.

"It's about to be on up in this bitch," Eraser Head said in a murderous tone as his eyes locked on the Mac 11 that sat right before his eyes.

The white van pulled up directly in front of Gmoney's house and sat for about 30 seconds, before seven wild ass Jamaican's hopped out the van with automatic weapons, and opened fire on Gmoney's house.

Gmoney sat on the floor behind a wall in the kitchen as he heard bullets ripping through his house, tearing shit up. "Fuck!" He cursed loudly as he gripped his A.K. even tighter, his heart pumping a hundred miles an hour.

Once the gunfire ceased, Gmoney shot to his feet, placing his back up against the wall. "Yo, Eraser Head you good?"

"Yeah I'm good," Eraser Head yelled as four Rasta's busting through the front door caught his Mac 11's attention.

With a sweep of his arm, Eraser Head sprayed the front door hitting one out of the four gunmen with a series of bullets, as he back peddled into the kitchen where Gmoney was.

"How many of them is it?" Gmoney asked.

Eraser Head held up three fingers as the gun shots continued to ring out. The gunfire seemed to pause briefly as Gmoney heard more people entering his home.

"Fuck this shit," Gmoney growled as he stepped from behind the wall, with his finger already on the trigger.

The gunmen quickly took cover as they saw Gmoney walking towards them popping shots. A wicked grin appeared on Gmoney's face when he saw the hit men scrambling for cover from the A.K. shells as they spit round after round, tearing up everything in its line of fire.

Gmoney eased his finger off the trigger long enough to see two more Rasta's enter his house. With a light squeeze on the trigger, Gmoney quickly sent the two Rasta's flying back out the front door.

One of the Jamaicans thought he had the drop on Gmoney from behind. He quickly sprung from his hiding spot, only to get two Mac 11 bullets popped into his skull.

Gmoney quickly turned around and saw a dirty Jamaican laid out by his feet, and Eraser Head holding a smoking Mac 11.

Gmoney gave him a quick head nod before he saw movement coming from the corner of his eye. Immediately, his A.K. followed the Rasta as he ran into the living room, ducking and dodging bullets.

"You take that side and I'll take this side," Eraser Head said as he tiptoed with caution over towards the leather sofa that sat in the middle of the living room.

The Rasta stood behind the sofa in a squatting position as sweat trickled down his face. Seconds later, shots flew through the sofa riddling the Rasta's body with bullets, killing him instantly.

"Fucking amateurs," Eraser Head growled as he spat on the dead Rasta's bloody body.

"Wild-ass Jamaicans," Gmoney mumbled as he removed the clip from his A.K. and replaced it with a fresh one.

"Yo I'mma go check up on Coco," Gmoney said as he headed towards the stairs, until movement at the front door caught him and Eraser Head's full attention. Both men quickly loosened up on their triggers when they saw Shorty enter the house with his gun in his hand, followed by four armed soldiers.

"Damn, did we get here too late?" Shorty asked, looking around at the murder scene.

"Nigga you know we don't play no games," Eraser Head boasted as he gave Shorty a pound.

"I see," Shorty replied with a grin on his face.

"I don't know what you grinning for," Gmoney snarled causing Shorty's grin to disappear immediately. "I said get here in 10 minutes. You five minutes late," he said, holding up the back of his wrist looking at his watch.

"Calm down G. I got here as fast as I could. Remember I had to round up a few soldiers, not to mention, two of them needed a hammer," Shorty pleaded his case.

"Fuck that got to do with you getting here in 10 minutes?"

"Nah, I was just saying...."

"You was just saying what?" Gmoney barked, cutting him off.

"I fucked up," Shorty mumbled, looking down at the floor.

"Time is very important," Gmoney told him as he draped his arm around the young soldier. "You can never get a minute back, you understand?"

Shorty nodded yes.

"You still my lil nigga. Keep your head up and you'll get 'em next time," G-money patted Shorty on his back.

Shorty was about to reply, until two cocktails came crashing through the front window.

"What the fuck?" Gmoney yelled as he watched his curtains catch on fire. "Did you see anybody out there before y'all came in?"

"Nah," Shorty replied quickly as he kept his .40 cal aimed at the front door. The whole time the fire was spreading, and spreading fast.

Yo, y'all watch the front door and make sure nobody don't come in. I'mma run upstairs, grab Coco, then we all gon slip out the back door," Gmoney instructed as shots began raining in through his windows from every angle, causing each man to hit the floor out of natural instincts.

Jimmy stood wide leg in front of Gmoney's house, sweeping his arms back and forth as shell's spit out his Uzi like fresh popped popcorn on the stove. Once the magazine was empty, Jimmy quickly removed it and replaced it with a fresh clip, and continued where he left off. Once that clip ran out, Jimmy tossed the Uzi in the grass, snatched a Beretta from the small of his back, and entered the house.

After Knowledge dropped off the last soldier, he wasn't quite ready to turn it in yet, so he decided to go swing by one of his tenderoni's crib who lived close by. He definitely needed to relieve some stress.

Knowledge wasn't upset that the stash crib had got hit. He was more upset by the fact of whom the stash crib got hit by. He had heard stories about the old time hustler, and really just wanted to kill him for bragging rights, and so he would be remembered as the guy who killed O.G. Rell. A thousand thoughts flew through Knowledge's mind as he pulled up on his Shorty's block.

Knowledge pulled up in front of the building he was looking for and quickly parallel parked the Expedition. "I hope this bitch is up," he huffed as he pulled out his cell phone that was only used for pleasure and entertainment. He strolled through the contacts until he found the number he was looking for. On the fifth ring, a girl with a soft voice answered.

"Hello?"

"Yo, what's good? This Knowledge. What you doing right now?"

"Nothing. Just sitting here watching Flavor Flav with his ugly ass," Tosha said in disgusted tone.

"Yo, I'm right downstairs. Come down to the lobby and let me in."

"Damn, you down stairs right now?" Tosha asked as she quickly snatched her scarf off her head and began raking her hair down with her fingers.

"Yeah, I'm right in front of your building as we speak," Knowledge said, looking up at her window.

"Okay, give a bitch 10 minutes so I can hop in the shower and freshen up real quick," Tosha told him as she quickly stripped down to her birthday suit.

"A'ight bet. I'mma run to the corner store real quick."

"Okay, I'll be in the lobby by the time you get back from the store," Tosha said, ending the conversation.

Knowledge smoothly slid out of the driver side of the Expedition and looked over both shoulders before he headed across the street, to the bodega that sat on the corner.

"Let me get four dutches and a pack of Newport's," Knowledge said as he tossed a 20-dollar bill on the counter. "Oh yeah, let me get a pack of those wet & wild condoms too," Knowledge suddenly remembered.

Rell sat back in the Honda and watched Knowledge enter the bodega. He glanced over at his shotgun that rested on the passenger seat, and then decided that his p89 would be better for the job. Rell slid out the Honda and swiftly walked over towards the bodega, holding his gun with one hand. Before Rell could even reach the bodega, he saw his victim coming out of the bodega. Without hesitation, Rell raised his p89 and pulled the trigger.

"I'm going upstairs to get Coco. If the flames get too high, I want y'all to be out through the back door," Gmoney said as he covered his mouth and nose with the bottom of his shirt.

"What about you?" Eraser Head asked as his eyes began to water from all the smoke.

"Don't worry about me. I'll be fine," Gmoney replied as he headed for the stairs. When Gmoney reached the middle of the steps, he heard gunshots popping. He quickly turned around and saw an Italian man standing in the doorway, blasting.

Jimmy looked over towards the steps and spotted his target. He quickly let off three more shots before throwing two shots in Gmoney's direction. The two bullets struck the wall inches away from Gmoney's head, leaving two huge smoking holes in the wall.

"Bitch!" Gmoney growled as he aimed his A.K. at the gunman with a murderous look in his eyes. Gmoney pulled the trigger and watched as the gun rattled in his hands.

When Jimmy saw Gmoney wave the A.K. in his direction, he quickly sprinted towards the bar area and dove over the counter, as he heard bullets whistling past his head.

Once Gmoney saw the gunman clear the counter, he made a beeline straight to his bedroom. "It's an Italian nigga downstairs. Go down there and take him out," Gmoney ordered as he tossed his A.K. on the bed next to Coco.

"I got you, boss man," the two soldiers yelled out as they hurried down stairs, so they could enter the shootout.

"What the fuck is going on down there? I can barely fucking breathe," Coco said in between coughs.

"We gotta get the fuck out of here," Gmoney said as his eyes locked on the window. From the look on Gmoney's face, Coco already knew what he was thinking. "I ain't jumping out no fucking window!" She snapped.

"You ain't got no choice," Gmoney said, staring at Coco like maybe this was a hallucination.

The loud gunshots coming from downstairs caused Coco to flinch a little before she responded. "Well I ain't feeling that plan, so you need to come up with a better one," she said, before breaking down into a coughing fit.

Meanwhile downstairs, Jimmy sat on the floor with his back against the counter. The heat from the flames had Jimmy's face sweating like he just finished playing three straight games of basketball, without taking a break. Jimmy took a short breath as he let the clip fallout from the base of his gun, before shoving a full clip back inside the handgun. On the count of three, Jimmy came up from behind the counter firing recklessly, not caring who he hit. Two of his bullets found fatal homes in the flesh of two of Shorty's soldier.

"Yo we gotta bail," Eraser Head yelled as he threw four shots over his shoulder, as he busted out the back door.

Once Shorty and his soldiers saw Eraser Head, head for the exit, they quickly followed his lead. Shorty and his crew continued to fire, back peddling out the back door.

When Jimmy saw that the coast was clear, he smoothly headed towards the steps. As he reached the bottom of the steps, he saw what looked like two bodies moving through a cloud of smoke. Without bothering to think twice, he aimed his Beretta at the two figures and pulled the trigger twice, then sat back and watched as the two bodies came tumbling down the stairs.

TEARS OF A HUSTLER 2

When Gmoney heard the shots come from by the steps, he knew he had to do something and do it fast. Having no other options, Gmoney snatched his .45 from his waistband and sent three shots through his big bedroom window, causing the glass to shatter, but not break. With an animalistic growl, Gmoney whirled around and grabbed Coco by her arms, and with extreme force, flung her through the shattered glass; not even taking time to see where she landed. Gmoney turned, let off three shots towards the bedroom door to keep the gunman at bay, as he hopped up on the windowsill, and jumped down into a pile of sticky bushes.

Gmoney quickly hopped out of the bushes, only to find Coco laid out in the grass howling in pain. Gmoney quickly turned his head as he saw Coco's ankle twisted in a backwards position. "Ahww shit," he cursed loudly as he scooped Coco up from out the grass, carried her over to the Yukon, and tossed her in the back seat.

As Gmoney ran around the truck to the driver side, he saw Shorty and his soldiers hop back in the whip they came in, and Eraser Head running full speed in the direction of the Yukon. Once Eraser Head was in the passenger seat, Gmoney backed out of the driveway. His braids flapped back and forth as he looked over both shoulders.

Jimmy finally made it inside the bedroom and saw that it was empty. "Fuck!" he cursed as he tossed his Beretta on the floor and hopped out the window, landing in the sticky bushes. When Jimmy hopped out of the bushes, all he could see was the Yukon flying down the street.

"Who the fuck was that Italian nigga?" Eraser Head asked out loud, as he tossed his Mac 11 out the window.

"I don't know, but you better believe I'm going to find out," Gmoney said, peering at the shrinking form of the gunman in the rearview mirror.

Knowledge exited the bodega with one thing on his mind, and that was Tosha's fat ass bouncing up and down on his dick. As soon as Knowledge stepped out of the bodega, all he had time to see was a muzzle flash, and a loud roar of a powerful pistol, before he felt a sharp and hot pain rip through his shoulder. The impact of the shot caused Knowledge to stumble back inside the bodega, crashing into the rack of potato chips. Knowledge hit the floor and automatically his hand grabbed onto the .40 cal in his waistband.

When the storeowner heard the loud gunshot bang out, and saw a hooded man come crashing into his store, he immediately reached for his shotgun that rested underneath the counter.

Knowledge had only made it to one knee when he saw the storeowner raise his shotgun from behind the counter. With the reflexes of an alley cat, Knowledge raised his .40cal and before the storeowner knew what was going on, two bullets exploded in his face.

Rell was about to enter the bodega until he heard two thunderous shots ring out. He placed his back against the wall and took a breath. On the count of three, Rell turned and threw his arm inside the store. He swept his arm back and forth, as he pulled the trigger, until he ran out of bullets and the chamber on his p89 jumped back. Once Rell was out of bullets, he didn't even check to see if he had hit his intended target. Instead, he jogged back to his Honda and fled the scene. About 90 seconds after the shots finished ringing out, Knowledge climbed back to his feet and slowly stepped out of the bodega with caution. Once he saw that the coast was clear, he jogged over to his Expedition. With his good arm, he opened the door and tossed his .40cal on the passenger seat as he climbed up in the driver seat. "Shit!" He cursed as he watched the blood flow out of his now limp arm. Knowledge threw the Expedition in drive and gunned the engine.

CHAPTER 32 A BLOODY MESS

Pauleena laid across the bed watching "The Five Heartbeats" in a lime green thong, with the matching bra. She sipped slowly from her glass of champagne as she enjoyed her favorite movie. Just as her favorite part was about to come on, Pauleena heard somebody banging on her room door like the police. She coolly grabbed her .380 that was lying on her bed within arm's reach, threw on her robe, and answered the door. "Fuck is you banging on my door like the fucking police?" She growled as she snatched the door open.

"Sorry Pauleena," Malcolm apologized. "But this fool Knowledge just showed up bleeding all over the place," he said, trying to read Pauleena's facial expression. "You want me to get rid of him?" Malcolm asked, cracking his knuckles.

Pauleena looked over at her surveillance monitor and saw four bodyguards standing around Knowledge, who clutched his shoulder. "Nah, take that fool in the kitchen and lay him on the counter," Pauleena instructed as she headed over towards her nightstand, and grabbed the cordless phone off of the charger. "Here you go brother," one of the Muslim bodyguards said as he offered the wounded man a cup of water.

"Nigga get that shit out my face!" Knowledge snarled as he slapped the cup out of the Muslim brother's hand. "I don't want no motherfucking water! Where's Pauleena?"

"I'm right here," she said, seeming to appear out of nowhere. "Fuck you doing showing up at my crib all bloody and shit?"

"I didn't have nowhere else to go," Knowledge said as he tried to lean up against the counter, but winced in pain. "I couldn't go to the hospital because I think the bodega camera might have caught me body something on tape."

"Damn!" Pauleena said, shaking her head. "Who did you hit?"

"A clerk at a bodega."

"I hope that shit was over some money," Pauleena said, trying to make sense out of what she just heard.

"It was an accident. I was out looking for the clown who been dropping all of our peoples, and hitting up all of the stash cribs," Knowledge explained himself.

"Well did you catch him?" Pauleena asked. But the hole in Knowledge's shoulder and his silence was enough of an answer for her. "What's this cocksucker's name?"

"His name is Rell. Now can you please call somebody to come over here and patch me up, before I bleed to death?"

"I got somebody on the way over here to hook you up. Be patient. He should be here in a minute," Pauleena told him as she helped herself to another glass of champagne.

"So do you have any idea who the Italian guy was?" Eraser Head asked as he, Gmoney, and about 12 other goons stood in one of the goons' apartment.

"Hell no!" Gmoney grumbled as he opened up a bottle of Hennessy. "Whoever he was, he had to be a professional," he said as he guzzled from the bottle.

"Who the fuck would hire a professional?" Eraser Head said out loud.

"I don't know, but you better believe I'm going to get to the bottom of this," Gmoney replied as he looked at his vibrating beeper.

"I say we just go to all the rival dealers and just start banging on they corners," Eraser Head said out loud. All the goons in the room seemed to be behind him one hundred percent. "I'mma sleep on it before I decide how I'm gonna play this one. But right now, we headed to Pauleena's crib."

"Why, what's up?" Eraser Head asked curiously.
"I don't know. She just paged me 911," Gmoney told him as him and all the goons filed for the exit.

"What the fuck is you doing?" Knowledge yelled as he pushed the doctor away from him. "Hey man, I'm just doing my job," the doctor shot back. "You want me to fix you up or not?"

"Let the man fix you up so he can be on his way," Pauleena said from the sideline. "Damn, this shit he doing hurt more than actually getting shot," Knowledge huffed. Pauleena sat on the sideline with a smirk on her face. "So how did it feel when you got shot?"

"Let me shoot you in your shoulder and you'll see how it feels," Knowledge fumed as the doctor continued to stitch him up.

"She'll never know what it feels like to get shot, because I will take the bullet or bullets for her," Malcolm spoke up with a sharp edge in his voice.

"Well let me shoot you, and then you can tell her how it feels," Knowledge said, trying to think about anything but the hole in his shoulder.

"I tell you one thing. If I ever do get shot, I won't be crying like a little bitch," Malcolm taunted. "I'll take mines like a man," he said as he pounded on his chest for extra emphasis.

"I hear you talking," Knowledge said, waving the big man off with his good arm.

Malcolm was about to reply until he heard a voice on the other end of his walkie-talkie tell him that Gmoney, and about four of his soldiers just pulled up. Malcolm clicked the button on the side of his walkie-talkie. "Alright send them to the kitchen."

"Fuck going on up in here?" Gmoney asked quizzically as he noticed the black doctor stitching up Knowledge's shoulder.

"That bitch ass nigga Rell been the one hitting up our workers and stash cribs," Knowledge huffed. "The nigga must have made me when I went to go check up on Trey."

Pauleena noticed Gmoney's whole facial expression change when he heard Rell's name.

"What happen with Trey?" Gmoney asked.

"That nigga Rell hit up the crib he was running and bodied the muscle."

"Then when you went to holla at Trey, the nigga followed you and popped you?" Gmoney asked.

"Yeah, but that's not even the worst part," Knowledge said, happy that the doctor had finally finished. "The worst part is that when this cocksucker shot me, I stumbled back into the bodega. And I guess the storeowner must have thought I was trying to rob him, so he pulled his shotgun."

"So you shot him?" Gmoney asked.

"Yeah and I think the store's camera might of caught all the footage on tape," Knowledge said with a hurt look on his face.

"Fuck!" Gmoney cursed. "When I catch this bitch ass nigga, I'mma blow his face off!"

"Don't forget we have to find out who that white, Italian guy is," Eraser Head reminded Gmoney.

"Oh, I didn't forget about that. I'm gonna get to the bottom of that."

"Who's this white guy?" Pauleena asked curiously.

"That's what we trying to figure out. Motherfucker burned my house down to the ground; a real professional," Gmoney pointed out.

"I'll look into that for you," Pauleena told him.

"Now, back to you," Gmoney said, turning to face Knowledge. "It looks like your career is over."

"I know," Knowledge replied with a sad look on his face.

"Cheer up. You know ya man gonna send you out on a good note," Gmoney patted him on the back.

"I know," Knowledge said dryly.

"Don't forget, we gotta leave and go to Miami tomorrow for Roy's birthday party," Pauleena reminded Gmoney.

"Oh shit…I forgot all about that," Gmoney said, massaging his temples. "A'ight bet, then I guess I'mma have to throw you a going away party tonight then," he said, looking at Knowledge.

CHAPTER 33 NO MONEY LIKE DOPE MONEY

Ali entered the visiting room with a confused look on his face. The C.O. on his block told him he had a visit. But when Ali reached the visiting room, he didn't see nobody he knew. Just as he was about to go have a word with the visiting room C.O., he heard a female's voice call his name.

Ali looked up and saw a woman who he had never seen before, waving her arms and calling his name.

"You know me?" Ali asked curiously, as he helped himself to the seat across from the woman.

"Nah, you don't know me. Gmoney sent me up here to deliver a message," the woman told him.

"I'm listening," Ali said nonchalantly.

"Well first off I wanna say it's a pleasure to finally meet you. I've heard so much about you. My older brother, Charles, used to work for you."

"I remember Charles," Ali replied in an even tone.

"My name is Tonya," she said, extending her hand.

"It's nice to meet you Tonya. Now if you don't mind, can we get down to business?"

"No problem. Well basically, Gmoney sent me up here to tell you he received your message and to tell you that he's working on finding a dope connect. And if everything goes according to plan, he should have something for you within a week."

"So I'm assuming you're the new messenger."

"Yes I am," Tonya replied with a warm smile. "Well, it was nice meeting you and hopefully, I'll be seeing you again next week,"

"If you want, you can see me every week," Tonya said flirtatiously.

"I don't think my fiancé would like that," Ali raised an eyebrow.

"What she don't know won't hurt her. You know how the game goes," Tonya said in a seductive tone.

"You got all my info right?"

"Yes Ali, I have all your info."

"A'ight send me a few kites (letters) and I'll keep in touch," Ali said as he got up from the table and headed to the back where a C.O. proceeded to strip search him, looking for any form of contraband. Once Ali made it back to his unit, he headed straight to Skip's cell.

Skip laid on the floor in his cell doing sit ups, when he noticed Ali step in his cell.

"What's good, my boy?" Skip said as he got up off the floor and gave Ali a pound.

"Just came back from the dance floor."

"Oh word, what's good with that thing?" Skip asked.

"Gmoney sent this fine ass messenger up here. She said shit should be coming in next week," Ali said, helping himself to a seat at the foot of Skip's bed.

"That's what I'm talking about, cause this weak-ass shit Loco working with is trash," Skip said as he threw his state green shirt over his wife beater. "Speaking of Loco, have you spoken to him about the new shipment?"

"Nah, I'mma holla at him in a little while, when we go to the yard," Ali said as he stood up. "Any word on who was behind the Lil Bit hit?"

"Nah," Skip replied, shaking his head. "I know Rose and his peoples had something to do with it, but I haven't heard anything concrete yet."

"Okay keep your ears open. I'm about to go to my cell and call Nancy. If you need to use the jack to call April or anybody, just let me know," Ali said over his shoulder as he made his exit.

"I'm glad you could come to pick me up," April said, bobbing her head to a Lil Wayne song that was on the radio.

"Don't mention it girl. It's the least I could do. We haven't chilled in mad long," Nancy said, keeping her eyes on the road.

"I know right. Sorry, but Little Michael is something else; can't tell that boy nothing."

"I know he's getting around that certain age," Nancy chuckled.

"How's Little Ali?"

"He's good, getting bigger and bigger every day," Nancy said as her and April's head jerked back violently.

The driver of an Escalade had just hit Nancy's Nissan in the back, smashing up the back of the vehicle pretty bad.

"What the fuck?" Nancy yelled as she hopped out of her car and made her way towards the Escalade.

"Damn shorty, that's my bad," the driver said, motioning towards the back of Nancy's car.

"You damn right that's your bad. Look what you did to my ride," Nancy said, waving her hands as if she was praising Jesus.

The driver held both palms up. "Calm down ma. Anything I damage I can pay for," he said in a calm, smooth tone. "My name is Marvin," he said, extending his hand.

$ilk White

As Nancy shook the driver's hand, she noticed he was a cutie. Marvin stood 5'10 and kind of favored the rapper Nas a little bit.

"Well Marvin, is your insurance going to pay for this?" Nancy asked with her hands on her hips.

"Insurance?" Marvin chuckled. "Nah, baby I only do cash," he boasted. On that note, his man slid out the passenger side of the Escalade.

"Cash huh?" Nancy said, looking Marvin up and down. "Looks like that's gonna run you about $2,500."

"That's it?" Marvin chuckled. "Oh shit how rude of me. This here is my man Smitty," he introduced his partner.

"What up?" Smitty said in a deep voice.

"Hi you doing?" Nancy said politely as she turned and faced Smitty.

Smitty had shoulder length dreads, with a face full of hair and a teardrop under his eye. Something about this man just screamed trouble, so Nancy placed her focus back on Marvin. "So what's good? How we gon do this?"

Marvin patted Smitty on the back. "Pay the lady."

With that being said, Smitty pulled out a huge wad of cash and peeled off 25, hundred dollar bills, and handed them to Nancy.

"We good?" Marvin asked with a warm smile.

"Yeah, we good," Nancy replied as she double checked, making sure the bread was straight. "Nice doing business with you," she said with a smirk as she spinned on her heels about to head back to her car, until Marvin grabbed her wrist. "Hold up I didn't catch your name."

"Nah, it's not even that kind of party," Nancy said, flashing her ring in front of Marvin's face.

"You flashed that ring like that's supposed to mean something," Marvin said, still holding on to Nancy's wrist.

"That means I'm already taken," Nancy said as she jerked her arm loose and headed back to her vehicle.

"It's all good ma. I'mma see you around," Marvin called out as him and Smitty climbed back into the Escalade.

"What was that all about?" April asked when Nancy slid back in the driver side of the Nissan.

"Nigga tryna spit game. You know how niggaz do," she replied nonchalantly. "I'll never cheat on Ali, so these niggaz should just quit while they ahead."

"So you not going to have sex ever again?" April asked.

"Yeah, with Ali," Nancy answered quickly.

"But he got life," April reminded her.

"And? So what you saying, you cheat on Skip?"

"No, I'm not cheating on Skip," April answered. "But Skip doesn't have life. He only have four and a half years left," she pointed out.

"I was nothing and I had nothing until I met Ali. Look at me now," Nancy said as she stopped for the red light. "Plus, Ali have this C.O. inside who lets us have sex in those trailers for the married inmates for $500," she informed her. "You can do whatever you want when you got money!"

"I'm not telling you to cheat on Ali. I was just asking you a question," April exhaled.

Nancy was about to respond until she heard her cell phone ringing. From the ringtone, she already knew who it was. "Speaking of the devil, this my boo right here...hello?"

"Hey baby, what's poppin?"

"Nothing, me and April was just sitting here talking about you and Skip; about to go get our hair and nails done," Nancy told him. "What you up to?"

"Nothing about to go hit up the yard in a minute, but I just wanted to hear your voice before I go."

"Ahww that's so sweet," Nancy sang, blushing like a little schoolgirl. "I can't wait to see you tomorrow."

"I can't wait either, but yo, let me go cause I see a C.O. walking around, doing his rounds."

"Okay, I'll see you tomorrow. I love you."

"I love you too baby, and don't be staying out too late."

"Okay daddy I won't," Nancy sang happily, as she hung up. "I love that man," she said, looking over at April.

"And he loves you too. When are y'all going to get married?" April asked.

"Soon; Ali wrote me a letter the other day asking me would I marry him."

"What did you say?"

"What you think I said?" Nancy said, looking at April as if she was crazy. "I said hell yeah," she said as the two busted out laughing.

"Well congrats girl. Can I be the witness?"

"If the people at the jail say its okay, then sure," Nancy said as she heard her phone ringing. She looked at the caller I.D. and didn't recognize the number. "Hello?" she answered.

"Hey girl what's up?" "Coco?" Nancy asked, trying to make out the voice on the other end of her line.

"Yeah it's me."

"Bitch where the fuck you been? I been trying to call you for the past two days."

"I'm in the hospital with a broken leg," Coco said, talking way louder than she needed to.

"The hospital? A broken leg?" Nancy echoed. "Fuck happened to you?"

"I was with Gmoney and some shit popped off. You know how that go. I'll fill you in on details when I see you."

"What hospital you at? Me and April gonna swing by there."

"Nah, you ain't gotta do all that. I'll be out this bitch tomorrow. But I can't talk on this phone for too long, so I'mma hit you up when I get to the crib tomorrow."

"A'ight girl keep me posted," Nancy said as she ended the call.

"What's going on?" April asked as soon as Nancy hung up.

"Coco in the hospital with a broken leg," Nancy said, keeping her eyes on the road.

"Who the fuck broke her leg?"

"I don't know. She said was with Gmoney and some shit jumped off. You know how that go," Nancy said, shooting April a private look.

"Yeah, you know I know," April replied, thinking back on when the racist cops had pulled her, Coco, Skip, and Gmoney over. Still to this day, she could still feel the officer's clammy hands running up her thighs.

"Well that's how it goes some times. We all knew what we was getting into when we started dealing with these men," Nancy said, breaking April out of her trance.

For the rest of the ride, the two rode in complete silence, both women in deep thought. Nancy stopped at the red light and reached down between the gears looking for a CD, when out of nowhere, a crack head began spraying some kind of liquid on her windshield and tried to wipe it off with a dirty rag.

"Yo, get the fuck outta here with that shit!" Nancy yelled as she beeped the horn.

The dirty crack head ignored the loud horn and continued to clean the windshield.

"Yo, you don't speaking English or something?" Nancy barked as she hopped out the car and snatched the dirty rag from the crack head. "I said get the fuck out...." Nancy's words got caught in her throat when she saw that the crack head was Christie.

Christie was getting ready to snatch her rag back, until she realized that the driver of the vehicle was Nancy. Like a sprinter at a track meet, Christie took off running down the block. Immediately, Nancy kicked off her heels and began chasing after her barefoot.

April quickly slid in the driver seat and followed Nancy as she chased the crack head down the block, causing pedestrians to look and see what was going on. After running for a block and a half, Christie began to slow up. That's when Nancy grabbed the tip of her shirt and somehow leaped on Christie's back, tackling her in the middle of the street.

"You steal from me after what I did for you!" Nancy growled as she turned

Christie over on her back and raised her balled up fist.

"Please Nancy, I'm sorry," Christie sobbed with her eyes closed bracing herself for the blow.

Nancy looked down at Christie and suddenly she unbaled her fist. Looking down at Christie brought tears to her eyes. "Get ya ass up," she said, helping Christie to her feet.

"Nancy I'm so sorry. Please forgive me," Christie sobbed, burying her face in Nancy's chest.

"Don't worry. I'm going to get you some help," Nancy whispered as she stroked the back of Christie's head.

"What the fuck is going on?" April questioned, pulling up to the scene. "What you was going to do; kill that crack head for trying to clean your windshield?" She asked confused.

"No, this is Christie; we have to get her some help."

"Oh my God," April said, covering her mouth with both hands when she got a good look at the strung out woman. "I'm sorry. I didn't know."

"It's cool. We just gotta get her some help," Nancy said as the two helped Christie in the back seat.

Nancy hopped back behind the wheel and headed to the nearest rehab clinic.

CHAPTER 34 SEE YOU WHEN I SEE YOU

"Okay, now tell me what exactly happened?" Mr. Goldberg asked, sitting back in his comfortable, not to mention expensive, looking chair.

"I told you. We went to my crib and motherfucker's tried to off the god. Long story short, my crib got shot up and set on fire," Gmoney said, getting to the point.

"Well was the house in your name?" Mr. Goldberg asked, pulling out a pen and a note pad.

"Nah."

"Well then, what's the problem?" Mr. Goldberg raised an eyebrow.

"The lady who's name the house is in, is one of my boys' mom's, so she can't do no time."

"Well then find me somebody who can," Mr. Goldberg replied with a steady face.

A warm smile appeared across Gmoney's face. "That's why I pay you the big bucks," he said as he shook his lawyer's hand and filed for the exit.

Once Gmoney and Eraser Head got back in their vehicle, Gmoney spoke. "Yo, find me a lil nigga on the team to do this time for us."

"Say no more," Eraser Head replied, as he pulled out into traffic. "Where we off to now?"

"Knowledge's going away party at the Holiday Inn," Gmoney answered as he turned up the volume on the radio.

Detective Nelson sat behind his desk putting together a master plan on how he was going to take Gmoney and his whole organization down, when Detective Bradley interrupted him.

"I think I got something that might put a smile on your face," Detective Bradley said with an evil smirk on his face.

"Lay it on me," Detective Nelson said dryly.

With the same evil smirk, Detective Bradley handed his partner a video tape.

"Great, another one of your porno's," Detective Nelson joked as he popped the tape in the old VCR that sat on top of his small T.V.

The smile on Detective Nelson's face quickly faded into a stone serious face. On the tape, Detective watched Knowledge murder the store clerk in cold blood. "Is this who I think it is?" He asked just to make sure he wasn't seeing things.

"Yup, it sure is...that cocksucker, Knowledge," Detective Bradley chuckled. "For a name like Knowledge, he sure is dumb."

"Let's get this warrant drawn up so we can go collar that prick."

"One step ahead of you," Detective Bradley said, holding up the warrant with a smile.

"I could kiss you right now," Detective Nelson said as he hopped up, threw on his jacket, and headed out the door.

When Gmoney and Eraser Head stepped inside the hotel room, the strong smell of weed, pussy, and perfume all mixed together attacked their nostrils. Inside the room, Uncle Luke's "DooDoo Brown" was blasting from the mini speakers, while strippers, hoes, chicks from the hood, and everybody was in their underclothes having a good time; a few didn't even have on clothes.

Gmoney turned and saw Eraser Head standing closely behind him. "Enjoy yourself brother," he said, patting Eraser Head on the back. With that being said, Eraser Head quickly helped himself to a seat on the couch and pulled a thick stripper down onto his lap.

Gmoney smiled, and then quickly made his way to the back of the room where he found Knowledge sitting on the bed with a bottle of Grey Goose in his hand, and a stripper's head bobbing up and down between his legs.

"No homo," Gmoney said as he sat down on the bed next to Knowledge. "You know you not supposed to be drinking, especially while you on them pain killers."

"Man fuck those pain killers," Knowledge huffed. "This my pain killer right here," he said, holding up the bottle.

"So this is it, huh?" Gmoney said in almost a whisper.

Knowledge let out a light chuckle. Knowledge let out a light chuckle. "All good must come to an end, but it was definitely fun while it lasted," he said, thinking back on all the fun times. "Better to leave the game this way, instead of the other two ways," Gmoney said half-jokingly. "So I guess when you leave here, it's back to business huh?"

"Yeah as soon as I leave here, me and the goons going to hop on the plane and head to Miami for Roy's birthday party," Gmoney informed him.

"I'm heading to Philly," Knowledge whispered.

"Don't worry. You know me and the goons gonna come through and visit you," Gmoney assured him as he grabbed the bottle of E & J that sat on the nightstand.

"You know I'mma be good wherever I go," Knowledge said, raising his bottle.

"I taught you well," Gmoney joked as he touched bottles with Knowledge and grabbed the nearest chick next to him.

"Yo I heard Coco laid up in the hospital," Skip surmised as him and Ali walked the yard.

"Word? What happened?" Ali asked, looking around the yard. "I heard some cats tried to off G-money and she was with him,"

Skip answered. "Damn, shit still popping out in the streets like that?" Ali wondered out loud. "You know shit don't change," Skip said as he grilled one of Rose's workers, as the two passed each other. "I can't stand them white motherfuckers!" "Don't even worry about them. We gon be busting they head's real soon," Ali said as the two walked up on Loco, who was surrounded by a pack of Bloods.

"My nigga Loco, what's poppin?" Ali said as he gave him a pound.

"Ain't shit, just chilling with a few of the homey's," Loco replied.

"Check it…I need to holla at you for a second."

"Yeah, I need to holla at you too," Loco said as the two walked a few feet away from the crowd, so they could speak in private.

"What's on ya mind?" Loco asked as he spat on the ground.

"Well basically, we been getting complaints about the dope you been getting. The shit ain't selling because the shit Rose and them putting out, is more potent.

"Yeah I know, but that's the best I can do," Loco said, looking over at Rose and the rest of the white brotherhood who stood across on the other side of the yard.

"Don't even worry about it. I got my man Gmoney sending us some pure shit. The shipment should be arriving in about three days," Ali said, trying to read Loco's face. "Everything will still be run the same, only difference is the new product."

"Nah, that's cool, I don't have a problem with that," Loco replied as he fished in his pocket and handed Ali a piece of paper.

Ali read the document closely before a smirk danced on his lips. "This shit says that your appeal came through."

"I know. My lawyer came and delivered the news to me yesterday. Motherfucker said I'll be out of here in three weeks," Loco announced proudly.

"That's what's up," Ali said as he handed Loco back the document.

"But what I wanted to ask you was," Loco leaned closer to Ali's ear. "Would you be able to get me some work out on the streets?"

"Definitely. I'mma set you up with my man Gmoney. He could use a little more muscle," Ali told him.

"As long as I'm getting paid, I'll do whatever," Loco said seriously. "Fuck that, I gotta eat…feel me?"

"I can dig it," Ali said, knowing how hard it was for brothers to get a job, especially with a felony. "You family now. And one thing we do is take care of family."

CHAPTER 35 HAPPY BIRTHDAY

Gmoney, Eraser Head, and four other goons stepped out of the airport terminal and slid into the awaiting limo.

"I love it out here in Miami," Eraser Head said, staring out the window, taking in the view.

"I love it out here too. But first things first, we gotta get our hands on some hammers," Gmoney said as he popped open a bottle of Grey Goose and turned it up as his face crumbled up.

"Yeah cause these country niggaz like to play with them choppers," Eraser Head agreed. "Plus, you know they hate New York niggaz."

As the two men spoke, the driver of the limo rolled down the thin glass that separated him from the passengers. "Check in that small box right there," he said, pointing to the box. "Pauleena placed three 9mm's in there for y'all."

"That's what I'm talking about," Eraser Head said, snatching the three burners from the box, handing them to three of the goons. "Y'all niggaz better not be scared to use these shits either!"

"Never that," a goon wearing a durag replied, admiring the handgun like it was a piece of gold. The limo pulled up in front of the club and outside looked more like a parade or a block party, instead of a club. "Damn!" Eraser Head said out loud, referring to the Miami women. "Bitches not playing no games out here."

"This what I live for," Gmoney slurred, as he slid from the back of the limo looking fresh to death. He wore a snug fitting white thermal shirt; his blue Tru Religions hung over his crisp, yellow construction boots. His braids hung to the top part of his back, while his blue Yankee fitted sat on his head at 45-degree angle.

As Gmoney, Eraser Head, and the goons headed for the entrance, they noticed a royal blue, old school Chevy with some big ass rims pull up in front of the club bumping some down south shit. Roy slid out the Chevy wearing all black, with way too much jewelry on. He had on three chains, a pinky ring, on each finger, and a big ass diamond studded bracelet.

"Birthday boy! What's good?" Gmoney said as he gave Roy a pound followed by a hug.

"Ready to get my party on," Roy replied with a warm smile.

As soon as Gmoney, Roy, and the crew stepped in the club, the heavy bass from the speakers slapped them in the face.

Mike Jones' "Drop and Gimme 50" was blaring through the speakers and the club was jammed packed, and popping.

$ilk White

As Roy and Gmoney snaked through the club, all the chicks reached and pulled at the tip of their shirts.

Gmoney cupped his chain in his hand as he continued to squeeze through the club.

Roy made sure he stayed close behind Gmoney and Eraser Head until this thick, caramel joint, with a nice weave grabbed his hand and pulled him towards her.

"Damn!" Roy said to himself. The caramel chick's ass was so big that he could see it from the front. "I'm about to bust this shit wide open," Roy said to himself as he cuffed caramel's ass and pulled her towards him as their bodies swayed to the beat.

Gmoney, Eraser Head, and the goons reached the V.I.P. section, but came to a halt. The big bouncer stood in front of the V.I.P section with his arms folded. "Get away from here!" He barked.

"What you mean?" Gmoney said with his face in a frown.

"You don't speak English? Get the fuck away from here!" The big bouncer yelled, unfolding his arms.

Gmoney and the goons took a step forward, but before shit got a chance to jump off, Malcolm touched the big bouncer's shoulder and whispered. "It's cool they with us."

With that being said, the big bouncer stepped to the side and let Gmoney and his crew pass.

"Faggot!" Gmoney hissed, making sure that he bumped the bouncer as he passed.

"You always getting into some shit," Pauleena smiled as she gave Gmoney a hug.

"Motherfuckers always wanna be tough," Gmoney said, looking back in the bouncer's direction.

"Fuck that nigga," Pauleena said, fanning her hand. "We came here to have a good time and celebrate my man's B-day. Don't want to fuck it up by having to bust a fool's head," she said with a smirk on her face.

Gmoney returned the smile as he checked out Pauleena's merchandise when she wasn't looking. She wore a skin tight, red leather one piece, with a pair of red pumps to match. The top of her one piece was in the form of a wife beater. On her wrist, she wore three woman bracelets on each wrist.

"Come help me drink this and shut up," Pauleena said, taking Gmoney out of his thoughts.

"Pop that shit open," Gmoney replied as he watched a few cats on the dance floor do a stupid dance he had never seen before. "These some dancing motherfuckers," he said, shaking his head, helping himself to a drink.

"Nah, these down south niggaz just know how to have a good time," Pauleena said, trying to do the Soulja Boy dance.

"Fuck all that. Who is these chicks you got up in this section?" Gmoney said, checking out the eye candy. "You stay with some bad bitches around."

"I keep a lot of male company around, so it's always good to keep some pussy around. That way, everybody ain't gotta be all rowdy all the time," she said, looking Gmoney up and down.

"Well if you don't want me all rowdy, then I think you should introduce me to this lovely looking sister with the blonde weave," Gmoney said, licking his lips as he eyed the half-naked woman.

"You'll stick your dick in anything," Pauleena sucked her teeth. "Come on." After Pauleena introduced Gmoney to miss thing with the blonde hair, she helped herself to another drink, as she looked at the sea of black, sweaty faces on the dance floor. Everything was going cool, until she spotted the person she was looking for.

Romelo stepped in the club with a pretty young girl on each arm, followed by two, seven foot, 300-pound bodyguards.

From where Pauleena was standing, she could tell that the older man was about his business from the way everyone cleared his path or broke their necks to shake his hand. For a man in his middle 50's, Romelo didn't look a day over 30. He wore his hair in a low czar, with his sideburns connecting down to his goatee. And to top it off, he wore an all-white tailor made, Armani suit, with a pair of white Stacy Adams to match. The red handkerchief in his upper left jacket pocket matched the red tie that hung neatly around his neck. As soon as Romelo and his entourage reached the V.I.P. section, a bouncer greeted him with a head nod, and stepped to the side.

"Hey gorgeous...let me get a couple of bottles of champagne over here," Romelo whispered in the waitress's ear, as he slapped her on the ass as she passed.

"It's popping in this motherfucker tonight," Romelo said to his bodyguard, as he placed his suit jacket behind his chair and took a seat.

"It's some nice talent in here," the head of his security, Tango replied, looking at the crowd through his dark tinted shades.

"Yo where you going?" Gmoney yelled out.

"I'm about to go holla at this old head real quick," Pauleena replied as her and Malcolm headed over to the other side of the club, where Romelo and his people were.

Romelo sat bobbing his head, sipping on some champagne as one of his tenderoni's whispered in his ear, telling him what she wanted to do to him, as she placed her hand on his dick in plain view.

Romelo had a smirk on his face until he saw Tango and his other bodyguard rush toward the V.I.P entrance.

"Sorry brother, this is a private party," Tango said, blocking Malcolm's path. "But you can definitely come hang out," he said, checking out Pauleena's goodies.

"She's not going anywhere without me," Malcolm yelled over the music. "You wanna run that by me again?" Tango's eyebrows rose over his sunglasses. "It's cool I'm a big girl," Pauleena said, placing a hand on Malcolm's chest.

"You sure?"

"Yeah I'm good."

"Okay, I'll be right here waiting for you," Malcolm said, his eyes still on Tango.

As Pauleena approached Romelo, she saw a curious look on his face. "It's cool, I come in peace," she told him, holding up both palms.

"Come in peace or leave in pieces," Romelo countered.

Pauleena brushed off the last comment, only because she was on a mission. "I think we need to talk."

"Money talks," he said in an uninterested tone as he sipped from his champagne flute.

"I only talk money," Pauleena replied, her tone a little more aggressive.

Romelo nodded and sipped some more. "Well, have a seat then."

"I'm going to get straight to the point," Pauleena said leaning forward. "I need a good price on some dope and word on the streets is, you the man to see."

Romelo took his time to reply. "So what did you say your name was again?"

"Pauleena."

"Pauleena, huh?" He said rubbing his chin. "I heard your name before. Word is, you the woman to see out in Florida and New York, if you want some good coke. Correct me, if I'm wrong."

"I don't know about all that. I'm just trying to get my hands on some dope that's all," Pauleena said, making sure she was careful with her words.

Romelo let out a light chuckle. "I like your style," he said, fishing around in his pocket. "Tonight, I'm here to party, but here's my card," he handed it to her. "Call me tomorrow and we can talk a little more."

"Thanks for your time," Pauleena said, sticking the card down in her one piece as she stood up to leave.

Romelo's eyes were glued to Pauleena's fat ass as it switched up and down in her red leather pants. "Now that's an ass!" He grumbled, helping himself to another glass of champagne. One of the girls on Romelo's arm sucked her teeth. "Damn daddy, is her ass fatter then mines?" She asked as she stood up and started shaking her ass in his face to Florida's song "Low."

"Hell naw her ass ain't fatter than yours," Romelo lied as he slapped the fat ass in front of him.

"Everything good?" Gmoney asked when Pauleena returned to the V.I.P. section.

"It's all good," she replied with a wink.

CHAPTER 36 THE STREETS TALK

"Take that shit the fuck off!" Rell growled as he pressed his p89 against the young worker's temple.

"Man you must not know who you fucking with," the young hustler grunted as he removed his chain from around his neck, and handed it to the gunman. "I work for Gmoney," the young hustler said proudly.

Rell and Debo busted out laughing. "Nigga shut the fuck up and gimme the mailbox key," Debo huffed as he searched the young hustler's pockets, while Rell kept him frozen at gunpoint. Once Debo found the mailbox key, he quickly opened up the mailbox. A smirk danced on his lips as he pulled two big stacks of money from the mailbox, and placed them in his back pocket.

"It's all good. I'mma see you again," the young hustler beamed, more out of pride than anything.

"I hope so," Rell chuckled. "Make sure you tell your boss Rell did this to you," he said as he popped a shot in each one of the young hustler's legs.

"Ahwwww shit!" The young hustler screamed out in excruciating pain.

"Enjoy your wheelchair faggot," Rell laughed out loud, as he threw the young hustler's chain around his neck as he and Debo made their exit, leaving the youngin laid out, leaking in the lobby.

Loco stepped in Ali's cell and saw him, Skip, and two other goons sitting down, chopping it up.

"My niggaz, what it's looking like?" He asked, giving everybody a pound.

"You tell me," Ali replied as he grabbed his tang container from out of the toilet bowl and took a sip, then placed it back in the toilet bowl to keep in cold.

"Just got back from seeing my lawyer," Loco paused. "I'm out this bitch in five days," he said with a smile.

"Congrats my dude," Ali said as he gave him a pound followed by a hug. "You got a place to stay or you need me to have one of my peoples hook you up?"

"Nah, I'm good. I'mma go stay with my girlfriend Monique," Loco replied with a sour look on his face.

"You sure that's cool? You know the two of y'all don't get along," Skip said, speaking for the first time.

"We'll be a'ight. Plus, she'll just be happy that a nigga is home...feel me?" Loco said in a light chuckle.

"Write down your address and I'll have my man Gmoney come pick you up from your crib the first day you get home, so he can straighten you out," Ali said as he slid Loco a blank sheet of paper.

Ashley laid on the bed with her face buried in a pillow and her ass poked up in the air. "Oh daddy, tear this shit up!" She begged as she bit down on her bottom lip and hissed as Gmoney's dick slid in and out of her wet pussy.

Gmoney started off with medium speed strokes as he listened to Ashley moan, and watched her fat ass jiggle and bounce back and forth with each stroke.

"Throw that shit back!" Gmoney demanded as his strokes started to speed up. Like a good little girl, Ashley did as she was told and threw that ass back, enjoying every stroke.

Gmoney spread both of Ashley's ass cheeks apart as he continued to thrust his dick into her hot, sopping wet pussy until his condom was filled with his babies.

Gmoney laid on the bed butt naked with his hands behind his head think about the good pussy he just received, when he heard the phone in the hotel ring. Only Pauleena had the number, so Gmoney already knew who it was.

"Yeah, what's up? He answered.

"Get dressed. I'll be over to pick you up in 45 minutes."

"Where we going?" Gmoney asked.

"I just called Romelo and he invited us to a party at his house tonight," Pauleena answered.

"In Syracuse?"

"Nah, he got a crib out in Dade County. Enough with the questions, I'll be there in 45 minutes," Pauleena said, ending the conversation.

Rell pulled up in front of the bodega, where about 10 to 12 hoodlums stood. "Oh shit! I was about to bust ya fucking head," a big man wearing a hoody growled as he gave Rell a pound. "I bet you wish it was that easy," Rell chuckled as he flashed the butt of his p89. "What you think, you the only one out here packing?" the big man asked. "The difference is, when they see me, they know I'm gonna bust my shit; while the rest of y'all niggaz is out here playing show and tell."

"Show and tell my ass," Big man shot back as he lifted the Jesus piece off Rell's chest. "I see you still out here eating good," he motioned towards the expensive chain that hung around Rell's neck.

"Oh this…I got this from one of Gmoney's boys," Rell boasted.

"You and Gmoney still out here going at it?" Big man asked.

"This ain't gon stop until one of us is dead!" Rell said, looking over his shoulder. "Some beefs are just everlasting, you know what I mean?"

"Yeah, I hear you," Big man said, shaking his head. "Y'all need to dead that shit. Cause you know I'm cool with both of y'all, and I don't want to see either one of y'all get hurt."

"This shit ain't gon never be dead until one of us is dead," Rell said as he slid a Newport between his lips. "Do me a favor…spread the word that I'm out here looking for Gmoney. No goons, no soldiers, just me out here by myself."

"I got you, and I'm going to be praying for the both of y'all," Big man said as he gave Rell a pound followed by a hug.

Pauleena and Malcolm slid out the limo, followed by Gmoney and Eraser Head. "This some a'ight shit right here," Eraser Head said, looking at the mansion.

"Old nigga getting that cake," Gmoney added as the four made their way to the entrance, where a bodyguard scanned each of them down with a hand held metal detector.

Once inside the mansion, Pauleena noticed that Romelo had a club area in his house. She also noticed that the dance floor was packed. Marvin Gaye's "I Heard it Through the Grapevine" was blasting through the speakers, while Romelo stood in the middle of the dance floor dancing with two chicks.

Gmoney expected to see an older crowd, but was shocked when he saw that the people who attended the party was his age and younger.

"I'm going to have a word with this nigga. You two try to find something to do," Pauleena said as she headed over to the middle of the dance floor.

"Yeah, I'mma find something to do alright," Gmoney mumbled as his eyes followed the ass on a stripper looking chick. "Yo I'm about to get up in shorty ear like some head phones. I'll be right back," Gmoney told Eraser Head as he excused himself.

"No doubt," Eraser Head replied as he watched Gmoney's every move closely.

"One more dance please?" A young woman begged.

"Okay baby, let me take a rest first. You know I'm an old man," Romelo winked at the young lady, as he and Tango stepped off and took a seat on a nearby couch.

"It's some fine ass bitches up in here," Tango said, licking his lips. "I know. Like this lil nice fine thing coming our way now," Romelo commented. "Big man, what's going on?" Pauleena asked as she walked up on the two men. "You tell me, good looking."

Pauleena was about to reply until Romelo cut her off. "No disrespect, but you fine as wine in the summer time," he said, using one of his old school, mac daddy lines.

"Thanks…I guess," Pauleena said with a smile. "Since I'm so fine, I hope you give me a good price on this dope."

"Have a seat," Romelo said, patting the seat cushion next to him. Once Pauleena sat down, he continued. "If you want me to give you a low price, you gon have to do something for me."

$ilk White

"And what's that?" Pauleena asked, rolling her eyes and snaking her neck.

Romelo laughed out loud. "Nah, I'm not talking about that," he laughed some more. "What I meant was, I'll give you a good price on the dope and you give me a good price on the coke," he said, signaling for one of his waitresses to bring him a drink.

"I don't think that would be a problem," Pauleena replied, shaking her head yes.

"But of course, you know it's a catch right?" Romelo smiled.

"I'm listening," Pauleena said in an even tone, as she grabbed a drink from the passing waitresses' tray.

"You see, the thing is this…I only wholesale," he paused to take a sip from his glass. "But my son, he breaks it down and distributes and supplies the streets. So if I give you a good deal on some dope, I would have to speak to my son and he'll let me know what area you can sell your dope at. But in return, you gonna have to give him an area where he can move the coke. One hand washes the other."

"Who's your son?" Pauleena asked curiously.

"Marvin," Romelo answered.

"Doesn't ring a bell," Pauleena said flatly.

"Well my son just walked in. I can introduce you two right now," Romelo said as he stood and waved his son over.

Marvin walked over with Smitty close on his heels, and a hood rat looking chick bringing up the rear.

"Pop's, what's good?" Marvin said as he gave Romelo a pound followed by a hug.

"Have a seat. I got somebody I want you to meet. This here is Pauleena, Pauleena this is my son Marvin," he introduced the two.

"What's up?" Marvin said with a nod of acknowledgement, and Pauleena did the same.

"I was just telling Pauleena here that I don't usually sell weight to hustlers from New York, because I know that's your playground, but she has something to bring to the table," Romelo said.

"Oh yeah? And what's that?" Marvin asked in a laid-back tone.

"In return, she gonna give us a good price on some coke, and give us a nice area where we can pump that."

"And what we giving in return?" Marvin asked.

"An area for her and her peeps to move the dope, that way nobody steps on anybody else's toes," Romelo explained.

"Nah, that's not gonna work," Marvin stated plainly. "She need us, we don't need her. Nothing personal, but business is business," he said as he stood to his feet.

"It's all good," Pauleena stood to her feet. "You right business is business."

"I'm sorry about this sweetheart. I wish things could have worked out," Romelo reached into his jacket. His revolver in its shoulder holster was revealed, but Romelo was going for his handkerchief.

"It's nothing," Pauleena replied as she turned her flute up, finishing the last of her drink. When she sat her glass down, she noticed the hood-rat chick ice grilling her. "You a'ight?" she checked the hood chick.

"Is you a'ight?" The hood chick shot back taking a step forward.

"What?" Pauleena barked as she slipped out of her heels. Malcolm quickly jumped in front of Pauleena before she got a chance to get a swing off.

"Come on bitch!" The hood chick said in a defensive stance. "I can't stand you bubble gum ass bitches."

"Yo, Moonie chill," Marvin quickly hushed her.

Seconds later, Gmoney and Eraser Head walked up. "What's poppin? Everything good over here?" Gmoney asked Pauleena, but he had his eyes on Romelo.

"Yeah everything good. Let's be out before I bust that lil girl's head up in here," Pauleena fumed.

"Bitch think she all that," Moonie raved. "I don't know why we just don't pop that bitch and take over her whole shit. Fuck is we being all nice and friendly and shit?"

"She's not the problem," Marvin told her. "She got Gmoney backing her up, and that nigga team is a little too strong right now," Marvin said honestly. "But don't worry. She's not going to last long. Chicks like her never do."

As Pauleena, Malcolm, Eraser Head, and Gmoney piled in the limo, Gmoney saw a familiar face heading towards the mansion's entrance.

The Terminator and Big Rodney entered the mansion and were immediately spotted by Tango. The big man threw his huge arm in the air and waved the champ and his bodyguard over.

"The champ is here!" Romelo yelled out as he gave the Terminator a pound, followed by a hug. "Come have a drink with me," he said as he handed the Terminator a glass of champagne.

"You know I ain't supposed to be drinking," The Terminator said, holding up both palms.

"Oh shit! I forgot you got this big fight in two weeks," Romelo suddenly remembered. "Should I bet on you?" He asked, trying to feel the champ out.

"Only if you wanna win some money," The Terminator replied with a confident smile.

"The Bully ain't no chump though," Tango added. "His last 10 fights, he won by knockout."

"That's because he wasn't fighting me," The Terminator retorted. "I also won my last six fights by knockout."

"I hope you not sleeping on this guy. Because the last real opponent you fought was that kid Spanky a couple of years ago," Romelo reminded him. "This guy ain't gon be no walk in the park."

"Man, the fight ain't going past six rounds," The Terminator said confidently. "Skills pay the bills around here. That big diesel motherfucker ain't got no head movement, his foot work is trash. Trust me; I might not even break a sweat."

"Well just be careful, because the Bully hits hard as a fucking truck!" Romelo said, helping himself to another drink. "What you doing out in Miami anyway?"

"I had a photo shoot to go to out here. I heard you was having a party, so I said let me swing by real quick."

"Well it's always great to have you," Romelo said as he noticed Marvin waving him over. "Excuse me for a second."

"Nah, I'mma get up with you later. I gotta be out," The Terminator said as he gave Romelo and Tango a pound. "A'ight I'll catch you at the Garden in two weeks," Romelo yelled over his shoulder as he disappeared through the crowd.

CHAPTER 37 HOME SWEET HOME

"I know I'll definitely be seeing you again," the red neck C.O. chuckled as he escorted Loco towards the barbwire fence.

"You crackers can kiss my ass," Loco replied in an even tone.

"Take it easy out there, my brother!" the red neck said, making sure he dragged out the brother part. Loco stuck up his middle finger as he gave his man, Gun Play a pound, followed by a hug.

"Damn nigga! I been sitting out here for like four hours," Gun Play huffed.

"You know how them crackers do," Loco said as he slid in the passenger seat of the hooptie. J.R. Writter's song "Grill em" blasted from the speakers, as Loco and Gun Play exited the prison grounds. "So what's good? What you been up to?" Loco asked as he rolled down the window, and inhaled the fresh upstate air.

"Shit, I just got out like two weeks ago myself."

"Word? What you was in for?" Loco asked curiously.

"I shot a fair one with a cop," Gun Play replied nonchalantly. "Motherfucker got mad cause I fucked him up, and he took me in," he chuckled. "When I got to Rikers, three C.O.'s jumped me cause that punk ass cop told them I snuck him."

"That's od," Loco chuckled, shaking his head. "What's good in the hood, you eating?"

"I be moving a little bud in the hood, that's about it. You know I make the majority of my money from juxes."

"Damn you still out here robbing niggaz?" Loco exhaled.

"I gotta do what I gotta do," Gun Play shrugged his shoulders.

"Well those days are over. I made a connection while I was up in the mountains."

"Word?" Gun Play asked, keeping his eyes on the road.

"Yeah, I hooked up with Ali while I was up in that shit hole."

"Who, that nigga from Harlem who fuck with Gmoney?" Gun Play asked.

"Yeah, Gmoney gon swing by the crib later on tonight. Basically, he got work for us. So I hope ya gun game still on point?" Loco asked.

"Come on B. what's my name?"

Gmoney stepped out of the bathroom with a towel wrapped around his waist, admiring himself in the mirror. "Damn that dude is fine," he said out loud, speaking about himself in third person.

"You ain't all that," Coco sucked her teeth as she sat on the bed with her cast leg hanging slightly off the bed.

"Don't hate," Gmoney shot back as he popped his "Rick Ross" CD in the stereo and turned it up.

"Turn that drive-by music down," Coco huffed.

"Oh I see, my boo want some attention," Gmoney said as he made his way over to the bed.

"Don't come over here playing," she warned.

"Shut up," Gmoney said as he pushed her down on the bed and planted soft kisses on her lips, careful not to lean on Coco's cast leg.

"You think you so cute," Coco whispered as she kissed him back.

"Thinking is for people who are not sure," Gmoney replied as he pulled one of Coco's titties from out of her sports bra, placed it in his mouth, and started sucking on it as if he needed it to live.

"Awe...shit," Coco called out in pleasure as she removed her sports bra. "What you doing?" Coco asked, seductively biting her bottom lip.

"Stop playing and give me my pussy," Gmoney demanded as he slowly pulled her boy shorts down her thighs and over her cast. Once the boy shorts were past her ankles, Gmoney dove in her pussy face first. He licked and sucked on her clit, while fingering her at the same time.

Coco clawed at the sheets as she purred out in ecstasy, as she felt herself releasing her creamy juices. Just as Gmoney was about to get his dick sucked, he heard someone banging on his front door.

"What the fuck?" Gmoney huffed as he grabbed his .45 ACP off the nightstand and headed towards the front door. When he made it downstairs, he cautiously peeked through the blinds and exhaled when he saw Shorty and Eraser Head.

"Fuck y'all fools want?" Gmoney asked, sticking his .45 in the small of his back as he stepped to the side so the two men could enter. From the look on Shorty and Eraser Head's face, Gmoney knew instantly that something was wrong. "What happened?" He asked.

"Shit is ugly out in the streets," Shorty said, shaking his head.

"Fuck he talking about?" Gmoney asked, locking his gaze on Eraser Head.

"While we was out of town, this chump Rell hit up a few of our spots and workers," Eraser Head paused to see Gmoney's reaction before he continued. "He going around telling everybody that you pussy and scared to come see him...."

Before Eraser Head could finish his sentence, Gmoney was already heading upstairs. Ten minutes later, he reappeared downstairs wearing all black, with his .45 sticking out the side of his waistband. "Let's go find this corny nigga and shut his fucking mouth for good," Gmoney steamed as he slid his hands into his black leather gloves.

"Don't forget, we gotta swing by Bushwick projects and scoop up the new soldier Ali recruited," Eraser Head reminded him as they headed out the door.

"A'ight we gon pick him up on the way," Gmoney replied as the trio slid in the Lexus truck.

"Yo I'mma go see what this chick talking about and I'mma get up with you later," Loco said as he gave Gun Play a pound and entered the project building. No matter how long a person is in jail, some things just don't change. Loco entered the elevator and made sure he stepped around the puddle of yellow piss that sat right in the middle of the floor. Loco counted the flights as the elevator reached the floor he had requested. As soon as he stepped off the elevator, he could smell weed smoke.

"I bet that shit is coming from this chick's apartment," Loco said out loud, as he reached the door he was looking for, and knocked lightly. He heard some feet shuffling behind the door before a woman's voice yelled. "Who is it?"

"Man just open the door," Loco huffed. A second later, he heard the door unlock.

Monique opened the door with a frown on her face, until she realized who was standing on the other side. "Oh my God," she screamed as she jumped into Loco's arms, planting kisses all over his face and neck.

"It took you long enough to open the door," Loco huffed as he laid Monique down on the couch. "I'm sorry baby," Monique whined as she unzipped Loco's pants and took him in her mouth.

"Damn that pussy was good," Loco said, breathing heavily as he put his jeans back on. "Why you putting your pants on for? You not gon stick around for a while?" Monique asked jokingly.

"Nah, I gotta go get this money," Loco replied in a serious tone.

"What?" Monique said the playfulness in her voice gone.

"Listen, I would love to stay here with you all night, but ma I gotta go get this bread."

"You know what? I don't even give a fuck do whatever you want. That's why I does me, cause niggaz like you never change," Monique snapped as she stormed to the bathroom and slammed the door behind her.

"She'll get over it," Loco thought out loud, as he heard someone knocking on the door. "Who is it?"

"The motherfucking mailman," the voice from the other side of the door replied. Loco peeked through the peephole and saw three men who he had never seen before.

"What's up?" Loco cracked the door.

"You Loco?" A man with braids that came to the middle of his back, spoke.

"Yeah," Loco replied quickly.

"I'm Gmoney," the man with braids extended his hand.

"Oh shit. What's good my nigga? Ali told me all about you," Loco said as he gave Gmoney and the two other men he was with, dap.

"Ali told me you was a soldier."

"All day," Loco replied.

"Good cause it's a lot of work that needs to be put in," Eraser Head said, speaking for the first time. "Here's some cash to get on your feet," he said, handing Loco a book bag, which held $10,000 inside.

"Good looking. I appreciate all the love y'all showing me, but I need a favor," Loco prodded. "I need y'all to put my man on too."

"Who's your man?" Gmoney asked curiously.

"My man, Gun Play," Loco told them.

"I don't know your man Gun Play, but if you want to put him on that's on you. I guess you can pay him out of what we give you, which will be more than enough," Gmoney explained.

"Okay that's cool," Loco replied.

"I hope you ain't scared to let that thang off," Eraser Head said as he handed Loco a 9mm.

Loco arched his brow. "I ain't never scared. I didn't get the name Loco for nothing."

"You'll get your chance to show how loco you are. We'll be back tomorrow to pick you up," Gmoney said and the conversation was left at that.

* ***

The next day, Loco stepped outside and saw Gun Play in front of the building, waiting for him. "What's good five?" He said as he and Gun Play did the Blood handshake.

"Out here early tryna catch these potheads," Gun Play said, scanning the block for potential customers.

"Fuck all this nickel and dime shit. Where all the homies at?"

"Which ones? It's mad Blood niggaz out here" Gun Play.

"Listen I'm about to go hit up 125th street and cop a couple of fits (Outfits). I want you to round up all the real Blood niggaz in the hood, and we gon have us a little meeting at the end of the week," Loco explained.

"Say no more," Gun Play said, as he sold a bag of weed to a customer out in the open.

"Listen, I'mma scream at you later before we roll out to the club tonight," Loco said as he flagged down a cab.

** * *

Gmoney parked his CLK 55 down the block from Club Mars 2112. "Open the glove compartment and hand me three stacks," Gmoney ordered.

"What you need all this money for?" Eraser Head asked as he handed Gmoney the stacks of money.

"So we can get our stunt on tonight," Gmoney said, turning to face Eraser Head. "We gotta let the streets know that we still got the strongest team out here, smell me?"

"I can dig it," Eraser Head said as him and Gmoney exited the Benz.

Gmoney slid out of the driver's seat wearing an all-black with a crisp pair of Nike Boots. The three iced out chains he wore around his neck, clanked, and clacked with each step he took.

As the two men bopped down the block, they could see the line spilling around the corner.

"Damn, the bitches is out tonight," Eraser Head said out loud, as he tossed a piece of Winter Fresh in his mouth. The two men got wicked looks and whispers, as they skipped the long line and headed downstairs to the main entrance. "What it's looking like in there?" Gmoney said as he palmed a hundred dollar bill and slapped it in the bouncer's hand.

"Its mad bunz in there tonight," the bouncer said with a smile.

"That's what I like to hear," Gmoney said as he and Eraser Head slid past the metal detector and entered the club. When the two entered the club, immediately the heavy bass from the speakers slapped them in the face, followed by the heat.

"Yo the V.I.P. section is this way," Eraser Head yelled over the music as he noticed Gmoney walk pass the V.I.P. area.

"Nah, we playing the dance floor tonight," Gmoney informed him as the two headed downstairs to the dance floor.

Meanwhile outside the club, Loco and Gun Play slid out the back of the cab looking like new money. "Damn this line is long as fuck!" Loco grumbled.

"Yeah, but look at all these hoes out here," Gun Play pointed out.

"I can't remember the last time I seen this many women in one spot," Loco admitted as the two hopped on the back of the line.

When 50 cent's song "I Get It In" came blaring through the speakers, the whole club went crazy. As Gmoney and Eraser Head snaked their way through the club, people he knew and a few people he didn't know greeted him by giving him dap. The two men reached the bar and each man ordered a bottle of champagne. Gmoney popped open the bottle and took a deep swig, when he noticed a thick sister with dreads that came to the middle of her back standing at the end of the bar.

"Damn that ass got my name written all over it," Gmoney motioned towards shorty at the end of the bar.

"Yeah, shorty is good money," Eraser Head said as he watched Gmoney head in the female's direction. "Yo see if she got a friend for me," he yelled out.

As Gmoney approached the woman at the end of the bar, he noticed she held a half-empty cup in her hand. Without asking, he walked straight up to the girl and filled her cup with champagne.

"Ummm excuse yourself," Dread head said, placing an open palm on Gmoney's chest.

"What's the problem?" Gmoney asked with a confused look on his face.

"You don't just come over here and pour that shit in my cup. For all I know, you could be trying to poison me or something," she snapped as she sat her cup at the end of the bar.

"Let me buy you another drink to make it up to you," Gmoney offered.

"That's all you had to do from the beginning," Dread head huffed.

A smirk played on Gmoney's lips. "What you drinking ma?"

"I'll take a Long Island Iced Tea, and my friend here," Dread head said, motioning toward her redbone friend who stood next to her.

"I got you ma," Gmoney replied as he waved Eraser Head over. "This my man E right here," he said, introducing Eraser Head to the redbone as he handed both women their drinks.

"So what's your name?" Gmoney asked as he turned up his bottle.

"Yolanda," Dread head answered with a smile.

"I'm Gmoney," he extended his hand.

"No, what's your real name?" Yolanda chuckled.

"Gmoney," he replied again with a straight face.

"So Gmoney," she made sure she dragged out his name. "Tell me something about yourself."

"Well I love money and I love beautiful women," he said as he held Yolanda's wrist, and slowly spun her around so he could get a good look at her ass.

"You like what you see?"

"Fa suga dell," Gmoney licked his lips.

Yolanda was about to respond until her favorite song came on. "This my song," she sang as she got in front of Gmoney and began shaking her ass.

Gmoney immediately placed one hand on her hips, threw his bottle of champagne in the air, and did his best to catch it as she threw it.

"Damn it's hot as fuck in here," Loco said with a frown, as he began sweating as soon as he and Gun Play stepped in the club.

"Let's hit the bar. This your second day home, I'm about to get you bent," (drunk) Gun Play yelled over the music as he lead the way towards the bar. As Gun Play tried to get the bartender's attention, he saw a familiar face over in the corner. When Uncle Luke's song "DooDoo Brown" came on, all the chicks in the club went crazy. "Yo Loco," Gun Play yelled over the music, trying to get his attention. "Yo," he gave Loco a nudge.

"What's good?" Loco asked as he bent down so he could hear what Gun Play had to say.

"Ain't that Monique over there?" Gun Play pointed over towards the corner.

Loco looked to where Gun Play was pointing and felt disgusted. Over in the corner, some guy had Monique tossed all up in the air, getting it in.

"I know you ain't gon let that shit slide," Gun Play instigated.

Loco didn't respond. Instead, he shot Gun Play a comical look as he headed over to the corner where Monique and the guy made love with their clothes on.

"Can I tell you something?" Yolanda asked as she turned to face Gmoney, her body still swaying to the music.

"I'm listening," Gmoney replied as he guzzled from his bottle.

"I think I like you," she said, batting her eyes flirtatiously.

"Oh yeah?" Gmoney replied with a smile as he looked at her perky breast standing at attention. "I think I like you too."

"So let me get your number," Yolanda pressed as she handed Gmoney her cell phone.

Gmoney quickly punched in his number and handed the cutie back her phone. Gmoney was about to say something else until a scuffle broke out over in the corner.

"Niggaz don't ever know how to act," Yolanda sucked her teeth.

"Yo that's that nigga Loco over there," Eraser Head yelled, leaning towards Gmoney's ear as the two squeezed and snaked through the crowd.

Loco walked right over to the guy, grabbed his shoulder, and spun him around so the two could be facing. The man was getting ready to say something, but the quick blow to his nose ended that thought. The man hit the floor, holding his nose with two hands.

Before Monique could even figure out what was going on, Loco and Gun Play were already stomping the guys face into the floor. "What are you doing?" Monique yelled as she tried to get Loco off of the guy.

Loco quickly turned and shoved Monique to the floor, as two big bouncers came and yoked him up, roughly escorting Loco and Gun Play out of the club.

When Gmoney and Eraser Head finally made it outside, they saw Loco and his man across the street arguing with the police.

"Yo come on. Leave that shit alone," Gmoney said as he draped his arm around Loco's neck and escorted him down the block. "What's that all about?"

$ilk White

"That motherfucker had his hands all over my girl," Loco huffed.
Gmoney and Eraser Head busted out laughing. "You making all that noise over a bitch?" Eraser Head said in between laughs.
"Y'all can laugh all y'all want, but she belongs to me," "Man listen," Gmoney began. "You need to get off that jail shit; it's a million chicks out here. Don't be a fool."
"Look at this faggot," Eraser Head nudged Gmoney. When Gmoney looked up, he saw Detective Nelson and Detective Bradley crossing the street in his direction.
"What's going on brother?" Detective Nelson said, letting that last word roll off his tongue.
"Fuck you want?" Gmoney asked dryly.
"You know what I want," Detective Nelson said, getting all up in Gmoney's face. "Where's your boy Knowledge?"
Gmoney laughed right in Detective Nelson's face. "I don't know."
"That's funny to you boy?" Detective Bradley cut in.
"Yup," Eraser Head said, taking a step closer, flexing his muscles.
"Whenever you ready boy," Detective Bradley said as the two continued to eye box.
"My advice to you...leave town A.S.A.P.," Detective Nelson said, forcing a smile.
"No thank you," Gmoney shot back as him and his crew walked off.
"I see I'm going to have to teach you a lesson, just like I did your friend Ali," Detective Nelson yelled at Gmoney's departing back.

CHAPTER 38 FINAL WORKOUT

"So are you going to use your speed to beat Marcus "The Bully" Jackson?" A white reporter asked the Terminator as he sat, getting his hands wrapped up.

"Absolutely," The Terminator replied nonchalantly. "I keep telling y'all, skills pay the bills around here."

"The Bully has tremendous punching power in both hands. How do you think your chin will hold up if he catches you with a clean punch?" Another Reporter asked.

"Listen man, I done been in 28 professional fights and 40 amateur fights. And guess what? I ain't been dropped yet, so I like my chances. You need to ask the so called Bully, how his chin is going to hold up because I'm definitely gonna be tapping his shit all night," The Terminator said in a matter of fact tone.

"Do you think this will be your toughest fight?" A lady reporter asked.

"Of course not," The Terminator replied quickly. "But I know for a fact this will be his toughest fight."

"Well I spoke to the Bully and he said the fight won't go past four rounds," a baldhead black reporter spoke strongly.

"So put your money on him then," The Terminator said flatly. "Put your money on him and I promise you will regret it."

"Enough with these damn questions," Mr. Wilson huffed as he held open the Terminator's left glove, so he could slip his hand inside. "This is supposed to be a public workout. You ain't been working out nothing but your mouth," he slightly scolded.

"I gotta give the people what they want," The Terminator replied with a smile. "This my gym and I'm the king of the ring."

Mr. Wilson heaved a deep sigh as he finished wrapping the last piece of tape around the wrist of the Terminator's gloves.

"I know all y'all reporters and cameramen can't wait until I lose, but guess what?" The Terminator chuckled. "It ain't happening. My name is west and I don't play that mess," he sang as he walked over to the heavy bag, and began punching it with all his might.

"This the Bully's ribs right here," The Terminator said, motioning towards the heavy bag. He threw left hook after right hook. The impact caused the bag to swing back and forth. After a good two-hour workout, Mr. Wilson kicked all the reporters and cameramen out of the gym. The only people left in the gym were Mr. Wilson, the Terminator, and Rodney. Mr. Wilson sighed loudly before he spoke. "In two days, it's going down."

"Don't worry, I'll be ready."

$ilk White

"You better be," Mr. Wilson yelled over his shoulder as he filed for the exit.

"I got this fight already in the bag old man," The Terminator yelled out as him and Rodney busted out laughing.

CHAPTER 39 STREETS IS WATCHING

"Fuck is y'all doing out here?" Shorty asked as he approached the two young hustlers, who stood in front of the building.

"What you mean?" The taller one out of the two asked.

"Fuck you mean, what I mean?" Shorty spat, with his face crumbled up.

"We out here getting this spread," the taller kid replied.

"Out here getting this spread, huh?" Shorty said sarcastically. "You two gotta be the dumbest niggaz in the world."

"Damn Shorty, why you coming at us like that?" The short kid spoke for the first time.

"Look around, you see anybody else out here?"

"Nah," the tall kid answered, looking up and down the block.

"It's task force Tuesday," Shorty huffed, shaking his head.

"Oh shit, it damn sure is Tuesday," the tall kid said, angry with himself for forgetting. "Yo Shorty, that's my fault. I forgot all about that shit," he apologized.

"It's narc's all around this bitch. Whatever y'all do, make sure it's in the building a'ight?"

"No doubt," the two sang unison.

"Y'all hold it down out here B.," Shorty said as he gave the two young hustlers dap, and then headed towards where his Acura was parked. He cautiously looked over both shoulders before he slid in the driver's seat and made the car come alive.

Little did he know, Detective Nelson and Detective Bradley sat in a yellow cab watching Shorty the whole time. "That little piece of shit is the muscle," Detective Nelson said with a disgusted look on his face. "We stay close to him and he's bound to lead us to a murder."

"Then once that happens, we can put the pressure on that scumbag, and hopefully he'll rat out Gmoney," Detective Bradley said as he pulled out into traffic.

"Make sure you stay at least five cars behind this prick," Detective Nelson warned. "This is our ticket to Gmoney."

"I wouldn't blow this for the world," Detective Bradley assured him.

CHAPTER 40 FIGHT NIGHT

"How you feeling baby?" Rodney asked in an exciting voice.

"I feel good," The Terminator replied as he sat in the locker room getting his hands wrapped up.

"All you gotta do is go out and do it just like we did it in the gym and you won't have any problems tonight," Mr. Wilson assured his fighter.

"I'm going to make you look good tonight," The Terminator said, winking at his trainer.

"I want a lot of head movement. Because when the Bully hits, he hits hard," Mr. Wilson raised an eyebrow.

"Come on, I know you don't think this chump can beat me?" The Terminator asked, clearly offended.

"I never said that," Mr. Wilson countered. "All I'm saying is to keep your head moving so you don't get caught with a big shot."

"I'm too smooth to lose and I'm too quick to get hit," The Terminator said as he stood up and began working on his footwork.

"This gon be a good ass fight," Eraser Head said as he backed his Range Rover into a parking spot and let the engine die.

"I don't care who wins. I just want to see somebody get knocked the fuck out," Gmoney slurred as he slid out of the vehicle. "Damn I'm twisted right now," he admitted.

"I'm kinda saucey too," Eraser Head said, with a hint of Grey Goose still on his breath.

"This going to be a good ass fight," Pauleena said out loud as she and Malcolm took their seats.

"Yes this is going to be entertaining," Malcolm agreed.

"It better be," Pauleena said as she saw Gmoney and Eraser Head headed in her direction.

"What's good ma, how you feeling?" Gmoney said, walking past Malcolm as if he was invisible, as he hugged Pauleena tightly. As he hugged Pauleena, he purposely brushed his hand across her ass. "Let's go half on a baby," he whispered in her ear.

Pauleena laughed out loud. "I give you some of this pussy and I'll have you working for free."

"The way you looking in that grey dress, I wouldn't mind working for free," Gmoney said seriously.

"You been drinking?" Malcolm butted in.

Gmoney looked at the big man, but didn't answer. "Who told this chump he can talk?" He said, looking at Pauleena.

"Leave Malcolm alone," Pauleena said as she sat back down and saw a familiar face on the other side of the arena sitting in the crowd. "Look at these clowns," she nudged Gmoney.

When Gmoney looked up, he saw Romelo and his bodyguard sitting about three rows away from the ring. Seconds later, Pauleena and Gmoney saw Marvin, Smitty, and Moonie snake their way through the crowd making their way towards Romelo and Tango.

"Yo, ain't that shorty you was about to get into it with at Romelo's house?" Gmoney asked, pointing at Moonie.

"Yeah that's that bitch," Pauleena said in an uninterested tone.

"What's good? You want me to go over there and slap that bitch for you?" Gmoney asked seriously.

"Nah, she get a pass just this one time," Pauleena told him.

The Bully stood in his dressing room, with his trainer and entourage, warming up. "I want you to go out there and pinch a whole in this guy's face," The Bully's trainer told him.

"I got this Walter," The Bully said confidently as he bounced up and down.

"The ref is here," one of his boys called out.

"Let him in," The Bully yelled.

"Good luck tonight," the ref said as he shook the Bully's hand. "Listen, I know you two don't like each other, but I don't want no foul play, no elbows, and keep them punches up, am I understood?"

"I got you," The Bully answered as he sat down so he could get his hands wrapped up.

"Do you have any questions?"

"Yeah, make sure when I unload on that bitch, he don't be grabbing me and all that," The Bully told him. The new all black S5 Audi pulled into a parking spot bumping 50 cents song "I Like The Way She Do It." Rell slid out of the driver seat wearing a royal blue L.A. Dodger fitted, a white thermal shirt, some black jeans, and a pair of old royal blue Pennies. A bad white bitch slid from the back seat and stood by his side, along with one of his shooters. When Rell stepped foot in the arena, he lit the place up like Las Vegas with all the jewelry he wore. He had on at least three chains, an iced out watch, and a foolish bracelet.

"Where are our seats?" The pretty, green-eyed woman asked.

"Way down in the front," Rell answered quickly as he threw on his shades and lead the way.

"I wish these niggaz would hurry up and fight already," Gmoney huffed.

"They should be coming out any minute," Pauleena said out loud.

$ilk White

"Get the fuck outta here," Eraser Head said out loud, as he nudged Gmoney with his elbow.

"What up?" Gmoney said, turning to face Eraser Head.

"Look over by the second row," Eraser Head said, pointing.

"What am I looking for?" Gmoney said, still searching the crowd.

"Look at the nigga with the blue hat on," Eraser Head said, still pointing.

When Gmoney finally realized whom Eraser Head was pointing to, he quickly shot to his feet.

"Chill, chill. We gon handle this nigga as soon as the fight is over," Eraser Head said, holding Gmoney back with one arm.

"Who's that?" Pauleena asked curiously.

"Rell," Gmoney answered with fire dancing in his eyes.

"Who, that corny looking nigga with the white bitch?" Pauleena asked making sure they were talking about the same person.

"Yeah he's a dead man walking," Gmoney said as all the lights in the arena went out. Seconds later, they began flashing as the Bully made his way towards the ring.

Over on the other side of the arena, sat Frank alongside him was Jimmy. "Hey Frank what's up with that moolie Gmoney?"

"What about him?" Frank asked as he stood up and cheered for the Bully.

"He's sitting over there on the other side. You want me to take him when he goes outside?" Jimmy asked in a calm tone.

"Nah, I'm over that. Let the moolie live," Frank told him.

"Let's go out here and get this done champ," Mr. Wilson yelled in the Terminator's ear as the two made their way to the ring. "Work your jab and you'll have an easy night."

The Terminator nodded his head, signaling he understood as Rodney swiped a fans hand off the Terminator's robe as he jogged up the steps to the ring.

Once both fighters were in the ring, the crowd went crazy in anticipation of what they were about to witness.

"It's show time baby," The Bully's trainer yelled aggressively as he applied Vaseline to his fighter's face. "This is what you been working for your whole life. Don't let nobody or nothing take this from you, you hear?" The Bully nodded his head yes, as he stared down the Terminator over in the other corner. He was completely in the zone.

"Both fighters to the center of the ring please," the referee called. "Okay I've spoken to both of you in the back already. I want a nice, clean fight. This is good," he said, pointing to both men belt lines. "Anything lower, is no good. Do y'all have any questions?"

Both fighters shook their heads no, at the same time.

"Okay good luck to both of y'all. Touch gloves," the referee said as the two fighters touched gloves, and headed to their separate corners.

"This first round I want you to work that jab," Mr. Wilson said in The Terminator's ear as he rubbed his shoulders. "The jab will set everything up," he said one last time as he exited the ring.

Once the bell sounded, the crowd erupted as the two fighters met in the middle of the ring. The Bully started the fight off with a powerful jab, followed by a right hand. The powerful blows bounced off the Terminator's gloves as he danced out of the way.

The Terminator took a couple of steps backwards so he could get a good look at how the Bully kept his guard up. Just by looking at the man's defensive stance, he knew that off the back he could hit him with at least two or three different punches, easy.

As The Bully came charging in, The Terminator took a quick step back and threw a swift left hook that landed on the side of The Bully's head. The punch caused the Bully's face to move, but the blow didn't seem to faze him, as he continued to come straightforward. "Stop running like a little bitch!" The Bully taunted.

The Terminator smiled as he threw two stiff jabs and danced out of the way before the two could exchange blows.

"Stop running and fight!" The Bully growled as he cut off the ring and managed to catch the Terminator close to the ropes. As soon he saw an opening, he took it. The Bully threw three vicious hooks upstairs, then went downstairs and threw four punches to the body.

The Terminator stood in his Philly shell defensive stance as he blocked most of the punches with his gloves and shoulder.

As The Bully continued to charge straight ahead, the Terminator caught him with two quick straight right hands, as the bell sounded, ending the first round.

"Get this man some water!" The Bully's trainer yelled as he shoved a long Q-tip up the Bully's nose. "Let me get a deep breath. This motherfucker don't want to fight, so you going to have to bring the fight to him. Keep going straight at him, just keep your head moving at all times," he told him.

"You see what I see out there champ?" Mr. Wilson asked as he squirted some water in the Terminator's mouth.

"What's that?" The Terminator asked, taking a deep breath.

"This guy is a sucker for counter punches, so I want you to stop all that sticking and moving bullshit. Stand in there with that chump and pick your punches. He's open all day. Let's make it happen," Mr. Wilson said in a regular tone as the bell rung, signaling the start of round two.

The Terminator started the round off with two stiff jabs. The Bully side stepped one of them and fired back with a left hook, and a straight right hand. The two shots caught the Terminator off guard, causing him to stumble off the impact. The Bully followed up with another left hook. The punch missed, but the tip of his elbow connected with the corner of the Terminator's eye.

The Terminator danced out the way and instantly felt the warm blood trickling down his eye. He pawed away as much blood as he could with his glove, as he saw the Bully continue to come forward. The Terminator threw a quick jab, followed by a right hook to the body before dancing out of range, pawing at his eye again.

"Stop running you little bitch!" The Bully taunted again as he blocked a jab and hook with his gloves, and fired back with a hard, straight right hand that landed in the middle of The Terminator's face, as the bell sounded.

The Terminator headed back to his corner and Mr. Wilson was all over him. "What the hell are you waiting for?" He barked.

"He's cheating!"

"I don't want to hear shit about no cheating," Mr. Wilson yelled as he splashed some water in The Terminator's face. "Stop waiting and go get it in," he yelled as the cut man did his best to stop The Terminator's eye from bleeding.

"I hurt that bitch!" The Bully said with an evil smirk on his face.

"That clown can't fight," The Bully's trainer said out loud, as he applied Vaseline to his fighter's face. "Keep going straight at him. He's going to break down in the later rounds watch," he told the Bully as the bell rung. At the start of round three, the two fighters met in the middle of the ring again. The Terminator started things off landing two out of three jabs.

"That's all you got bitch?" The Bully snarled as he bobbed his head from side to side, and fired a jab of his own.

The Terminator quickly stepped back and countered the jab with a sharp left hook, followed by a straight right hand. The hook landed perfectly on the Bully's jaw, causing his mouthpiece to fly out his mouth, while the straight right hand dazed him a little bit. Once the Terminator saw that he had the Bully hurt, he went in for the kill; throwing punches from all angles, causing the crowd to rise to their feet. Once the punches started raining in, the Bully quickly grabbed the Terminator's arms and held on for dear life.

"Get the fuck off me!" The Terminator growled as he snuck in an upper cut, while the referee separated the two.

"Come on bitch. That's all you got?" The Bully slurred as he backed up into the corner.

The Terminator threw a quick jab that snapped the Bully's head back, and then threw a six-punch combination as the bell sounded ending the round.

"That's what I'm talking about. Just use your head and you got this fight in the bag!" Mr. Wilson yelled as he squirted some water in the Terminator's mouth.

"What the fuck are you doing out there?" The Bully's trainer yelled as he splashed water in his fighter's face. "Turn this shit into a dog fight you hear?"

"I got you," The Bully replied as he stood for the next round.

At beginning of the next round, the Bully came out letting his hands fly.

The Terminator stood in his Philly shell defensive stance as he blocked six of eight shots. He could tell by The Bully's movement and body language, that he was beginning to run out of gas.

The Terminator landed six punches in rapid succession, before The Bully decided to fire back with a wild hook. The Terminator easily sidestepped the hook and landed a sharp upper cut that wobbled The Bully. As the Bully felt his legs buckle, he knew he had to do something. As the Terminator came in for the kill, he threw a hard hook. The Bully managed to duck the hook by inches, and countered with an uppercut below the Terminator's belt, dropping him instantly.

"If you do that again, I'm taking a point!" The referee yelled as he pushed The Bully to an empty corner, while The Terminator laid on the floor clutching his family jewels.

"Come on champ, shake it off. You got five minutes to get yourself together," the referee told him, as the crowd continued to boo The Bully for the cheap shot. Two minutes later, the Terminator was up walking around gingerly.

"That nigga did that shit on purpose!" He yelled out to Mr. Wilson.

"Well whip his ass then!" Mr. Wilson yelled back.

"You ready to go?" the Ref asked excitedly.

"Yeah I'm ready!" The Terminator replied as he and The Bully met up in the middle of the ring again. The Bully threw two jabs followed by a hook. The Terminator ducked the hook and came up with a vicious uppercut that dropped the Bully straight on his face.

Once the Terminator saw the Bully hit the canvas face first, he knew he wasn't getting up. The ref made it to the count of 10 easily.

"That's what I'm talking about," Mr. Wilson sang happily, as he jumped in the Terminator's arm.

"Can't nobody beat you! You the fucking man!" Rodney yelled as he lifted the Terminator up on his shoulders.

"I'm out," Gmoney said as he kissed Pauleena on the cheek.

"Where you going?" She asked in a worried voice.

"I gotta go handle some business," he replied, nodding in Rell's direction.

Pauleena didn't respond. She just kissed Gmoney on his cheek and hugged him tightly. "Be careful," she whispered in his ear.

"I got you ma," Gmoney told her as he and Eraser Head spun around and headed in Rell's direction.

$ilk White

"Fuck!" Eraser Head yelled. Rell had somehow managed to blend in with the crowd.

"I called the goons, they outside. No way he should get passed them," Gmoney said as he and Eraser Head took hurried steps towards the exit.

"Keep your head and eyes open," Rell said to his shooter as he held on to blue eye's arm.

"I got you," the shooter replied as he spit the street razor that he had stashed in the side of his gums, into the palm of his hand.

"Yo go grab the ride. Me and Brittany gon wait right here," Rell said, tossing his young shooter the keys. "Hurry the fuck up too," he said, looking over both shoulders. Rell knew that nobody was strapped in Madison Square Garden. That's why he chose to stay there until his young boy pulled up front. If anybody ran up on him, he could handle a fistfight. As Rell and Brittany stood in the lobby, Rell noticed three suspicious looking guys strolling around the parking lot. Something about the men just screamed trouble.

Loco, Gun Play, and a Y.G. (young gansta) from the hood strolled through the parking lot looking for Rell.

"Yo, what this nigga look like again?" Gun Play asked.

"I don't know. Eraser Head said money got braids and a royal blue hat on, with mad chains on," Loco said out loud.

"Man, we ain't gon never find this nigga!" Gun Play snapped.

"Come on let's go!" Rell said when he saw his shooter pull up front.

"Money right there got on a blue hat, and mad chains," Gun Play said, pointing at the man and white woman sliding in the Audi. Gun Play thought about popping off, but the two police officers walking around, cancelled that idea.

"These niggaz know better than to try something down here on 34th street," the shooter said with a smirk as he pulled off with his .45 sitting on his lap. As the Audi pulled off, Rell saw Gmoney and Eraser Head, exit the building. For a split second, the two made eye contact. Each man, giving the other a murderous glare.

"That was that clown right there," Gmoney said as he watched the Audi peel out of the parking lot.

"Come on. If we hurry, we can catch that pussy!" Eraser Head said as the two raced to the car.

The Audi came to a stop directly on the side of an all-black van on a low-key block.

"Baby take the car home and I'll see you later," Rell told her as he and his shooter exited the Audi and slid in the van.

TEARS OF A HUSTLER 2

Once inside the van, the two men traded their nightclothes for black jeans, black sweatshirts.

"Tonight we going hunting," Rell said as he loaded his Moxberg shotgun with the pistol grip. "You ready to get your feet wet," he asked, looking at his shooter for a response.

"Only one way to find out," the youngster said confidently.

"We ain't gon never find this motherfucker," Eraser Head said in a lazy drawl, as he cruised down block after block looking for the all black Audi.

Gmoney jiggled the white foam cup he was holding before taking a sip. "He's hiding like a little bitch. Fuck it; let's go hit up the club. I'm tired of looking for this chump," Gmoney said dryly. Eraser Head noticed that Gmoney hadn't been himself for the past two weeks. "Yo, you a'ight?" He asked in a concerned tone. "Yeah, I'm good," Gmoney answered, showing a weak smile. "I just feel like my man Mitch, from Paid in Full right now. I need to be around some love tonight, smell me?"

"I got you. I know the perfect spot," Eraser Head said as he made a sudden detour.

CHAPTER 41 PARTY TIME

Alfonzo stood outside on 31st, between 7th and 8th Ave, in front of club Rebel. He loved working security at the nightclub cause for one; he got to look at beautiful women all night. And two, he got paid to look at beautiful women all night. Things couldn't have been going better for Alfonzo, until he saw Gmoney walking towards the front entrance with five goons behind him.

"Alfonzo, what's good?" Gmoney said as he gave the bouncer dap.

"Ain't nothing good," Alfonzo said folding his arms. "You know you banned from this club."

"Banned?" Gmoney echoed. "Banned for what?"

"Remember awhile back, you and a couple of your buddies came in here and almost stomped a guy to death?" Alfonzo said, refreshing Gmoney's memory.

"Come on B. That shit happened like a year ago," Gmoney pointed out.

"Don't matter how long ago that was, the guy sued the club. So therefore, you and your peoples are banned from this club," Alfonzo said as if it was his club.

Gmoney sucked his teeth. "Yo nobody asked you all that. You letting us in the club or not?"

"I already told you no!" Alfonzo said way louder than he had to, trying to impress a few chicks who stood in the front of the line.

"A yo fam, what's really good?" Loco stepped up. "We just want to have a good time tonight. Why you fronting for?"

"Listen new jack," Alfonzo began. "I don't even know you, so why are you even talking to me?"

Loco sighed loudly as he turned and snuffed Alfonzo, sending him stumbling back towards the entrance. Before he knew what was going on, Gun Play and two other goons were on the bouncer like a pack of wolves.

Gmoney and Eraser Head sat back watching Loco and his goons put it in.

"I like this guy already," Gmoney said with a smile.

"Me too," Eraser Head added as he continued to look on. Seconds later, five big bouncers came running towards the fight, but they quickly came to a halt when Gun Play backed out his .357. "Back the fuck up," he growled as he waved the cannon back and forth. "We out," he yelled as Loco and the other two goons all took off running back to their car.

"Be out, there go five-o," Gmoney yelled.

Gun Play quickly took off running down the block. Before he bent the cover, he made sure he tossed the burner down a sewer drain.

"Are these men giving you problems?" Four uniform cops asked as they walked up.

"Yeah get them out of here!" Alfonzo growled, pointing at Gmoney and Eraser Head.

"Okay come on fella's, let's get going," one of the officers said as he grabbed Gmoney's arm.

"Do me a favor…don't put ya hands on me!" Gmoney said as he jerked his arm loose.

"Make a move!" The officer snarled getting all up in Gmoney's face.

"Come on, we out. Fuck these crackers," Eraser Head said as he pulled Gmoney away. "They only tough when it's a lot of them anyway," he waved the officer's off.

"Get somebody up here to shoot this bitch up!" Gmoney ordered.

"I got some goons on their way up here now. They should be close by," Eraser Head as he pulled out his cell phone and dialed a number. On the forth ring, a deep voiced man answered.

"Yeah what's up?"

"Yo junior, where you at?" Eraser Head asked.

"I'm right around the corner from the club. It's popping in there?"

"Fat motherfucker at the front door fronting. I need you to send a little message."

"Say no more I got you," Junior said as he ended the call.

"It's done," Eraser Head said, flipping close his phone.

"Let's get up outta here before I have to wash somebody up," (beat them up) Gmoney huffed as he slid in the passenger side of the Benz. Once inside the vehicle, he grabbed some ice from out of the bag in the back seat and dropped a few cubes in his foam cup, before filling it up with Hennessy.

"It's any left for me?" Eraser Head asked as he slid behind the wheel.

"Yeah its cups and ice in the back," Gmoney told him.

Eraser Head fixed him a quick drink, and then pulled out into traffic.

A block away, Rell sat in the all black van, along with his young soldier. "You ready to do this?" The young shooter placed his Mac 11 on his lap and nodded his head yes.

"Let's ride out," Rell said from behind his ski mask. The young shooter rolled his ski mask over his face, and then pulled out into the street.

"I'mma go see Ali tomorrow," Gmoney said, staring blankly out the window.

"Word? You sure them crackers gon be cool with that?"

"Yeah, Mr. Goldberg said everything is cool."

"That's what's up," Eraser Head said as he made a left at the light. "Tell that nigga I said what up."

Gmoney nodded and sipped some more. "I got you."

"I gotta give it to him," Eraser Head began. "He been down for a minute and never said a word."

"That's what real niggaz do," Gmoney said as he noticed two PYT's (pretty young things) strolling down the block. "Yo pull over!"

The two ladies took a few steps away from the curb when they saw the Benz come to a sharp stop. "Damn, what the fuck?" A girl wearing a short jean skirt barked.

"My bad ma," Gmoney apologized as he grabbed his .45 from under the seat and tucked it in the small of his back, as he slid out the passenger seat. "Where the party at ladies?"

"We was on our way to Rebels," Jean skirt announced.

"Nah, we just came from there. Ain't nothing happening over there," Gmoney said as he leaned up against a parked car.

"You sure?" Jean skirt asked, flashing a smile.

"It's dead over there," Eraser Head said, adding himself into the conversation. "So what's good? Y'all got names?"

"I'm Nicole," Jean skirt said, pointing to herself. "And this here is my girl Trice."

"I'm E and this is my man Gmoney," Eraser Head said, introducing the two.

"Yeah, this the club right here. Pull up at the end of the block," Junior ordered as he loaded his Desert Eagle. Once the driver pulled up at the end of the block, Junior slid out of the passenger seat with his gun hanging by his side. He counted to three in his mind before he raised his gun in the club's direction, and let off eight shots in rapid succession. As soon as the shots finished ringing out, Junior hopped back in the vehicle, not caring who he hit or if he had hit anybody at all. Once Junior was back in the vehicle, the driver quickly pulled off.

Gmoney sat leaning against the parked car talking to Nicole, when he heard some shots go off. From the sound of the shots, he could tell that the shots came from a few blocks away. Immediately, he looked over at Eraser Head and flashed a smirk.

"There them motherfuckers go right there," Rell said out loud as he rolled down his window, and aimed his shotgun at his target. Once the van got close enough, he pulled the trigger without hesitation.

As soon as the thunderous shot went off, Gmoney quickly tried to duck behind the parked car that he was leaning on, but he was too slow. Two pellets, from the shotgun, landed in the top part of his shoulder and collarbone. He quickly dropped down to the ground, pulling Nicole down with him.

"Yo ma, get down!" Eraser Head yelled as he grabbed Trice down behind the parked car, next to the one Gmoney and Nicole was hiding behind. He quickly pulled his 9mm from his waistband. "Yo, G, you a'ight?"

"I'm good!" Gmoney yelled back as he felt his warm blood running down his arm. "Y'all niggaz wanna play?" He said out loud, as he snatched his .45 from the small of his back with his good arm.

Rell hopped out the van and aimed his shotgun at the parked car that Gmoney stood behind, and pulled the trigger.

Gmoney and Nicole squatted behind the parked car as broken glass rained on top of their heads.

Rell and his young shooter slowly inched towards the parked car.

Once Gmoney heard the footsteps getting closer, he reached his arm over the hood of the car and let off three shots. Once those three shots went off, all hell broke loose. Eraser Head quickly sprung from behind his hiding spot and began popping shots at the gunmen. When the young shooter saw Eraser Head spring up from behind the car, he aimed his Mac 11 at the man and pulled the trigger.

Once the machine gun went off, Gmoney quickly sprinted from behind the car, crouched over letting his .45 bark. One of his bullets found a home in Rell's upper thigh, causing him to stumble backwards and lean up against the van for support.

When the young shooter saw Gmoney make his move, he swept his arm in G-money's direction and pulled the trigger. Two of the bullets from the Mac 11 ripped through the back of Gmoney's leg, dropping him in the middle of the street.

Gmoney hit the ground, looked up, and saw Rell standing in the line of fire. Instantly, he raised his .45 and let off six shots in rapid succession. One of the bullets landed in Rell's neck, while the other five found homes in his chest, killing him instantly.

The young shooter looked over and saw Rell laid out in the middle of the street. Before he could turn his focus back on the target, a bullet ripped through his shoulder, causing him to drop his Mac 11. Not knowing what else to do, the young shooter sprinted down the street clutching his shoulder.

Eraser Head quickly reloaded his 9mm and began chasing the young shooter up the block.

"Fuck!" Gmoney cursed loudly as he laid in the middle of the street in a pool of his own blood. He winced in pain as he reached down in his pocket with his good arm, and pulled out a broken up blunt and lighter. "What a motherfucking day," he chuckled as he threw a piece of the blunt in his mouth and put fire to the end of it. He laid on the ground for about 45 seconds puffing on the blunt, until he heard a car come to a screeching stop and a familiar voice. "Gmoney is that you?" Carl asked as he rushed over to Gmoney's side.

$ilk White

"Some corny nigga got the drop on me," Gmoney said, flashing a weak smile.

"We gotta get you to a hospital!" Carl said as he lifted Gmoney's upper body into the car. Gmoney screamed in pain when Carl put his legs in the car.

"Sorry for getting blood on your seats," Gmoney apologized. "I'mma cop you a new whip when this shit is over."

"Don't even worry about it," Carl replied in a neutral tone.

"Yo, you got a phone on you?"

"Nah, I left my shit in the crib," Carl said in a shaky voice.

"Damn I wanted to call Coco and let her know what's going on," Gmoney said in obvious pain.

"I'll call her for you when we get to the hospital," Carl told him.

"Good looking my nigga," Gmoney said as he closed his eyes and tried to relax as Lil Wayne's song "Misunderstood" pumped through the speakers. Five minutes later, Gmoney opened his eyes to the sound of Carl's cell phone ringing.

"I thought you left your jack (phone) in the crib?" Gmoney asked suspiciously.

"Nah, this phone is prepaid and it only got like one minute on it," Carl stuttered.

"Where the fuck we at?"

"We here right now," Carl said as he pulled in a dark alley.

Gmoney laughed out loud. "Youz a real bitch ass nigga," he said with a smirk on his face.

"No, I'm a real O.G." Carl said as he pulled out his .357 and aimed it at G-money's head. "You and ya boys been running around all wild and shit. I asked you a thousand times to just ask them to move from in front of my building with that bullshit, but I guess a hard head makes a soft ass." "I could have twisted ya shit back in the lobby that day."

"That's the difference between y'all young niggaz and a real O.G. We don't play," Carl snarled.

"So do what you gotta do then," Gmoney said, flashing his trademark smile. The last thing Gmoney saw was the muzzle on the .357 flash.

"Punk motherfucker!" Carl said as he slid out the vehicle, threw his hoody over his head, and headed down the block like nothing happen.

After chasing the young soldier five blocks, Eraser Head gave up. He quickly tossed his 9mm in the trashcan, and then headed in a totally different direction. Eraser Head made it about a half a block, when a Lincoln pulled up on the side of him. "Fuck!" He cursed as he kept on walking straight thinking it was the police riding up on him. A woman's voice caused him to stop and look. He breathed easy when he saw Nicole and Trice in the back seat of the cab. "Get in!" Trice yelled.

Eraser Head quickly slid in the back seat with the ladies as the cab driver quickly pulled off.

"I gotta go back and get my man!" Eraser Head said.

"Someone picked him up already," Trice told him.

"You sure?"

"Yeah some guy with a baby afro dragged him in his car," Nicole said, confirming the story.

"A'ight bet," Eraser Head said, feeling a little better inside. Before the cab driver dropped the ladies off, Eraser Head and Trice traded numbers. "I'mma call you probably tomorrow a'ight?" "I'll be waiting," Trice replied flirtatiously as she and Nicole headed towards their building. Once the ladies were gone, Eraser Head gave the cab driver directions to Pauleena's house. On the ride, Eraser Head pulled out his phone and made a quick call.

Shorty stood in front of a building in the projects poppin shit with about six to eight other soldiers. "Yo what's good? Ya mom's cooked tonight?" He asked one of the soldiers.

"You tryna be funny, you little ugly motherfucker?" The soldier shot back as all the men around them fell out laughing.

"What? You know me and ya mom's go way back," Shorty laughed as he answered his vibrating boost phone. "What's the deal?" He answered.

Grab all the soldiers you can find and strap up. Gmoney just got shot. I'mma meet you at the spot in an hour," Eraser Head said, ending the call.

"Yo tell ya mom's she better have my slippers waiting at the door for me when I get home," the soldier continued as soon as Shorty got off the phone.

"It's on, Gmoney just got hit. Round up all the goons and have 'em meet me at the spot in an hour," Shorty ordered as he and three soldiers jogged to his car and peeled off.

$ilk White

Detective Nelson and Detective Bradley sat across the street in an unmarked car, watching Shorty's every move. "I think we got something good!" Detective Nelson said excitedly as he watched Shorty and three of his soldiers jog to the car and pull off into traffic.

"I hope so, cause I'm tired of following this piece of shit around all fucking day," Detective Bradley huffed.

Shorty reached the stash crib and double-parked on the corner, as he and the soldiers headed upstairs. Twenty minutes later, the detectives noticed six cars pull up in front of the same building.

"I told you something big was going down tonight," Detective Nelson said with a smile as he watched the men head in the same building. He quickly pulled out his cell phone and called for back up.

"We about to go push these niggaz shit back!" Shorty said, holding a double barrel shotgun. Each man in the apartment was armed with more than one gun.

"Yo, I just got word back that it was Rell and his peoples," a soldier announced, reading a text message out loud.

"Fuck that! We going hunting," Shorty said out loud as he and all the soldiers exited the apartment. Once outside, each man hopped in the vehicle he came in. Before Shorty could switch the gear from park to drive, a cop car came to a screeching stop directly in front of his car. Seconds later, flashing lights were everywhere. "Fuck!" Shorty cursed as he searched for an escape, but it was no use. He and his whole crew were boxed in.

CHAPTER 42 I DON'T BELIEVE IT

"Out of nowhere, bullets just started flying from everywhere," Eraser Head said, replaying the story.

"So where's Gmoney now?" Pauleena asked with a concerned look on her face.

"I have no idea," Eraser Head said with a hurt look on his face.

Pauleena quickly walked to the living room and turned the T.V. to the news.

"Breaking news: Gerald Williams, better known in the streets as Gmoney, was found dead tonight in a stolen car parked in an alley. Police are saying this murder is believed to be drug related. Also, tonight several men who worked for Williams were caught hours later with loaded firearms. Police say Williams and his crew were at war with another crew over territory. We'll have more details as this story develops," the reporter said.

"Fuck!" Eraser Head cursed as the tears silently rolled down his eyes.

"Where the fuck were you when this happened?" Pauleena yelled, getting all up in Eraser Head's face as tears rolled down her face.

"I was chasing one of the niggaz who shot him," he told her as she buried her head in Eraser Head's chest.

"Don't worry. We gonna find the niggas who did this," Roy said, "just fucked up that most of the soldiers just got knocked." (Locked up)

"I told Shorty to wait until he heard from me to make a move," Eraser Head raved. "Motherfuckers don't never listen!"

"Ahwww hell naw," Knowledge said in a defeated tone as he watched the news from his living room in Philly. "Why all the bad shit gotta happen to the real niggaz?" He asked himself as he shook his head in disgust. At times like this, Knowledge wished he were still in the game. Deep down inside, he felt that if he were with Gmoney when it went down, he would still be alive.

EPILOGUE A NEW BREED

"Damn that shit is crazy," Marvin said, shaking his head as he and his crew sat listening to the reporter.

"At least he had a couple of years to enjoy all that money he made," Smitty said, looking on with the rest of the crew. "So what's next?"

"We gonna take over all of Gmoney's old spots and get it poppin," Marvin said with a smirk on his face.

"What about Pauleena?" Smitty asked.

"Fuck that bitch! Either she runs with us, or get ran the fuck over," Marvin answered.

"That's what I'm talking about," Moonie said excitedly. "It's about time. I never liked that bitch anyway. What have she done to deserve her spot? She probably won't even bang out for her shit!"

"Well we definitely about to find out," Marvin said out loud as he turned off the T.V.

"To be continued!!"

Tears of a Hustler PT 3 Now Available

Books by Good2Go Authors

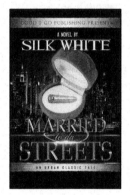

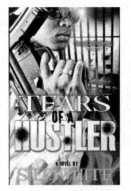

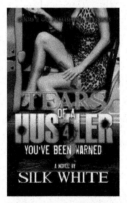

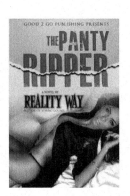

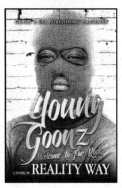

Good2Go Films Presents